PRAISE FOR SUSAN ISAACS AND

### RED, WHITE AND BLUE

"Who the heck is our best popular novelist? The nominee from this quarter is Susan Isaacs. . . . Isaacs is a comic realist, an astute chronicler of contemporary life in the tradition of . . . Anthony Trollope. . . . During the course of her career, Isaacs has produced eight novels that, with their humor, suspense, and equal grasp of male and female psychology, are unlike anything else on the best-seller lists."

—*Ft. Lauderdale Sun-Sentinel*

"The jauntiness and frothy exuberance of Susan Isaacs's style in her eighth novel carries you along as if on a wonderful joy ride. She is superb at quick character sketches, the deadly battles between fathers and sons, family frictions and generational antogonisms. Her effervescence convinces you that everything will turn out all right in the end. Which it does. But just barely."

—*Providence Sunday Journal*

"Fiction done well, and done with a difference. . . . A sophisticated storyteller, with a wry view of the world."

—*Washington Post*

"Filled with humor and well-drawn characters . . . reminiscent of Isaacs's multigenerational, best-selling *Almost Paradise*. . . . It's a tribute to her ability that you'll not only care deeply about the subject but also about the characters to whom she entrusts the job."

—*San Antonio Express-News*

"Is there anyone better than Susan Isaacs at wrapping a romance inside a larger, topical tale? . . . Most readers will find it hard to resist her scrappy heroine and her exuberant examination of the overlapping roots of an American family tree."

—*Glamour*

"Ms. Isaacs is not only                                    d."

*ella*

"With keen humor and fine characterizations, the bestselling Isaacs's multigenerational saga explores the nature of American identity. . . . An absorbing chronicle of the American character."
—*Kirkus Reviews*

"An intriguing story. . . . A tale as timely as today."
—*Denver Post*

"Susan Isaacs has . . . a knack for entertaining her reader with the details of American pop culture. . . . Isaacs has taken on a formidable project: to write a multigenerational family drama that is also a romantic comedy and a murder mystery and a serious consideration of weighty issues like anti-Semitism and assimilation—all without losing her sense of humor or her eye for the entertaining detour."
—*New York Times Book Review*

"Generates a good bit of suspense (and sexual heat)."
—*Orlando Sentinel*

"Fans of Susan Isaacs can look forward to *Red, White and Blue*."
—*At Your Leisure*

"A perfect winter beach read. . . . Breezy, inventive, and very satisfying. . . . You know when you crack open a Susan Isaacs's novel you're getting a fun read. . . . This entertaining yarn is also a multigenerational saga with a twist."
—*Women In Touch*

"Isaacs has the Midas touch with whatever she writes. . . . A model of what popular entertainment ought to be but rarely is: a medium that provides escape without turning the mind to mush."
—*Newsday*

"Isaacs's latest is entertaining, yet in examining anti-government paranoia and the politics of hate, it poses deeper questions about what it means to be an American."
—*Library Journal*

**"SUSAN ISAACS WRITES WONDERFUL BOOKS. THEY'RE LOADED WITH WIT, CRAMMED WITH**

MEMORABLE CHARACTERS, ENDLESSLY ENTERTAINING, AND BEAUTIFULLY WRITTEN."

—*Los Angeles Times*

"Ms. Isaacs is a master of the smart, accessible novel."

—*Wall Street Journal*

## *LILY WHITE*

"A big, fat, happy feast of a book. . . . [Isaacs's] most confident and appealing. . . . [She] is both funny and piercing, a highly satisfying combination."

—*New York Times Book Review*

"Riveting. . . . Best of all is the character of Lee, smart and sassy . . . self-deluded at the same time. Her good-humored, self-knowing, self-mocking voice is a treat for the ear."

—*Boston Globe*

"A well-written, moving story that will keep the reader engrossed all the way."

—*Miami Herald*

"A one-volume vacation reader."

—*Los Angeles Times*

"Stunning. . . . [Isaacs] has created an ingenious novel that breaks out of the mystery genre. In fact, it sets the genre—in which, typically, the killer is brought to justice—on its ear."

—*Cincinnati Post*

"Shiny fun, jampacked full of story."

—*Atlanta Journal*

## *AFTER ALL THESE YEARS*

"Entertaining and imaginative. . . . Isaacs scores again with this relentlessly funny portrait of the rich, old-line and nouveau. The plot rewardingly twists, the characters charm and Rosie carries the day. . . . A delightful summer cooler."

—*People* magazine

"You gotta laugh. . . . Susan Isaacs has always done awfully well in her entertaining fiction, and she's done it again in *After All These Years*."

—*New York Times Book Review*

"Once again Isaacs proves a dab hand at rattling skeletons in the closets of Suburbia—here murder and adultery are skewered with this author's typically savvy wit."

—*Publishers Weekly*

"Bursts with energy, razor-sharp dialogue and memorable characters."

—*Detroit News*

"Terrific."

—*Detroit Free Press*

"Fabulous beach reading."

—*McCall's*

## MAGIC HOUR

"Vintage Isaacs. . . . *Magic Hour* is like polishing off an entire box of chocolate-covered chocolates. . . . Fun."

—*New York Times Book Review*

"Clever, unexpected, drum-tight. . . . The plot is streamlined and the time-frame is short and the voice we hear is witty, and coming-at-us real."

—*Washington Post Book World*

"A wonderfully rich, sensual sort of novel. . . . The dialogue rips along with panache, with sharp and surprising turns, always funny, always fun."

—*Detroit News*

"A delightful blend of obsession, comedy, romance, movies and murder."

—*San Francisco Chronicle*

"A witty and sexy page-turner."

—*Pittsburgh Press*

"Elegantly funny and original. . . . Long after the handcuffs are snapped shut you're likely to find yourself smiling fondly at the memory of Susan Isaacs's one-of-a-kind characters."

—Anne Tyler, *Vogue*

## CLOSE RELATIONS

"Jane Austen brought up to date. . . . Highly amusing."

—*Atlantic Monthly*

"An entertaining novel by a witty, wry observer of contemporary life."

—*New York Times Book Review*

"A delightful read."

—*Publishers Weekly*

"The gritty political detail and the fairy-tale ending in this page-turner are equally appealing."

—*Library Journal*

"Both a witty analysis of big-city politics, family relationships and the singles scene in Washington and New York, and a fairy-tale love story in which the heroine finds her Prince Charming almost despite herself."

—*Publishers Weekly*

"Both Marcia and her creator are clever and bright. . . . Besides being simultaneously romantic, feminist and political, the novel is also a satire: of Jewish mothers and success-orientation, late-marrying Irishmen, American political campaigns, WASP mores, and human relations."

—*Best Sellers*

*Also by Susan Isaacs*

*Novels*
LILY WHITE
AFTER ALL THESE YEARS
MAGIC HOUR
SHINING THROUGH
ALMOST PARADISE
CLOSE RELATIONS
COMPROMISING POSITIONS

*Screenplays*
HELLO AGAIN
COMPROMISING POSITIONS

*Nonfiction*
BRAVE DAMES AND WIMPETTES:
WHAT WOMEN ARE REALLY DOING
ON PAGE AND SCREEN

# Susan

# Red, White and Blue

# Isaacs

HarperPaperbacks
*A Division of HarperCollinsPublishers*

**HarperPaperbacks**

*A Division of* HarperCollins*Publishers*
10 East 53rd Street, New York, NY 10022–5299

This is a work of fiction. The characters, incidents, and
dialogues are products of the author's imagination and are not
to be construed as real. Any resemblance to actual events or
persons, living or dead, is entirely coincidental.

A hardcover edition of this book was published in 1998 by
HarperCollins*Publishers*.

ISBN 0-06-109310-6

HarperCollins®, ✶®, and HarperPaperbacks™ are trademarks of
HarperCollins Publishers, Inc.

First HarperPaperbacks printing: August 1999

Printed in the United States of America

Visit HarperPaperbacks on the World Wide Web at
http://www.harpercollins.com

❖ 10 9 8 7 6 5 4 3 2 1

*To the Thanksgiving crew*
Andrew Abramowitz, Elizabeth Abramowitz,
Elkan Abramowitz, Adam Asher, Benjy Asher,
Bobby Asher, Diana Asher, George Asher,
Henry Asher, Janice Asher, Sara Asher, David Kenty,
Joanna Kenty, Nora Kenty, Caroline Lane,
Ed Lane, Eric Lane, Judy Lane, Kate Lane,
Lizzie Lane, Maggie Lane, Cynthia Scott,
Leslie Stern and Rob Stoll
*with love*

# Descendants of Dora Schottland

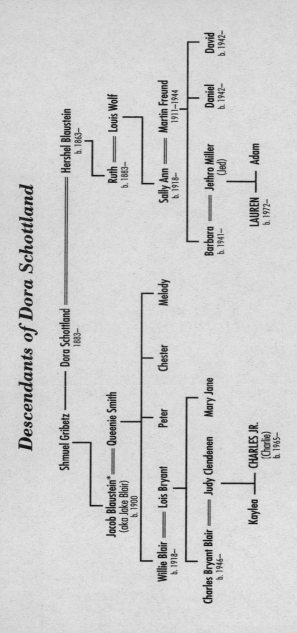

*Note that Jake, the illegitimate son of Dora and Shmuel, has his stepfather's last name.

# Preamble

If the Statue of Liberty and Uncle Sam had come together for a one-night stand, guess who would have popped out nine months later? Charlie Blair, Special Agent, FBI. What an American!

First of all, Charlie looks the part. He's tall, commandingly tall, over six three. In this country, that is the precise height at which men begin to meld into gods. Second, he is lean, naturally hard-bodied, although the full-length mirror on his wife's closet door, which he avoids, would reflect the sad truth: His lonely man's diet of Whoppers with cheese, fried onion rings and Dairy Queen vanilla cones have caused his once-tapering waist to thicken. His virile block of a jaw is starting to puff up like the Cheez Doodles he scarfs while spending his evenings switching between ESPN and the History Channel.

In other words, if there were a Mr. Law Enforcement beauty contest, Charlie wouldn't make it past the semifinals. And that's not even taking into account his ears, which are on the large side. They stick out like the handles on the cream-soup bowls his wife insisted had to be part of their dinner set. Two kinds of soup bowls? he'd puzzled, probably too loudly, in the middle of Fine China. Yes, Charlie, two kinds, Stacey answered in her husky voice. One bowl for, like, vegetable soup and the other kind for cream of mushroom, cream of tomato, cream of asparagus. Each time Stacey said "cream," she all but licked her lips, making the word sound thick and steamy. Back in those days, he usually got blindly aroused by anything she eroticized—a word, a coffee spoon she licked, a scarf between her fingers. But that particular time, his mind's eye caught a glimpse of limp asparagus tips floating in a sea of nauseous green cream, a pale skin corrugating the surface. A sense of doom he now realizes he should not have laughed off descended upon him. So, funny cream-soup-handle ears.

Furthermore, the bridge of Charlie's nose is squished and wide, while the nose itself has meandered off center ever since six years earlier, in Atlanta, when he got whacked in the face with the butt of a Winchester wielded by the girlfriend of a bank robber he and another agent were bringing in. Instead of going by the book and straightaway wresting the weapon from her hand, Charlie succumbed to her bubble-gum-scented, gun-moll prettiness and commanded, his voice dropping to its deepest he-man register: Hand the rifle over, sweetheart. On the rare occasions when he can bear to think back on it, he is awed by his own idiocy. Besides getting him a broken nose, his two seconds of sexism ended with the other agent's getting a bullet in his backside and Charlie's being demoted to his present post.

Just as well, really. There is no place in the upper echelons of the FBI for a guy like Charlie Blair. He's too independent to be a successful bureaucrat. Sure, he's smart as the best of them, but the director's chair, which must of necessity swivel in all directions—toward Congress, the executive branch, the public, the press, the law enforcement community—is not for him. Charlie loves his country, is proud to serve and truly believes the words of the

FBI's motto: Fidelity, Bravery, Integrity. However, he is not an organization man. By instinct and upbringing, Charles Bryant Blair, Jr., age thirty-four, is a cowboy. He pretty much lives by the code of the West: You take care of yourself. You help your neighbors. Government exists to keep the peace or wage war.

A cowboy? When we first come upon him, the day he volunteers to put his life on the line, he does not, at first glance, appear to be anything so mythic. Not even at second glance. Check him out in that dreary government office of his. He stands still as a photograph, staring out the window at coffee-break hour. The watery late-winter sun that manages to pass through the dirt-streaked glass reveals what might appear to some to be not much more than a pasty-faced, time-frittering bureaucrat (albeit a tall one with broad shoulders). He seems mesmerized by the only color in this dead day: a lackadaisical yellow cyclone of a Juicy Fruit wrapper and a crumpled Post-it swirling around the parking lot in downtown Cheyenne, Wyoming, going nowhere.

Cheyenne, as Charlie could tell you, is not the most electrifying city in America. It sits six thousand feet high on that broadest of plateaus, the Great Plains. It does boast a nifty rodeo, and a full fifty-four percent of its male citizens actually own cowboy boots, but it feels as much midwestern as western. If it were levitated and plunked down in some less-than-thrilling corner of Indiana, it might seem as if it had been there forever. In the day's weak light, our hero Charlie appears as flat as the landscape. But really, he is not.

Soon he will become the man he was born to be, once he gets out of that city, once he has driven west across his home state of Wyoming to the mountains he came from.

There, sunlight will bring out his natural high color, the piney dawn frost will make his eyes shine. Charlie will begin to feel so alive again he'll even look like a different man. No more pallid, paper-pushing G-man. Why, in the shadows of the Tetons, one of those Hollywood moguls tear-assing around buying up acreage might be tempted to slam on the brakes of his pickup (a rusty, dented thing with a gun rack—*so* authentic, *so* Wyoming). He'd call out to Charlie, "Hey, pal, don't think I'm nuts, but I want to screen-test you!" Not conventionally good-looking, but as the Hollywood type knows so well, riveted as he is by Charlie's prizefighter's nose, dazzling eyes and shock of black hair, pretty-boy looks come cheap and go no place fast.

And what would the ladies think of Charlie if they could see him in the right light, away from Cheyenne? Don't ask! It's not just his eyes, the color of the sky at noon over Mount Moran in May, that would curl their eyelashes. He also has that I've-got-a-secret smile in which only half the mouth actually moves. As Charlie is well aware, his smile can be pure male magic. In fact, he could tell you that the only woman immune to his appeal is his wife, Stacey.

Now, don't go getting the wrong idea. He isn't any narcissist, raising his eyebrow seductively at himself in his rearview mirror, tucking his shirts in tight to accentuate the babe allure of his still-splendid chest. Nor is he one of those aw-shucks fictional westerners, the paradigmatic cowpoke, the sort described as "utterly unaware of his own attractiveness." Please. Charlie knows what he's got.

Yet he is no runaround. Even though Stacey has long since moved out of his bed, out of his house, out of his state, over to Colorado Springs so their twelve-year-old daughter, Morning, can train with one of the top coaches in American figure skating, even though each month Stacey demands more of Charlie's salary to pay for life among the aristocrats of the ice world, even though they no longer have anything to talk about beyond the triple Lutz problem in Morning's technical program, even though he will never forgive himself, much less Stacey, for letting her pressure him into giving his only child such a shamefully attention-grabbing name, even though the flower of southern womanhood he married, that once-hot honeysuckle, is now a formidably fleshy matron whose formerly dimpled chin has transmogrified into two pouches of flesh that obscure her neck, even though they have not had sex for twenty-eight months (and if Stacey did offer it, Charlie would go along only because he wouldn't be able to think of a courteous way to say no), even though he cannot remember what made him once think he loved her, he has kept his marriage vows.

Why? Charlie Blair's got character. Not just loyalty. He has never added an extra nickel to an expense voucher, never deducted even one illegitimate cent from his taxes. All his life he has stood up to bullies. He is polite to strangers, surprisingly tender to people who need tenderness. He is a man's man who values women. There is not a morning or night that he does not pine for his lost daughter. He loves his mother with remarkably little ambivalence. He is incredibly good to his sister, Kaylea, even though she is executive vice president of Friends of the Herd and engages in stupidly provocative, pro-bison tactics that enrage and humiliate him.

But Charlie has more going for him than plain old rectitude. To be sure, he is, literally, a straight shooter, qualifying repeatedly in the top one percent of all agents. He has other talents too. Having grown up on a ranch, he can wrestle a steer and rope a calf with sufficient authority to have qualified him for a career on one of the lesser rodeo circuits. When he goes fishing, trout all but hurl themselves at him. He knows enough about carpentry and plumbing and electrical wiring to make his dream of building his own house perfectly realizable. His grandmother taught him to bake a dazzling variety of fruit breads, from apricot-raisin to pineapple-pistachio. And while these particular skills would not secure him a calves'-embryo leather CEO chair in L.A., or the top floor of a crystal palace on Wall Street, they attest to what sort of a fellow he is. Patient, practical, strong, self-reliant.

The best of America, that's Charlie Blair. It is sad, then, to report that he hasn't had a genuinely happy day in sixteen years.

His speakerphone squawks: a meeting in the conference room. Something's up. The big boss is here. No, not the really big boss but Special Agent in Charge Gene O'Donnell has driven up from his office in Denver. Gene is a short, bald guy built along the lines of an isosceles triangle. Whenever Charlie sees him, he tells himself, Don't think of Dopey the dwarf, but he always does, even though he knows the man isn't the least bit dopey, that if anything he's too cerebral. Gene is now doing what he does best, talking in measured terms.

"We've got a serious situation here." Gene stands at the head of the conference table. The six FBI agents who constitute the Cheyenne office are seated. Gene oversees the office but seldom visits it. He gets edgy away from the dedicated phone line on his Denver desk—which goes straight to the director's secretary's desk—and drives up only during a crisis, which happens so infrequently in Wyoming that he needs a map to recall where to get off I-25.

"A situation?" The head of the Cheyenne office, Wally Woodruff, grips the edge of the table, white-knuckled at the possibility of felonious activity on his turf. He no longer has time for crime, what with five boys under twelve, all with elaborate before- and after-school sports schedules, and a wife back up at the University of Wyoming getting her RN, who announced a year earlier that she had cooked her last supper.

"Over in Jackson," Gene replies. "Wrath."

Jackson! Charlie sits up. The town may be almost four hundred miles northwest of Cheyenne, but it's less than fifteen minutes from the ranch on which he was born and raised, the ranch he loved, now lost to him forever.

Wrath? Charlie tries to recollect. Right, he'd heard about some jerks calling themselves Wrath who moved down into Jackson Hole from the northernmost part of Wyoming sometime last year. This intelligence did not knock his socks off: Radical organizations thrive like spruce in the West, and Wrath is just one more.

Charlie recalls that the bureau has an informant within the organization, a Gulf War veteran trained in demolitions, Russ Something.

"Russell Dillard made contact last night." Gene stops to sigh. "Wrath pressured him to bomb a store in Jackson that just opened, a place owned by a Jew." All the agents' spines straighten. A bomb? Charlie knows why: Oh sure, now and then some domestic terrorist group does real damage, but mostly the culprits are nutcases who act alone. The FBI often hears about them when the rest of

America does. "Russ swears he didn't have a choice." Gene's Irish complexion is taking on a green tinge. "He had to set the bomb because they were literally watching over his shoulder. But he set it to fizzle. Deliberately made it go off at three A.M., when the store was closed, so's no one would get hurt."

"Wrath is claiming responsibility?" Charlie is skeptical.

"Of course not. Group making the claim is something called Free America Cadre. But that's a made-up name. There doesn't seem to be a Free America anything. We're ninety-nine point nine percent sure it's Wrath. Fact is, someone phoned Denny Rettig—that right-wing radio guy, the one who sounds like John Wayne. The caller said Free America made sure the bomb fizzled on purpose and at a time when no one would be in the store. It was only meant as a warning. If the warning is received and if foreign elements leave Wyoming and go back where they came from, there won't be more serious warnings." He shakes his head. "Funny thing is, when this Rettig talked about it on the air, he kept harping on the 'foreign elements' business and left out that the store owner is a Jew. Besides the white supremacy stuff, Wrath is anti-Semitic. Looks like it's got ties to some militia groups, some other big-time anti-Semites."

Charlie asks, "Nothing in the message about 'We're putting a bomb here because this guy's a Jew'?"

"No. And the talk radio fat-mouths and the regular media are both treating the 'foreign elements' thing like it's an anti-immigration protest. Not giving it much play at all."

"I don't get it," Wally cuts in. "How come Wrath isn't claiming responsibility?"

"Because, Wally," Gene says in the too-slow voice of someone trying not to get riled at blatant stupidity, "it's still a state and federal crime, planting the bomb plus the civil rights aspect. Why the hell would they admit to that?" Charlie knows Wally is not stupid. But his life outside the FBI, once so simple, so satisfying, has changed. The world has changed. "Man of the house" no longer has any meaning. He walks around permanently exhausted, perpetually befuddled. "Wrath is a public organization," Gene adds.

"I must be missing something in translation," Wally says.

"It means," Charlie explains patiently, "that we know who Wrath's leaders are. If they claimed responsibility, we'd go in and arrest them."

"Oh *that*." Wally rubs his forehead with his fingertips to hide his flush of shame behind his hands.

Charlie speaks again. "I guess the question is, is their call to that radio guy just a response to Russell's fizzle? Did they expect to claim a big blast and it didn't happen, so they had to make chicken salad out of chicken shit? Or could Russell be lying and they really did tell him just to make it a warning?"

"I wish to Christ I knew," Gene answers. "All I do know is that the 'foreign elements' business is not the main point, from the bureau's point of view. At least not right now."

"What point is the main point?" asks one of the newest agents.

Gene O'Donnell growls: "We cannot let one of our informants get messed up with bombs! What if something like that came out? We've got to get moving. We need to get on top of the situation inside Wrath. It's not just a matter of controlling Russell Dillard. It's making sure Russ is passing on genuine intelligence, not bullshit to keep us off his back—or Wrath's back, if he's two-timing us." Gene turns his head, deleting Wally and the others from his line of vision. He speaks to Charlie as if they're alone in the conference room. His tone changes; his words are hesitant, more reflective. "When push comes to shove, we need better intelligence on Wrath than Russ can give us, stuff that the U.S. attorney could build a case on. Russ is a liar and maybe a psycho. Personally, I wouldn't use him as a witness in small-claims court. We've got to have someone, especially now that they've gone active in the Jackson Hole area. How dangerous are they? What are they planning? Jesus, do you know how many tourists go there every year?"

Charlie feels a chill of dread. He knows radical groups commit crimes. They rob banks or run guns or sell drugs to pay for their arsenals. They extort. They assault. They even kill on occasion. But so far, they have appeared to be waiting for Armageddon to come before waging war. They live more to hate than to fight. Is this fizzle of a bomb so near his heart's home a single crazy act—or the start of something that could end in terrible slaughter? He stops torturing a paper clip and glances up. Yes, indeed, he is the one Gene is talking to.

"Russ is one of them," Charlie remarks, "not one of us. We turned him, right?"

"We caught him in a bank robbery, trying to balance the books for a crew called the White Army. Half the guys in the White Army were in Wrath. You know how it is. You can get the same fifty guys in three or four organizations. Anyhow, when the Army folded, we told Russ he had to stay in Wrath."

"But at the time Wrath was no big threat?" Charlie asks.

"The data didn't support that this was a group that would actually go and do anything!" Gene snaps, as if the bureau has some objective standard by which to ascertain who, among the legions of crazies in America, will go forth to maim and kill.

Instinctively, Charlie knows now is the time to make his stand. He rises, leans up against the wall. Now that he and Gene are the only two on their feet, their exchange becomes a private conversation between equals. Well, not quite equal: Charlie towers eight inches above Gene, although he's smart enough not to lower his head or give his boss any overt sign that he realizes he is taller. "Send me to Jackson."

"What are you talking about?" Wally barks from his seat, a high-strung toy poodle bark. He can't afford to let Charlie go anywhere, and Charlie knows it. While Wally is out of the office, carpooling to preschool, Charlie is reading the daily Digest of Arrests and Investigations and the weekly Statistical Summary of Criminal Activity for him, as well as monitoring the rookie agents' caseloads. "You're not the one who makes the assignments here, Charlie. I am. *I'll* decide if anyone from here is going to Jackson."

Charlie ignores him. "No anchor on my ass," he informs Gene. His words come steady, slow. Well, he's supposed to sound laconic. He's a westerner. But his heart isn't supposed to be fluttering maniacally fast, like a hummingbird's wings, and it is. He's man enough to admit it's not the three cups of coffee and two Dr. Peppers he already downed this morning that is causing this turmoil. It's that there's a chance of going home!

His long-gone wife and daughter have left him desperate for family, and he would give almost anything to have Sunday dinner with his mother—even though it would probably be some horrible, healthy cheeseless pizza studded with broccoli. He would love to try snowboarding with his sister, who keeps assuring him, It's a piece of cake, Charlie. He yearns for home, to once again wake every daybreak and turn in each night under the protection of the mountains, shielding, eternal. A boy who grows up on the Maine coast will always need the scent of salt in the air. A boy who grows up near the Sonoran Desert has to hear at least a whisper of wind. Charlie must look upon his mountains to feel complete. "You know, I come from just south of Jackson."

"No kidding?" Gene murmurs.

Charlie understands Gene's "No kidding?" is pure bull, that the man knows precisely where Charlie comes from. Most likely, he called personnel in Washington to double-check before he bothered to leave Denver. "Nobody here knows that area like I do," Charlie says quietly.

"I hear you," Gene snaps, running his fingers over his domed, Dopey-looking forehead to remove the beads of perspiration that have begun to form. Charlie understands the sweat: Gene remembers Waco and Ruby Ridge as well as he remembers his own title, and he fears being scared witless by those awful legacies as much as he fears taking any action that will end with him sitting at a long table and talking into a microphone before the House Subcommittee on Crime. He's also probably regretting having begun this conversation in front of the other agents, but Charlie is damn well not going to let him wiggle out now, gracefully or not.

Charlie is dying from lack of purpose. Every other weekend in Colorado Springs he lies in bed staring at the broad back of his wife, who is the only woman in America who does not want to analyze relationships. *Stacey, talk to me. What's happening to us? Charlie, what is there to say? Do you think I'm living here by choice?* Every other weekend, he finds his daughter, Morning, has receded from him even more. Once his pleasure, his great pal, she is now a distant, tiny, twirly thing on ice.

He's got to have some life in his life. He says, "No one in Wrath will know who I am, Gene. All those guys come from way up around Sheridan. Anyway, I haven't been around Jackson much for, jeez, fifteen, sixteen years."

"I'll let you know."

"Name me one guy who'd be as right as I am to go in undercover?" Charlie demands.

"Who said anything about undercover?" Gene does not like being caught asking for the precise thing he actually wants. "You did not hear that from me. That has to come through Washington to me. Then to you . . . or whoever, if ever. And trust me, Charlie, they have a database full of guys who can do this."

"I know. I was just putting in my name in case having someone go undercover turns out to be necessary." Charlie is trying to back off. He has to work harder to sound more offhand, less desperate. Washington is wary; it would automatically disqualify as unstable an agent too anxious to risk his life. "All I was trying to say is I'd fit like a hand in a glove. You let them send someone out from Domestic Terrorism or even one of your boys from Denver, Wrath might be able to sense he's not Wyoming. I'm the real thing."

"It's not up to me. This is a situation that has to be

weighed. These don't look like militia guys just shooting off assault weapons and their big mouths on weekends, and believe you me, Charlie, I don't want to have to answer questions on how come I recommended you for what turns out to be a suicide mission."

Charlie checks his watch, a Timex with a dent beneath the winder. "Eight hours, Gene, and I'm there." He knows he's not being cool. But all cool will get him is lost in a database. "Twenty-four hours after that, I could have a place to live and a job and get to work checking out your informant, seeing how much of a powder keg Wrath is."

"Cut it out with the undercover stuff, Charlie!" Gene's snarl is so harsh that Charlie knows his instincts are right: His boss and probably his boss's boss want a man inside Wrath.

"Hey!" Wally jumps up. "Don't I get a say in this?" Charlie and Gene do not even glance at him.

"Okay, Gene. I've forgotten it. No undercover."

"It's a dead issue unless you hear from me, personally, to the contrary. It's not your decision to make, Charlie. I mean it."

"I know you do." He knows he's going.

Three weeks later, at the exact minute that Charlie tosses into his suitcase his old Smith & Wesson, which lands on a pair of jeans so worn they have the texture of velvet, a young woman in a town called Shorehaven on Long Island in the state of New York is debating whether she should pack her Wonderbra for Wyoming. Telling you this is not meant to make her sound frivolous, for that is certainly not the case. In fact, having mentioned that Charlie Blair is a hero of this story, it is time to present our other hero: Lauren Ruth Miller, the child Anne

Hutchinson and George Washington never had.

Lauren is twenty-seven years old and has hair the color of fire. Since she cannot stand being stereotyped as a tempestuous redhead, she subdues the sparks she inevitably gives off by pulling back her blaze of hair into a braid or ponytail. She hardly ever wears makeup, although she well knows she's running the risk of looking like an anemic loser. Now that she's temporarily living at home again, her mother, Barbara, repeatedly leaves burnt sienna blushes and dusty rose lipsticks—department store bonuses from cosmetics companies—on Lauren's dresser with overly cheery notes: "Hi, sweetie! Not a hint (I swear!), just an offer. If not interested, put back on my bathroom sink. XXXOOO, Mom." Lauren is convinced Barbara believes that all it would take for her to be Pentagon correspondent for the *Washington Post* and happily married is a little makeup. Occasionally she's tempted to oblige, for both their sakes, aware of the transformative witchery of a touch of brown mascara. But then, what if nothing happened?

Not that she has money to throw away on makeup. Having given up a perfectly good job in Ohio covering the criminal courts for the *Columbus Star* and taken a huge salary cut in order to get back to New York, she is working as reporter, book reviewer and advice-to-the-lovelorn columnist at the *Jewish News,* a paper whose absentee owner, busy cataloging his collection of Tibetan tanka scroll paintings, has long since forgotten, especially as it came to him as one thin wedge of a humongous inherited pie.

Look at Lauren over there, sitting in front of her computer. Her dark eyes appear to be focused on the letters that fly across the screen, but as she types "Mr. Gruber claimed his petrochemical plant in Haifa 'is a hundred percent not polluting the bay,'" all she can think about is how to get away. She loathes her job. Yes, she is Jewish, and sure, growing up around New York brings with it a pride in Semitically surnamed Nobel laureates, a smattering of lively Yiddish phrases and a knowledge that Passover follows Purim that follows Hanukkah, but her beat—Jews—which she assumed would be a piece of cake, has turned out to be difficult for her, almost impenetrable. This world of synagogue-goers and latke-fryers and Zionists and Dead Sea Scroll scholars and numerologists and Hebraicists and cardiologists' Torah study groups is as alien to her as the Vatican, and more unwelcoming, for a cardinal would not look as askance at her lack of knowledge as do so many of her subjects: What, sweetheart, what? You don't know the difference between kiddush and kaddish? Lauren what? Miller? What? Non-Jewish Miller?

When at last she types "#" at the end of the piece, she exhales a weary sigh, one that comes so naturally since she's been at *JewNew* she no longer hears it. A year earlier, in Columbus, leafing through *Time* or *Newsweek,* she came across one of those "Fifty Young Americans Who Will Make the Future Bright" roundups. Suddenly she realized she had missed the boat. She was too old to be a prodigy. Not only that: Even if she had worked faster, harder, she obviously lacked the stuff to ever be first rate. A prodigy would be covering a war by now, hunkering down with insurrectionists, tossing out questions in Albanian or Zulu. But Lauren's only foreign language is Latin, which she chose because her mother said French is so mellifluous and her father said Spanish is so practical.

By now, a genuine Young American Who Will Make

the Future Bright would have been able to make banner headlines by tracing an inadvertent aside after a press conference all the way up to the White House, or at least the statehouse. Lauren's biggest journalistic coup was getting Columbus Criminal Court Judge Farley Boccherini to admit that he should not have let a sequestered jury in a rape case go out to lunch at the Splendid Lotus Chinese restaurant, where the assistant DA prosecuting the case, known to eat sesame noodles there almost every day, was brazen enough to smile in the direction of the panel. Ninety minutes later, the jury voted to convict. Her revelation wound up on page nine of the *Star*.

But if it doesn't take congenital optimism to be a reporter, to believe that today's routine assignment might lead to the big story, it at least takes an innate gift for not giving up. A second later, Lauren's natural buoyancy returns, and she plasters a cheery expression on her face, blinks her eyes a couple of times to make them twinkle. One more time, energetic, earnest, she enters the office of the editor in chief, whom she despises because she knows in her heart, head and gut that he doesn't care. How could anyone not want the big scoop? The truth is, all Eli Bloom cares about is maintaining the number of subscribers so that at his annual meeting with the paper's owner's accountant, he can proclaim that *Jewish News* is one of the great Jewish newspapers in the country, a lie the accountant, Paul Rooney from the Bronx, is too polite to dispute, even though the publication looks pretty crummy to him.

"Eli?" Lauren opens his door, smiling. As usual, Eli Bloom has propped his forehead on his fist, convinced it makes him look as if he is contemplating the nature of God's covenant instead of napping. He is kidding himself, but even if he knew this, he wouldn't care. He is seventy-six years old, bored by high-spirited reporters like this redhead with the long, pale eyelashes. "Can I have a minute?" she asks. Three, four days a week, she's after him for the same thing, and he's worn to a frazzle by her. Well, not just her. Eli is bone weary of Reform, Conservative and Orthodox Jews, Reconstructionists, Hasidim and Cabalists. He is also wiped out by the mere thought of atheists, agnostics, neo-Nazis, Holocaust deniers, to say nothing of run-of-the-mill goyim. However, he is too exhausted to clean out his desk and retire.

"I don't got a minute, Red."

"Lauren. Lauren Miller. Listen, we're going to be the only Jewish paper in the country that doesn't have a reporter in Montana or Idaho doing a piece on radical groups." As she's done for the past six months, she hands him a menu: "Militia, Christian Identity, White Supremacy, Posse Comitatus, Freemen." Eli doesn't look up. "Basically, they all think the only good Jew is a dead Jew."

Eli's gravelly exhalation sounds like the final sigh an ancient machine emits before it conks out forever. "By you this is news?"

"Yes. Each time, it's always news."

"Forget it. We don't got the money for fishing expeditions."

"It won't take that much!" Eli responds to Lauren's petition by readjusting his dental plate with his tongue. He hasn't reported a story since 1957, when he covered the arrival of UN troops in the Gaza Strip for the *New York Post*, and even back then he didn't give a damn. "Come on, Eli." His indifference sparks her fervor. She marches over to perch on the edge of his desk, lean in and eyeball him, but she stops herself. She does not want to give any signal that might be interpreted as a feminine wile, although she is savvy enough to realize Eli probably has not been wowed by a wile since mid-century.

"Iowa ain't in the cards for you, sister." Eli tests his dentures by clicking them together a few times, but he appears dissatisfied. "Iowa? We can't even afford carfare to New Jersey." She knows he uses that line with everyone on staff. While she has a soft spot for cynical old reporters, she realizes Eli is not cynical, merely sour.

"It's Idaho, not Iowa, which of course you know. And what's going on there is right up our alley." She unfolds a sheet of paper she has tucked into the back of her spiral-bound notepad. "Listen to this. I got it off the Web ten minutes ago: 'WE BELIEVE that the Canaanite Jew is the natural enemy of our Aryan (White) Race. This is attested by scripture and all secular history. The Jew is like a destroying virus that attacks our racial body to destroy our Aryan culture and the purity of our Race. Those of our Race who resist these attacks are called "chosen and faithful." John eight, forty-four; One Thessalonians two, fifteen; Revelations seventeen, fourteen.'"

Eli takes a long, deep breath. When he exhales, the air comes out as a moan. Preoccupied with proving his fatigue, he leans his head back against his chair. His mouth hangs open. Lauren guesses even his uvula is hanging limp, not that she's tempted to look. "We got plenty of anti-Semitic incidents without having to go cross-country, spend an arm and a leg," he mumbles. "You want to write about out there, get it off the wires or on the Web."

"But this is significant. It's a movement. I don't know about numbers or the strength of it. That's part of why I should go. What are all those people who've never met a Jew in their lives doing obsessed with Jews?"

"The eternal scapegoat."

"Eternal scapegoat is no answer. It doesn't explain why. These people are our fellow Americans. We damn well should want to know who they are, what they're like. And why do they think this way? Are they a threat? Or just a small group of paranoids who keep switching, one week saying Jews are secretly running the world, the next week lawyers?"

"Lawyers?"

"Just think about all those anti-lawyer jokes about greed and sharks and all that. You know what they are? Recycled anti-Semitic jokes. Go ahead: Substitute 'Jew' for 'lawyer.' Listen, I've spent months reading their garbage. I want to get an inside view."

"No, you don't. You want us to send you out there so's you can write a big, splashy story that will get you a job on the *New York Times*."

Actually, her secret ambition is to be New York bureau chief of the *Los Angeles Times*, covering the great gray city she loves, flying cross-country once a month to confer in a room overlooking a sun-bleached street lined with palm trees. But Eli's accusation is close enough, so she makes her pro forma protest: "I promise you, when the *Times* calls me, I'll tell them no, thanks. I'd much rather stay at *JewNew* and write about Sephardic folk-rock bands."

"Like I tell you every time, no."

"A story like this could put us on the map."

"Girlie, who do you think you are? Nellie Bly? Anyhow, what do you know from this kind of stuff?"

"I covered the criminal courts for the *Columbus Star*. I

know from murderers, child molesters, arsonists, wife-beaters. I can handle these guys."

"Get outta here." He manages to lift his hand off his desk to point a knob-knuckled index finger at the door. "I got things to do. So do you."

It is not simply that Lauren wants leverage to pry herself up and out of the *Jewish News*. While this may not be a great story, it is a damn good one. For the paper. For her. Because, she thinks, people can spout *E pluribus unum* till they're blue in the face, but assimilated as she is, she suspects that many of her fellow citizens, her fellow and sister Americans, believe that she, Lauren Ruth Miller, New York Jew, is not as authentic an American as, say, a farmer in Tennessee or a car salesman in Oregon—or a sociopath dribbling over *The Turner Diaries* in the Sawtooth Mountains in Idaho.

The following week, when Lauren finally comprehends that her journalist's weapons, information and perseverance, will not move Eli Bloom, when he tells her to stop cheppering him already and assigns her the opening of Milk@Honey, a kosher cybercafé in Great Neck, she quits *JewNew*.

Eli calls her to the office, tries to lure her back with a raise: The kid, after all, is a workhorse. The workhorse refuses, telling him she's heading west, as a freelance. When he doesn't believe her, she slams down her plane ticket—actually an utterly invalid ticket written, solely to be slammed down, as a favor by her mother's travel agent friend, Elaine, who has warned her that if she tries to fly on it she'll be . . . God knows what. Maybe arrested.

So Eli says that once she hands in two articles, a book review and three weeks' worth of "Ask Aunt Sara" advice columns, he'll send her to Montana for two weeks. Not one day more. However, three days before Lauren is to leave, one of her contacts at the Anti-Defamation League calls. A few weeks ago, she says, a bomb fizzled in a just-opened video rental store in Jackson Hole, Wyoming, which is owned by a man named Mike Pearlstein. Dirty-movie store? Lauren asks. She cannot risk getting side-tracked by some overzealous anti-porn crusader who, for all she knows, could turn out to be a pro-Semite. No, her contact replies, a regular video store. You know, like for *Beauty and the Beast*.

Lauren's heart flutters so fast it feels like one extended beat. Not the usual losers and lunatics vomiting over the Internet. A real bomb! Without consulting Eli, she calls the airline and cancels her reservation to Butte. Is there a plane to Jackson Hole, Wyoming?

After two weeks' training, Charlie Blair heads west from Cheyenne in the Ford pickup the bureau's undercover operations unit has given him. A six-pack of Dr. Pepper is on the seat beside him. The O'Kanes' *Tired of the Runnin'* blasts from the tape deck. He tingles with anticipation. That very same day, Lauren sits in seat 18A, flying in the same direction on an American Airlines flight to Denver. She reads Hofstadter's essay "The Paranoid Style in American Politics," dips one of the Almond Sunset tea bags she's brought with her into a cup of hot water, and tingles too.

All right, so Charlie and Lauren tend to tingle when they feel excited. That can hardly be called a bond between them. So it's a good time to ask: Is there anything our two heroes share, aside from the mere fact that they are citizens of the same nation?

Yes, many things. But the fact is that although they

will never know it, Charlie Blair and Lauren Miller have a great-great-grandparent in common. They are family. Third cousins. Thus, they are not merely going to the same place: They come from the same place.

So before we join them in western Wyoming, we ought to look back about one hundred years, to when the story of our two American heroes began.

# Becoming American

# 1

On a glacial December afternoon in the final year of the last century, a certain Herschel Blaustein, a thirty-six-year-old winemaker from a shtetl not many kilometers out of Cracow, stood on the lurching deck of the SS *Polonia* and snatched the chapped but finely shaped hand of Dora Schottland, a fifteen-year-old orphan from somewhere east of Budapest. At the very moment the Statue of Liberty came into view, his great, blue-stained fingers closed over her diminutive reddened ones. When at last he found the words (Yiddish words), they came close to being blown back to Europe by the cruel wind. Still, Dora was able to hear them. "Marry me, my little American prune shnecken." He had rehearsed "apple shnecken" the night before, but at the last minute realized that apple was too prosaic a pastry to entice a romantic and sparkly eyed young girl.

Dora was already sick to her stomach—thanks not only to the roiling waters of New York Harbor but also to being two and a half months pregnant, courtesy of one Shmuel Gribetz, a slick piece of work with blue eyes from Belarus, who had passed himself off as an itinerant Torah scribe on his way to Vienna, except—Shmuel had confided to her as the sun set—he was praying that he would not have to enter that thrilling, sinful city without the company of a good Jewish wife. As the moon began to rise, he sighed: I love you, Dora. When it reached its height, he beseeched her: Marry me, Dora, my angel. Without actually taking their vows, they consummated them at midnight.

Now, with "prune shnecken," Dora's nausea became unbearable. She was no dope: To acquiesce to prune shnecken was to concede the end of dreams. Such turbulence inside her! Her poor head spun like a windmill. What little food she had been able to swallow that morning—burned beans, rank water, stale bread—sloshed violently from gut to throat to gut again, again and again, like the foam-topped swells crashing against the *Polonia*. She grew so wretched that she began to understand the deathly magic of those nightmare tales they told below on stormy nights: A nice girl was out on deck, minding her own business, when all of a sudden . . . Oy! Overboard!

Oh, overboard! The solace of no more. She could feel the warmth of that icy black water as it claimed her body for its own. Yet even as her vision narrowed so that all she could see were whitecaps rising, branching into thin plumes—pale fingers beckoning, Come here, Dora, come to me, sweet girl—even as she yanked her hand out of Herschel's paw and took one step, then another and another, rushing to get to the rail, to hurl herself over it, her head was lifted by . . . Who knows by what? By God? Or maybe it was simply that her cheek was slapped so hard by the wind she was forced to look westward. In that instant, her black eyes met the unfathomable copper eyes of Liberty, the Mother of Exiles, and in them Dora found the strength to turn back to Herschel and enunciate her first word of English:

"Yes."

So here we are, just about a hundred years later. Are any of Herschel's or Dora's descendants aware of this fleeting vignette in their histories? Do they even know there were two people named Dora Schottland and Herschel Blaustein? Well, Lauren Miller does have a vague image of her progenitors, although she doesn't know their names. What she pictures is two resolute figures, a tad on the swarthy side, standing at the rail of a ship. Look! There is Great-great-grandpa, thin-faced, with a regal beak of a nose: Imagine a five-foot-six-inch Abraham Lincoln with a skullcap. And right beside him is Great-great-grandma, careworn in her shabby dress and black babushka. This great-great-grandma of Lauren's imagination is twenty-five or thirty years old. She's slightly pudgy. Okay, built like a matzoh ball. Seen close up, her face is already scored by a cobweb of fine lines—she has come from a land without moisturizers. In any case, Lauren envisions tears streaming from their noble immigrant eyes. She hears them sobbing, "America! America!"

Despite Lauren's natural assumption that this touching scene is drawn from ancestral memory, the two faces were actually suggested by a few frames near the end of the movie *Yentl,* which she happened to glimpse one night in May 1997, as she was flicking through the channels on her way from Comedy Central to Conan O'Brien.

There is no such affecting image for Charlie Blair. He has heard vague references to a Jewish great-great-something, but he is more intrigued by reports of an Indian forebear. That's where he gets his black hair from. A Cheyenne or an Arapaho woman. Whatever. No one in the family remembers much about her, except that she was a beauty and a chief's daughter.

Fine, you say. Nice, the ancestor stuff. Now can we get back to Lauren and Charlie? Not quite yet. We need to look at Herschel Blaustein and Dora Schottland and their

children and their children's children. We need to understand the process by which our two American heroes
became Americans—and whether that great journey
from there to here had any meaning.

Last, but definitely not least, as we leave this century,
isn't it time to inquire: What is an American anyway? It's
a critical question to think about now, what with all the
virulently anti-government rhetoric abroad in the land.
We ought to ask: Now that we've gotten here, what holds
us together? What do all of us, with our different American experiences, have in common? Is there an American
character? Are Americans somehow different from Euro-
peans and Africans and Asians? What, besides a couple of
random genes, do this western mountain man and this
eastern suburban woman share?

Herschel was not an utter schlemiel, but when his son
Jacob came into the world six months after his marriage
to Dora and she groaned to him, her face drenched with
sweat after the first hour of labor, that the baby was going
to be premature, he believed her because he loved her. His
little doll, that's what he began calling her after she
seemed to get tired of prune shnecken. She was a doll—
small, dainty, with huge black eyes and a pink bow of a
mouth. A living doll. Now his doll was saying it was
coming premature. Fine, okay, premature.

Therefore, it was only natural that Herschel believed
his beloved when, after the baby arrived, she explained—
her voice raspy after shrieking through her fourteen hours
of labor—that it was not at all unusual for two dark-eyed
parents to bring forth a blue-eyed boy. See, girls of dark-
eyed parents always have dark eyes, that's true. And that's
why he might be a little confused. But boys are different.

Boys could have eyes as blue as—she chewed her lower lip—as blue as, uh, some beautiful blue thing in Cracow.

Cracow! Herschel thought, his eyes suddenly awash. Dora, ecstatic that her diversionary tactic had worked, reached up and wiped away a drop of wetness meandering down her husband's stubby cheek, a gesture so tender, so rare, that it turned his tears to chest-heaving sobs. Ah, his beloved wife, his beloved city, coming together in one sublime moment. True, he had never precisely lived in the city, but on a clear day, he had been able to make out the spire of Wawel Cathedral. And he'd been to Cracow, five times, and drunk tea and eaten poppy cakes in a café. The last time, he was sure the waiter had nodded, remembering him. Practically a regular customer. How he'd loved sitting on that little chair, watching fine ladies stroll by on the arms of . . . gentlemen? More likely princes! And one of *them* had nodded too!

With such memories, who needs reality? Thus, Herschel forgot his true life, forgot the sting of the saliva of Polish peasants on his face, forgot his boss's own spit-flecked tirades, forgot the ever-present odor of chicken feces and rancid onions that pervaded the shtetl in which he'd lived. From the first storm-tossed, wind-lashed night on the *Polonia,* his heart, stricken with terror, yearning for solace, turned back east, to home shores. The ship perversely continued west, but Herschel found peace in borrowed dreams, wealthy, fragrant, Christian dreams. Then and for years to come, he was amazed and outraged to find himself in America. What dybbuk had possessed him and made him turn his back on his beautiful Cracow?

Now, deep in his favorite fantasy, of bringing Dora back home (dressed in a fine fur cloak, shiny black, like her eyes), he did not notice Minnie the midwife's scandalized slit of a mouth. Nor did he hear her "Mr. Blaustein!" or her thunderous "Tsk!" as she pointed out his son's blue eyes. He hurriedly counted out three dollars in coins and, feeling like a big shot, stuffed a jug of Schwartzbaum's Garden of Eden Best Malaga—a concoction that tasted more of grape fungus than of grape—into the fissure formed by Minnie's crossed arms and formidable breasts. Cracow! He sighed as the midwife's aggrieved stomping down the stairs made its way into his consciousness. Coarse woman. Made for America. Not like his little doll, not like the fine ladies of Cracow, queen of all cities, on whose outskirts he had worked as a fine winemaker.

Here, in this treeless hell of New York, the only work he could get was as a common laborer. Every day except Saturdays found him at Schwartzbaum's, all the way over on Hudson Street, bent double, shirtless, like a bum, sticking his arms down into the barrels ten hours a day and paddling, feeling for bits of skin and seeds on the bottom that might have gotten past the sieves. Head down the whole time, so when at last he stood up straight to go home, like a regular person, he was all the time dizzy.

Even more terrible than his shameful job was the effect it was having on his little wife. He had never been a fellow who appealed to ladies, because he wasn't exactly handsome. He knew it, what with such a low forehead—although sometimes he thought it was that he had high eyes. Once, when he passed an organ grinder, a fresh-mouthed boy pointed to him and shouted, Monkey Man, Monkey Man. But the last few months, even his little Dora, who had sworn she thought him . . . all right, not handsome, but manly . . . well, he sometimes sensed she didn't want him to touch her, and not because she was big with child. Look at his hands! It wasn't just his fingertips anymore, a little blue stain. Everything, from his nails to his elbows all the way up to the hair under his arms: purple.

Herschel peered over at the tiny, fuzz-covered head that rose above the swaddling. Premature? The baby *did* look small. Dear God, what had they needed this baby for? He had to get Dora out of this place, home to Cracow. She would love it there. He had tried putting away a few pennies toward the voyage, but she had pined for milk, eggs—cheese, even. Such a little doll could eat a block of farmer cheese the size of a brick in one sitting. What could he save now, with a third mouth to feed? Not that this baby would be eating for a while. If ever. Premature babies hardly ever lived. Everyone said so. So Herschel consoled himself by staring at this newborn boy and pondering: What do I do with the body if it dies during the night?

One year and two weeks later, when Dora went into labor again, Herschel was at work, feeling for grape seeds, so she had to carry little Jacob down two flights to Mrs. Heimowitz's place, even though he screamed and kicked and clawed to get free. The little stinker was so strong.

In truth, the tantrum was only in part due to Jacob's filial devotion—quite a small part, as sixteen-year-old Dora had never actually exhibited any behavior that might be construed as mother love. However, if the toddler did not seek succor from her, he was already shrewd enough to understand that, for him, what she had to offer was the best deal in town. He had to stick with her. Then, too, he sensed that her desperation to get rid of him meant something interesting was about to happen. Jacob loved excitement. The snorting horses and the clanging bells of the fire engine, the shouts and grunts and bloody noses of a fistfight on a hot summer night . . . This time, he was going to hang around to see what was up.

"Stop kicking! Stop it! Stop it!" his mother cried.

Why should he stop? What was in it for him? He knew he would get nothing—not a sweet, not a crust of pumpernickel—from closefisted, consumptive Mrs. Heimowitz. But Dora ignored his screams and even his kicking as she staggered down the unlit stairwell, leaving a trail of amniotic fluid in her wake. "Mamamamamama!" he wailed. His cries might have wrung the hearts of the uptown charity ladies who now and then traipsed through the fetid hallways of Lower East Side tenements, yearning to do good, but on that particular day he was out of luck, as most of the ladies were at a tea in a town house on Gramercy Park, eating petits fours with wee candied violets on top, listening to a speaker address the issue of a dearth of public bathing facilities for the poor.

"Shut up, you little bastard!" Dora screamed into her son's ear. She wished she had a third arm so she could give him a whack across the face. Instead, she kicked at the door to Mrs. Heimowitz's apartment.

"Go away!" Mrs. Heimowitz bellowed in Yiddish, thinking it was the rent man, the one with a thick walking stick that he never leaned on, just held up in the air, like he was going to bring it down and klop you on the head if you didn't pay up. "I'm dying from the typhoid. Don't come near me. Any minute they're coming with the quarantine sign."

"It's me. It's Mrs. Blaustein," Dora called out. "It's my time."

Mrs. Heimowitz opened the door, just a crack, but that was enough for Dora, who used her year-old son as a battering ram. The next minute she was inside, in the murky front room where Mrs. Heimowitz and her four children worked making cigars. "I don't got time now," Mrs. Heimowitz panted, her chest making dry, rattling sounds with each breath. "We're behind." She grabbed the cylinder of tobacco out of her eight-year-old's fist—the girl was too slow—and began expertly rolling the outer leaf in a spiral up the cigar. "Faster, faster!" She lifted her hand as if to smack the girl, and the child sped her pace. To Dora, she said, "Go somewheres else. Can't you see I can't watch no baby?"

Dora set Jacob—"Mamamama!"—on the floor, filthy not just from the winter's grime and coal dust and rat droppings but from a compacted carpet of tobacco shreds. When the six-year-old ran low on tobacco at the end of the day, she would scrape her fingernails along the floor to meet her quota. "You watch him, Mrs. Heimowitz, I give you fifty cents," Dora lied. "A dollar if the baby don't come by tonight."

Then, with remarkable adroitness for a girl in her condition, Dora was out the door, up a flight of stairs, before Mrs. Heimowitz could even rise from her chair. Three steps up, Dora was stopped by a contraction, forced against the wall, gasping, moaning, until the pain passed. All right, quiet. No sign of Mrs. Heimowitz chasing after her. That lying old witch, she was the reason Dora was pregnant again. Listen, Mrs. Blaustein, Mrs. Heimowitz had whispered one morning as they passed each other by the outhouse in back. You want to not get another baby soon, you know what you do? No—tell me. You get up right after your husband gets offa you and come outside here to the toilet. You sit and cough hard as you can for five minutes. It makes it all come out. I swear, on my lit-

tle Solly's life. Once I got the TB and was coughing all the
time, I never got pregnant again.

Now Dora shivered with dread: When she got back
to her apartment, would the midwife be there, waiting
to help her? The minute her pains started, Dora had
shouted out the window to Mrs. Feingold: "Get Minnie
the midwife! Hurry! It's my time." Had she been wrong
to trust Mrs. Feingold—a woman so slothful it was
whispered her husband had to wash dishes—to actually
pick herself up and run the four blocks over to Ludlow
Street?

Another baby. That Herschel! Couldn't he keep his
thing in his trousers? A big man with such a little thing,
like a boy would have, and not even red, like Shmuel's big
one, but purple, like it was one more thing he couldn't
manage to keep out of the wine. He ought to be ashamed
of it, tiny disgusting purple worm, hide it away, say to
himself, Thank God I have a son! Now nobody ever has to
see my thing again. Even though he didn't know the
truth about the son. That moron Polack, couldn't he
count? And every night he had to have it. Every night!
Even when he wasn't supposed to, when it was her time of
the month. Maybe she should go find a rabbi who could
stop him, but what could she say to a rabbi? She couldn't
talk to a man about things like that. And there was
always the risk that hearing her story, the rabbi would figure out Jacob was a bastard and tell Herschel. And even if
she could say, "He does it to me when it's my time," what
would a rabbi tell her? Push him off? She pushed him
every night, and it didn't stop him. Nothing stopped him
and his purple thing. But the rabbi probably wouldn't
tell her to push Herschel off. He'd say, Don't you want to
make your husband happy? And her husband always told

her, Don't be so modest, my little doll. See? Doesn't it feel nice?

Dora made it up the second flight of stairs and staggered down the hall to her apartment, lurching through the front room, on the air shaft, to the back room, with its filthy little window. And there was Mrs. Feingold, where she had been a half hour before, sitting on a cheese crate!

"Where's Minnie?" she tried to scream, but she was so hysterical she could only get tiny gulps of air, so at first Mrs. Feingold did not hear her. "Minnie the midwife!" Dora cried, over and over, till the next contraction took her breath away.

Mrs. Feingold made a megaphone of her hands: "She's coming."

"You're lying! You didn't go, you lazy *bummerkeh*!"

Mrs. Feingold's chins dropped in consternation. "Shut up, you stinky greenhorn," she brayed.

"You didn't go!"

"I did too!"

"It doesn't matter. It doesn't. . . . Help me now! Please, please go get her."

Four hours later, Dora, too spent even to moan, much less scream anymore, delivered her second child and its afterbirth by herself. Then she passed out. Herschel found the infant girl, bloodied from birth, howling from hunger. He shook Dora until she woke, then handed her what appeared to be—he sighed wearily—a healthy baby girl with a robust appetite. Another mouth. Dora would have to get piecework. Hats or ladies' coats or cigars like the lady with tuberculosis on three, by the stairs. He shook his head. It would be two, three weeks, even, before he could start doing it to Dora again. He loved her, his baby doll, but he had to admit he was exasperated. She had sworn to him she knew what to do so she wouldn't have another baby after Jacob. Now look.

And that is the story of how the next generation, Jake and Ruthie, came to be born in the golden land.

Wouldn't it be lovely, then, to say that after five or twenty years in America, Dora came to her senses and learned to love her hardworking husband and feel tenderness toward her handsome son and sturdy daughter? Wouldn't it be heartwarming if Herschel awakened one morning and grasped that his family was composed of real people, not a baby doll to play with at night and two extra mouths that sucked up his chance of going home to Cracow? It would be, but this is for the record, the truth about what really happened here in America.

The truth is that Dora and Herschel Blaustein spent the rest of their lives together with him thinking her a doll equipped with tiny breasts and a vagina for his delight. She was his only pleasure in the godforsaken country he hated. As for Dora, she remained true to Shmuel Gribetz. She explained to herself that Shmuel's running off after one night of love was not running off. He'd gone for a walk and been beaten by hooligans, so hard that it left him senseless for a few months. With every fiber of her being, Dora believed Shmuel had returned, heard she had gone to America, and followed to search for her. Every day until she died of a heart attack at fifty-six, she searched the crowds for his face.

The closest Herschel got to Cracow was the Polish sausage he took in his lunch pail every day. Dora became pregnant four more times and had four abortions, the last such a butchery that, at age twenty, she became sterile.

It took boldness to leave the old world and come to the new. Alas, whatever vigor Herschel and Dora possessed was spent in emigrating and starting a new marriage in a strange new land. America was too much for them. Nevertheless, the hopefulness and tenacity that manifests itself as pioneer spirit was part of their essence. Admittedly not a big part. But by some mysterious whirl of the double helix, it was passed along to both their children.

Jake Blaustein didn't call his teacher a whore without provocation. Mrs. Morrison, a sourpuss who whooshed her ruler through the air the way the Three Musketeers swished their swords, had clunked him on the back of his neck and called him a loafer because he hadn't looked up the capital of Connecticut, even though she had thundered at him the day before: You, with the dirty shirt, you better know the capital of Connecticut by tomorrow or else! Yeah, well, he did know it—Hartford—but he wasn't going to give that scrawny old whore with her ittybitty teeth the satisfaction. Thweck! The metal straight-edge of the wooden ruler cut a paper-thin line on his nape. When he clapped his hand back there, he could feel warm wetness. Blood!

"You hoo-ah!" he roared at her—and was instantly gratified by the chorus of gasps that flew out of thirty-two fourth-grade mouths, by the look of horror that passed over the hoo-ah's face, contorting her beaky nose and pointy chin till they almost touched—although that witchy look was quickly replaced by rage as she snatched his left ear and dragged him down two flights of stairs to the principal's office.

The truth was, at age nine, Jacob Blaustein did not yet know what "whore" meant. He simply knew from hanging out with the twelve- and thirteen-year-old bad boys over on Eldridge Street that it was the worst thing you could call a lady. He did know, however, the meaning of "Serves you right, you little bum," which was what Mr. Anderson, the principal, blared at him after Jake turned to display the evidence of Mrs. Morrison's cruelty: the bloody line on the back of his neck.

"Don'tcha call me a bum, you dumb Swede son of a bitch!"

So Jake got his ears boxed by Mr. Anderson. A particularly powerful blow to the left ear—the very one Mrs. Morrison had been schlepping on—permanently knocked out fifty percent of its hearing. But as his father screeched "Bum!" into his right ear that night, he didn't have to say "Wha'?"

Anyways, Jake thought, they was always calling him bum: his old man, his old lady, the neighbors. They could all take a long walk off a short pier. "Nogoodnik!" his old man screamed, the big tub of schmaltz. Jake looked down at the purple hands that were grabbing his shirt. The cuticles on his father's thumbs were stained so dark they were black semicircles. Jake tried to slip out of his father's grip, pulling away, scratching at the huge hands, but he backed up into the gas meter. Suddenly, the purple ape bastard started to shake him. Bang, bang, bang, over and over, Jake's head crashed against the metal. "Bum! You bum!"

The big boys on Eldridge Street were always getting into trouble—Stinky Levitz had a dent in his skull from a cop's nightstick. You could actually feel it. But when their fathers got after them like this, their mothers would always run between the boys and their fathers, sobbing, "No, no, no, don't you lay a finger on my baby." Except where was *his* old lady? Looking like she was staring out the window, but really gazing at her reflection in the glass, making eyes at herself like she was pretty, not dried out like last year's apple you find in your new desk the first day of school, acting like she was alone in the room and nothing was going on. "Bum, if you don't behave I'll kill you. The next time, they'll kick you out for good, not just a week. You hear that, you stupid bum? What do I gotta do to make you listen?"

His sister, Ruthie, would stop it the right way, not just by shouting "No, no, no." She'd grab the old man's arm with both her hands, which wouldn't stop him, but then she'd dig in her nails, breaking the skin, and he was scared of that because the wine would burn. Once she even bit him, right on his hairy purple forearm, to stop him from beating Jake with a skillet.

Except Ruthie was probably at the library now, reading a book. She read the ones that didn't have pictures. She'd come home, big blabbermouth, and start trying to tell them the stories she'd read, like "Once upon a time," and go on and on, even when they told her to shut her mouth, nobody wanted to hear stories about a king named Arthur. Like someone would really name a king Arthur. Sometimes, though, he'd force himself to listen, at night in the bed he and Ruthie shared in the back room. What the hell, it was better than listening to the grunting the old man made and his mother's Get offa me! every night. Anyhow, he knew how much he owed Ruthie, his skinny little eight-year-old sister. So once in a while he'd listen while she whispered herself blue in the face about Lady Somebody and knights and hooey. Yet with all her books and sucking up to teachers, she was willing to sink her buckteeth into the old man's arm. God, she was a pal! He wished for her sake she was prettier. It really wasn't fair he got the looks and she got the brains. Not that he was dumb. He was good with numbers, and when he played moshie for money with the big boys, he was the one who could keep track of everyone's marbles—even with eight or ten boys in the game—and they all trusted him, which was a laugh, har-har. Unless they found him out, in which case some poor schmeggege on a tugboat was going to spot his carcass floating past Hell's Gate. He'd heard if you crossed the Eldridge Street boys, they'd just as soon kill you as look at you.

"You do this again, you bum, and I'll kill you!" Herschel was screaming. No longer content with rhythmically banging Jake's skull against the metal of the gas meter by shaking his shoulders, Herschel grabbed his son's face and smashed his head back, over and over, faster and faster.

Right before he passed out, Jake swore to himself that when he got big enough, he'd give it back to his old man in spades.

He didn't. By the time he was eleven, he was out of the house more often than not. He dropped out of school entirely, working first as a runner at Spotty's, a poolroom in the seamy Tenderloin district, then, in 1913, as a messenger for Bill Quinlan, a very small Tammany Hall ward heeler, and finally, at age fourteen, as aide-de-camp for an imperceptibly bigger pol, Gentleman Jim O'Flaherty. Jake's duties ran the gamut from dousing Gentleman Jim's pocket handkerchief with bayberry oil every morning to seeing home Gentleman Jim's lady friends late at night (while Gentleman Jim hurried home to Mrs. O'Flaherty) to collecting and counting Gentleman Jim's share of Tammany's graft. Jim said, "Jake m'boy, you're a whiz with figgers."

Jake rarely returned to visit the two-room tenement on

the Lower East Side his parents lived in for all the years of their marriage. At first he slept in the vestibule of Gentleman Jim's house on Twenty-second Street or in the back room at Spotty's, on the soft felt of a broken pool table. Soon, however, between his salary and the percentage of his patron's bribes he distributed to himself, he was able to rent a fine room in the Union Hotel, with a washstand and a brass cuspidor and running water. During his fifteenth year, Jake returned home just once, and that was because he had a dream in which Ruthie was caught in a terrible blaze in a big building, like the Triangle Shirtwaist fire. In the dream, she was standing at a window— her face burned to a crisp, black crackles flying off of it, like bits of flaming newspaper, her pigtails blazing—crying, "Jakie! Help me!" Perhaps the dream came because, while collecting Gentleman Jim's payoff from a Mr. Zwick of Stuyvesant Frocks, he noticed one of the violations Gentleman Jim was getting paid to forget: All the knobs had been taken off the insides of the doors on the floors where the girls worked, so they could not sneak outside for fresh air.

Or he may have gone home knowing that now fourteen-year-old Ruthie worked thirteen hours a day in a button factory, and she had to be crying out for something from him. Okeydoke. She had been the best pal ever. So he came to see her with a box of caramels tied with a red ribbon and a big, fat Shakespeare book. Right away he was sorry, because his brave little Ruthie began to bawl. "Jakie, come home, please, please." He didn't know what to do. Then she was hugging the book to her chest, then setting it down to hug him, but she was fourteen, and even though she was still skinny, she had—he felt himself turning scarlet from the shame of thinking about his sister—bosoms. And she was still so plain, just a minute short of ugly, not like all the girls who hung on to him, nice girls, whores, every one of them a looker. Who would marry a girl who looked like Ruthie? Who would get her out of there?

And his mother, the whole time of his visit staring at him like she'd never seen him before, rubbing the lapel of his fine worsted jacket between her thumb and index finger, and not a word, not even a hello or goodbye. His old man, that schmendrick, wouldn't budge from the table, sitting there shoveling huge forkfuls of kasha into his fat yap, eyeballing his slender, blue-eyed son in his pearl-gray suit and maroon cravat. And when Ruthie realized he was backing out toward the door, she whispered, "Jakie, take me with you. I swear to God I won't be any trouble. Please, Jakie."

Jake swore he'd come back for her. He even decided to skim a little more off the top of Gentleman Jim's take. That way, he could pay a good matchmaker an arm and a leg to find Ruthie a decent husband—a fella who wasn't afraid of a bath, a fella who wouldn't mind a bookworm. He'd give her and the fella money for a feather bed and a pair of silver candlesticks, that's what he'd do. But he never got the chance.

The day after Washington's Birthday, 1917, Rocco Biondo, an asphalt contractor, happened to run into Gentleman Jim and began to grumble about the fifteen bucks a week boodle—"You greedy harp"—he was paying. Gentleman Jim said, "What are you talking about, you dumb guinea? It's ten bucks." At the same moment, they both said, "Jesus Christ, it's that little sheeny!"

If it weren't for Gentleman Jim's lady friend, Rosalie, who was, after business hours, sixteen-year-old Jake

Blaustein's girl and who ran to Jake's room to tell him Gentleman Jim was looking for him with a derringer in his pocket and gave him kisses and fifty bucks and a ride in her brougham to Grand Central so he could get out of town fast, Jacob Blaustein would have been history and Charlie Blair would never have been born.

He hopped a train to Chicago. By the time he got as far as Buffalo, he'd already made seven hundred bucks playing jackpots, a poker game. By Fort Wayne, he was nearly three thousand bucks ahead. Right before Kokomo, a card sharpie named Little Moe, who said he was from Providence, joined the game. Jake realized it would be politic to lose, because Little Moe would figure out which end was up in two seconds and rat on him. So he lost five hundred on purpose and got off at Chicago. After painting the town red and getting rolled by a blonde named Felicity, he was down to his last hundred, so he hopped another train west. There was no sense going east. If you were in need of a new situation you headed west. Not finding much action, Jake arrived in Denver with only thirty-six bucks, and it was snowing something awful.

Fortunately, he found a big game of stud on a train out of Rock Springs, with a bunch of cowboys coming back from selling their cows who were so dumb they didn't know from the name Jake and kept calling him Jack. But not so dumb that one of them didn't have the money to take a parlor car all to himself. It had a fancy wood table and red plush chairs and thick draperies that turned all hours into three A.M. and a humidor with fat, expensive cheroots. The schnook kept saying, "Help yourself, pardner." The train had slowed down to a crawl, so Jake had plenty of time to win big.

Except outside of Warren Junction there was a

momentary lapse in the cowboys' stupidity. They caught on that their new pal, New York Jack, by palming cards, had cheated them out of five thousand smackeroos. They ran through the train. Jake ran faster. Between the cars, freezing. God almighty. A regular icebox. And snow? Oh boy, was it snowing! Two cars before the caboose, he saw he was going to have to give back the money. He flung it behind him.

But they still kept coming. Pick it up, you schmoes, he yelled, pick it up! But no, they weren't going to stop. He was going to have to jump for it. Well, all right, the train was creeping along. But he had nothing on him except a few coins and a box of matches. In the coach car right ahead of the caboose, he grabbed a valise out from between the knees of a hick in a glen plaid suit, who started wailing, "Stop thief!" Jake ran to the rear platform of the train.

Whew, it was cold! Snow! God in heaven, the wind! What the hell was this, all this snow? Was that why the train was creeping along, because the motorman couldn't see where he was going? Snow was coming so fast it hid the entire world. Not a tree, not a house, not a rock could be seen. Wind whooshed past his face, swiping the air in its wake, so he could hardly fill his lungs. Jump into this? Or face those farshtinkener cowboys—with their guns?

On the coldest day in 1917, Jacob Blaustein leaped into the state of Wyoming.

Ruthie Blaustein was no beauty, but she was prettier than her brother Jake thought she was. True, a little underendowed in the chin department. In profile, her top teeth looked as if they were trying to devour her lower lip. Her brown hair was indeed so lackluster that seconds after you left her company you'd have no idea what was on top of her head. But she had inherited her mother's black eyes, and they so lit up her plain face that the man who had the cheese pushcart on Rivington Street was moved whenever he saw her. He'd always say (in his native Sicilian dialect, since he assumed that a child with such fine golden skin must come from his homeland), "You're a beautiful girl. You got eyes like Messina olives." He'd also slice her a chunk of provolone and present it with a little bow. Since no one had ever told her not to take cheese from strangers, and being as how, even at seven years of age, Ruthie was astute enough to comprehend that he not only meant her no harm but for some strange reason wished to make her happy, she would offer a diffident smile and a "Thanks, mister," and hurry off, her thin-soled shoes making faint shushing noises on the cobblestones. She would wait till she rounded the corner onto Orchard Street before wolfing down the cheese.

Ah, the sweet saltiness of it, the silkiness as it eased its way down and soothed her grumbling stomach. What a good way to get praise, Ruthie thought. Warm words, followed by good food.

Not eating was often a sensible alternative to mealtime at the Blausteins'. Dora did dreadful things to a chicken. The family was forever pulling little horny shafts from between their teeth; at the end of a chicken dinner, there would be tiny fans of feathers at the edges of their plates. Well, Dora had grown up in an orphanage and been a mopper, not a cooker. She assumed the way to cook a potato was to boil it until it dissolved in the water.

As for warm words, Dora had none, lost as she was in her daily dream: that she would accidentally collide with a tall, handsome man on the street and he'd say, Excuse me, lady, and she'd gasp, Oh dear God in heaven, it's you, Shmuel!

Herschel, of course, could do nothing to make up for his wife's lapses. All Ruthie got from her father was a purple-handed wave and a morning and evening 'ullo. "'Ullo, pretty girl. Gimme da butter." "'Ullo, Rut'ie. Go downstairs and get me t'ree cigarettes," at night. She found it intriguing how her father could say his name, albeit with a bit of an accent—"My name is Hoishel Blaustein"—but otherwise had no awareness of the existence of the letter *h*. When she and Jake whispered at night in the back room, their brother-sister language was devoid of aitches.

"'Ow are you? Are you a 'appy boy?"

"No, I would be a 'appy boy if that big ape would stick 'is 'ead in a pile of 'orse—"

"Don't you dare, Jakie!"

Ruthie doted on her brother's verve, his shining blue eyes and sleek dark hair, on the lopsided grin that passed across his face when she managed to amuse him, on his valor and toughness, his refusal to be cowed by his father's curses and slaps and kicks, even though she knew Jake was sometimes so bad he deserved them. She wanted so much for him to be a 'appy boy that at age eight, she took over making dinner, having figured out by watching her friends' mothers at their stoves that feathers are not a condiment served with poultry and that potatoes ought not to be presented in a liquid state.

Having successfully supplanted Dora in the kitchen, at age eight and a half she negotiated a deal with her father: As her mother did not find laundry an appealing chore and three out of every four weeks forgot to do it, no matter how often she was reminded, she—Ruthie—would take on the wash and also cook the porridge every morning, without the black crust they were used to—in exchange for a half-dollar a week. Herschel had gaped at her, amazed. "I gotta pay for dat?" he asked, both befuddled and irate. "You want nice white porridge?" she inquired. He agreed to her terms.

Proudly, she split the money fifty-fifty with her brother, who, for his half, did what he always did in the family's two-room fourth-floor walk-up. Nothing. Not that Ruthie expected anything. She knew she was so different from Jake that they might have come from different families, except, thank God, they hadn't.

When her teachers at P.S. 147 first saw that name again, Blaustein, on their rolls, their teeth clenched. But by the time Ruthie had reached fifth grade, the mere mention of her name was music so sweet that it lifted their Irish and Yankee hearts. In a school jammed with voracious readers and ardent arithmeticians—the ambitious children of immigrants—she stood out not by virtue of her fine mind, although she had one, not by her passion for knowledge, although she possessed that too, not even by her gender, because even in 1910 there were girls who were not afraid to be smart, but by her absolute lack of competitive spirit. When twenty-five voices rang out, when twenty-five arms shot into the air and waved frantically: "Ooh, ooh, Mrs. Moore! I know it! I know it!" Ruthie's was never one of them. Her teachers loved her because she was pure: She loved learning for its own sake. When no one else could explain the annexation of Korea by Japan or stand up and tell the class what a cumulonimbus cloud was, they would simply say, "Ruth Blaustein."

She never once let them down, the faculty murmured over their bread-and-butter sandwiches at lunch. Better

still, Ruth never—like all the others, even the best of
them—got that smug little smile on her face when she
had the correct answer. Actually, the only time they ever
saw her smile was when they offered her a book to read:
Yes, that's right, Ruth, you may take it home with you.
Just make sure to return it in good condition. Not that
you would do otherwise. Perhaps, Miss Rollenson
observed to Mr. Quinn, she does not smile because of her
teeth. Quite prominent. Except, Miss Godey chimed in,
she does smile for that desperado brother of hers whenever
he comes prancing around the schoolyard. When she sees
him, her whole face lights up. Pity. Miss Williams sighed:
What will become of her? Secretly, each and every teacher
longed for the same thing for Ruthie: that she would
grow up to become one of them. She was so trustworthy,
so settled, so precise. They could actually envision her,
fresh out of normal school, short, thin, in a dark-gray
dress. When they would assign her the chore always given
to the newest teacher, collecting tea money, Ruth would
not, even for an instant, resent the responsibility.

So each and every one of them was stunned—"I am
beside myself!"—when, the following term, eleven-year-
old Ruth Blaustein left school to work in a factory, sand-
ing down the rims of pearl buttons.

Ruthie thought: They all think it's the worst thing
that could happen. It wasn't *so* bad. She shuddered, recalling how poor Miss Godey actually came to call, breathless, her corkscrew curls sticking to her wet forehead after
climbing all the stairs. And how Miss Godey almost
plotzed when she turned and saw Herschel's purple arms,
to say nothing of the black hair on his belly poking out
from the rips in his undershirt. And you could see how
Miss Godey wanted to throw up from the smell of Mrs.

Rabinowitz's stuffed cabbage. Or maybe she was able to smell that Herbie Krauss kept peeing in the hall because he could never make it down the stairs and to the toilet in time. Ruthie herself couldn't usually smell it, except on really hot days, but she bet a Christian lady with a starched white collar and cuffs could, even though they said in school we're all created equal.

Ruthie really wasn't positive about that, because it seemed pretty obvious to her that Jews could count faster and Christians could smell better. That's just the way things were. During arithmetic, when Miss Rollenson was up at the blackboard with the problem If on summer vacation you gain two pounds in July and lose three pounds in August and when you get back to school you gain four pounds, what is the change in your weight, eight boys and three girls—Ruthie was one of them— knew the answer before Miss Rollenson. On the other hand, when Ruthie was head monitor and had to go into the teachers' room on an errand, they were always having their tea: "Ew, hello, Ruth. So nice to see you." What were they always doing with the tea? Smelling it. Sniff, sniff, before they took a sip. Or one long inhalation. What was to smell? It was always tea, wasn't it?

Anyway, Miss Godey stood right on the spot where the splintery wood floor never failed to make a week-of-beans squeak and begged her to come back to school: Please, Ruth dear. Please. Her mother didn't say boo, just stared at Miss Godey's pale-blue coat with its two rows of buttons and lambskin collar, and her father said, She's gotta go to woik. We need the money.

The truth was, they did need the money. Her father's back was starting to go, and her mother couldn't summon the energy to peel a carrot, much less stand on her feet twelve hours a day in a factory. You're so intelligent, Miss Godey pleaded, taking Ruthie's hand between her soft, buttery ones. You could be a teacher, Ruth. She turned to Herschel and Dora: Wouldn't you be proud to see your daughter a teacher? They looked at Miss Godey as if she'd asked a question in a language they'd never heard.

Even if she wanted to stay in school, Ruthie thought, she couldn't now that Miss Godey had climbed the dark stairs to their flat, seen the chair with the stuffing coming out of it, the table set with the chipped and cracked plates, none of them matching. Now that she'd seen her parents, her father with six teeth missing and her mother, who hadn't combed her hair in a week.

Besides, the factory wasn't as terrible as everyone said. Some of the buttons were cut from mussel shells, and on the days when a new shipment came in, it smelled so deliciously fresh and fishy, like the East River on the brightest spring day. Ruthie had gotten so good at imagining that she didn't have to close her eyes. Instead of seeing the pile of buttons before her, waiting to be buffed, she could picture herself down at the pier, with a cute boy who was carrying a picnic basket, like the fair-haired boy in the picture in her second-grade reader. She'd never forgotten him. His name was John: John will eat meat and bread. Of course, *that* John lived on a farm and had a puppy and was a goy and the meat could be ham, but the John who would take her to the pier for a picnic was Jewish. John Levine—and he'd have pirogi and a jar of lemonade in his basket.

The other girls at the factory were all right, not that any of them would ever come in first in a spelling bee. But the foreman would let them talk softly to each other as long as the owner, Mr. Beale, was out, though the old skinflint was usually stomping up and down the aisles, his head swiveling right and left like he was going to catch one of them pocketing a button, which he never did. In fact, she was the only one who *didn't* steal. The other girls weren't so—what was that word?—meticulous.

Meticulous. You lost your vocabulary doing factory work, there were no two ways about it. That wasn't all. Her shoulders and neck formed a perpetual triangle of pain. If she wasn't careful how she held the buttons, her thumb and index finger would bleed. On the other hand, she liked being the big wage earner in the family, liked it that she did the shopping instead of having her father hand over his pay envelope to her mother and her mother racing downstairs two seconds after he left and spending half of it on nougat. Sure, Ruthie was always tired and wished she didn't have to cook supper and clean up, but if she didn't, they'd have to eat her mother's barley soup, and you'd ask yourself, What in God's name did she do to barley soup that would make anybody who tasted even a drop want to grab at their throat and go Pluch!

What did make Ruthie sad enough to cry was how much she missed the learning. She had no one to explain how a motorcar worked, or to tell her more about Tamerlane. She had fallen in love with Tamerlane right before she left school, even though he had a gimpy leg. She liked to think of herself as his Mongol queen, although she wished that instead of being a Mongol, he could have yellow hair like John.

The worst part of going to work was being so weary that most of the time she fell asleep over the books she took out of the library. She'd wake up in the morning not knowing if Anne Boleyn had lived or died. When she found out, she got so upset with Henry VIII that it ruined her whole week: She had been so sure that in the end he would change his mind and take Anne back and live happily ever after, and Elizabeth and Mary would play together in the gardens of Hampton Court and be best friends as well as sisters.

Somewhere Ruthie Blaustein had read that Love Conquers All. She believed it. Someday love would come and conquer her.

# 2

What the hell? What kind of snowstorm was this? And that wind! Jake Blaustein hefted the valise he'd grabbed from the yokel on the train and held it like a shield in front of his face. Listen, growing up on the streets of New York, you knew from weather. He'd heard wind before. During snowstorms, roaring down the air shafts between the tenements, making buildings shudder. During hurricanes, whipping sheets of rain so hard against the windows he'd been sure the panes were going to crack. But nothing like this. No New York woo-woo-woo wind out here, taking its time, catching its breath between woos. God in heaven, what state was this? Colorado? (Was there something above Colorado before Canada?) It sure as hell wasn't New York. Out here it was one endless *wooooooooo!* It never stopped. He couldn't stand the howl. Like a wild animal. He wanted to cover his ears.

His poor, freezing ears. But he had to keep holding up the valise, because the wind was driving the snow at him—hard snow, tiny ice pebbles more than flakes. Straight at him. Who in God's name ever heard of sideways snow?

His hands. He couldn't feel them now. Numb. Except that when a part of you went numb, it wasn't supposed to hurt, and inside all the numbness, his hands were on fire. Not that he could see them anymore, the snow was coming so fast, striking him in the face like it had found a way

to sneak around the valise to get him right in the eyes.
God, what he wouldn't give to be back in New York,
with a bowl of lentil soup. To be with people who said
hello if they knew you but if they didn't, they minded
their own business. With people who didn't shove out a
hand they hadn't washed since they stuck it up a cow's ass
and say, Howdy, I'm Earl Thurston from up in Cootie-
ville, and then tell you their life story. New York, with a
shave with hot lather and a steaming towel, where weather
didn't kill people.

To be with Ruthie again, to have her beside him. Oh
God, he didn't wish this terrible cold on her—the way
the icy agony crept up your fingers to your hands, then
your wrists, your arms. You could feel it killing off your
flesh inch by inch. But if his little sister was here now, she
wouldn't be staggering around like he was, like a chicken
without a head. She'd say, Jakie, I have an idea! And her
wise black eyes would be like hot coals, burning with life.
Together they'd plow through this storm, following her
plan, whatever it was: shoulder to shoulder, the two
Blausteins, warming each other, saving each other.

Jake lowered his head a fraction of an inch, trying to
discern the train tracks beneath the snow, but they had
disappeared. There was no sign there had ever been a
train, or people in it. The whole world, earth and sky, had
turned white.

When he'd jumped for it, the snow had been up to his
shins. It had soaked through his shoes in less than a
minute—but to look on the bright side, it had cushioned
his fall. And probably those meshuggene cowboys in
greasy suede vests that stunk to high heaven wouldn't
come looking for him—especially since he'd just lain
there till he couldn't hear the train anymore. If they had

braved the snow and wind to step out to the back of the train for a look, they'd have seen him lying there, and they'd have said, Yup, dead as a herring. Smart, Jake complimented himself. Yeah? If he was such a genius, how come when he'd finally gotten up, the back of his suit, from the bottoms of his trouser cuffs to the top of his collar, was soaking wet? Two seconds later, the wet had turned to ice. Brilliant.

Now what was happening? His eyes! He couldn't see! He was petrified to put down the valise, that he'd lose it in the snow, so he tried rubbing his eyes with his wrists, but his wristbones tapped against something hard. What? What was it? Oh God, both eyes had iced over. Easy, easy, you'll work yourself into a tizzy, and then where will you be? Gotta keep your wits. Trying not to panic, Jake turned around and let the wind whip his back. He squeezed his eyes shut tight, praying they would thaw, or at least that the ice would crack enough so he could see. Nuts to the damn valise. He tried putting it down so he could cover his eyes with his hands. But his fingers had frozen to its sides.

Was this going to be it? Was he going to freeze to death holding some rube's valise? Why hadn't he opened it the second the train was out of sight? It was probably crammed full of knit hose, wool vests, fringed scarves—oh, his neck was so cold. You'd have thought if you were freezing to death it would be your feet or your nose that would bring you the most pain, but it wasn't his hands anymore. It was his neck, on the whole left side, between his ear and shirt collar, where each icy snow dart pinged him, stabbing the thin skin. What he wouldn't give for a scarf! If he'd opened the damn valise he could have had one, and—who knows?—maybe a big felt hat with a brim to keep the snow out of his eyes. Now that he couldn't see, he was probably walking around in circles.

Or, for all he knew, walking a straight line—and with the next step he'd fall off the side of a mountain. Because right before those shtunks found out he'd been bamboozling them, a couple of fifties from the top of his pile had slid off the table, and that's when he'd realized the train was climbing. What are we, in the mountains or something? he asked, and they looked at him like he was a knucklehead, and the cowboy who kept twirling his nose hair while he studied his cards gave a stupid hick laugh— a-hoi, a-hoi—and the one who wore his trousers over his union suit said, Sure we're in the mountains, Jack. Sure, except he said it Sherrr.

He *was* walking in circles, he was almost positive. Was he actually going to freeze to death? Funny about dying: Jake clearly understood that lying down in the snow would be the death of him. He'd have thought that would make him want to keep going, even if it was in circles. But the snow he could no longer see called out to him like his feather bed in the Union Hotel after a big night. He could see it in his mind's eye, white and warm and fluffy. Oh, he was so tired. He tried to lie down. But his legs were so stiff he couldn't get his knees to bend, and he had to keep staggering on.

Ten minutes later, a big yellow dog began to bark at him, not that Jake could see or hear it. His five senses had all shut down. Yet he was still alive, if barely, his deadened legs plowing the snow.

But Queenie Smith, mostly Shoshone (not Cheyenne or Arapaho, as later, ignorant family historians claimed), with a touch of Scot and a hint of Dane—Warren Junction's blacksmith—heard her lost mutt calling to her over the shrieks of the blizzard. Crazed with relief, she threw on her coat, pulled on her boots and, with her well-muscled shoulder, heaved hard against the wind and snow to force open her door. Wyoming born, Wyoming bred, she knew enough to prop it open. In two shakes of a lamb's tail, she grabbed her shotgun and rammed the muzzle between the door itself and the jamb so the storm couldn't slam shut the door and, before you knew it, freeze the latch, leaving her locked outside so one of the boys would have to scoop her into a wagon at the first thaw and when he'd take his first swig that night he'd tell the others: Old Queenie sure was ripe! and one of the others would add: But not ready, for once in her life. But after they laughed they would probably drink to her—"Best damn blacksmith in three counties!"—and a couple of them might feel bad enough to get roaring drunk.

"Butter!" she hollered, and her beloved dog replied from not fifty yards away. "Get over here!" Now, what's she doing all the way across from the depot on a day like this? Then Queenie saw what: Butter, half mastiff, half collie, was slogging through the neck-high snow in circles, herding a crazy white man in a blue suit away from a wood fence he seemed to think was a door and kept banging into.

Queenie realized this was a killing wind. If she went over and tried to help the man, she could get knocked flat. Even if she made it, there was enough sun glaring off the snow that she could end up snow-blind and not be able to find her own way back home. If anything happened to her, what would become of Butter? And she didn't have much more in her one-room cabin than a couple of dressed rabbits and some dried corn cake and a bottle of whiskey one of the boys had given her for mending the shaft of his carriage, and this white man would probably be starving to death, so he'd eat her out of house and home. And he'd probably have frostbite real bad, and if there was one thing that made her sick, it was caring for frostbite.

But in the end Queenie said, Aw, damn, and went and got him, because she couldn't stand not knowing how this sucker got to Warren Junction in a blizzard, wearing only a blue suit. She was a patsy for a good story.

Truth be told, Queenie mused on the third day, when he finally opened his eyes, he was a pretty boy, and though it shamed her, she had to admit she got silly for any jasper with blue eyes. And her mostly Shoshone. Like Nogood Smith, her second husband, who two years before he keeled over finally did teach her his trade, credit where credit's due, the old geezer. But these eyes weren't that weak blue like old Nogood's, always watering. Nope. Every once in a while the boy would blink them open and look deep into hers without seeing anything. She sat by him on the edge of the bed. The sun reflecting off the drifted snow illuminated the one-room cabin. She couldn't get those eyes out of her mind; she could see them in her mind's eye even as he slept. Such a blue! The purest azure, outlined as if by the finest nib in blue-black ink. And those dark lashes against the whitest skin—except for the fever flush that reddened his high cheeks and his forehead. Glossy black hair, almost like an Indian's; it was that black and thick. A little on the skinny side for her, and his dingus didn't have a sheath, which was something she'd seen only once before, and she'd seen more dinguses than she'd care to count. That man told her the army surgeon done it to cure hiccups that had been plaguing him for eighteen months.

This one in her bed now: His hands were smoother than the bolt of velvet she once touched in a store in Casper, where Queenie had met her first husband, an Arapaho named Pete. She was saving up to buy a couple of yards for a cloak—crazy, sure, but what the hell—except then most of Pete's sheep got sick and died. With those velvet hands, it was clear as day this boy wasn't from Wyoming, although it was a damn shame she'd had to chop off his little finger. But after she'd finally warmed his hands under her arms, it was amputate or let the rot spread. At least she'd saved his ears, which she hadn't thought she'd be able to do. Not just a pretty boy, Queenie decided. A beautiful boy. But a boy. Couldn't be more than sixteen or seventeen. She was thirty-six.

"Hello," he whispered.

She let out a little scream, because she didn't think he'd be right enough in the head to speak for a while. "Hello. How'd you get to Warren Junction in a blizzard in a blue suit?"

"Jake," he said.

She could hardly hear him. "Come again?"

"My name is Jake."

"Queenie Smith."

"Water."

"Water or Waters?"

"Can I have some water?"

"Oh, sure." She went over to the stove, got the pot with the melted snow, because her pump had frozen worse than it ever had, and brought it over and held it up to his lips. But he'd forgotten his thirst. He was staring, his eyes wide in horror, at his bandaged hand. "You had the frostbite. Just a little finger, which, considering, isn't too bad."

"Who did it?"

"Me. Where you from?"

"New York."

"That explains it."

"Explains what?"

"Explains you was thinking it was a doctor that did it. This is Wyoming. Anybody waits for a doctor, they get put to bed with a shovel. We do for ourselves here."

"You got me out of the blizzard?"

"Carried you must've been fifty yards."

"Thank you."

"Welcome."

"You cut off . . . ?"

"Didn't like doing it, believe you me. Just the sound made me want to puke. And trying to fix a poultice out of what I have in the larder was something. How come your dingus don't got a sheath?" He looked confused, so she pointed. "Where's the thing around the top of it?"

Look at him, face all pink, then red, but he looked prettier with each change. "They cut it off in my tribe when boys are babies."

"Your tribe!" She laughed. "You're a white man."

"But that's what happens." He smiled, red going back to pink.

"You're talking through your hat—'cept your dingus don't have a hat."

They both had a good laugh at that, though he didn't have the strength to laugh out loud. Just sort of shook and smiled. "I'm a Jew."

"I've heard of them. That's a tribe?"

"Well . . ."

"What's your last name, Jake?"

She wasn't bad-looking. Big, bigger than he was.

Huge hands, broad shoulders. Schnozz like a half a pickle. But beautiful copper skin and full lips. Coal-black hair in a heavy braid that looped around and then got pinned on top of her head. It must be beautiful loose, flowing down to her waist. Bosoms you could get lost between, and even though he was thirsty as hell, he could feel he was getting ready to get lost. Now she was helping him sip the water. He was dreading saying Blaustein and then having her, like all of them, say Huh? and he'd have to say it three more times, then spell it, then tell them it meant blue stone in German because goyim out this far never even heard about Yiddish, although she was an Indian—that was pretty obvious—so he wasn't sure if that made her a goy or something else. Something else, he decided. So instead of saying Blaustein, his tongue stopped right at the top of his teeth and slid down a little, and he said, "Blair. Jake Blair."

"How old are you, Jake?"

"Twenty-one," he lied, but naturally she knew it.

"How old are *you?*" he inquired, even though he knew you never asked a lady her age, but with her you could.

"Twenty-five," she lied back, but of course Jake was on to her.

He grinned and she smiled and he kissed her, somehow sensing she wouldn't smack him in the face for taking such a liberty. Instead, she slipped out of her dress— God almighty, he thought, no bloomers!—and they made love till the cows came home, which was three months later.

By that time, Jake was on a horse, riding around the county peddling the dress patterns and needles and thread and scissors that were in the valise he had stolen, and they were living happily ever after, man and wife, and

Queenie was back at her forge, pregnant with Special Agent Charlie Blair's grandfather, William.

Ruthie Blaustein believed in love. It sustained her, and in her sixteenth year, as she hurried along Third Avenue on a cold day in March in the dank, gray shadow of the El, it finally came upon her. Or rather, Louis Wolf, a handsome devil of twenty-seven (being hurled out of Mikelson's Saloon after standing the boys a round and then not having a red cent with which to pay), collided with her. "Am I dreaming?" he demanded, as he gently took her arm and helped her up. But he did not let go. "Or are you my dream girl come to life?"

Nowadays, even the most naive girl would roll her eyes at a line like that, but in 1917 it sounded fresh, at least to Ruthie. Naturally, she had no magazines or TV shows to clue her in. The only movies, at the nickelodeon, were silent on everything, the language of Don Juans included, and besides, she had gone only twice, to see a ballerina and a trained horse. The girls at the factory talked about boys all the time, but what they spoke of were stolen kisses or myths of German-Jewish Prince Charmings coming down to the Lower East Side in search of a wife— a modest girl with a pure heart—having wearied of all the pampered heiresses paraded before them.

Had Ruthie any experience at flirtation, she would have wrenched her arm out of this masher's grasp and fled. If she had been wiser in the ways of the world (like her female descendants—her daughter, her granddaughter, and her great-granddaughter, Lauren Miller, and other, future girls), she would have known that men who drink at two in the afternoon often lack a certain steadfastness and that being pitched out of a bar and grill is not a good character reference. But no one had ever flirted with her before.

And just look at him! Tall, with an immense silky brown mustache, wearing a suit and a shirt with a starched collar. And so gallant, like a knight, the way he had knelt to help her up.

"Forgive me," he was saying. "I have been too forward." He held out his right hand and said, "My name is Louis Wolf." He had pale eyes; she couldn't tell for certain if they were gray or green. "Can we shake hands and be friends?"

She hesitated. Her fingers were so dry and callused from holding buttons that her hands felt more like pieces of machinery than the soft, feminine objects such a man would want to hold.

"Are you that offended by my behavior?" Louis demanded.

"No. Of course not," Ruthie replied.

Oh, she couldn't believe it! When he shook her hand, not only did his big right hand envelope hers, but he also held the back of her hand with his left, so she could feel the warmth of him from both sides. It was so exciting it made her embarrassed, as if they were doing something on Third Avenue that married people did. Yet it was such a tender gesture. Nothing to be ashamed of. All her life she had been waiting for this, the heat of someone's skin against her own, the reassurance—I am holding you, I will never let you down—of flesh against flesh. She turned her head away so he could not see how homely she was. Before she turned back, she jutted out her jaw, so her chin wouldn't appear so weak. He demanded, "Am I going to have to guess your name? Esmeralda. No? Phoebe? Penelope?"

If she was going to talk, she had to pull in her chin, which was too bad, because he would realize she wasn't pretty. Smile? She didn't dare. Her two top front teeth were so crooked they practically made an X. But if she didn't smile he would think she was not only ugly but a crabby old maid to boot. So she smiled and said, "Ruth Blaustein, Mr. Wolf. I guess, with my name, you must know exactly what I am."

"I do? What are you?"

"Another dull girl from downtown." He smiled. What kind of smile? Pleased, maybe at the two *d* words she'd used. Two words with the same letter like that had some name; Miss Willard had told her about it one afternoon after school, when she was showing her a poetry book, but now for the life of her she couldn't remember the word. Wait! She could. "The alliteration doesn't make me any more poetic."

"The way you speak tells me you're anything but dull. I find you—now that we are alliterating—decidedly delightful."

She was unaware of it happening, but somehow they were walking, together, away from the humid darkness under the El, out into the sunlight along Fourteenth Street, past elegant store windows, one with mannequins dressed in spring coats with brown braid trim, another with giant jars of walnuts and almonds and some huge, gleaming ball of a nut she had never seen before. "We could average out 'dull' and 'delightful,'" Ruthie found herself saying, "and find something that just means 'nice.' Except I am out of *d* words. So let me just tell you that besides living downtown, I work in a button factory. My parents still talk as if they got off the boat last week. And you know how people say, 'I don't have a nickel to my name'? Well, I do." She reached into her coat pocket and pulled out thirty-eight cents. She was about to announce, "My dowry," but caught herself in the nick of time. "My assets. All of them."

"Do you think I'm a ne'er-do-well looking for a girl with assets?" Louis was pressing his hand over where his heart was. The light had gone out of his eyes; he looked genuinely hurt.

"No, of course not."

"Because I'm not. I do all right for myself."

"I'm sure. . . ." Oh God, she had offended him! His head hung, and below his generous mustache she thought she saw the pink of a quivering lip. "Tell me about yourself!" she urged, assuming the lively manner of Hannah Sternberg, the most popular girl at the factory, who everyone said knew how to make boys eat out of the palm of her hand, an image Ruthie found more revolting than intriguing. "I would love to hear your life story, starting on your birth day."

So he told her that both his parents' families had come over from Germany in the late 1840s, because there were bad times over there. At that second, there must have been some mysterious meeting of minds, Ruthie decided. Because just as she was peering into his gray or green eyes and thinking: Jewish?—she prayed that if he wasn't, he wouldn't think she didn't believe that all men were created equal—he added, They were Jews, of course.

Then he told her how his father had owned a men's hosiery factory on Canal Street, but the roof caved in during the blizzard of '88 and he lost everything and had to go to work for his biggest competitor, a man who made inferior goods, and this broke his father's heart. He died when Louis was still a child. His mother, Ann—Ruthie's heart fluttered at the Americanness of the name—had married again, a man named Marcus Landau. You know Landau's, the department store? It was too fancy for Ruthie to *know,* although of course she'd heard of it. He's from that family.

But Louis hardly ever saw them, because they were always traveling abroad and because Landau was wildly jealous of Ann's love for Louis. He would not let his stepson into the house except once a year, on the High Holy Days, although Louis's mother would sneak out as often as she could. They took tea at Carswell's.

Ruthie glanced around and was startled that they were now walking up Fifth Avenue and that the buds on the branches of the trees were beginning to swell for next month's bursting. Just then, the mysterious meeting of minds happened once more. Louis suddenly comprehended that she was beginning to wonder how come he kept talking about what hotel his mother stayed at in London when she was traveling—and hadn't said one word about himself. That instant, he explained, he was a bookkeeper at Jamison's, a store down on Hudson Street that sold fine stationery.

"A bookkeeper," she said.

"You're disappointed," he observed.

"What?"

"That I'm only one step above a clerk."

"A bookkeeper is a fine job!" To tell the truth, she *was* a little disappointed. She'd thought a man with such a fine carriage, wearing a suit with a matching vest, must do something extremely refined: be a violinist, manufacture teacups.

"You're right to be disappointed," Louis said. "I'm disappointed in myself. Even though my father had nothing to leave me, I could have made my way in the world better than I did. But I was headstrong." He did not look headstrong, Ruthie thought. His eyes closed for a moment, as though he could not both look at her and keep control of the upheaval inside him. Without the light shining from those fine eyes, he appeared weary, almost beaten down. There were deep lines perpendicular to the corners of his mouth, so deep they looked like scars. Emerging with him from the shadow of a building canopy, Ruthie saw that his fair skin had lost the rosiness it had when she first encountered him. Now it appeared sallow, almost yellow. "Headstrong. I drank, I gambled, I caroused."

"Oh," Ruthie said. "I've never met a man who caroused before."

He allowed himself a swift but sweet smile. Then his melancholy returned. "I lost job after job. My last employer, Mr. Stoddard, a spice importer, a wonderful man—he often took me to the opera—told me I had a weak character. He was correct."

"He was not!"

"He discharged me on the spot, and he was right to do so. I was habitually late. And then I could not account for two hundred dollars. What else could he do?" Louis stopped and leaned against a streetlamp. His chin dropped onto his starched collar. The memory seemed too much for him.

"What else could he do? He could have given you another chance!"

"No, my dear Ruth. I did not deserve one. But at least"—he stood straight and adjusted the sleeves of his jacket—"at least what he did brought me to my senses. It has been a brutal two years, but I am climbing out of the hole I dug for myself. I've paid back every cent of that money."

"So you took the two hundred dollars?" Ruthie inquired, trying to sound as if she knew it was the sort of thing businessmen did every day.

"Good God, what you must think of me! No! Please forgive me. I should have been clearer. I have no idea what happened to that money. Perhaps I marked it down as received when it had not been, or made some other error I was never able to trace. Maybe it was stolen. It doesn't matter. I was responsible, and at least—at last—I have finally lived up to my responsibilities." He smiled at her, a wide, generous smile. "You are a rare young woman, Miss Ruth Blaustein. You are intelligent *and* kind. Now, I have a bit more than thirty-eight cents. May I buy you an ice cream soda? Please. I want to be with you, if you can bear more of my company."

So she had a strawberry soda, and three weeks later she married him.

Within six months, Ruthie Wolf was pregnant. And seven months after that, very pregnant. That was why she was shocked when Louis grabbed her arm, dragged her from the corner she was cowering in and smacked her across the face, first with the back of his hand, then with the flat of his hand, then with the back again. She covered her cheeks and temples with her hands, and he roared, "Don't you dare laugh at me!"

The "Shhh" escaped before she could control it, but she didn't want the other residents at the rooming house to hear them fighting again, because every time she walked outside she'd get dirty looks from them, as if they were trying to understand what she could have done to make such a handsome, courteous man—he held doors, remembered their children's names—so angry that he had to holler at the top of his lungs and pound the walls of their room in frustration. And now he'd hit her, and then hit her again and again. He'd raised his hand to her once, a year earlier, but quickly put it down. She'd seen him gripping his thigh, sinking his fingers into his own flesh, hurting himself to protect her. But not this time. Dear God, her jaw. The pain radiated to her teeth and into her ear.

"Don't you think I have any pride?" He had never been this loud before. His yelling rattled the teakettle. If Jakie were still here, if he knew what Louis was doing to her, he'd grab the hand that hit her and crush it inside his until you could hear the crunch of breaking bones. He'd kill him. "Answer me!" he screamed. Her teeth felt loose. What if they fell out? He raised his hand again. "Answer me!"

"You were telling me about the salesman's job for the dairy and you started laughing, so I . . ."

He crossed his arms over his chest and looked down at her in the middle of the room, where he'd dragged her. She could see the muscles bulging beneath his shirt. His lips pressed together to form an angry gash. She waited, breathing as quietly as she could, afraid to move, afraid to speak. "Am I an embarrassment to you?" he finally asked. His voice was softer now, but she understood she should not be relieved. "Because I can't get work?"

"No, Louis. Of course not."

He hadn't worked a single day since they'd been married, when he claimed his boss had discharged him because he took time off for the wedding. Their marriage was six hours old when she knew her husband to be a liar. Either he had been fired from his bookkeeping job at

Jamison's long before or, perhaps, he had never worked there at all.

So Ruthie stayed on at Beale's Buttons, while Louis went out to look for work. Soon she learned that his elaborate narratives of walking the baking or icy pavements, of interviews with boorish managers and stonehearted proprietors, were stories. Good stories: While he was telling them, her heart would sink at his despondency, her eyes would fill. But the instant a tale ended, Ruthie knew it to be yet another lie, that he had spent his streetcar fare at the tavern.

"There's not a day in the week that I'm not all over the city, begging for work."

"I know that, Louis," she whispered. How her ear hurt, outside and all the way inside. Oh God, the loose teeth. Was her face swollen? She wanted to touch it but was afraid of what he would do if she reminded him he hadn't been a loving husband.

"Maybe that's what's wrong," he ruminated, as if they were having a regular conversation, as if he hadn't just struck her, as if she weren't sitting on the cold wood floor, her legs forced apart to make room for her belly. "I must seem too eager to please, too eager to roll up my sleeves and do whatever has to be done. They must think: Hmm, something wrong with that fellow. Why is he so desperate for work?"

She knew then that for the next few months, his stories would be how he went out and acted confident, not desperate, how he told Mr. Schmidt of Ace Breweries or Mr. Jeffries of Bushwick Plumbing Supplies that he was ready, willing and able to do what they wanted done. But then, perhaps around the time their child was a year old, his thinking would change. He would suddenly determine that, no, he hadn't appeared self-confident at all; he had seemed bold: They must think I'm too eager to please.

"I am talking to you!" he was shouting. Ruthie had not been aware that her hand had drifted up. Her right cheek was swelling so much her eye was closing. Mr. Beale had her working on the smallest buttons now, the costly ones made of the yellow shells from Manila, and she needed both eyes. He grabbed her hair and jerked back her head, forcing her to look up to him. "Why can't I have respect when I'm talking?"

"I'm sorry, Louis."

The morning after the first time he'd come home drunk, drool flecked with vomit on his chin, shirt buttoned wrong, his apology was heartfelt: I swear to you, Ruthie, I'll never, ever do this again. But after the second time, although he himself continued to believe that the drinking was an aberration for which he was truly, truly sorry—look at his tears, which proved it—she knew it would happen again.

Yet after the first three months of her pregnancy, she felt a glimmer of hope. She would come home from the factory, and Louis would massage perfumed cream into her hands before she put supper on the stove. She knew he must have pilfered the cream, Essence of Rose, from an uptown apothecary, but she tried to force herself to enjoy its sweet lubrication and not think about Thou Shalt Not Steal.

As she grew bigger, he helped her with the corset that restrained her belly so no one at Beale's would notice her condition and she could continue working. They made a joke of it, Louis's ineptitude with the hooks and eyes and strings. Never drunk, never a coarse word, so she'd begun to dream that he would like this change in himself, would like the sweet, sober Louis, and that his restraint would last throughout her pregnancy. No, in truth, throughout their lives.

"If you can't respect your husband, who can you respect?" he bellowed. "Who? The man in the moon? Mr. Beale? Let me tell you something: You're fooling yourself, because the minute he knows about your condition, you're out on your ear, and what will become of us?" Perspiration outlined his mustache, dotted his forehead. "I asked you a question!"

She saw his fingers flex and stretch, his hand begin to rise from his side. "If you hit me again," Ruthie whispered, "my eye will close. I won't be able to polish those little buttons. He'll cut my wages."

"Is that my fault?" But he did not hit her again.

The following week, the foreman called her into Mr. Beale's office, and Mr. Beale, his thin nostrils distended in distaste, looking somewhere over her head so he would not have to look at the belly she could no longer hide or at the purple and yellow skin of her healing black eye, told her to leave the premises.

She could not go home. From the factory, Ruthie walked straight to the Chatham Square library and read about divorce. She would need a lawyer, but she had only eleven dollars. What could she do for her baby? At six o'clock, sitting back in the hard wood library chair, her eyes closed for a moment so she would not have to look at reality, she heard the low bong-bong-bong-bong-bong-bong of a church bell. The Catholics!

At six-fifteen, she was lying to an Irish priest who looked like a snowman, telling him her name was Mary LaRosa—the name of her best friend at P.S. 147. The father gave her a glass of milk, then a piece of paper with a name—and ten cents for carfare. She lied once more and swore to him she would go to confession tomorrow. From the church she took two streetcars and prayed to God to forgive her for lying. Then she found the ferryboat. It took nearly the entire voyage for her to pull her wedding band off her pregnancy-swollen finger, but when she did she sighed with a satisfaction that was pretty close to exhilaration. Squeezing it in her fist, she got ready to hurl it in the Hudson River. Her muscles flexed, her arm went back, but halfway through the pitch she slipped the gold band into her pocket. When the boat docked, she took another trolley across Jersey City and sold the ring to a pawnbroker for three dollars. Then she walked two miles to the Mother Margaret Devlin Home for Wayward Girls.

Two months later, she brought forth a daughter she named Sally Ann. *Sally?* Sister Therese inquired politely. Yes, Sister. Sally Ann. It was the most American name Ruthie could think of for a child who, she knew, was going to be in need of a land of opportunity.

# 3

It wasn't exactly a porch, but with each of their four children, Jake and Queenie Blair had added another room to the cabin, and after the youngest, Melody, they wound up with some extra planking. Of course, Jake didn't know which end of the hammer was up, so Queenie and Willie, the oldest boy, extended the eave of the roof so it hung over a narrow platform. They had just enough lumber to make a platform that would accommodate a couple of rocking chairs, although if you rocked too far back you'd bang into the house. But you could sit there in the cool of a summer's night after the children were asleep and watch the gold moon rise into a silver mist of stars.

That's where Queenie was when she spotted Jake returning home, coming down the incline that led to the town of Warren Junction, which comprised a general store with a post office inside and a gas pump in front, and a deserted depot for a train that no longer came through. In spite of the gas pump, Jake still had to get around on a horse. Sure, there were surfaced roads all around the county now, pretty smooth, oiled gravel, but who could afford a car? Not the Blairs, not with the drought so bad. Water holes were dry, grass had burned up, and everything and everybody seemed to be covered in dust. Maybe two or three of her regulars could afford to pay her; the rest gave her promises or a bunch of beets or legs off one of their scrawny lambs.

So after eleven years in Wyoming, Jake was still stuck on a horse, and, Queenie had to admit, Jake on a horse was one sorry sight. He sat stiff-legged in the stirrups, as if Pal, the gentlest horse west of Nebraska, were a bronco planning some neck-breaking surprise.

"Kept the wolf from the door again!" she thought she heard him calling out as he crossed over the tracks. He reached into the side pocket of his jacket, pulled out something. . . . Ah, a handful of money. He held it up for only an instant, then shoved it back so he could have two hands to grip the reins and the saddle horn.

"Good going!" Queenie called back, rising up from her chair. Gosh, how her heart was beating! It didn't realize she wasn't a girl anymore. She oughtn't to be giddy with love. She ought to be guffawing to beat the band. Just look at him on that horse! Arms tight to his body, he was trying to pretend that he was at home in the saddle, hated the thought he would soon have to dismount. Jake was the tenderfoot of all tenderfeet. But she'd take him over any horseman, white or Indian, she'd ever met. She knew his handful would be only dollar bills, twenty or thirty dollars for a whole month's trip all around Wyoming. Probably just sold pinking shears here, some throat lozenges there.

Not that any peddler—though Jake called himself a salesman—could make much of a living these days. Bad times had struck Wyoming ten years before it slammed the rest of America. Hardly anyone could buy what Jake was selling, which was whatever portable items he could get on credit from his jobbers in Cheyenne: tinned sardines, corset strings, breeching straps. But it didn't matter to Queenie whether he came back with five or fifty one-spots. Just so long as he came back.

She and ten-year-old Willie would keep the wolf away from their door. Jake? She no more believed her husband could stop a wolf than she believed Blair was his last name. But what the heck, Queenie would have been the first to say: So what if he wasn't what he pretended to be? So what if he'd told so many lies he wouldn't know the whole truth if it snuck up and bit him on his rear end? He made her writhe with pleasure by night and laugh till she nearly peed by day. And the very sight of him! His tight little rear. His blue eyes. And how she loved the feel of his smooth New York hands on her! Her life with Jake was far sweeter than anything she had ever hoped for, even in her grandest dreams. All right, so he had sputtered B-b-b before swiftly picking the name Blair. Some sheriff back east was looking for a Brown or Barker for some annoying infraction she couldn't care less about—rum-running, homicide.

Whatever happened in Jake's life before the blizzard didn't count. That's why men came west, to start all over again. And in this new life, Jake Blair was good as gold. She woke many mornings with lips still swollen from his night's kisses. So why should she care if he wanted to ride out in the mornings and meander back at dusk with only a nosegay of sunflowers to show for his day's work? Or if he wasted whole days shooting pennies with the ranch hands while they waited for her to shoe their horses? She had arms like iron and a trade that kept them from starving even during the hardest times, like these. What's more, for the ten months a year he wasn't traveling, at day's end Jake would hand her a lemonade he'd made himself, with a lemon circle floating in it. Or a whiskey and water when it got cold: Here, Queenie honey. Sit down. Put your feet up.

True, he wasn't the best father in the world to the boys, but he was sweet as sugar to the little one, Melody, bringing her a nosegay all her own, telling her that story about Goldilocks—he called her Brownielocks because of Melody's dark hair. Jake didn't seem to know what to say to Peter and Chester, the seven- and eight-year-olds, big-featured, heavy-muscled boys with skin so tough it seemed to be fashioned from the same hide as a cowhand's chaps. But at least he would reach out to pat their heads as they raced past him, and they'd call out "Morning, Pa!" and smile—genuine, big-toothed smiles—at him.

But Jake and their oldest, Willie, were another story. Maybe it was that Jake was a man who could never shy away from a looking glass. And here was a ten-year-old chip off the old block—except the chip was handsomer than the block. The boy had her broad shoulders and Jake's slim hips, skin that turned the deepest bronze in high summer and astonishingly blue eyes, Fourth of July eyes. Willie's beauty was a living, breathing reminder that Jake Blair wasn't the cock of the walk he made himself out to be—not even in his own house. Or maybe it was that Willie understood from the time he was seven or eight that he'd gotten stuck with his father's share of the work—the share his mother couldn't manage—while his father lived the life of the spoiled son of a fancy family.

Father and son were so overly obliging to each other they might have been living in one of those cities where men blew their noses into white handkerchiefs: "Morning, son. How are you this fine day?" "Fine, thanks, Pa. Mind if I grab me a slice of bread?" In a way, Queenie was glad they were so polite, because if you pried up the rock of their good manners, you might not want to look at what was underneath. Maybe nothing. Maybe something real ugly.

When she thought about it, the boy was one hell of a mix of them both—with her strength and nimble fingers and his father's dance-hall grace and cleverness about what makes people tick. Willie was the smartest of all her children too, so you'd think she'd just say, What do you know, we got it right on the first try! and sit back and be content to have such a fine boy. But she worried about him most.

Unlike the rest of the Blairs, Willie seemed to accept whatever came his way. Where was his fight? Tell him he couldn't go someplace because he had too many chores, and he'd say, Gee, that's right, I'll get to 'em. Or if one of the younger ones grabbed the mixing bowl Willie had been hanging about waiting to lick, he'd shrug and say, Oh, what the heck, and probably offer them the spoon to boot. Where did his—what was it?—sweetness come from?

Not from Jake. Jake could charm a fox into giving back a chicken—yes, indeed—but he'd never give anything himself, not one single thick black eyelash, unless he got something better for it. Sweetness? Not from her. She'd always found a way to get what she wanted, but never with sweetness. Early on, Queenie saw that girls who used honey to get what they wanted got only what men would have given them anyway. Nothing got in her way, especially not sweetness.

Jake dismounted, and he took her in his arms with such luscious indifference she immediately knew he hadn't spent his whole time away selling saddle strings. Some other woman had been doing wife's work on him. Well, she'd make him forget whoever the girl was, although it wasn't getting any easier to vie with those pretty things—she knew in her heart they were still young and juicy, and at forty-seven, Queenie didn't have much juice left. Those young girls always managed to leave Jake with a memento—a strand of yellow hair on his drawers, perfume rubbed off on his shirt, which smelled better than bluebells.

So Queenie forgot her worries about her boy Willie. In fact, for the next day or two she forgot about Willie entirely.

Which was all right with Willie. He would have been surprised to learn his mother thought about him as much as she did. Surprised, but not particularly gratified.

By the time he was . . . what? He tried to recall, scratching his head: seven? eight? Anyhow, by the time he stopped being a little kid, he understood where the Blair children stood in the family. Last. Okay, not strictly last, Willie had to admit. But they sure weren't first.

He sat on Sugar, a cranky, swaybacked nag. From atop the rise that stood on the far side of town, he gazed down into the flat bottom of the bowl of land, over to the small triangle of packed dirt that was his family's place. His home. He hated it. For years he'd dreamed of living in the little house he saw once on a sampler up on the wall in some friend's kitchen: "Home Sweet Home," sewed in little-bitty X's, with the prettiest X house with X smoke coming out of a chimney and a big old X tree beside it.

But then Willie saw Piggy Pearson's house. Piggy, the man he worked for; Piggy, the biggest sheep rancher around. While the Blairs' house was like a bunch of wood crates nailed together, the Pearsons' was fine, solid, made from the smoothest logs ever. Big, two stories. It had a brass doorknob that Mrs. Piggy polished with a white cloth. The Blairs' door had an ugly iron bar his mother had hammered out, purple-faced, sweating buckets, in her brick forge.

His mother. Willie this, Willie that. Willie, I'm counting on you, boy. You're such a sweet boy. But he couldn't count on her. Working her own flesh and blood half to death so's Jake Blair could have his cigs, his whiskey, his flower-smelling hair oil. So's Jake Blair wouldn't up and leave her. Caring about a man like that more than her own flesh and blood. It was like Jake was her firstborn and her son Willie was some orphan she'd been forced to take in.

By the time he was old enough to think, Willie knew his parents weren't people who lived in a Home Sweet Home house. Now, he wasn't saying his mother wasn't a good blacksmith. Even Piggy Pearson had nodded in agreement when one of his men was going on about how fine a toolmaker Queenie Blair was. But what good did that do Willie? First of all, she was still an Indian. Every time he got into a fight, some stupid kid—a friend of the guy he was punching—would be yelling, Your ma's a squaw, so after the one fight, he'd have to go and beat up the friend. And second, even if she was a white mother, what kind of lamebrain would want a blacksmith for a mother? A mother with muscles in her arms a steer wrestler would pine for?

Willie was done with his day work at the Pearson ranch, but unable to bear leaving, he turned his back on his own home and rode to look at Piggy's spread once more. The view never failed to make him catch his breath. That's how much its beauty stirred him up. The valley went on almost forever, shimmering, now green, now brown, in the summer's terrible heat. But even the dust in the air over Piggy Pearson's was finer. It made everything look like it was touched with gold. On the far side, snow-streaked mountains rose, and the sun, flashing off patches of ice, created flares of dazzling light. Beneath, in the mountains' violet shadows, sheep grazed, hundreds of puffs of clouds on a grassland sky.

All that land. All those sheep. That perfect house with white curtains down to the floor that you could see through—not because they were cheap or had holes but, as Mrs. Piggy explained in her soft lady's voice, because you were *supposed* to see through them. A four-wheel-drive Winther. It all belonged to one man!

Piggy, with his short piggy legs and hair that stood up on his near-bald head like hog bristles. Piggy, who when he hired Willie for day work wouldn't waste words on the likes of him, saying what he wanted done. Why should he, when he knew how desperate the Blairs were for the dollar or two cash money he'd pay? So he'd point, and somehow Willie would understand that most of his ranch hands were busy, so he wanted the boy to finish trimming hooves and checking for foot rot. Jeez! Did that ever stink! Or to clean all the knives and shears. Piggy pointed so often and spoke so seldom that when Willie imagined getting back at him—not just slugging him but beating in his ugly pig snout—the response would be not a frightened apology but a terrified, hoggy snort.

Still and all, if there were only two men in the whole wide world and Willie had to pick one of them for a father, he'd pass up Jake and pick the Pig. Part of what was bad about the father he'd gotten stuck with was like one of those long columns of numbers you got in school, small numbers, all in the ones column. But after you added them up—what do you know?—they were out to three places! Small numbers: Jake's trying not to sound like he was from New York City, calling women "maaaa'am." Sounding like he *was* from New York City, saying to George Carter, the second-biggest rancher, "I hee-ah youh younga boy jerned the ahmy." The way he smiled at himself when he shaved. How he greeted each dish at every meal with that deafening smack of the lips. Small numbers.

Once in a while his father would give Willie a wink or a big fat grin, and Willie would scold himself. You're cuckoo hating him. He's so friendly. He loves you like a son . . . well, because you are his son. But Willie's heart told him his father could win the blue ribbon in a winking contest, and that big fat grin was the same big fat grin he had for everybody. Willie understood Jake so well because he'd gotten more than just blue eyes from his father. He'd gotten the easiest wink and the fastest smile. The difference was, Willie never threw them around the way his father did. He was saving them up for when he needed them. For when he was old enough to go out and not work like a slave—trimming hooves, hauling feed, to pay for his father's cigs. To work to buy a place in the world for himself.

Maybe he could have lived with all his father's small numbers if there weren't larger ones, ones nobody in the family talked about—though everybody else did.

Jake letting his wife work like a dog. Jake sitting in his armchair or his rocking chair, his thrones, during the *day*, ten months a year, ordering his kids around like he was the king and they were the slaves: "Get me my cigs!"

No, not like he was the king. Like he was the queen. That was the biggest number of all, the one in the thousands column. Bad enough Jake Blair parted his hair; worse that it took him half an hour each morning to get the part perfectly straight, and then he'd spend the rest of the day smoothing back the sides with his palms, like he was some girl at a dance.

Not just letting his wife do a man's work. He *couldn't* do any of the things a man was supposed to do. Split a log. Ride like the dickens to join up with the fire brigade. Shoot. Teach a kid what kind of lines to use with different weights of fly rods. Ride out with a kid someplace, just for the heck of it, and camp under the stars. Who needs a father to teach him six ways to shuffle cards?

It was almost suppertime, but Willie saw no smoke rising from the chimney in the house. The only smoke came from the chimney of his mother's forge. Soon as he got back, Queen Jake would be ordering him to run outside and see what was keeping his mother. His mother would yell at him to get going and fry up some bread to make hot bread sandwiches, but no—Wait, Willie—before that she needed him to shovel some coal. And he'd do it.

Willie could do a man's work and a woman's work. Not only could; did. But the thing that got him in the pit of his stomach was that if something terrible happened, there was no real man to protect them. From a storm that blew the roof off. From a crazy tramp. Some nights, Willie lay in the bed he shared with Chet and heard the roar of a mountain lion far off, and he got scared thinking that someday there would be something a woman couldn't do, some horror that would finally make his mother scream, or even faint. Then it would be up to him. And he was ten years old.

So yes, he would take Piggy any day. Because nobody

got a smirk on his face when Piggy came by. Because he once saw Piggy patiently showing Piggy junior how to tie a figure-eight halter hitch. But most of all, because if Piggy were his father, he would wind up with the only thing he wanted in his life—a ranch to call his own.

Chewing tobacco could turn the inside of your mouth uglier than a horse's asshole. Going to whores could give you the clap. But most of the time, those small human frailties wouldn't kill you. Besides, at least a plug of tobacco tasted sweet, and for five bucks a whore would do you front and back and give you a shot of whiskey. Nevertheless, by the time he was twenty-two, Willie Blair had accumulated wisdom enough to know that his particular weakness, his craving for rich girls, was not likely to bring him anything much but pain.

Here he was on a dull gray day, that first day of autumn in the year 1940, walking down the street in Jackson, Wyoming, on his day off, bathed, shaved, looking for a good time. He didn't doubt for a minute he could find it. Why wouldn't he? He had money in his pocket and an easy smile. And, in truth, he was devilishly handsome. But despite having Jake's thick black fringe of lashes, Queenie's jutting cheekbones and a mouth heaven-sent for kissing, Willie Blair was no pretty boy. He had left home before he was fifteen to make his way in the world. The hard life, eking out a living in hard country, had chiseled and lined his face, so he looked closer to thirty-two than twenty-two. His brows slanted down just enough to make him look as if he had a sad story, even when he laughed.

Willie knew his idea of fun was fifty feet farther down the street. Fun certainly could not be had in the ice cream parlor he was passing; in fact, the faded pictures of opu-lent cones and cherry-topped sundaes made him quicken his pace. But just as he did so, his eye was drawn beyond the plate-glass window. There she was, inside, near the counter.

The perfect rich girl. She was peering at the ceiling with a look of someone in conflict: chocolate or vanilla? How did Willie know the girl was rich? That air about her. By now, he was an expert. She wore a sweater around her shoulders as if it were a shawl, its arms tied in front. Only a rich girl would be winding a lock of hair around her index finger while debating chocolate or vanilla, because any regular girl's mother would have slapped down her hand years earlier to break that dreamy, sexy, hair-whirling habit and snapped, Cut that out, missy! Besides, a regular girl's hair would never be as glossy as this girl's, rich brown with red shining from its depths, like the sideboard in the Double T dude ranch's dining room.

Jeez, it made him redder than a beet every damn time someone asked him where he was working at and he'd have to say the Double T. As if it was a real working ranch. He'd fallen so far from that dream. Well, he'd really had no choice. Everything came down to money. If you happened to look like what some millionaire doctor's wife from Minneapolis believed a cowboy ought to look like—and not the way most cowboys really did, what with their rotted teeth and busted noses and red, ropy scars from knife fights—well, the owners of the Double T would pay you double what any other rancher would. Furthermore, if you had enough brains to smile at the guests in a shy way and say, "Mighty nice to see you, ma'am," you'd soon be earning triple.

Willie took a deep breath and opened the door. For a moment, the sugar smell and the sight of the girl's hair falling across the shoulders of her creamy white sweater made him light-headed. He stood, unable to go farther, until the proprietor called out, "Let's not let the flies in, friend!"

It wasn't that Willie Blair was shy, afraid rich girls wouldn't give him the time of day. They would. Sometimes a lot more than the time. No, he held back because he knew their power over him. When he came to Jackson Hole and started at the Double T, dreaming how he'd build up his stake real fast, he'd expected to laugh at them—rich girls, rich women. But that was before he noticed their perfection. It took his breath away. Every inch of them was taken care of: There were no hangnails, no stray hairs beneath an eyebrow, no shirts with fraying collars, no boots run down at the heel. At seventeen, he had been too awed by their flawless femininity—to say nothing of the presence of their husbands, or fathers—to make a move. But he hadn't had to; they moved. "Oh, Willll! I'm having trouble with my saddle pad." "Willieee, honey. Can you help me down?" For his first half year at the Double T, he was sure he had gone to heaven. So many women for the taking. Such dizzying perfume. Such shocking softness.

It took nearly two years before he realized what he was to them: another activity offered by the dude ranch. They might cry out, "Oh, Willie, I love you!" but when they were ready to go home to Ohio, he learned love did not mean bringing home a cowboy to introduce to friends at the golf club. He felt sorry for all the ranch hands who believed they would someday be able to convince one of those rich girls to give them the magic kiss that would turn them into the prince of Cleveland. Not that Willie would ever want Cleveland. In Cleveland, in Indianapolis, in Milwaukee, there was no perfect silence, no sweet, wind-waving grasses, no elk grazing in the shadow of a mountain. Back east were big-bellied men and wives with red nail polish. They had no sense of the significance of a ranch, of land and livestock; they were people who could be satisfied by a mowed lawn and a poodle dog.

Each one of those rich girls, those women who had raked his back with their fingernails and wept at the thought of parting, had packed up and gone home. Not a single one said, What the heck, Willie, I'll stay one more week. Not even: I'll stay one more day. Sure, they cried out, I love you! What they meant was they loved getting from him everything they couldn't get from their lardy-assed husbands: the feel of a cowboy between their legs, giving them the ride of their lives.

But this girl here, still pondering chocolate or vanilla, wasn't like any of them. No stockbroker's daughter out for a midnight ride: She was rich, all right, but a western girl. She stood firm, feet apart, not lounging on one leg to show off the curve of a hip. She might even be local, so she wouldn't be leaving the following week, weeping on the depot platform, swearing to write—although not a single one of them ever did, no matter how many buckets of tears they'd shed.

The proprietor was cooling his heels till she made up her mind, a contented—no, a respectful—smile on what looked like a normally mean mouth. Sure enough, seeing that Willie had come in, he gave a snort that all but said, Single scoop, and I bet you'll pay me in pennies, piker.

So Willie told him, "Chocolate ice cream soda," as he came up to the counter and stood right beside the rich girl. She had that faint sheen they all had, like just-picked pea pods. It drove him nuts. Still, he couldn't believe he was actually wasting his wages on a soda. What the hell was possessing him? The fact that she was rich? What good was that going to do him? The proprietor bent his head to scoop out the ice cream, and Willie, aware the girl was looking at his profile and trying not to stare, felt a rush of pleasure at knowing that when he turned to her, she'd get all blushy.

Which she certainly did. "Hello," he said, sensing that with this western girl, it would be foolish to start with the "Howdy, ma'am, I'd be mighty pleased to make your acquaintance" stuff. No, not foolish: disastrous.

Her already blushing cheeks became rosy, then scarlet. "Hello," she said, but a little coldly. Now, why was that? She was trying, but she definitely couldn't keep her eyes off him. She wasn't such a beauty the men were kicking down her door. Not that her individual features were bad. In fact, they were kind of pretty. "Trying to decide between which two flavors?" he inquired.

"Strawberry and coffee." Her eyes slanted up a little, what Willie supposed they meant when they talked about bedroom eyes. She had a cute enough pug nose. Puffy, kissable lips. The problem was, she had a big, round face, so all those nice features bunched up in the middle and she wound up looking like the man in the moon's sister.

"You from around here?" he asked.

"Not too far." The proprietor, who had turned away to get a bottle of milk out of the icebox, pivoted around as if to prevent Willie from perpetrating some horrible crime against the girl. But she smiled reassuringly—Nothing I can't handle—so he turned back. "What about you?" she asked.

"I'm from a little town about three hundred miles northeast of here. Warren Junction. But now I'm working over at the"—he drew a slow breath—"Double T."

"The dude ranch?" Now it was his turn to flush. Worse, she caught him doing it. A Wyoming girl would realize that no man starts out in life saying "I work in the tourist trade." He was mortified. "What do you do there?" she asked.

Well, he wasn't going to make excuses. "Anything the boss wants me to."

"Flirt with the guests?" she asked, in a fresh, flirty tone he sensed she'd borrowed from some movie star.

He turned away from her. "Hurry up with that soda," Willie snapped at the proprietor.

"I'm sorry," she said. "I didn't mean—"

"Forget it." It took forever until the soda was finished, as if the bald bastard of a proprietor was stretching out Willie's humiliation by stirring in the chocolate syrup with insolent slowness. Each clink of spoon against glass seemed separated by minutes. Willie could feel the girl right beside him. What he couldn't sense was whether she was still feeling bad or had already forgotten him. He dropped his dime on the counter and took the soda over to a table, so his back was to her. The last thing he wanted to do was drink the damn thing, but he wasn't going to give her or the proprietor the satisfaction of leaving.

Even before he could put his straw in the glass, she was sitting across from him. Since it was a small, round table, her knee was brushing his. "I'm truly sorry that I hurt your feelings."

"You didn't—"

"I know I did," she insisted. "I didn't mean to. It's just that I have this unfair idea about . . . about good-looking men."

"And I'm . . . ?"

"Well . . . Sure. Of course you are. Darn it, you know you are. Anyway, I always think the handsomer the man, the crummier the personality."

"How crummy am I?"

"I don't know. Maybe you're not at all crummy. But do you understand what I mean? Handsome men are so used to girls being thrilled just to *be* with them that they never feel obliged to do anything. Like be nice. Make conversation."

"I haven't told you my life story yet."

"I'd like to hear it," she said, too quickly, too enthusiastically, and started blushing again.

"How about: My name is William Blair. People call me Will or Willie."

"Mine's Lois Bryant."

"People call you Lois Bryant?"

"Just Lois will do fine."

"All right, Lois. I suppose a girl of your social class expects a fellow to get up and get her an ice cream soda."

"What makes you think my social class—"

"Strawberry or coffee?"

"Strawberry cone, please." He could tell she was trying to think of a nice way to offer to pay, so he quickly went over to the counter and bought her a double-deck cone, a scoop of each flavor.

It was funny: For the first time with this kind of girl, he wasn't letting his eyes and his smile do all the work. Instead, he was working hard at being the nicest, non-crummiest person in America, asking her if she wanted some of his soda even before he took his first sip. Suddenly, he was yammering away—making sure not to say "ain't"—like it was the first time in his life he'd been given permission to talk.

Here he was, going on about his family, about everything he'd done since he left home at fourteen and a half. He found himself trying to entertain her, the only thing he could think to do with a rich girl. What the hell else could someone like him, a ranch hand with a hole in the elbow of his good, day-off shirt, do to impress her? So he talked.

He told her right off about being half Indian, even though most people didn't take him for that. Half Jew too. He couldn't figure out why he was telling her, because what he wanted to do most was impress her. But there he was, going on about his first job after he left Warren Junction. It was over in Idaho, during a wild windstorm, and he was cleaning out stalls when the muck blew back in his face. He knew this definitely wasn't the kind of thing you should tell a rich girl, about wiping horse shit out of your eyes, but here he was, blabbing on. And about logging larch up in Montana one summer and getting his arm pulled out of the socket so many times he learned to push it back in himself.

After she stopped laughing, Lois said, "I bet it hasn't been as easy as you're making it out to be."

"It wasn't so bad."

"Willie," she said quietly.

"Okay, it was pretty bad. Still is. Dude ranch." He stared into his soda glass, surprised to find it empty. "A lot of nights, even now, I pine for my mother and my brothers and my little sister, Melody. Sometimes I even wish I could play a few hands of pinochle with my old man, which only goes to show you. Must be crazy with homesickness."

"How come you don't go home?"

"I sometimes want to. That first year I left, I kept kicking myself for being so darn stubborn, for not apprenticing to my mother so at least I could learn toolmaking—even if horseshoeing was a dying trade. But times got to be so bad, I knew I had to leave and send a little money back home so they wouldn't go hungry. And now . . . You get to a point where you just can't go back, except for a Christmas visit."

She gave him not just a sweet smile but a girl-who-goes-to-a-dentist brilliant white smile, without a single bad tooth. "You mean because the space that used to be there for you has closed up?"

"Yes!" Now, how did she know something like that?

They walked around town for a while, and while the sun did not come out and shine for them, the vast gray sky brightened so it was almost silver. Lois suggested a drive. When Willie said he didn't have a truck or a car, Lois replied simply, "I do," and led him to a convertible they had passed on their walk. Just as he thought he was going to have to say goodbye because he couldn't bear the embarrassment of a girl driving him around in her car, she slipped the keys into his hand.

"You're pretty decent for a spoiled rich girl."

"You're pretty smart for a dumb cowboy."

He drove into the mountains, not that he had to do much driving. The damned car seemed to have wings that lifted it above the road. Lois told him she was born at her family's place, about fifty miles south. Her mother had died giving birth to her, and her father had taken her and moved to a big house in Cheyenne. They returned to

Jackson Hole for a few weeks at a time throughout the year. It had always been just the two of them: Daddy and Lo-ey. "There's never been a father like him," she said. "Least none I ever heard of. You know what he did? Learned to make braids so he could fix my hair every morning. And he read me Hans Christian Andersen stories every night."

"And now?"

"Now?" She rested her head on the back of the seat and closed her eyes. "Now he has cancer."

"I'm sorry to hear it. Bad?"

"Lung cancer. He hasn't got much longer. He's come back to the ranch to die." Willie slowed the car. What the hell . . . ? His chest felt like it was being pressed through to his back. Even though the convertible top was down, he couldn't get enough air. Finally, he spotted a grove of young aspen where he could pull over. He turned off the engine.

"To die," he managed to repeat. But it was not the word "die" that was suffocating him. It was "ranch." He was afraid. All the prayers he'd never prayed were, nonetheless, being answered. Too much was riding on this moment.

"Yes, to die."

"I'm so . . ." He didn't know what to say. She lived on a ranch? They kept coming back to stay there? They were rich. Therefore they must own the ranch! "I'm so sorry, Lois." He reached over, put his arm around her and pulled her close to him. He could sense from the angle of her head that she thought she was about to be kissed. However, Willie understood delicacy was called for. He dared not give her what she expected every man would easily give. He tried to take a deep breath. Yes, thank goodness, his chest was expanding. Instead of lowering his lips to meet hers, he gently rubbed her cheek with his finger. "You're just about the last person in the world who deserves such . . . such tragedy, Lois. I'm sorry there's nothing I can do to make it easier on you."

Make it easier on you? he had wanted to shout out to the whole valley. I'll make it easier! I'll run the ranch after your old man's gone!

For four months, he focused his energies and his talents, his heart and his soul, upon showing her how worthy he was of a ranch like the Circle B. But sixteen weeks after they'd met, what were the results of his efforts? Lois whispered to him, "You don't love me, Willie."

He could barely hear her words, although he could feel her humid breath misting his already wet ear. His other ear picked up an exhausted cough from her daddy's distant bedroom. "What do you mean, I don't love you? You're talking nonsense, Lo!" Oh, swell. He'd meant to sound cooler than a May breeze, but he sounded cantankerous. Worse, gurgly. Well, that shouldn't have come as a big surprise, since here he was, drowning in his own sweat under Lois's feather quilt in Lois's bed, in Lois's bedroom in her daddy's ranch house. Why did they have to have such huge amounts of steam hissing through the radiators? Sure, it was cold out, but every night when he shinned up the downspout to get into her room, he got hit with so much heat it felt like the Bryants were trying to make Wyoming hot enough to grow bananas.

"I'm not talking nonsense," Lois was coming back at him. He touched the velvet lobe of her ear. It was, of course, dry, and she smelled like expensive soap. "Why do you tell me you love me when you don't? Don't you know me by now, Willie? Tell me, do you think I'd rather hear a sugar-coated lie or a painful truth?"

Holy Jesus, was he ever sweating, giving off that terrible wet-wool stink, like an old ram on a hot, rainy afternoon. When he'd climbed through the window a couple of hours earlier, he'd muttered, Gosh, it's kind of warm in here, but—like every other night—Lois said it was freezing outside. And naturally, she wouldn't let him take anything but his jacket and boots off. Not even his sweater.

To think how smug he'd been that first day! He held back so long in the convertible that Lois had finally kissed him. They'd spent the next hour mouth-to-mouth. Oh, he knew getting further would be a challenge, but he was so used to getting what he wanted that he just assumed: Good as done. He'd get to first base the next time, second base the time after that, and once she asked—the way they all did—How do you feel about me, Willie? and he said, Uh, gosh, Lo, I think I'm falling in love with you, he'd be sliding into third, even home. So there he'd been that first night up in her room, the smuggest guy in the world. Because Lois was clearly and completely wild about him: mesmerized by his looks, taken with his charm, touched by his life. He was sure the plan he had would work. In less than a week he'd be in the saddle with her. Then, before the thought could even cross her mind—Wait a minute, isn't this how some girls get in the family way?—he'd have her knocked up. Then her old man wouldn't have any choice. He'd have to say yes to Willie as a son-in-law.

It should have been easier than pie. Sure, Lois was always kidding around about how he used his looks the way a southern belle uses hers, but her knowing didn't give her immunity. Willie had never had a girl this gone on him—Lois practically wept with joy every single time she saw him. Some nights when he was climbing in over the windowsill, he'd see actual tears in her eyes and was embarrassed for her. Couldn't she hide it? But when he threatened never to see her again because if she wouldn't let him put his hand under her nightgown, she obviously didn't love him, obviously didn't think he had character, all she'd said was, It's not right, Willie. So he didn't show up for two nights. When he returned, she sobbed with relief. But still she said, No, Willie.

It's not as if he had all the time in the world. The minute old Charlie Bryant popped off, they'd have to call in the sheriff to control the crowds, that's how many suitors Lois would have.

Now a new stream of sweat sprung up in his sideburn. It kept pouring down his jaw onto his neck, tickling like a son of a bitch. But he couldn't wipe it away, because he was busy holding Lois's hands and gazing at her with what he hoped was a look of love. "I do too love you," he snapped. "You know what I don't love? You calling me a liar."

"Shhh! All right. Maybe you just *think* you love me," she conceded into his ear, the less sweaty one, thank goodness. "But you know what's really drawing you here? Not me. My daddy's ranch." How could he have been stupid enough to tell her about looking down over Piggy's spread back home, dreaming it was his? "You know and I know the ranch is what you really love."

"That just shows what you don't know, Lois. I only *like* your daddy's ranch. If it was bigger, sure, I'd love it. But it's not even three thousand acres."

Here he was, sneaking out in one of the Double T's trucks every night to drive down to the Circle B. The second they found out about it, which sooner or later they would, he'd be fired. Meanwhile, however, for someone taking crazy risks, he was being as sane as he could be. He'd leave Lois by three A.M. so he could get two hours' sleep before working a twelve-hour day. Then, biding his time till everyone was asleep and he could get the truck once again, he'd drive back to his real job, trying to knock up Lois Bryant. Except the sicker the old man got, the less time Lois was willing to devote to romance. The only thing she seemed to crave for the last month was tenderness, which was a pain in the ass when you're lying under a heavy quilt with blue balls, sweating like a pig.

"Oh, Willie, what am I going to do if he dies?"

"Easy, honey."

"Don't tell me it'll be all right."

"I won't lie to you."

"I know that, Willie. Thank you," she said, and immediately started to sob again. He had to give her credit: Thank you. In fact, he couldn't get over that no matter what she was doing—going for a hike, licking an ice cream cone, yes, even blubbering because her daddy was dying of lung cancer, to say nothing of getting all hot and bothered three nights earlier when they were soul kissing and carrying on and for the first time he managed to slide his knee between her legs and, even though he couldn't maneuver the nightgown out of the way, was rubbing her so good she started making those little kitten noises in her throat—Lois always managed to be nice. Not just polite. A nice person. Somehow all that richness—the maids, the fancy car, the doting daddy—hadn't spoiled her. Willie held her in his arms and pulled her close and stroked her hair, silky rich-girl hair that smelled like she washed it every single day.

Willie was amazed that the old man had come back to die on the ranch where he'd been born. Knowing you were going to die! Jeez. Although he kind of understood the old man, admired him for coming back, although not for leaving this gorgeous land for the high life with all the other absentee cattlemen in that hellhole Cheyenne, drinking gin and playing billiards and the stock market.

"I wish you could meet him," Lois whispered.

"I wish I could too."

Lois had stopped the waterworks. Just sniffling now. "You probably wouldn't like him at first, because he's always ordering everybody around—'Do this! Do that!'—but before they can get started, he's yelling, 'You're doing it wrong, you numskull!'" She grinned at the memory, and for that one second, she looked pretty. "Once you get to know him, he really does have the softest heart in the world." Willie had heard from the old-timers at the Double T that Charlie Bryant was the hardest ass in the West.

"Well, maybe he is tough with his men. So what? He sounds like a good father. More than that. A good man."

"That's exactly what he is!" Lois whispered. Even in moonlight, he could see her face take on a glow of amazement, like he'd said something brilliant no one had ever thought of before. He felt a rush of excitement, blood in his brain, a burst of hope he hadn't felt since Lois started saying no to him. "A good man," she was repeating. He kissed her forehead, then her eyes, and tasted the salt on her still-wet lashes. His mind was racing ahead to triumph. He was already inside her, and then . . . Yes, she was definitely a virgin, and he'd have to make sure they changed the sheets so the girl who made the bed—

"Willie, what do you think is going to happen to the Circle B when my daddy dies?"

"Jeez, Lo!"

"What?"

"It's not nice to be talking about things like that before they happen."

"Daddy and I talk about it every day. Except when he's too tired or doesn't have the breath."

"Well, that's between you and him."

"You never thought about it, not even for one second?"

She waited for the lie. He wouldn't give it to her. "Of course I thought about it." He flung off the quilt and sat up, his back toward her, and felt around with his foot for his boots.

"Willie," she whispered, moving over to his side of the bed so she could reach and hold on to his arm. "Please don't be angry."

"What do you expect, Lois? That I'll tell you all the terrible things you want to believe about me? You want me to say someone told me, 'Oh, there's that rich Bryant girl from the Circle B,' and so I ran after you? Okay. Except it didn't happen. You want me to say, 'I expect you'll be inheriting the ranch and I want to marry you so it'll be mine?' Fine. But it so happens I walked into that damn ice cream parlor because you were playing with your hair with your finger and it got me all hot. And I don't know if your daddy is passing the ranch down to you or selling it to high rollers from Texas and leaving the money to some chorus girl he met in Denver or somewheres."

"What do you think?"

"If I was your daddy? Well, I'd've been born on the Circle B, and I guess I wouldn't be able to bear it going out of the family." Willie reached over and turned on

Lois's lamp, a funny china thing shaped like Cinderella. The lacy shade was the top of her ball gown. He wanted more light. He wanted to be able to look her right in the eye. He also knew it wouldn't hurt for her to be able to see his face in the lamp glow. "If I was your daddy, I'd know I raised a damn smart girl. A damn fine girl. The last thing she needs is a mixed-blood cowboy, who's never got past ninth grade and who doesn't have a pot—pardon me—to piss in, to tell her how to run it."

He heard the brush of her nightgown against the soft sheet as she sat up and pressed herself against his back. He felt her breasts, that wondrous combination of soft and hard, as her arms recaptured him. "Oh, Willie!"

"What?" His voice sounded even colder than he had tried to make it.

"I love you."

He grabbed her wrists and flung her arms off him. "Now it's my turn to tell you the same thing you told me," he said, not turning back to her. "You don't love me. Maybe you have a schoolgirl crush. Maybe you just need someone strong to get you through this bad time. But you can't love someone you don't trust."

"I trust you." He saw his boot sticking out from under the bed, but he didn't bend to put it on. He just sat there. Did he have her? "I know you won't lie to me, Willie." Did he? Sure enough, her voice got high, shaky, so girlish it sounded phony, except he knew she couldn't help but speak the truth: "And I do too love you."

"And what about me?" he asked, turning back to her, as he got busy undoing what seemed like the thousand stupid buttons that had kept her neck and her chest hidden from him. "Do I love you? Or am I just some no-good opportunist trying to rope me a rich girl?"

Her fingers ran over his high cheek, his perfectly squared jaw. "You really do love me."

And the thing of it was, as he kissed her mouth and her neck and, finally, the valley between her breasts, that he found he was indeed in love with this smart, good-hearted, straight-shooting girl, this about-to-be heiress, the future Mrs. William Blair. Not madly in love. But deep enough in love so that both of them could believe in it for the rest of their lives.

*"College."* Ruthie Wolf uttered the word to her eighteen-year-old daughter, Sally Ann, in the tone a rabbi would use to invoke God. "How can you *not* go?"

"Mom, just listen."

"You're going to say we're in the middle of a Depression. Don't you think I know that?" Ruthie made a sweeping gesture, as if to point out an entire shanty-town, scores of people shivering under the newspapers that were covering them—Hoover blankets, they called them. But in that particular moment on that particular Sunday, a June day so clear every bird in Manhattan tweeted its praises, there was no want to be seen. Their walk was on Park Avenue.

They had long since passed out of Harlem and its panoramas of need. Up there, passing a church, they had nodded to a group of women in their Sunday best. Together the women had once made a rainbow. Now their dresses were almost white and nearly translucent from a decade of washing. They had seen a man with a little girl, both barely able to walk, not stricken by the same disease but simply so hungry they hardly had the strength to get down the street to a breadline.

But here, on this stretch of Park Avenue, the Depres-

sion seemed a nasty rumor, unfounded, untrue. Sally Ann
Wolf took in the insolent castle of an apartment building,
its awning stretched before it like a supercilious nose.
"You think college is only for boys?" Ruthie was saying.

"Mom, I know——"

"You know the phrase 'Smart as a whip'? Whatever
that means. Smart as a Charles Dickens reader: *That*
would make some sense. You could be a Charles Dickens
reader and studier, listen to professors who've read everything he wrote five or six times! With what I bring in
these days, thank God we can still have a roof over our
heads. All right, that leaves the question of things like
food open to discussion. Listen, Sally Ann, you know me.
No baloney. I have never shielded you from the truth.
And the truth is, you can do it!"

"Mom, the truth's good. Okay? I'm crazy about it. It's
another thing to say what's my truth is your truth. The
way I see it, I have no choice. I have to work. Mom, we're
poor."

"That's not the American way," Ruthie said, "giving
up without a fight. Aren't you even going to try?"

"The American way isn't to tell yourself phony stories
that all end 'and they lived happily ever after' when they
don't."

"But it is!" Ruthie insisted. "They're not phony stories. They're incentives. You know what the difference
between Americans and everybody else is?"

"Yes. We're gullible. We believe our own fairy tales."
Sally Ann was so tired. She wasn't a quitter; she just
wanted to rest. Well, rest and work two jobs. But every
time she brought it up, her mother practically jumped up
and down and waved the flag in her face.

"So maybe we're a little romantic," Ruthie conceded.

"So what? We all believe tomorrow will be better. What's wrong with that?"

Sally Ann tried not to roll her eyes. "We're a nation of children, that's what's wrong. All our movies have to have happy endings. We can't face the world."

"Movies." Ruthie rolled her eyes and exhaled contemptuously. "You have a first-class mind."

"No I don't. I'm just bright."

"You're more than bright! Why movies when you can read a book, use your imagination?"

"We were discussing college, not movies." Now, why did she say that? As if her mother needed a reminder.

"College," Ruthie said, giving both syllables respect, then nodding her head in deference. "But I'm the first to admit, we do need the money you earn. You know my pay was cut."

"So how can I—"

She stopped as her mother shook her head vigorously: No negative talk! Ruthie was distracted by a passerby, a woman in a beige silk-shantung suit, so flawlessly groomed she looked like a walking statue. "That could be you," she said to Sally Ann.

They walked without speaking for a block, passing, it seemed, only rich people, as if she and her mother were the only two New Yorkers not sufficiently ashamed by their bargain-basement dresses to keep off Park Avenue.

"Get a load of him," Sally Ann observed to Ruthie to break the ice of their silence. A uniformed doorman with braided epaulets and brass buttons was guarding the entrance of a massive white apartment building. "Like an army officer from some make-believe country in . . ." She was about to add "an MGM musical," but she let her voice trail off.

The doorman, meanwhile, observed Sally Ann back. True, she was no Park Avenue girl, not even Central Park West, not in that cheap dress. Nevertheless, she walked the way the beauties walked, with her head back, like she didn't have to watch out for cracks in the sidewalk. Her long dark hair, pulled off her face by a wide turquoise ribbon, bounced cheerily on her shoulders. He touched the brim of his cap.

"A make-believe country in what?" Ruthie snorted. "In a movie, right? You're complaining you can't find the money for college, but you have money for movies." She stopped snorting to glare at the doorman.

"You scared him, Mom. He could have been your son-in-law."

"Bite your tongue and spit out three times!"

"But he's got a Park Avenue address."

"You're laughing, but with a bachelor of arts, you could get a Park Avenue husband. You could have a subscription to the opera *and* the Philharmonic." Ruthie patted Sally Ann's cheek, and they kept walking. No more talk of movies. No more talk of college.

Ever since the girl could remember, Sally Ann and her mother had taken their Sunday walks through every part of the city. Walks? Hikes. Her earliest memories, though, were not of strolling across the Brooklyn Bridge or of visiting the giraffe in the Bronx Zoo, but of sitting in the infinite security of her mother's lap, her head on the pillow of Ruthie's bosom, as the subway hurtled them toward the starting point of that week's route.

Freezing rain, blistering dog days, it didn't matter. Walking was educational. Walking was free. So they tramped through a forest in Staten Island and collected leaves so they could go to the library and look up what trees they'd seen. Strolled along Sheepshead Bay and stopped to talk to the fishermen about their catch and, more than once, went home with a flounder for dinner. They had heard their footsteps echoing in the empty fortresses of Wall Street on the first Sunday after Black Tuesday.

And always, even if it meant an extra subway fare they could barely afford, they wound up at a museum. Girls who had fathers might be bought an ice cream cone on Sundays, but Sally Ann had a mother who brought her culture. Vermeer's paintings: "He didn't rush through those brush strokes, let me tell you! Look! What are you staring into space for? Nothing's in space. Vermeer's right in front of your nose!" Ninth-century armor: "That Charlemagne was no dope when it came to chest protection." Every Sunday was an opportunity to learn more.

"Mom, listen." Sally Ann spoke carefully. "We both know there's a Depression now. Agreed?" Be fair, Sally Ann wanted to argue. I know better than you. Didn't I write "President Roosevelt and the Federal Emergency Administration of Public Works," which had won Abraham Lincoln High School's coveted Yetta B. Feigenbaum Social Studies Award at graduation and placed third in the all-Brooklyn competition? Sally Ann Wolf was a girl who understood what was what.

And really, how often did she actually go to a movie? Three, four times a year? It wasn't that she slacked off. Hadn't she rushed out and gotten a second job after school, working the steam tables at the Brighton Cafeteria—six to ten, seven nights a week—the very day after Mr. Tsung, who owned the Oriental Pearl Trimmings plant, where her mother was now forelady, confided to Ruthie that he wasn't sure if he could stay in business;

most of his customers were padlocking their doors forever? And even when Oriental Pearl did manage to remain open through that disastrous Christmas season of 1934, hadn't Sally Ann stayed on at the Brighton, dishing out cauliflower that was as exhausted as she was? She knew firsthand about the Depression. Deny it? FDR or no FDR, she could see no end to hard times. And Sally Ann was so loyal to FDR that she could not even bring herself to go to the Young Communist League's square dance although she knew for a fact that Selwyn Klein would be there. These hard times were simply not college times. That was it. Dreams didn't pay for books. Her mother wasn't fair.

But just like her first cousin Willie Blair (who, of course, knew of her existence no more than she of his), Sally Ann had a great deal to say to her parent that had to be left unspoken. She made silent speeches to her mother nearly every night, the only time she was actually alone, in the privacy of her room. Naturally, Sally Ann knew "privacy" was not the precise noun, considering that their second-floor apartment was level with the elevated subway line, and if she forgot to draw her shade BMT riders could look into the living room, see her on her Murphy bed and, by the light of the subway car, count the number of moth holes in her yellow wool blanket.

In her facsimile of privacy, she did concede that she was lucky to have such a mother. How could she not? Another woman in Ruthie's shoes would have skedaddled, with or without her baby, not owned up to twenty-five irate nuns two days after giving birth that she was not Mary LaRosa, not Catholic and, what's more, not going to give up her baby for adoption. What courage!

Her mother had more than courage, though. She had

wisdom. How many other women would have had the judgment to walk the streets of Brooklyn with her baby, studying faces, and pick out a woman—Mrs. Jirásek, with her big cheeks and big smile, standing in front of a house with her five small children encircling her big hips—and make a deal right on the spot for her to watch Sally Ann every day while Ruthie went to work at Beale's Buttons' biggest competitor? Her mother had honor too. What other woman would still be sending two dollars of her pay every single week to the nuns after eighteen years, Depression or no Depression? How could New York City waste money on monuments to war heroes when they had mothers like Ruthie around?

Still, the things unsaid. What eighteen-year-old girl wants to spend her Saturday night listening to the Philadelphia Orchestra on the radio with her mother? What eighteen-year-old girl wants to spend her Sunday schlepping down Park Avenue, then over to the Metropolitan Museum to sit through a lecture on Egyptian tomb paintings from the eighteenth dynasty? What eighteen-year-old girl doesn't have time for a best friend, or even a good friend, what with two jobs and a mother who never had time for a friend either? What eighteen-year-old girl has never been kissed, except by Selwyn Klein, the Party's foremost recruiter in all five boroughs, the Communist Clark Gable without the mustache—who, when she finally told him she wouldn't join the Party, acted as if he wanted to snatch the kiss back? What eighteen-year-old girl who'd pulled straight A's in high school wasn't finally ready for some fun?

And what girl wouldn't look up that proscribed name Louis Wolf in the Manhattan phone book every year and—from the time she was twelve and allowed on the

subway by herself—walk by those two or three or four
addresses time and time again, looking for a shiftless,
vicious dandy? A man with her prominent cheekbones,
her high forehead, but with bloodshot gray-green eyes.
And what girl, on turning eighteen, wouldn't finally
knock on the door of each of those Louis Wolfs, armed
with a clipboard and a pencil: Good morning or Good
evening, I am Miss Cohen from the Bureau of the Census.
Are you Mr. Wolf? Just a few questions, sir.

Sally Ann had dreamed of him reformed, in a three-
piece suit, working at Landau's, his stepfather's department store. Behind the Swiss Watches counter. No, better,
upstairs in the executive offices. A vice president, a silk
handkerchief in his breast pocket. May I help . . . , he'd
start to ask, but his voice would trail off because he knew!
He was looking into the mirror of her and seeing himself!
He'd take her to a restaurant for lunch and she'd have a
chicken sandwich with the crusts cut off and then he'd
say, Come, dearest, let me bring you to Miss Jones in Better Dresses. She'll help you choose a dinner frock for
tonight.

Or not reformed. Frail, yellow with cirrhosis, living in
a seedy room in a flophouse. Yet when she would tell him
who she was—I'm Sally Ann Wolf, Father—tears would
spill down his sunken cheeks and he'd whisper "My little
girl" with such loving-kindness even the gin fumes
wouldn't bother her.

She never found him.

She did find a third job, working a mangle, pressing
sheet after sheet after sheet in the subbasement laundry of
the Madison Arms Hotel. From the Madison Arms, it was
a half-mile walk to Hunter College, where, night after
night, semester after semester, Sally Ann Wolf, against

her better judgment, began to believe in the American dream.

"Tuna on rye toast with lettuce and tomato. And a vanilla Coke, please." Of course, after five days in a row, all Tunafish Man would have had to say was "The usual." Sally Ann Wolf would have flown from behind the counter of the Lexington Coffee Shop, smashed through the swinging door into the kitchen and shouted, "Fresh-toasted rye!" She'd warn the cook, Joey, None of your toasted-at-six-A.M.-and-reheated stuff.

And give me a prime center slice from the reddest tomato in midtown Manhattan! Extra tuna salad! And make sure it's spread thickly all over the bread, not just piled up in the middle to make the sandwich look expensive.

"Will there be anything else, sir?" she inquired, pencil poised.

"No, thank you." He was peering straight into her eyes when he said this, so she took her deep breath. Then, just as she'd rehearsed the night before at Hunter College with her friend Denise Silverstein—during the break between History of Art II and the American Labor Movement—she forced her facial muscles to relax. Then she smiled at him. Denise had given her no choice, demanding, Where is doing nothing getting you, Sally Ann? Nothing will get you nothing! So, her best smile, which showed her single but spectacular dimple.

But what was she getting back? Nothing! He might have been a statue by Donatello: Apollo on Coffee Shop Stool. Manly, pensive, and as impassive as a block of marble. Flames of mortification scorched Sally Ann's cheeks: Oh God, he thinks I'm smiling at him for a big tip. . . .

No, that I'm a gold digger out to nab a guy in a three-piece suit. No, worse, much worse—one of those desperately jolly girls who's never had a boyfriend in her life. Okay, so big deal. I've never had a boyfriend. He must think I've got a hopeless crush on him. Well, that's true, but—

Look! Suddenly, he was smiling back at her! Not one of those fake Dr. Lyon's Tooth Powder grins that show all thirty-two teeth and add up to nothing. Definitely not one of those snooty acknowledgments that, yes, he knew the lusty serving wench adored him and he thought it touchingly sweet. No, this was for real! Happy surprise, as if he hadn't expected her to notice him and was glad—no, excited—that she did. But wait! What was this? Was he blushing? Come off it, Sally Ann admonished herself. How could it be a blush? It was merely high color. A guy with a maroon striped tie and a vest that matched his suit and a white shirt with a collar that looked as if it were ironed on him must smile twenty-three hours a day, at everyone from titans of industry to household help. But hold on a second. Yes! He actually *was* blushing! His warm olive skin was suffused with red. The tops of his perfectly shaped ears . . . almost purple.

Maybe it was true: Jane Shalam, the other waitress, had told her fourteen times, Tunafish Man has a *mad* pash for you. Jane was a pretty blonde; she was the one the customers got the mad pashes for. Jane said, If you don't believe me, ask Joey. And Joey, the egomaniac cook who was perpetually swishing his spatula in the air as though acknowledging Louis XIV's homage for his cheddar cheese omelette, conceded that Tunafish Man wasn't coming into the Lexington only for the cuisine—even though all the salad dressings were homemade, Sally Ann, and you find me one other coffee shop north of Forty-second Street that can make that claim. Together, Jane and Joey got blue in the face trying to convince her that sure, a busy guy in an expensive suit might drop in once in a while for a quick bite but not every single day, and yesterday, Sally Ann's day off, he looked like he'd been punched in the suck when he didn't see her at her station behind the counter. What if he's married? she'd demanded of Jane. Stop it! Jane insisted. You think I can't spot those types a mile away? Do I know men or do I know men? But what if this one time Jane was wrong?

Sally Ann's hands were trembling by the time she brought out his plate from the kitchen. She pictured herself tripping on a stray pickle slice, sliding up to the counter, crashing to the floor in front of him. But everything was okay. Uh-oh, not okay for him. After three days of nudging, Joey had finally given in and made an extra-generous sandwich. But Tunafish Man must have squeezed it too tight, because a thick glob of it plopped from his uplifted half-sandwich right into the sleeve of his dark-gray suit jacket. He set down his food and tried to root around in his sleeve beneath counter level, trying to find it, without apparent success. Meanwhile she was standing there like a lukshen kugel, lacking the presence of mind to get into the kitchen and let him find the offending tuna glob in privacy. He bolted out of the Lexington without looking at her again. Not even a nod goodbye in her general direction.

She was dazed, nearly numb, like a person who has just received terrible news, although she managed to comprehend that he had left two quarters, a princely tip, a here-you-go-now, don't-bother-me-again tip. Sally Ann leaned across the counter. The tuna glob was neither on his plate nor on the floor by his stool. The rest of her shift, she could not rid herself of the image of him at a great mahogany desk, an American flag behind it. An indignant snarl would be curling his archer's bow of an upper lip as a putrid tuna odor emanated from the silk lining of his jacket. She realized she would never see him again.

Suddenly, the term "lump in her throat," that commonplace of heroines of historical novels—princes being a callous lot—took on real meaning. Sally Ann's maroon-tie prince was gone. Thus, forty minutes later, when old Mrs. Fessenden snarled, "Don't just stand there, gimme another napkin and some club soda," after gravy from her Yankee Pot Roast Plate dribbled onto her jabot, some of the tears that had been welling up in Sally Ann's eyes found their way out.

As she gave the counter her final wipe of the day, she admitted to herself that this grief at having Tunafish Man walk out of her life was pitiful. Downright crazy, even. Look at her, never had a date, never been kissed, except by Selwyn Klein the Commie, and she was painfully aware that didn't count. She was the only girl in her class at Abraham Lincoln High School who wasn't married, except for Hilda Bronstein, a known nymphomaniac, and Ina Zuckerbrot, who looked like the Discus Thrower with a wig. So why shouldn't she have tears in her eyes?

Maybe she should heed the advice of Denise Silverstein, her friend from Hunter, a girl wise beyond her years: get a secretarial job—even though the Lexington was a gold mine, with its East Forty-third Street location and its big-spending lunch crowd. Is it *such* a big deal, Denise had demanded, if you only make twenty-five dollars a week instead of thirty? I know you want to take the pressure off your mother, but when your boss says Take a letter, Miss Wolf, you'll be sitting down, like a lady. Imagine a life without bunions. And listen, Sally Ann, you're pretty. You know you are. Some exec is sure to grab you up. For five bucks a week more, do you want to risk winding up being Mrs. Joey? Sally Ann hadn't had the heart to tell Denise that the Mrs. Joey position was already filled.

By the time she left the Lexington at three that afternoon, Sally Ann was exhausted. Sure, every day her arches ached, her ankles wobbled, her arms and wrists got shooting pains, but this time her fatigue was not from slinging corned beef hash and eggs at six o'clock for the breakfast crowd, from standing through lunch until the last crumb of grilled cheese and tomato was consumed. For three years she'd been waking up five days a week at four forty-five to get in to work from Brooklyn. She was always tired. Well, at least she wasn't working three jobs anymore, as she'd done when she started Hunter.

Whatever she yearned for in life—and she was nothing if not a great yearner—she was going to have to get for herself. She was willing. True, she'd probably be ninety by the time she got her bachelor of arts, but she'd get it. Except that now, standing outside, breathing in the air with its autumn nip, its acrid perfume of coal dust and bus exhaust, Sally Ann doubted her own strength. She had come so far, but maybe that was because she'd been pushed. Even as she dismissed as melodrama unworthy of a Hunter College student the thought "I cannot go on like this," she felt that indeed she could not. Something was dying inside her. Maybe it had perished already.

The wind, a nasty bit of business left over from a hurricane in the Carolinas the radio had been warning New Yorkers about, whipped down Lexington Avenue, blowing her hair into her eyes and mouth. She lacked the verve to lift her hand and push it away. Even as she asked herself, Okay, what's really going on with me? the answer came that her strength was being sapped by the prospect of a future as loveless as her present and as bereft of passion as her past. She was her mother all over again. Despite the insight, she was unable to come up with any reserve of vitality. It was not so much the four-pound *Art of Raffaello* weighing her down as her own lonely soul. Oh hell, the library book was a day overdue. It was Friday afternoon, so she had no classes; she did not think she had enough strength to trudge uptown to Hunter just to return it.

"Hello."

On an ordinary day she might not have bothered to look up, because what man except a masher would be saying hello to her right in front of the Lexington Coffee Shop at three in the afternoon—or ever? But there was something energizing in the timbre of those two syllables —*Hel-lo*—that gave her heart enough muscle to bang against her chest. And when she looked up . . . Tunafish Man!

"I can't say, Funny meeting you here, can I?" he was inquiring. "I mean, you work here." She must have been staring at him like Miss Nincompoop 1940, because suddenly his ears were fuchsia and he was stammering, "I'm the vanilla Coke—"

"And tuna on rye toast with tomato. Hello." She transferred Raffaello to her left arm and stuck out her hand. "I'm Sally Ann Wolf. Nice to meet you." He was the perfect height. More slender than she'd thought. But not too slender. Because she wouldn't be comfortable being held by one of those Fred Astaire–slim men whose hips might measure less than hers.

His hand enclosed hers. Perfect. Not rough, but not girl soft either. "Martin Freund," he said. A gust of wind nearly tore his hat off. When he slapped it back into place with his left hand, he left a dent in the dark-gray felt. "Marty. I'm, uh, just on my way back from a meeting. Going to my office." His head tilted in a downtown direction. "In the Lincoln Building. Forty-second and Vanderbilt."

She couldn't believe it. He *was* shy. Okay, he must be about twenty-seven or twenty-eight and, true, he had an office job. But he clearly didn't know what to say next. Neither did she. Oh God, too many seconds were passing! "What kind of an office do you work in?" popped out of her mouth.

"A law office. I'm a lawyer." He said it casually, as if he inhabited a planet on which every man was a lawyer. And she liked it that he said lawyer, modestly. Not attorney, highfalutinly.

"A business kind of lawyer or Clarence Darrow?" A newspaper delivery truck cut off a taxi, and horns blared, curses were exchanged. She had to shout her question again over the din.

"Business." She must be smiling at him—yes, she was—because a small, sweet smile passed across his mouth. "Very dull, actually. Corporate stuff, some real estate."

"Do *you* find it dull?"

"No, actually. I mean, it's not riveting, but it's interesting." She felt Marty's hesitation after "riveting," that it might be too big a word for a waitress. Part of her was tempted to say, Hey, buster, I know from riveting. I go to Hunter.

Maybe he was realizing he'd been hanging around a

lamppost with a nonriveting waitress for a ridiculous amount of time, getting blown apart by a crazy Carolina wind, and he should get back to the Lincoln Building and find someplace else for tunafish. But he was staying right where he was. "That looks like a heavy book you're carrying."

"I have to get it back to the library," she muttered.

"May I see it?" She handed it to him. "Raffaello," he said respectfully. Then he opened it and started leafing through. Oh God in heaven, he was going to think she had taken it out of the library to look at penises! "Do you like art?" he asked.

"I love it. My mother and I go to museums every Sunday." Nuts! Was there *anything* she could have said to sound more old-maidish? "I'm taking an art appreciation class at Hunter, although my major is history."

"American? European?"

"American."

"Is that where you're headed now, up to Hunter?"

"Just to return the book. I don't have classes Fridays."

"Well, I don't . . ." He had broad shoulders for a slender man. And what looked like a powerful chest. She wondered if it had hair on it. She hoped so. Curly chest hair, not the dense, straight kind too many of the men with their open shirts at the Brighton Beach Cafeteria had, as if their mothers had had liaisons with raccoons. "I don't have anything pressing at the office. It's such a nice day." The wind from Carolina screamed down the avenue. Marty swallowed. "Would you mind if I kept you company part of the way?"

"Sure." Say "I'd love that," she ordered herself. "That would be nice."

By the time they reached the library, Sally Ann Wolf

learned that Marty Freund was twenty-nine, that he'd gone to City College and NYU Law School, that his family lived two blocks from Yankee Stadium, that his father was a taxi driver and that Marty had taken the afternoon off from Steinberg & Mendelsohn, Counselors-at-Law, because once and for all, after five days of the torments of hell, he had to know if he was lapsing into some strange form of bachelor insanity or if the beautiful girl with the luminous black eyes behind the counter at the coffee shop he had stopped into that first day only because it was one forty-five and it was raining and he was starved was truly as wonderful as she looked.

"Well?" Sally Ann asked. "Am I?"

And Marty answered, "So much more wonderful, I can't begin to tell you."

# 4

Machinist's Mate Third Class William Blair gazed past the palm fronds at the thousands of pinpoints of light in the night-black sky that arced over the middle of the Pacific Ocean. More stars here than even in Wyoming. He thought: This goddamn smear of stars may be the last thing I'll ever see.

His foxhole was a three-foot-deep depression in the sand thirty feet from the shore. It kept oozing water. His uniform was soaked. When he wiggled his toes, his boots made squishy noises. He shivered in the tropical night under the camouflaging blanket of palm leaves.

One of the guys in the foxhole, the one from Tennessee, sighed in wonderment. "Evah seen s' munny stars?"

Vance, from Sacramento, growled back, "Shut your fucking mouth, fucking cracker jerk. You'll get us killed."

Tennessee har-har-harred loud enough to be heard in Tokyo. Then he gurgled at Sacramento, "Ya thank the Jap pilots kin blubba blubba me?"

Jesus God, they had so little time left. Why were they wasting it giving each other the business? Didn't they realize they had dug their own graves on this beach and now were lying in them? Hell, burial would be a cinch. Shovel back the wet sand, and Admiral Yamamoto would be sitting right over them in a canvas chair, a rum punch in his hand, planning his attack on San Diego.

How much past midnight was it? What the hell did it matter anyway? They would all be goners before dawn. The lieutenant commander, a college professor from North Dakota with yellow horse teeth, had announced, "The attack, very likely"—he'd said "veddy likely," that buffoon—"will come soon. By the dawn's early light, as it were, if not before." The upshot of it was, in the rare moment Willie wasn't living his own death—the crackling of his skin as he became a human marshmallow, that final scream of agony as a bomb's impact vaporized his balls—he kept hearing not only "by the dawn's early light" but the whole damn "Star-Spangled Banner."

Now, to make his last hours on earth even more unbearable, the chest pains were coming back. He turned onto his left side, but that did not relieve his misery. God almighty, was he ever tired, swinging back and forth between his own harrowing death, "The Star-Spangled Banner" and now, once again, the pain by his heart. Earlier, around nineteen hundred hours, he'd almost staggered over to the chief petty officer. "Listen, I cannot spend the night in this foxhole. Please, I've *got* to get to the dispensary." He'd been a hundred percent positive he was going to drop dead. But then he'd belched. Now, buried deep in his chest, squeezed between ribs and spine, to the right of his heart, he could feel the cause of his suffering: a baseball-sized lump. Long after his body was shipped home to the Circle B, buried and decomposed to dust, it would still be identifiable: navy food. Fifty, sixty years from now, when Lois's time finally came, they'd dig six feet down, and his son or daughter—Christ, now he'd never get to know which—would ask, What are those metal things in my daddy's grave? And some old-timer would say, Them's dog tags from the war—and would you look at that! A navy cheese sandwich right alongside them!

*Join the Navy! See the World!* That's what the poster in the recruiting office had said. What the poster hadn't spelled out was the rumor he'd been fool enough to believe: Soldiers in the army get killed a lot quicker, so become a sailor! That was the whisper Willie kept hearing around Jackson Hole. Fool that he was, he hadn't doubted it for a minute, for the simple reason that no one was saying it out loud. Had he actually believed the War Department was telegraphing, in unbreakable code, top-secret intelligence to Bob Freemantle down at the gas station and Scotty Pease over at Silver Spur Plumbing and Heating? And that's why Willie Blair, gullible fool, was now stretched out in a foxhole on Midway island, waiting to die.

"At the twilight's last gleaming" broke into his thoughts. What was that moron songwriter talking about? Twilight? Was it "dawn's early light," or wasn't it?

Anyway, he'd rushed to enlist in the navy even though he was aware that if he played it smart, he had a chance of getting a deferment. Running an essential agricultural enterprise, which Lord knew the Circle B was. But fat chance of asking for a deferment, being married to Lois: Right when they heard about Pearl Harbor that Sunday, she'd simply assumed he'd be aching to fight for his country and the only reason he'd hold back would be to spare her, it being so soon after their wedding. A quick ceremony, because she was pregnant. Naturally, she'd had to go and blab it to the minister, because it wouldn't be right not to be truthful, especially to a man of God. So all through "Do you take this woman," the Reverend Cockeye Tipton kept giving him dirty looks, although technically the old geezer was, as always, surveying the bridge of his own nose. A somber ceremony, and a fast one: Old Charlie Bryant had given up the ghost at the end of the first week of November, right around the time Lois missed her monthly. Never woke up from his coma, so he never knew a grandchild was on the way. Never found out about the existence of Willie Blair, thanks be for small favors. Because if he had, there'd have been hell to pay. He might even have had someone take Lois up to that doctor in Billings to get rid of the baby. I know you'll be wanting to enlist, Lois said to him just hours after they heard the sickening news from Hawaii on the radio. She was giving her beautiful hair its nightly hundred brush strokes and grieving. All those ships. All those poor dead sailors.

In that instant, coming back in after brushing his teeth, wearing his new, striped husband pajamas, his arms went all tingly with fright: Enlist? But he just chuckled and said, Want to get rid of me so soon? She'd set down her silver brush and rushed over to throw her arms around him. Oh, Willie, she said into his shoulder, you know I love you more than life itself. And he did know it. The problem was, if he didn't act like he was dying to fight for his country, she'd think he was a chicken or, worse, maybe even like a Nazi or something. How could a girl with high standards like Lois love a chicken or a Nazi more than life itself? Oh God, if he could only hold her one more time, feel her warmth against his belly, his thighs, sniff her sweet, clean, rich-girl hair.

A week after December 7, him and Joe Whitcomb, who owned a spread over near Dubois, drove to Casper through a terrible snowstorm to sign up for the navy. Married just a few weeks, there he was driving with the likes of Big Joe, laughing every time they went into a skid, gabbing about pickup balers like they were old buddies, even though a month earlier, before Lois was Mrs. William Blair, Big Joe wouldn't have wasted spit on him.

Now, less than six months later, he was seeing the world, like the navy promised. On a tropical island paradise, courtesy of Uncle Sam, midway between Los Angeles and Tokyo, under palm leaves at the back edge of an endless strip of beach. Except instead of girls in grass skirts with giant bare bosoms, he was rubbing shoulders and asses with three other guys in a foxhole, more guys dug in more foxholes on either side of them.

"Cowboy?" The guy from Tennessee called him. They'd played cards a few nights before, and after Willie won forty bucks off him, the guy mumbled something about Willie having been born to play poker. You bona play pokah. "Cowboy?"

"What?" The pain from the cheese sandwich had worked upward from his chest to his throat. It felt raw, like a little boy's sore throat, each time he swallowed. When the bombs began to burst, it would probably be too sore for him to scream out in terror, and without that release, being blown to bits would be even more excruciating. What would dying feel like, in that unspeakable instant? Was it a violence, a pain beyond imagining? That's what scared him most, having to bear agony, even for just a second. Your whole damn life would add up to nothing because of the enormity of that torment. Or was he shaking in his boots for nothing? Did toes and liver and dick go flying apart so fast that you truly didn't know what hit you?

Oh jeez, his mother. Would the navy send a telegram to them? Or would Lois have to get a message to them in

Warren Junction? They didn't have a telephone yet. Would she send them a letter? Dear Queenie and Jake? Dear Mom and Dad? She'd spent only a couple of hours with them, the day of the wedding, and he couldn't remember if she'd called them anything. Dear Mr. and Mrs. Blair: I don't know if there is any right way to say this and it breaks my heart to be the bearer of such sad news but . . . She wouldn't be able to drive all that way to tell them, not a woman in her condition. But Lois was so damn plucky. What if she tried and the pains started coming and she was all alone on some crappy rutted road through the Absarokas, her screams echoing through the mountains, unheard?

So frightened. He wasn't like the other guys, who were probably just now getting a little jumpy. No, he was all but pissing in his pants. Pure yellow, that's what he was. Not just now, in the shadow of death. From his first day on Midway, two months before, he'd been scared shitless. He'd spent half his time off sitting on the can, doubled over with the trots.

His terror had all started because the navy found out he had mechanical skill—big surprise, the son of a blacksmith. Anyway, they gave everyone a bunch of tests. Then a couple of officers sitting around a table asked him to make a weapon out of some junk—wire, a sheet of tin, some screws—so he did. They decided he was some kind of genius who could rig anything, which only went to show how fucked up the navy was. His first day on Midway, they'd put him in charge of a detail making antiboat mines out of sewer pipe. Within five minutes, all his pleasure in the warm sun, the thick, salty air, vanished for good. Because it hit him—like the lightbulb going on over somebody's head in the funnies: They weren't going to set those mines around the coral reefs to keep away American ships. No, they were *expecting* the Japs, and soon, because they weren't waiting for matériel to come by ship from Hawaii. They were counting on Willie Blair. A week later, when they asked him to come up with landmines for the beach, he was double sure: Soon he'd be a dead man. Still, he'd devised antitank mines from cigar boxes, filling them with twenty-penny nails. He couldn't believe, making that first one, how he was shaking inside—like an old engine with a rough idle—although miraculously his fingers were precise and steady. Later, he'd had one of the guys in his detail paint bull's-eyes on the landward sides of the mines. He'd said, If their tanks don't set them off when they come ashore, we can get in one last shot from the foxholes, take a few Japs with us to kingdom come. Some hillbilly from Arkansas said, You are some damn cowboy! and everybody started laughing and yelling Ya-hoo! like he was Errol Flynn in *Dodge City*. How come those dumb clucks hadn't realized they were days away from being turned into a pile of shit and bone dust?

He'd been right as rain to be terrified. The enemy *had* been on its way. Just a few days ago, Horseteeth from North Dakota gave the enlisted men the word: Japanese aircraft carriers were steaming toward Midway.

Any minute now, Japanese dive-bombers would strafe the island. Once he and the other sailors and the marines way down the beach were dead, their intestines hanging out like a bunch of slaughtered hogs, their blood seeping into the sand, Midway would belong to the gooney birds and the Japs.

Someone from the telegraph office in Jackson would drive up to the house, and Lois would learn the baby would never know a father. It is with deepest regret, blah, blah, blah. Willie pictured her gasping, embracing her pregnant belly—she must be so big by now. The telegraph boy would have to lead her, staggering, her face soaked with tears, over to the big brown wing chair. And her having just lost her father. Like a throne the wing chair was, the old chair Charlie Bryant had sat in. Now it was Willie's. Right before he left for basic, Lois had asked, Is it okay if I re-cover it in a green plaid, Willie?

"Yuh thank blubba dubba dubba?" the Tennessee guy was asking him. For the life of him, half the time he couldn't figure out what southern guys were talking about.

"What did he say?" Willie asked Roger, who was a shoe salesman from New Hampshire; Roger said "radah" for "radar," but at least you could understand him, and he, for some reason, could understand them.

"He's asking, 'Do you think the Japs are *really* going to attack before dawn?'"

Willie did not have to answer. In that instant, miles out in the Pacific, there were explosions they could not hear. A second later, however, they watched as two aircraft fell into the sea in flames, like matches dropped carelessly after a cigarette was lit. "The bombs bursting in air." Fucking song wouldn't go away.

Roger asked: "Is it stahting, Cowboy?" Vance from Sacramento called out to him, "Cowboy, you think it's all gonna be out at sea, or are they coming in?"

What the hell made all of them decide he was the expert? But Willie said, "It's starting. Bet they'll be flying by to drop a few."

"So? Does that mean we're dead?" a new voice, thin with fear, demanded from another foxhole.

"No," he called out. Tiny flares of red erupted along the horizon. "They'll most likely go for the seaplane hangars or the ordnance shop." Of course we're dead, shit-brain.

"It's horrible," Roger said softly enough that Willie knew the words were meant for just him.

"What?"

"Seeing those bursts of light in the sky. Not hearing anything." Roger was right: The battle was too far off-shore for the sound to carry. No whistles of bombs, no grumbles of planes taking off from aircraft carriers, no shouts so you could know who was getting the worst of it, them or us. "What do you think, Cowboy?"

"It is pretty damn horrible, Rog," he said softly. For a few minutes, the weight of the silence blanketed them as heavily as did the darkness, muffling the scratch of a boot digging into sand, nervous sniffling from two foxholes down. "On the other hand, once we start hearing explosions . . ."

Roger tried to chuckle, but it came out a cough. "Well, if we don't make it, it's been great—"

Willie cut him off. "Hell, no. I'm feeling lucky tonight."

"You just saying that, Cowboy?"

"You know I don't sling the bull, Rog." How come they all believed him? Looked to him for comfort? Why the hell had they named him sheriff? Did they think he was the guy in the white hat who was going to pull out his six-shooter and blast the bad guys? He heard Roger let out the breath he'd probably been holding since the first two planes went down. The other guys started to make normal noises, letting go of some of their terror—gulps, farts, throat clearing. But suddenly, Willie became

aware that their human sounds were being drowned out
by the distant drone of planes.

"Ours, Cowboy?"

"Why would ours be coming *toward* Midway—unless
ours were chasing theirs?"

The drones grew deeper, louder. From somewhere
across the island, booms of antiaircraft batteries began,
the firings coming closer together until it was almost one
hideous bang of defensive fire that nearly drowned out the
noise of the planes.

Was it daybreak? Or were the bombs lighting up the
sky? Daybreak! And out of the sky came a Japanese
bomber—

"Cowboy," someone was calling out, a stretched, desperate voice, "what kind of plane is that?"

"A Zero," he said, not having any real idea what the
hell it was, only that—Jesus God!—he could actually see
the doors of the bomb bay opening. What was it, less than
a quarter mile down the beach? The bombs were coming
out! He could see them! So damn big. In the newsreels
they looked like such silly little turdlike things. And he
could hear the sound they made as they fell. Screams. And
then the blast! The ground trembled. The wet sand sides
of the foxhole began to give way. Willie turned to the
direction of the hit: The powerhouse had been bombed,
to the north. Now all that was left was a giant column of
fire and black smoke so thick it looked solid. He'd been
saying, Don't worry, they're going for the seaplane
hangars. But he'd forgotten completely that the plant
powered every damn light, every piece of equipment, on
the whole island.

The Japs were coming their way, strafing the beaches
now. Not just that one plane that had bombed the power-

house. No, three smaller planes, silvery white, like gulls, were flying toward them, planes with—oh Jesus!—those Japanese suns. Their guns blasted as they flew, throwing up skyscrapers of sand. One plane headed inland and, with a sickening burst of automatic fire, took out the dispensary, less than five hundred feet away, the very place where he'd wanted to go, where he'd almost begged to go. Then it turned back toward the beach. It was coming right toward them.

"Lois," Willie said aloud. Let her be my last thought, my last word. Lois. The baby. Lois. But the damn "Star-Spangled Banner" began to play in his head again. He could hear the tight-ass opera singer who'd been singing before the third game of the World Series games last year, when he'd lost five bucks on Brooklyn, and her squealy voice was drowning out Lois. "O say, does that star-spangled banner yet wave . . ."

And suddenly, the three planes banked and flew off to sea. Gone!

Roger was punching him in the arm. "You were right, Cowboy!"

Minutes later, all of them were climbing out of their holes, racing toward the orange flames and sour smells of the dispensary to see if there was anyone, anything, to be saved. Horrible. It looked like a giant campfire—with voices. "Here!" "Help, oh God, save me."

Willie heaved smoldering wood aside, grabbed red-hot pipes with his hands, pulling them back so some skinny little guy could squeeze inside a tight triangular opening between overlapping boards to try and reach one of the voices. Christ, his palms, his fingertips, hurt so much he wanted to cry like a baby. Wah! One after another, sailors became machines, hauling concrete and steel, wood and glass. Searching for nurses, doctors, patients. A deep voice cried out, "I can't feel my belly!" Then the voice became a scream.

The jerk from Tennessee turned out to be stronger than an ox, tossing aside an I-beam like it was a toothpick. But there was a twisted bed frame that he couldn't seem to move. Willie stepped around the line of men to help him lift it. It felt bolted to the center of the earth. Uhhhh! they cried as they strained with all their strength, but it wouldn't budge. Its sharp edges cut into what was left of the flesh on Willie's burned hands. Another man joined them, some squat, muscular guy Willie had never seen before, with brown, horseshoe-shaped pouches under his eyes. At last, with one final screaming grunt, they succeeded. Looking down, they saw the dead, white-shoed leg of a navy nurse. Only the leg. The rest of her was someplace else.

"Mah God!" The Tennessee guy tried not to retch. He failed.

The muscular guy (whose maternal grandmother had landed in America from Naples the day before Herschel and Dora Blaustein had) closed his eyes and muttered something. A prayer, Willie guessed.

Willie held his burned hands against the cool of his cheeks and forced his eyes from the leg. He made his mind stop wondering which of those brave girls it belonged to. He turned back toward the line of men and—shit!—the damn lyrics came back, in that squealy lady opera singer voice. "O'er the la-and of the free . . ."

"Y'okay, pal?" asked the short guy with muscles.

"I'm okay. You?"

"Ditto."

Simultaneously, they took a deep breath and walked

over to what looked like the jagged edge of a girder. Jeez, heavy as hell.

"So where ya from?" the muscular guy managed to grunt.

"Wyoming. You?"

"Brooklyn."

Willie was about to say, Hey, I lost five bucks on your fucking Dodgers last year, except he heard the rapid clomp! clomp! of boots. Past Brooklyn, over the heads of Roger from New Hampshire and Vance from Sacramento and all the other guys, beyond the mountain of charred two-by-fours, he saw the fatigues of a platoon of marines running over to help. For the first time in his life, Willie Blair, looking from man to man to man, understood he was part of something even greater than three thousand acres in Wyoming.

And though he hated it, goddamn hated it, to be prisoner of a song that wouldn't go away, he found himself mouthing "'. . . and the home of the brave.'"

"'Deck the halls with boughs of holly . . .'" A chorus of cheery Christians was still caroling over Macy's public address system, even though it was the day after Christmas. Their yuletide harmonies spread across the seventh floor, shivering the tinsel on the Boys' Coats sign, swirling around the flushed, damp-faced, clench-jawed crowds of gift returners, over a display of little-girl dummies in tiny military-style coats and miniature WAC and WAVE caps outside the Little Miss Muffet Shoppe, past the artificial snow on the Layettes counter and underneath the closed door of the studio of Mr. Fitzwilliam, Photographer of Children. "'Fa-la-la-la-la . . .'" Not a single square inch of the store, of New York, of America, Sally

Ann Freund thought, was safe from the season's relentless joy, although Mr. Fitzwilliam, clearly anticipating the arrival of the Freunds, had moved his peewee Christmas tree against a wall and stuck a pint-sized crèche in a corner so only the back of the manger was showing.

Not that the children were old enough to need a real explanation that they were having a Hanukkah picture—not a Christmas picture—taken to send to Daddy. She had made the appointment too late for Marty to get it for the holiday, a dumb move. Sure, she'd been preoccupied, writing the fifth draft of her paper on Veblen. But the truth was, nothing she was doing—including babbling on and on, page after page, about conspicuous consumption—was as important as what Marty was doing: fighting Nazis. How could she not have taken a minute to think that every mother in the five boroughs would want a photograph of the children this time of year? So she'd sent off a tin of brownies and *The Greatest Love Poems of the Ages*. Probably every semiliterate girl in America was sending that slender book to her soldier this year. But unlike all those guys who would think: Gee, smart *and* romantic, and that's why I love her, but would wind up littering Italy and France and Belgium with "Let me not to the marriage of true minds admit impediments . . ." and "Ah love, let us be true to one another . . . ," Marty would keep it in his knapsack, read every single line.

Sally Ann finished posing Danny and Davey, the two-year-old twins, around a neat pyramid of alphabet blocks. Naturally, the second she turned her attention to three-year-old Barbara—whomp! The boys knocked over the perfectly poised blocks and began stacking them into a daring, precarious tower.

"Sorry," she murmured to Mr. Fitzwilliam, a large-bellied, florid man with a halo of white fuzz for hair. His cherry lips were permanently downturned, as if he'd been compared to Santa Claus one damn time too many. However, he had a disconcerting habit of flashing a smile every few minutes, as if recalling that surliness was bad for business.

He was smiling now. "Please don't apologize, Mrs. Freund! Heavens, we *want* children to feel comfortable here." He made a sound back in his throat that Sally Ann assumed was his standard delighted gurgle. "Boys," he tried to enthuse, "that is really something you're building! What is it?"

The twins looked across the studio to their year-older sister for an answer. Her back was toward them; she sat cross-legged, hunched over by the crèche. "The Statue of Liberty," she called out, not bothering to look. She turned the crèche around and was filling her hands with Mary, the Magi and Baby Jesus. Then she stuffed several lambs and a cow under her chin. "Is the daddy here?" she called out to Sally Ann.

"Heh-heh." Mr. Fitzwilliam chuckled wearily and warily, although not without goodwill—even after Barbara stood and held up Baby Jesus to the photographer's glaring lamp, examining him suspiciously. "Heh-heh." Lately, both in this Yule season or at any old time, Sally Ann sensed little but goodwill. After three years of war with Hitler, America loved Jews.

"Where is the daddy?" Barbara insisted.

"In the army," Sally Ann said softly as, one by one, she extracted the figures from Barbara's pudgy, knuckleless toddler hands, offering her instead a teddy bear, a prop whose matted brown coat indicated that it had been dribbled, sucked on and gnawed by a number of Mr. Fitzwilliam's young clients.

"With *my* daddy?" Barbara stroked the bear tenderly, her dark eyes so serene she might have been mimicking the beatific expression of the three-inch wooden Madonna now safely back in the crèche.

"You never know." Her mother sighed, coaxing Barbara down beside her brothers. She gave the skirt of the little girl's velvet dress a final flounce, smoothed out its lace collar, straightened the boys' plaid bow ties, then stepped back behind the photographer to see what their portrait would look like. Wow!

What beauties her children were! They could be triplets, with their ravishing black curls, jet-black eyes and peachy skin. She and Marty were good-looking enough, but not dazzling—except in each other's eyes when the bedroom lamps were low. How had they managed to produce three such flawless children? Her eyes fell then to her own alligator pumps. As always, she was filled with remorse that she was so shallow as to be moved not by substance or spirit but by a superficial quality like beauty. Her children's loveliness was irresistible. She was compelled to study it up close, bask in it. She often hovered over the three of them like . . . well, like a normal mother might.

Having grown up bathed in the blazing light of Ruthie's unremitting mother love, Sally Ann was astounded by her own lack of maternal passion. Hurt, too, as though someone had neglected to give her a quality that was rightfully hers. Oh, she loved the children, but the truth was, once she finished gazing at their glorious fringe of black lashes, once she received an answer to How's my big boy? or Did my big girl have a good night's sleep? they were fairly boring. Given the choice between adoring them and a good book, she'd rather read. She envied the mothers in the playground who seemed to be endlessly thrilled by each string of drool down a tiny chin, by every less-than-bon mot of their toddler.

"Boys and *girl*!" Mr. Fitzwilliam gushed in the manner of professionals who feel they must enchant the young. "Can you smile?"

"Yes," Barbara answered carefully. She obviously thought it was an addlepated inquiry, but being a courteous child, she did not remark on its silliness. The twins, taking her lead, as they always did, nodded solemnly and repeated, "Yes" and "Yeth."

"Well, give Mr. Fitzwilliam a big smile," Sally Ann instructed. "We want to send a smiley picture to Daddy." So Barbara beamed, and the twins followed her by breaking into huge, goofy grins, as if to display all their teeth at once. Sally Ann found herself smiling back at the sheer joy on their faces, then smiling inwardly in relief at once again finding evidence that, yes, she was a normal mother. They were such sweet-natured kids. It should be easier for her. Of course, she had taken psychology: She knew all about ambivalence. Yet how appalling it was to discover it in herself, to overhear herself thinking, as they blanketed her cheek with sweet, moist good-morning kisses: Leave me the hell alone.

"Your husband's in the army, Mrs. Freund?" the photographer asked, when he put new film into the camera.

"Yes."

"Do you know where he is?"

"In France, or maybe Belgium. In his last letter, he went on about the big box of chocolate bonbons he bought me two Christmases ago. What he actually bought me was a sweater set and some opera records for Hanukkah." Mr. Fitzwilliam was nodding his head—up, down, up, down—in congenial brotherhood. "I figured 'chocolate' was a clue."

"What our boys won't do to get by those censors!" He chuckled. Instantly, she regretted her openness, recalling all the Don't Be a Blabateur warnings. But with his jolly red weskit and his froth of Santa hair, Mr. Fitzwilliam did not look like a spy, despite his bogus jollity and his sour cherry of a mouth. Except what would the Nazis do? Send in a secret agent with a Teutonic accent and a dueling scar? "What does your husband do?"

"In civilian life, he's a lawyer. Now he's a medic with the Five hundred fourth Parachute Infantry."

"Oh my!" Mr. Fitzwilliam's white brows saluted respectfully. "He jumps?"

"Yes. At first I thought: Has the army lost all reason? I couldn't get him to climb up a stepladder and change a lightbulb because he said he didn't like heights. But in October he wrote that jumping out of planes was 'invigorating.'"

"Amazing what we can do . . . I mean, when push comes to shove." For just an instant, Mr. Fitzwilliam's sad red round face glowed with possibility. If not for a mere decade or two, *he* could be leaping from planes. "Well, with any luck, he'll be back this time next year. Probably sooner. My next-door neighbor's boy came home last week. And things do seem to be looking up, don't they?"

"Well, far be it from me to tempt fate, but I was thinking last night: Gee, wouldn't it be funny if he came home before the photograph of the children got to him?"

In the taxi going home, the children were weary from smiling, dopey after a half hour of flashing lights. Their lips and fingers shimmered red and green from the candy canes she had used as a reward for good behavior. Barbara and the boys climbed on her lap, leaned against her. Deep-blue fibers from Sally Ann's coat clung to their candies and in turn transferred their stickiness to her. She closed her eyes, inhaling her children's pepperminty sweetness.

Sally Ann could not believe how her life had been transformed. In September 1940, she was a waitress with rapidly falling arches and a hopeless crush on the Tunafish Man. Now, a little more than four years later, there was an apartment on the Upper East Side and—

"Good afternoon, Mrs. Freund." The ancient doorman, brought out of retirement to serve during the war, wheezed as he helped them from the taxi. Then he doffed his cap to Barbara politely, modestly, but with dignity, like Eisenhower greeting the troops after the Normandy invasion. He demanded of the twins, as he always did: "All right, which one of you is Danny today and which one of you is Davey?" as he ushered them into the building.

Kindly doormen and a hairdresser named Monsieur René and a Chinese rug in the living room. At the beginning, she'd been stupefied, like a dope addict, by the richness of Marty's life: the silk lining of his suit jackets; the clouds of buttery rolls at his favorite restaurant. Then, after they were married, by the richness of her own life: her monogram, *sFw,* on hankies, bed jackets, towels, pillow slips; a silver sugar bowl; plush velvet orchestra seats on which to sit and hear Mozart, see Ibsen.

All that softness, that conspicuous consumption, was supposed to keep the haves anesthetized so they couldn't feel pain—their own and the pain they caused the have-nots. I like being rich, she confided. Marty laughed. Come on, Sal. We're not rich. We're upper middle class. What do you know? she shot back. I slung hash for enough years to know from rich. No, she hadn't felt anesthetized at all. She'd felt wonderful: protected, cared for, loved. All right, she'd always been loved, by her mother. But since that day he had waited for her outside the Lexington and then walked her up to Hunter, she'd not only felt loved; for the first time in her life, she'd felt happy. Alive.

Oh, how she wanted Marty back. He really was Prince Charming. His kiss had brought her to life. His kisses. His beautiful body. How she longed to roll around with him in bed, making love all day, all night.

Except when they were talking. Was Harlan Fiske Stone the best choice for chief justice? What was the best moment of your childhood? Was there something in our natures that dooms us to making war, or is it something in our culture? God, those fantastic conversations long into the night. Like asking each other: Could it happen here? Could what happened to the Jews in Germany, the Jews all over Europe, happen in America?

Of course not! Marty had argued. It's different here. We're Americans. We're part of this country.

I thought you knew history, she countered. We were Spaniards in 1492, weren't we? We were Germans—

What happened during the Depression, he demanded, when the country needed a scapegoat? Nothing happened. That's your answer, Sal.

What about Father Coughlin?

Well, what about him? He spewed his dreck and nothing happened to us. Listen, sweetheart, this is America. We're not the outsiders living among a homogeneous people, the way we were before the Inquisition. We're just another drop in the melting pot. Relax, you're part of the soup. You're safe here.

When times get really bad, she replied, you think they won't be looking for a Jew or two to take the rap?

Times *did* get really bad. You were young and pretty—and damned lucky to get work. But a lot of people couldn't get one job, let alone three. Did they go around looking for Jews to blame? Did they, Sally Ann?

All she wanted was passionate talk, passionate love. Oh dear God, how she missed the feel of him, naked, hairy, damp from sex. How she missed just looking at him. Across the breakfast table. Taking off his coat when he got home from the office.

What was she without him? Mrs. Freund, in an alpaca coat, with three children. Almost but not quite alive. In the elevator, she glanced down at them. Amazing. Three such little ones. Six glittering black eyes—her eyes—staring up at her. "Hi, sweeties." She sighed.

As Sally Ann opened the apartment door, she heard her mother's voice. "Hellooo!" After he got his induction notice, Marty had pressured her to have Ruthie stay with them while he was gone. You'll need to get out once in a while, take a walk, go to a concert. This way, you have a built-in baby-sitter. They'd argued back and forth:

I can manage on my own.

Of course you can. But wouldn't you like a little help?

Listen, she said, do you *know* what it's going to be like to get rid of her once you get home? You'll need the Corps of Engineers to dream up a way to pry her out of here.

Come on, he'd entreated. We'll be doing a mitzvah. She's so lonely. I always feel so bad when she leaves to go back to Brooklyn, to that empty apartment. You're her life, Sal. I'm the bad guy who kidnapped you.

Don't be ridiculous. She adores you.

"I'll be right there," her mother was calling. "I have a chicken in the oven."

"Grandma always has a chicken in the oven," Barbara observed.

"You're telling me." Poverty had taught Ruthie well, so wartime shortages were no impediment. She could stretch a chicken as if it were rubber, which is what it generally tasted like, but still—

"My babies!" Ruthie cried. The children careened into her arms. "Sally Ann, how did it go? A nice picture to send to my handsome son-in-law?"

"I think so, Mom." The apartment was redolent of roasting chicken, cinnamony applesauce. Sally Ann's heels clacked comfortably against the hard oak floor of the foyer as she hung up her coat between a Persian lamb jacket and a plaid wool cape. "The kids seemed relaxed enough, except for the lights." She imagined all the paratroopers in a circle around Marty, looking down at the photograph and saying, Hey, aren't they great-lookin' kids?

"Why don't you take a little rest, Sally Ann? I can give them a bath, some dinner. Read to them. I went to the library today."

A rest? Sally Ann thought, as she lay on her bed in the darkening room. God, it was depressing, the way night fell so early. Wait, not just her bed. Her bed and Marty's. With him away, she never trespassed, always staying on her side. Each night, her final act before sleep was to reach out her hand and, for a minute, warm the cold sheet on which he would have slept.

What did she need a rest for? She wasn't working three jobs, the way she was in high school, or on her feet ten hours at a stretch at the Lexington. She had a woman to clean twice a week, a mother to cook and baby-sit. All she had to do was take the kids to the park, have lunch or go to matinees with the wives of the lawyers in Marty's firm, read to wounded soldiers at the hospital on Mondays and Fridays, and show up at Hunter Tuesdays and Thursdays for History of Economic Thought and her New Deal seminar. And have her nails done: I think today . . . hmmm . . . Deep Claret, Beatrice.

Sometimes she wasn't certain what she was becoming without Marty. Or had she already become it? She ran her thumbs over the edges of her long, well-shaped oval nails. Marty would groan when she raked her nails down his back. She loved the noise he made in bed. Sometimes, he told her, when I get out of the shower, I turn around and look at my back in the mirror. You know what? I get all worked up again. The twins had been just five weeks old when he'd gone off to war. The doctor told her she and Marty would have to wait for six weeks after, but of course they didn't. I'm not hurting you, am I? he'd asked, and she'd laughed. Are you kidding?

She didn't even hear the doorbell, but a moment later, there was her mother opening her bedroom door without knocking, saying, "Someone for you, Sally Ann." Quickly she put on her shoes and rushed down the hall into the foyer. She had this crazy idea that Marty had come home and decided to surprise her. No one would believe that a lawyer could do an outrageous thing like that, but Marty was full of surprises.

When she saw the peaked cap of the Western Union boy, she knew what the surprise was. Oh, she had worried about it all the time. How could she not have? But in her heart of hearts, she had known he would come home safe to her.

"We regret to inform you Sergeant Martin Benjamin Freund was killed in the line of duty on December 16, 1944, while his regiment was repelling an enemy attack in the Ardennes Forest in Belgium. . . ."

At the end of January, letters came from the men in his unit. Buzzy. Jim. Henry.

I'm so sorry . . . such a great guy . . .

My condolences to you and your children who I know for a fact Marty loved . . .

If you want to know what happened . . .

Our captain was hit. Marty had on his hat with the Red Cross on it and his armband and went out to pull the captain back behind the line . . .

A German sniper . . .

. . . shot him right in the heart, so he never knew . . .

I pray to the Almighty that you find comfort in knowing your husband died a hero for his country . . .

He loved you, Mrs. Freund. You'll always have that and your three fine boys.

# 5

Soon after he came home from the war, early in September of 1945, William Blair took his wife, Lois, and drove out to the Grand Teton to watch the moon rise. At first it appeared gray over the mountain, but it brightened as it climbed, and they stood with their arms around each other against the chill of evening. Moonlight made their skin glow—a little silver, a little gold—as though they were slightly better than human. Well, they had been on the side of the angels. And the angels had won. The war was over.

At last, Willie thought, the world the way it should be: the only sound the wind across the grass, the chirp of cicadas, the bugling challenge of a distant elk.

"Willie, I think"—Holy Christ! If she'd screamed Boo! in his ear he wouldn't have jumped more—"I think we should talk."

"What?"

"Easy, honey," she soothed. "We should talk. Just, you know, regular conversation."

"All right."

"What's it like for you, being home?"

"It's good." He was surprised at how far the snow line had already crept down the mountain. It would be a bitter winter.

"Willie."

"What?" Okay, he'd better be cautious. Even though

she kept telling him "I'm so glad you're home" and, over and over, "I love you, I love you, I love you," as she served him up pan-fried trout for breakfast and steak for lunch and roast beef for dinner—plus a devil's food cake with a half inch of thick sticky white frosting that could tempt God Himself—ever since he'd been home he wouldn't have been stunned if she'd laid down her fork and said, Look here, Willie, we made a terrible mistake, getting married.

Truth of the matter was, they'd spent most of their courting days in her bed, whispering their life stories. They told each other everything there was to tell. So why didn't they know each other? If right now someone asked him, Hey, Willie, does Lois like to go to the movies? he wouldn't have had the foggiest notion, although it was probably yes, because would a girl who loved to say I love you *not* like to go to the movies? But they'd been man and wife only a little more than a month before he went to war. The important things they knew about each other could be written on the inside of a matchbook.

What if she'd fallen for someone else while he was gone and hadn't had the heart to write him a Dear John letter? But who could it be? Greg, their foreman, was nearly seventy and kept his teeth in his back pocket most of the time. Her old man's lawyer, Kunkel—Willie couldn't remember his first name—who had taught her about being an executrix, wore Coke-bottle-thick glasses. On the other hand, the boys in town were always talking about how it looked like Counselor Kunkel stuffed a pair of socks into the front of his Levi's.

"I wish you'd talk to me, Willie. Are you really happy, being home?" He had to be really careful here, because if he said yes too enthusiastically, she might just think: It's better to get it over with fast, before he settles in. On the other hand, if he said, "No; I wake up in the middle of the night after dreaming about a piece of nurse's leg, seeing strands of muscle dangling over a knob of bone, and also I got a god-awful scary pain in my gut the doc swears is only nervous indigestion, real common with boys coming home—why the hell I keep feeding it I'll never know— and there's a perky little girl with your eyes and my mother's blacker-than-black hair named Mary Jane and you picked that name yourself, never once wrote me asking what name I'd like, no more than you asked if I'd be willing to go along with Charles Bryant Blair if it was a boy"—well, then Lois might think: Gee, if he's so miserable, why don't we get it all over with in one fell swoop. "Willie? Are you . . . ? You're so quiet."

"I'm happy, Lo. I'm just not used to talking all the time."

"Didn't you talk with your buddies?"

"Sure, but different talk. What do you think, I said, 'Gee, buddy, you have eyes like emeralds'?" She lowered her green eyes, and even though it was too dark to see, he knew she was blushing. A hopeful sign.

All right: The gospel truth was that her eyes didn't come anywhere near emeralds. They were more like the green of sagebrush. But that wasn't what you said to captivate a woman who really doesn't need you around, except maybe as one of those gigolos, and truth be told, he was losing his looks. Sure, he'd always be thought of as handsome compared to what you saw Friday nights strolling around Jackson. Nowadays, though, it wasn't only the usual plug-ugly cowboys who'd been kicked in the face once too often. He'd come home from the war to find the valley had become an even bigger damn tourist trap. Friday nights, he'd hear a thunder of clunks, boot heels against wood walks. Tourists. The harmonious hodgepodge of Americans who'd been his buddies in the navy, the guys he'd, well, kind of loved, repulsed him now that they were descending on Wyoming. That first night in town, Willie found himself recoiling from them all, from too-white California teeth stained by their first chew of tobacco, from Kentucky potbellies straining the buttons on their leather vests, from beady New York eyes devouring his lean cowboy looks, wishing they could be him, buy him.

But they'd be buying worn goods. It unsettled Willie that he couldn't come up with a manlier word than beauty, but there you had it: His beauty had faded. And while he was thinking about going downhill, how about his physique? It wasn't so great anymore: a little scrawny, like most of his juices had trickled out into the Pacific Ocean.

But his worst worry wasn't in the mirror. It was realizing that Lois didn't need him to run the Circle B. She could do it herself. All the time Willie was gone, he kept waiting for her to write him: What should I do? Doc Birdsall says there's some new stuff for pinkeye in the herd, and how much should I buy or should I just wait till fly season? But no, all he got was a mile-high stack of love letters. Fact of the matter was, either she'd sat by her old man's side so long his shrewdness had rubbed off on her or she'd been born smart.

Like just that morning, after breakfast. He was still hungry, so she was making him cinnamon toast and she asked, Before next breeding season, do you think we ought to set a target weight for each group of same-size heifers? He'd said something brilliant, like, Huh? So she explained: That way, we could figure out a feeding plan that would make sure to get them to that weight. He'd said, You know something, Mrs. William Blair? You are one damn smart woman. She'd gotten all blushy, almost girlish, saying she was so glad he agreed. Agreed? In his entire life he wouldn't have come up with an idea like that.

The whole situation shook him up because after all his planning, nothing was happening the way he'd thought it would. Like, before he married Lois, he was positive he could run a ranch. He knew he would love it. It was so clear he could actually picture it: him riding out, like Piggy Pearson, sitting up there on his horse, watching the hands do all the hard work. He'd be yelling, Hey, you dumb oxes, you're doing it all wrong! But in the few weeks he'd supposedly been the big cheese, before he left for the navy, he realized that running a ranch had less to do with hard-trailing a herd than with reading about stuff like recommended snow loads for the roofs of livestock buildings—and he was a lousy, slow reader. Well, it also had to do with drinking coffee with other ranchers, which wasn't half bad, but then the talk always got down to the quality of their forage, and he wanted to smash his cup and scream, Let me out of here!

When he was away, he hadn't allowed himself to think about how disappointing it had been; there was too damn much else to worry about. But deep down he'd known after a single week of marriage—after a week of being top dog of the Circle B—that as much as he longed to possess the land, to be out there on it from sunup to sundown, he wasn't cut out to run a ranch. He was born to work one. Get out there, ride with the boys. Being the man he'd dreamed of becoming all his life had turned out to mean—of all lousy things—being a businessman.

He might as well be an insurance broker or operate a slaughterhouse. That's how goddamn numbing it was. You were out there breaking your back like any old ranch hand, because the truth of the matter was, the men wouldn't respect you if you just sat on your ass and gave orders. You couldn't sit on your horse at the end of a hard day and watch the sun set orange and purple and be filled with joy. No, when day was done, you put your truck in gear and sped back to the house, where you had your reading to do and your ledger, and your cattlemen's associations to attend—to say nothing of being a good husband to the wife who made it possible for you to have the job of your dreams, the job that bored you blue.

What in God's name could he do about being bored for ninety percent of his life? Become an absentee owner like old man Bryant had been? Live in Cheyenne and eat food with sauce? He could no more live in a city than live underwater. He was caught in the trap he himself had so cannily set.

"Willie?"

"I'm happy to be home. Can't you tell?"

"Don't get the wrong idea. It's just that you hadn't actually *said* you're happy." He must have sighed or snorted or something, because she flapped her hands in front of her face, a flibbertigibbet gesture not meant for a smart girl like Lois Bryant Blair. "Please, honey, don't get upset with me," she said.

"I'm not upset, okay? I'm happy. Wouldn't I be crazy not to be? In fact, I'm . . . Whatever the word is for the best happiness in the world, that's what I am now that I'm back with you." She slid out from under his arm and stood in front of him, savoring, he sensed, how much taller he was than she, and Lois was one tall girl. Her head tilted back. Her eyes closed. So he kissed her, lightly at first, then harder until she was breathless, moving right into him as if her hips had radar. "But Lo—"

"What's wrong?" She pulled back. Her eyes and mouth, small in the roundness of her large face, appeared even smaller, for suddenly they were tight with wariness. No, with out-and-out fear. Just two seconds after he'd told her how much he loved her, here she was, petrified he was going to say, So long, sweetheart! For a moment, Willie's chest swelled with confidence, with power. In like Flynn, that's where he was. The job he didn't want was his for life. And all he had to do to keep his employer content with his performance was to maintain in her a perfect balance between bliss and terror.

"I saw some pretty bad things over there. I'm kind of . . . I don't know. Shook up."

She held his face between her hands. "Willie, I've been reading, hearing on the radio. So many men are going through the same thing. It's *normal* to be shook up. You wouldn't be human if you weren't."

He pulled back his head so his face slipped out of her grasp. "I don't know. A little human is one thing. Weakness is another. I want to be the kind of father Mary Jane can be proud of. And most of all, I want not to be a burden to you. You know, this morning when you were talking about the heifers' feeding plan? I was thinking I wouldn't have come up with that in a million years."

"You would have if you were here last spring and—"

"No. You're a natural, Lo. You see the big picture. I'm no good at management stuff like that."

"I won't let you say that about yourself! Willie, you don't give yourself enough credit. You've always been better than you think you are." She set her hands on her hips, meaning to appear reproachful, but he sensed she couldn't help but think about his not being a natural. If she permitted her brain to do what it was capable of doing, she'd realize *she* was the best man for the job. Jeez, maybe that wouldn't be so bad. If she would only get rid of him now, before he got too old to learn a trade, before he got too crazy about Mary Jane, too used to three hot squares a day on gold-banded china plates.

"Look, Lois, maybe I should just go off for a little while by myself—"

"Don't say that!"

"—to try and—"

"No!" Her cry was so harsh, so loud, it brought the land to dead silence, almost like a coyote's cry.

"I'm not saying—"

"Please, Willie, no!"

"All right, baby. All right." He drew her in to comfort her.

In the process, their son, Charles Bryant Blair, was conceived.

Willie called him Chuck right from the beginning, because bubbling just beneath the surface of his consciousness was the recollection of Lois's jabbering about Daddy one night when the old man was still alive and laboring for breath in his room down the hall. Daddy hated being called Charles—too darn eastern!—but Chuck was worse: It's like calling yourself Meat! Lois, naturally, called the baby by her daddy's name, Charlie, but since most everybody on the Circle B and over in town seemed to want to either revere or eradicate the memory of old Charlie Bryant, the boy became Chuck Blair.

He grew up to be a strapping, fine-looking fellow. Folks who saw him with Willie would smile and say, Gosh, like father, like son. Still, Willie knew his son wasn't genuinely handsome, not the way he had been. True, Chuck's features were almost copies of his, but the boy's were set in a Moon Pie of a face. So even though he was tall and strong, he always looked like he'd been allowed too much ice cream, like a spoiled city boy.

Well, he was spoiled. By Lois. Oh, she was strict enough about his not using swear words and not chewing with his mouth open, but all Chuck had to do was open his eyes wide. Whatever he was looking at he'd get. Presto! Lois would put half an apple pie on her boy's plate, and the à la mode would be a double scoop. When the boy was in seventh grade, Lois took him for skis, and Chuck—who worked at skiing the way a boy his age ought to have worked at school or chores—came home with a two-hundred-dollar pair. All Willie could think was that it was a miracle he didn't have a stroke, that's how mad he was. When Chuck was in ninth grade, he was hunting ducks with a Browning Superposed, for crissakes. When Willie banged his fist on his chest of drawers and yelled, all Lois said was, Calm down. We're not doing all that bad, what with the ranch and my daddy's other investments—and what's money for if you can't do something nice for your children?

Not that she indulged Mary Jane that way. Whenever the girl asked for anything, which was rare, Lois would tell her, I have to discuss it with your father. But even if he was there and overheard them and said, Aw, go ahead, most of the time Lois somehow didn't get around to it. When Willie would bring it up, Lois would say, You really favor her, don't you.

Well, Mary Jane was a pretty thing, tall, broad-shouldered, graceful. With that long dark braid almost to her waist, she looked like his old schoolbook pictures of that Shoshone woman, Sacagawea, who led Lewis and Clark. And just like the Indian, his one-fourth-Shoshone daughter could always be relied on. By the time Mary Jane was nine, if there was an emergency with one of the animals, he'd call on her to help him. She wasn't only dependable. She was clever too, always coming up with new ways to do things. And all you had to do was say, Good job, Mary Jane, or just plain old thanks, and she'd go back and work twice as hard.

Chuck, on the other hand, did only what you asked him to do, and you always had to ask twice. Even when he was grown, seventeen years old, a senior in high school, no less, he was helping Willie plant some more rows of trees on the windward side of a tree belt so's to better catch the snow. Each time Chuck finished lowering a tree into the ground—doing a half-assed job most of the time, not digging deep enough, stuffing it in and cramping the roots—he'd look over to Willie as if to ask, Well? Am I done yet? To be fair, he never actually spoke the words, but you'd have needed hay for brains not to know what that look meant. A couple of the ranch hands were working alongside them, and Willie was shamed that his son was such a shirker. Was Chuck that dumb or thoughtless that he believed transplanting twenty-five trees was anybody's idea of a high old time?

Had Willie asked Chuck, the young man might have said, No, transplanting trees isn't anybody's idea of a high old time. But he was not asked, nor did he volunteer an answer. A few years later, however, by the time the mid-sixties rolled around, and Chuck would simply have told his father to take his spruces and shove them up his ass. Okay, he conceded to his girlfriend, Judy, one night when they were out drinking, I guess I need to know how the Circle B works because someday it's going to be mine, but couldn't he just *tell* me how? But at least these days his old man was starting to know enough not to keep bugging him about ranch shit. "Pardon the language," Chuck added.

"Oh, I am shocked," Judy replied, letting her jaw drop open, clasping her hands over her heart and then, overdoing it as she often did, intentionally falling off her barstool, laughing too hard, like she did when she was watching *Bewitched*, which in his opinion wasn't all that funny either. Of course, if he told her to take it easy— they were at the bar in the Blue Snake, not at her family's kitchen table—she'd tell him to go soak his head, and she'd keep on laughing. All the other people at the bar would think: She is one live wire, but she's so cute it doesn't matter that she's a handful. And besides, she's a Clendenen. Why, the Clendenens almost beat the Indians into the valley. Anyhow, that big guy she's with seems to be managing her just fine.

Chuck realized that only he was able to see how her hilarity diminished at his rebuke, as if he'd turned down her brightness knob just a little. "What I'm saying is . . . ," he began again slowly, giving her the chance to get up off the floor and get serious again, which she did, he was pleased to note, in record time, "he's always given my sister the benefit of the doubt. As far as he goes, she's Saint Mary Jane."

"Well, aren't you Saint Charles to your mother?"

"I don't think so."

"Not that there's anything wrong with that," Judy chirped quickly. "*I* think you're a saint." She flashed her smile.

"Thank you, my child." He made the sign of the cross in the air.

"Any old time, Saint Chuck." As usual when in her company, Chuck found himself grinning. He became a mirror reflecting Judy. She was little, barely over five feet, but she had the world's greatest grin—glistening Chiclet teeth rimmed with generous red lips. Sometimes she looked like a smile on legs.

Judy lifted her beer stein—how she could order a beer in the middle of January was beyond him—and gazed at the thin layer of white that was all that was left of the head, but she didn't drink. She wiped the condensation off the glass with a napkin. Then, her chore complete, she set the glass back down. "Don't you like getting out there, pitching in, helping your dad on the ranch?"

"No. *You* like to pitch in and help your dad. They don't call your boots shit-kickers for nothing. You're never happier than when you're knee-deep in cow flop."

"Ankle-deep. But think about this, Chuck: When you're helping him, you're helping yourself. The Circle B's going to be yours one day." He saw what everybody couldn't see because they were too dazzled by her exuberance—that this ownership business was a sore point with Judy. The sorest. Clendenen Ranch, her family's spread, which bordered the Circle B on the south, would go to her older brother. Should anything happen to Brock, she'd once confided, it would pass on to one of the younger boys. And if something happened to each one of them, it would go to any tramp walking by on the road, as long as he had two hands and a weenie. But it

would not go to her, even though she was the only one of
the five kids who gave a damn about the place. Who
loved it, to be perfectly honest. She told Chuck she
thought he was an absolutely perfect person except for
the fact that he didn't give a darn about what was his, the
Circle B. "Even if it's not in your blood to get out there
and work side by side with him, it at least should be in
your financial interest."

"What the hell does he need me for to warm up some
calf's frostbitten teat?"

"Sometimes you get a whole bunch of animals that
get hit real bad, and you need as many hands as you can
get—"

"You don't have to draw me a picture." He signaled to
the bartender for another Jim Beam. Until it came, he
traced the beer logo on a wet bar coaster with his finger
and did not look at her, although she ostentatiously
shifted in her stool, took off her headband and combed
her shoulder-length blond hair with her fingers, and
recuffed the sleeves of her red sweater. At last, his drink
came, neat, in a shot glass. He wished he could down it in
one gulp, but he'd tried too many times and choked and
coughed like the feeblest dude, so he acted thoughtful
and took small, introspective sips. "If I'd decided to stick
it out in college, do you think he'd be calling me there,
saying, Chuck, you better get home quick 'cause I got
some frostbitten teats that need warming? Excuse me: the
*calves* got frostbitten teats."

Judy grinned. "Who doesn't, this time of year?"

He knew she was trying to jolly him out of the funk
he always fell into when talking about his father. All
right, he'd let himself be jollied. "I wouldn't mind
defrosting yours."

"Where? In your car, with your busted heater? They'd turn blue and fall off."

"Where else can we be alone? Your place? How about in the kitchen? Your mom's probably putting up hog's brain jelly or whatever she's canning this week. Your dad would have his shotgun out if I took one step up toward the bedrooms. How about the living room? We could keep your brothers company watching *I Spy*."

"That's what you'd rather be doing than defrosting my frosties."

"You're nuts, Judy. Do you know that?"

"I'm not nuts. You can get my frosties six other nights a week. You only can get that black guy and the white guy being cool once a week."

"They *are* cool. Going around the world, spying, playing tennis."

"Chuck," she said, halving a peanut with her teeth.

"What? No one's going to pay me to play tennis?"

"You got it."

He laughed, but the thing of it was, no one was really going to pay him for doing anything. At least not very much. Oh sure, he could get a job teaching cross-country skiing or—if he felt like knocking himself out, which he didn't—earn a little more taking tourists to backcountry and show those slickers who thought they were hell on skis what it took to give up chair lifts and tows and climb. What it felt like to hurtle downhill with the speed and power of an avalanche in awesome mountain quiet—the way the world must have been on the seventh day. How could his old man think it was a life worth living to ride around in cow shit all day on the flatness of the ranch, just looking at the mountains now and then? How could he not yearn with all his heart to *be* in the mountains?

What the hell are you fit for? his father once yelled at him. What *was* he fit for? He could lead pack trips once June rolled around. Bartend and shake up Moose Juice and frozen daiquiris all summer. But the sad and sorry truth was, the only job with a future in Jackson Hole was being Willie Blair's son. Lois Blair's son too, but even though his mother owned the damn ranch, even though she was the real brains behind it, even though she had a soft spot in her heart for her son, she always came down on the side of her husband when push came to shove. All the times Chuck came to her to say, Hey, Mom, this or that isn't fair, she'd get that big-eyed dippy look, the kind the dumbest blondes in movies get, and say, Gosh, honey, I don't really understand what's going on, and besides, I wouldn't want to come between you and your dad. She tried to make up for it by slipping him money on the side, but it was never enough to do anything important, like buy a Mustang, which his old man sneered at, saying it was a hunk of tin and he needed it like a second asshole.

"I could be a ski instructor someplace like Vail or Squaw Valley," he told Judy.

Give her credit: She was the girl next door, and she'd confessed she'd loved him just about forever. And they'd been going together for six years. Any other girl in her position would have slammed her beer onto the bar and ripped him to shreds for that kind of going-away talk. Or tried to make him feel guilty, like, Well, do what you have to do, don't worry, I'll be fine. But each time he talked about moving on—maybe going into the air force and becoming a jet pilot or opening a ski school down in South America, she'd do just what she was doing now: Look him straight in the eye and listen to his plans as if he were talking about some mutual friend of theirs.

Patience, that's what she had. Guts too, come to think about it, because a couple of times she'd been smart enough to catch him doing a little cheating. No big deal, just some tourist or a local girl throwing herself at him so hard the only way to stop her was to screw her blind, deaf and dumb. Judy never said, How could you do this to me? Nothing like that. Just told him that she knew. Not even that she was disappointed in him or hurt. Just that she knew.

It wasn't that she couldn't get anybody else. In high school, she was president of 4-H and captain of the cheerleaders. Sure, she was small, but good things came in small packages. She was as sexy as she was cute, like a short *I Dream of Jeannie*, although she had a bit of a Bob Hope nose. And with her great smile, she really was Most Popular Girl. Nevertheless, right from the start she'd made it clear to everyone that Chuck Blair was the only boy in her life. The only man in her life.

"I was also thinking a little about looking into training for the biathlon. When I was watching those guys at the Olympics, I kept thinking: I can ski as good as they can. And I can damn well shoot a whole lot better." He put the shot glass to his mouth for another sip, but it was empty.

She really was a patient girl. Waiting since tenth grade for him to pop the question. He knew the faster he popped, the better, what with Vietnam hanging over his head. Except he'd been saying that to himself for a year, and he couldn't get the words off the tip of his tongue. He knew marrying Judy would be the right thing. It made sense. She was a great skier and a really good lay. The human pretzel, he called her. And she was almost always in a good mood. Her spirit was so terrific it was contagious. People loved to be with her. And her family liked him, his family liked her. If he was doomed to stay on the ranch, well, she'd be a big help.

Sometimes, like now, after a few drinks, he came so close to asking, it took his breath away once he sobered up. But other times, when he was slightly bagged, he'd start to think that maybe the reason she was so damn patient was because she'd really had her eye on one thing since sophomore year at Jackson High. Not on him. On the Circle B. He was going to inherit a ranch and she wasn't, so what's a ranch-hungry girl like Judy Clendenen to do? Marry a ranch, that's what.

But that kind of thinking would take one cold bitch, and if there was one thing his Judy was, it was a warm-hearted, fun-loving, sweet girl. So sweet. She really did look like Jeannie, sitting up on that barstool, her feet in red socks wrapped around the base of the stool, her boots—cute little boots—down on the floor. Like Jeannie, with those slanty-up blue eyes, except when you saw her profile, then you couldn't help but think of Bob Hope. But she must have known her nose wasn't her best feature, because even when they were driving, she'd scrunch around so her full face was toward him. It hit him suddenly: how touching it was that she always wanted to put her best face forward for him. She loved him so much, all the time, was always thinking of him. He owed her.

Chuck realized he'd just been sitting there, thinking, not talking, for how long? A minute? Ten minutes? So he leaned over and took her little hand in his—her left hand, her ring hand, although he couldn't be completely sure, being a little bagged—and said: "Judy Clendenen, will you marry me?"

\*　　\*　　\*

Of course Sally Ann knew Marty was dead. But so many mornings, just before daylight forced her to look at what had become of her life, she would lie in her husband's arms. Kissing him, her lips would get roughed by his night growth of beard, making them even more sensitive to each successive touch, each variation of pressure. Instead of just circling her arms around his back, she would clutch his strong shoulders. His muscles swelled in her hands, forcing her fingers apart. Marty's own hands slid down her body—oh, the heat of them—and he would moan and say, Sweetheart, I can feel it, you're ready for me.

Her mornings with him were the only part of her life she could bear. She knew they were fantasy, but before each ensuing hour of every day pressed down upon her, harder and harder, crushing any possibility of joy, she allowed her mind its comfort. For those transcendent minutes, Marty's spirit was truly embracing her. The God Who she was now certain could not exist was nonetheless permitting Martin Freund, Esquire, to put his affairs in order before he had to withdraw, allowing Sergeant Marty Freund, the medic, to ease his wife's heartache with visits to her sickroom.

An hour past dawn on the first anniversary of his death, Sally Ann awoke sweaty, shaky, heart thudding, not from a terrible dream but from the realization that she had just missed Marty's last visit and now he was gone for good. Down the hallway, she heard four-year-old Barbara whispering, like a fussbudget schoolteacher: Shhh, Danny. Davey, let Mommy sleep.

Everything Sally Ann had experienced in those months since the Germans shot her husband in the heart—the whoosh of voices, the scuffing of pajamaed children's feet and her mother's slippers on the way to the kitchen, the sight of winter light so lacking in strength that it could barely illuminate the dark wood slats of the venetian blinds, the earthy aroma of Wheatena—seemed less than real, as if she were experiencing her life as a theatergoer with a particularly bad seat.

She longed for the simple faith of other war widows she read about. Those women's soldier boys hung around the Pearly Gates, faces reflecting the white luminescence of angel wings, biding their celestial time until they could be husbands eternally. If not faith, then Sally Ann yearned for an answer. If not an answer, help. Two weeks earlier, when she had taken the children up to the Bronx for their weekly visit to Marty's parents, she'd gone out for a walk, alone, and—Why the hell am I doing this? she asked herself—went to see the Orthodox rabbi who had married them.

"Time. It takes time," the old rabbi said. At first she'd been so grateful he hadn't asked if she believed in God, and so humiliated by breaking into loud, barking sobs she could not control, that she hadn't noticed he was talking to his cuticles. "That's why we say kaddish for eleven months." His accent was *mittel* European; he pronounced "that's why" as "dot's vy." It was like sitting across from half of an old Jewish vaudeville routine, except the rabbi was no comedian. He came from a country where nobody was laughing.

"It's been twelve months," she replied.

"Are you a machine that can be turned off to stop making grief?"

Even when she leaned forward, it was hard to hear his voice. She could be eavesdropping on counsel he was offering some other, invisible sorrower. Sally Ann had no doubt he had offered up this solace hundreds, thousands of times: to mourners insensate, mourners silently weeping, mourners insane with grief. It seemed to be exhausting him to do it yet again. And why couldn't he look at her? Was it some weird Orthodox thing with women, like not sitting with them in synagogue? How can I get out of here? Okay, I can say, Yes, you're probably right, Rabbi, and time is a great healer, and thanks for talking to me. Because she knew what he was going to say, even as she was hiccuping and weeping, pouring out her heart to him: Listen, sweetheart, go home, take care of the *kinder*. Don't worry you don't feel no love for them. It's just that you're still in shock. Who wouldn't be, what with such a loss? You're young yet. You'll see, you got a luffly life ahead of you.

Yet she remained in the stiff-backed chair with its squeaky oilcloth-covered seat. "What if the deadness inside never stops?"

"It will. The pain will lessen." A recording of a recording might have been playing inside him with this message, that's how remote he sounded. "At least you have the comfort that your husband died a soldier, able to fight them like a man. Not gassed like vermin, like . . ." He sighed, one of those loud, old-world, old-people exhalations that would normally amuse her. But this rabbi appeared older than old, now that she looked. More like a dead man. Cadaverous hollows in his cheeks were barely covered by a gray beard that seemed as if it would become dust if he only had energy enough to stroke it.

His eyes left his cuticles and, avoiding her, moved over to the spines of the books in his shelves and then, quickly, out the window of his basement study, to the knotted roots of a great tree, which were cracking the sidewalk.

Sally Ann sensed that, like her, the rabbi was only going through the motions of life. He, too, was being forced to witness a play. Unlike her, though, he had not been granted a seat for the performance, not even a lousy one. He was center stage in the epic war drama that was being staged in the town in which he had been born, a depraved pageant of shrieks and stinks and fire that would never end.

"I hate them," she told another rabbi the following day. A very American rabbi, a man not much older than Marty, the assistant rabbi at a large Reform temple on Fifth Avenue. No gassed aunts and uncles for him, no baby cousins run through with bayonets. So American he might have been waiting on Plymouth Rock to greet the *Mayflower*. "The only time I'm able to feel anything at all, it's hate."

"The Germans?" he asked drearily, as if daily he was assailed by yammering hordes of Jews crying, Germans! Germans!

Come on, she told herself, give the guy the benefit of the doubt. Maybe he's asking politely. Maybe you misjudge him. Yet when she'd walked into his beige office, she'd felt he'd taken her in with one fast glance and, in that blink of time, gone from appreciation to courteous indifference, from finding her an appealing woman to seeing someone not quite worthy of his level of pastoral service. Was it her unplucked eyebrows? Her unfashionably short coat, clearly from the days of the wartime fabric shortage? Were her breasts so large as to be low class?

With close-cropped hair, tan suede elbow patches, private-school vowels, and tight lips, he looked bitter and Protestant, like an instructor who had been denied tenure at Vassar and was now forced to deal with her ilk, Hunter students, females with thundering opinions and dentalized *t*'s.

"Of course it's the Germans I hate. Who else? For what they did to us. For what they did to my husband." The rabbi was nodding—at her predictability, she thought. "Marty was a medic. He wore the Red Cross, for God's sake, and they still shot him in the heart."

"No," the rabbi said. "*They* did not shoot him. One German shot him." Then he added, "Let me offer you something a very great man once said." Sally Ann waited for the wisdom of Maimonides. " 'I do not know a method of drawing up an indictment against a whole people.' It was Edmund Burke who said that," the rabbi began to explain. "He was—"

She interrupted. "I know who Edmund Burke was, and I'm pretty sure he said that right before the Revolution. He was talking about *us*."

"Jews?"

"No, no. About Americans. But trust me, if Burke knew what we know about the Germans, he'd have kept his mouth shut."

"If we hate them as a group," the rabbi said, standing, inching toward the door, "are we any better than Nazis?"

So she concluded that the faith of her foremothers had nothing to offer. But how could it, when she herself had no faith? Sally Ann retreated even further from the life and the laws of her people than Dora and Ruthie had. Without Marty beside her to explain the rituals—the lighting of the candles, the blessings over the wine—they became foolish foreign exercises. Happy holidays seemed hurtful, the somber ones too depressing to be borne. Repetition of ancient prayers, even the simple, soothing rhythm of them, might have comforted Sally Ann, but her grandparents had left their Hebrew in the shtetls, perhaps thinking that language useless in a new world, or the prayers risky in a land of Christian English-speakers. Like so many college students, she had read from Aquinas's *Summa Theologica* and Barth's *Epistle to the Romans*, studied Buddha's Four Noble Truths and the Eightfold Path, but was utterly ignorant of the Talmud, except to bandy about the pejorative "Talmudic scholar." There was no God in Sally Ann's universe. She simply had to go it alone.

However, the existential void she was confronting was a nicely furnished one. Between Marty's insurance and her widow's benefits, she could have managed a modestly pleasant life with the children: excursions to Central Park, visits to the library and the Museum of Natural History, ice cream sodas on birthdays. She might have bought herself smart, if not chic, clothes, taken an economy cruise, had her hair coiffed once in a while by Monsieur René and, sooner rather than later, met a man decently enough disposed toward her children so that she could marry him.

To be sure, there was not enough money for Sally Ann to remain on the Upper East Side, or to dine out in restaurants or hear *Tosca* from Dress Circle seats. This was determined by Ruthie, who had come to stay when Marty left for the army and who never went home. She took over their finances—and everything else—in the years after the war. She had to.

Sally Ann stayed in her bedroom for days at a time. Whenever she did come upon little Barbara with her satellite twins, she would pat the three small heads or give their cheeks the airy kisses of a distant relation. As the second anniversary of Marty's death passed, she began going out again, but only to the movies, that pastime her mother had always regarded as frivolous.

But Sally Ann simply had to see John Garfield. She was drawn to him. She could refuse him nothing. In the years before the war, she'd hardly noticed him, although once she had remarked, Gee, Marty, he looks a little like you, except he has a fat nose. Marty had shaken his head, chuckled and patted her cheek. Can't resist us up-from-the-streets Jewish guys, can you? But having passed a newsstand and spotted the actor on a *Photoplay* cover, Sally Ann began seeing John Garfield almost daily. She would sit through double features two or three times in order to watch him in *Body and Soul* or *Force of Evil*. In that popcorn-perfumed darkness, she forgot she had three children, forgot that her mother would grab her the minute she walked through the door: Tell me, *what* do you think you're doing? Sally Ann, this is crazy, this is— Her whole world was now the man on the screen. The times he was not in a scene, she waited, restlessly, as if someone had summoned him out of the room on patently foolish business.

Ruthie Wolf's torrent of mother love may have overwhelmed Sally Ann, but now, divided by three, it helped to make up for what the children did not get from their mother. Ruthie brought the same doggedness to running the Freund household that had allowed her to rise from sweatshop worker to factory foreman. The rent was too high? We need a new place to live? All right. In battle gear of sensible black oxfords and a gray raincoat that could deflect a monsoon—but with an expensive hat with a long blue feather, so building superintendents would know they were dealing with a lady—armed with an umbrella and a pocketbook full of ten-dollar bills for bribes, weapons with which to combat the postwar housing shortage, Ruthie took her three grandchildren and scouted most of the length and all of the breadth of Manhattan, pointing out the buildings of architectural significance along the way.

In 1948, she found them all a home on Riverside Drive on the Upper West Side, in a building that had not been elegant since the First World War. Nevertheless, it was not too much of a comedown. The hallways were drab, but they did not reek of garlic and unsuccessfully toilet-trained toddlers. The day and the night doormen, while not in snappy, Upper East Side livery, were sober.

The apartment Ruthie found was grand in size if not in style. While the bedrooms were barely larger than penitentiary cells, the public rooms were capacious, seemingly designed for families of diplomats: a graceful entrance gallery; a living room large enough for a ball; a formal dining room in which the family could sit around their small and decidedly informal table and watch the sun set flaming red across the Hudson River, as if it were trying to burn up New Jersey.

As the forties faded into the fifties, Sally Ann's melancholy seemed to lift, perhaps because time had, indeed, healed, or because John Garfield was gone. He had been blacklisted. No longer allowed to make movies, he could have no more assignations with her. One December, she pulled up a chair beside her mother at the dining room table. For the first time since Marty had died, she peered at the family's checkbook. "Does it balance?" she asked her mother. The second the words left her mouth, she knew the answer. "I mean—not balance. I know you're good at all that stuff. I mean, what do you think of our financial situation?"

"What do I think?" Ruthie screwed the cover back on her pen and shrugged, as dramatic a shrug as her arthritic shoulders would allow.

"I know I've been a little . . . abstracted since Marty . . ."

"And now?"

"I don't know. I guess I'm coming back to myself."

"You've still got your youth—"

"Ma, I'm thirty-three."

"Your youth and your looks. Listen, Sally Ann, you walk down the street and men still turn around for you. Their eyes follow you. Don't tell me they don't, because you don't notice. I do. You have a way with you."

"I don't want another husband."

"Well, we'll have to make do—"

The nine-year-old twins rushed into the apartment following their after-school play, their cheeks brilliant from their basketball game, their hands gloved with city soot. They kissed their mother politely, then leaned against their grandmother, bookends squeezing a much-loved volume. "Can we afford a television?" Danny demanded.

"No," Ruthie responded brusquely.

"We're the only ones in the whole neighborhood—" Davey began.

"Good. You'll be the only ones who aren't idiots." Without bothering to appeal their case to their mother, they moved on to the kitchen. "An apple *or* a slice of cheese," Ruthie shouted after them. "Not both!"

"Maybe we should get a television," Sally Ann said. "For us, for the news. And a half hour a day for the kids wouldn't be so terrible."

"Find me the money."

"Oh."

"That's why I brought up the subject of maybe you getting married again."

"What should I say to the man? 'I don't love you, but I want a DuMont?' We'll do without television. Did you go out and marry someone you didn't care about to help raise me? No. You worked, I worked."

"But don't you want to be able to send the children somewhere to college where they can meet classy people, go to football games with all that 'Boola-boola'? Study with great minds?"

"There are great minds at Hunter and City and Brooklyn and Queens. And if they need 'Boola-boola,' they can get scholarships. I don't have to get married for them to have a good education." Sally Ann closed her eyes for a moment to shut out her mother, but there was no longer anything to distract her in her darkness. In the six years since his death, Marty's heated presence had cooled and solidified. He was now more a household saint than a burning spirit. "I guess I should go back to work," she said.

She was hired by Johnson Flag and Banner, Incorporated, the company that had the contract for the City of New York, the State of Connecticut and the Knights of Pythias. "Manufacturing Old Glory Since 1898," it proclaimed on its letterhead. There had been only forty-five stars on the union then. "The union's the blue part, the upper corner nearest the staff," Clyde Johnson III told her. A big man in his fifties, more thickset than corpulent, he seemed composed of solid chunks rather than indentable flesh-and-blood parts. He looked as though he should be operating a jackhammer rather than running the second-largest flag company east of the Mississippi. "Now, this may be . . . confusing, but on other

flags that part is called a canton." It was hard to hear
him. The clacking of industrial sewing machines in the
factory combined with the rumble and squeals of traffic
in the Bronx drowned out his soft basso voice. "But not
on the American flag."

"Yes, sir." She was sitting so close to the edge of the
chair near the side of his desk that she almost slid off. She
really didn't know exactly how secretaries ought to sit,
although if she remembered correctly, in movies they
never put their whole behinds on chairs. Then again, she
wasn't actually a secretary. She had been hired as a receptionist. However, it was understood that Sally Ann would
fill in for Mr. Johnson's right hand, Ethel, during lunch
hours and vacations. "I know."

"You know?" He seemed befuddled by her response,
gazing around his office as if looking for a sign as to what
to say next. There were only the moth-eaten colonial
American flags Mr. Johnson's father had collected. Snakes
coiled or with forked tongues sticking out, warning
DON'T TREAD ON ME. Crossed swords proclaiming LIBERTY
OR DEATH. A stately pine tree on a faded yellow background crying AN APPEAL TO GOD. On the wall behind Mr.
Johnson's Duncan Phyfe desk was a flag with just an
anchor, which, more peaceably, suggested HOPE, but since
this was not in Mr. Johnson's purview, he simply kept
silent and chewed on his upper lip.

"Right after you offered me the job last week, I went to
the library and looked up 'flags' in the encyclopedia. They
had a diagram that showed all the different parts of the
flag. It said 'canton' on the upper left. . . ."

"Yes?" Mr. Johnson said encouragingly.

"But there was an asterisk, and the footnote explained
how that space was called a 'union' on the American flag."

"Oh." This time the monosyllable had a contented ring to it. "So you know . . . ?"

"Yes, Mr. Johnson. All the parts of the flag, at least the ones that were in that diagram."

"Good," he murmured, although she couldn't actually hear the word. But she saw his mouth form it before he closed his eyes to concentrate on dictating a response to a letter from the deputy assistant secretary of the Department of the Interior regarding contingency plans if Alaska or Hawaii should achieve statehood. Forty-nine stars? Fifty stars? Good God! "'Dear Harold: Thank you for yours of the fourth. . . .'"

Sally Ann tried to swallow, but her throat wasn't working. Dictation. They had tested her typing skills, listened to her telephone voice, found them acceptable. But in what probably was an oversight, no one at Johnson Flag and Banner had asked the simple question: Do you take dictation? Well, she did not, but she was going to figure it out right now. Fortunately, Mr. Johnson was a man of few words. Even more fortunately, he was not comfortable even with these, which gave Sally Ann time to write what he said verbatim.

The following day, during Ethel's lunch hour, Mr. Johnson asked, "Fixed up my . . . , Mrs. Freund?"

"I'm sorry, Mr. Johnson. I wasn't able to hear you."

"I see you fixed up my punctuation."

It was his grammar she had corrected. As she typed his letter, she found herself changing a word here and there as well. But she was unable to admit it, because her mouth was dry with fear. So she merely nodded. He'd caught her. What was the worst that could happen? The family could survive without her working. But boy oh boy, she didn't want to be fired. It was so exhilarating to have a job again, to be on the subway shoulder to shoulder, arm to arm, with people with a purpose: X-ray technicians and factory workers and keypunch operators and salesmen. To be putting on lipstick and rouge and a freshly ironed blouse, kissing her mother and the children goodbye—See you for dinner!—buying the *Herald Tribune* in the morning and the *Post* every night and consequently possessing once again that bracing I-belong knowledge: what plays had opened; how the money for polio research was being spent or squandered; which Democrats might be able to do something to contain the Republicans.

True, saying, "Good morning, Johnson Flag and Banner, Incorporated," and having to carry a sandwich in a bag for lunch because the only decent place to eat in that particular corner of the southwest Bronx was La Stella— an Italian restaurant only Mr. Johnson and the other factory owners could afford—wasn't exactly what most people would call a glamour job. But advertising agencies and publishers wanted peaches-and-cream executive secretaries fresh from the Seven Sisters colleges, not a widow with seventy-two credits from a city college, no matter how bright she was.

Still, how she shone in the Bronx! What a worker! She awoke thinking: I've got to call Helen at Crestview Notions and Trimmings to order more gold cord and tassels for the Shriners shipment. She drifted into sleep contemplating that bucolic paradise represented by the Vermont coat of arms.

Early the following year, Sally Ann replaced Ethel. By June, Mr. Johnson no longer had to dictate to her. That mysterious bond between boss and secretary had been forged, one mind linking itself to the other. Sally Ann knew not only what was going on at Johnson Flag and

Banner, but also what Mr. Johnson wanted to do about it. By the end of that year, she was in charge of his entire life, including buying Christmas presents for his wife, his two grown daughters, their husbands and their children. When Mrs. Johnson called from Scarsdale the Monday after the holiday, she told Sally Ann in enraptured tones: You wouldn't believe what I got for Christmas, dear. Or maybe you would. Wait, of course you would. You are an absolute treasure. Thank you, thank you! Chinchilla!

Seven months after that, Clyde Johnson took Sally Ann out to lunch at La Stella, to celebrate her second anniversary at Johnson Flag and Banner. Actually, she had been dreading the lunch, because she could not imagine sustaining a conversation with him for more than sixty seconds, much less sixty minutes—except for debating about how to up the Girl Scout order. Also, there was the matter of eating: She had tried discussing it with Ruthie, but the truth of the matter was, her mother was getting a little senile lately; she kept asking why *she* had to go out to lunch with Sally Ann's boss, so Sally Ann just said, Never mind, Mom, he called to say he can't make it, then she sat her down in front of the new television and put on the *Voice of Firestone*. But after a discussion with twelve-year-old Barbara, who was so mature she was more like a friend now than a daughter, it was decided that to order spaghetti was to risk a blouseful of tomato sauce and humiliation.

So she was desperately studying the menu, which didn't have one word of English—what was this, Palermo or the Bronx?—trying to find some word that might mean "macaroni" and could be tucked, nondrippily, into the mouth, when Mr. Johnson reached across the bread sticks, took her hand and said, ". . . love you."

"Excuse me?" she said, knowing he could not possibly be saying what she thought she heard. She wished she hadn't taken psych and read *A General Introduction to Psychoanalysis*, because then she wouldn't be so chagrined at her own mishearing. What had he actually said? Maybe recommending some fancy Italian dish—they all ended in vowels—or maybe a cocktail or something.

"I love you," Mr. Johnson was repeating. His steely-haired block of a head started to descend in embarrassment, but being a man who, five days a week, faced LIBERTY OR DEATH, he did not dare be fainthearted, so he added, ". . . Sally Ann."

"Oh." She had no idea what to say, only that she had to say it. What was he expecting? I love you too, Clyde? Clyde? His name was so awful, so clunky. How was she going to call him that without making a hideous gulping sound with the *C* and the *l*? And she didn't love him. Or did she? Maybe he was some kind of mind reader, picking up signals from her subconscious that, despite her conscious mind's not knowing, were broadcasting: I'm crazy about you, Clyde baby.

Well, she could say something mealymouthed: I'm so grateful for the warmth you seem to feel toward me, Mr. Johnson, but— But what? Oh boy, he was waiting for her to say something. He looked like . . . Was he going to cry? Get mad? How dare you not love me, with the Christmas bonus I gave you! If he gave her the heave-ho, what would become of her? Oh sure, she could go to some lesser flag company, Stars and Bars or Fiedler's Fine Flags, but that would mean being a regular secretary. Well, she was a secretary here, of course, but she was . . . well, she felt she was actually helping him run the company. "I don't know what to say."

". . . like me?" he asked.

"Do I like you?" He bobbed his big head up and down. "Of course I like you, Mr. Johnson."

"I wish you'd call me Clyde."

If she called him Clyde, would he expect her to take off her girdle and do God knows what? Okay, she had to admit she had wondered once or twice what it would be like doing it with a non-Jew and how an uncircumcised one would look—would there be some primeval gag reflex triggered, or was it a taboo because it looked so thrillingly different, so wonderful, although she couldn't imagine what could make any of them look all that great—and also what it would be like to do it with someone like Mr. Johnson, who was probably over six feet tall and built like a block of cement, except for his chin, which hung loose and quivery, like a pelican's pouch. All right, to be honest, not how it would be with someone *like* Mr. Johnson: She had, on occasion, imagined being naked against his bigness.

But this wasn't fair, pulling this on her without even a hint, going from Mrs. Freund, does the blue on the Hadassah order look too indigo? to I love you, Sally Ann. But what could she say without risking getting fired?

"This isn't fair," she said. Those words popped out of her mouth. She couldn't believe it.

"What?"

And they kept coming. "If I say I'd rather call you Mr. Johnson, you'll get angry—"

"No."

"—and in a couple of weeks or months you'll find you don't like my work and you'll—"

"No."

"And if I call you Clyde, you'll expect . . ." She felt a

shiver of fear and excitement when, instead of saying no to that one, he waved over the waiter and asked him to bring the special antipasto platter and to tell Mario to put extra of that good white cheese on it, to make it nice for the lady. It was a far longer sentence than Sally Ann had ever heard from him, and while she was touched by Clyde's solicitousness, she was too nervous to eat anything, especially some white Italian cheese she'd probably never even seen before, although if it was like the stuff on the tray at the next table, it looked like American cheese, except without the color. "I mean, you're not saying, 'Call me Clyde because I want us to be friends,' are you?"

"Um," he said, and she realized she had thrown too many words at him and he wasn't quite sure how to answer her question. Not that he was stupid. On the contrary, he was smart about business, definitely smarter than his father had been. Mr. Johnson II or Jr. or whatever they called themselves had spent a fortune buying antique flags and furniture to show off in the Bronx, where no one ever came except Johnson employees—who thought the flags stank and went pyew all the time. According to Fay the bookkeeper, who came in three days a week, the middle Mr. Johnson almost ran the business into the ground. ". . . something more than friends, I hope."

What was more than friends? She realized he hadn't said a word about Mrs. Johnson, or, Gee, I'd love to meet your kids, which might mean . . . No, she told herself. You're too old to be silly. Not *might* mean. Does mean. Does mean he isn't thinking about marriage. Does mean he wants me to be his paramour. Or maybe nothing as romantic as a paramour. Maybe he wants one of those awful arrangements you overhear in conversations on the subway, where two girls from a steno pool are talking about a third, saying, She stays late every single night, and it ain't dictation she's takin' from him, if you get my drift. On the other hand, he knew she had three children and a mother who was a little forgetful, so he wouldn't have thoughts of setting her up in a love nest with lots of negligees from Saks Fifth Avenue, would he?

How could she ask him what the rules were? He'd think she was being greedy and then he'd remember all the terrible things he'd ever heard about Jews and he'd probably say something goyish to himself, like, This is a fine kettle of fish I've gotten myself into. She said, "This isn't an easy conversation, is it?"

"No."

"Well, I think we have to have it anyway." She couldn't believe she'd said that, but he actually seemed relieved. His head was bobbing up and down in agreement, although he wasn't actually talking. "If I were to call you Clyde, I would still work for you?"

"Yes," he said, his eagerness mixing with surprise that she had asked such a question.

Now what? "Have you given this thought, I mean about how . . . ?" He nodded, a definite yes. "Tell me what you've been thinking."

"Me?"

"Yes."

"That we'd . . . I can't leave Mrs. . . . I mean . . . But I would get us a nice place somewhere, where we could be, could spend time."

"I couldn't . . . I'd have to get home."

"Me too," he said, and they gave a simultaneous nervous, monosyllabic chuckle. "I don't want you to think we would just . . . We could talk, you know, about whatever. Ourselves, the business . . ."

"No matter what happens," Sally Ann said, "this conversation has already gone on too long for me ever to be . . . to feel safe about my job. What if you don't like me after a couple of weeks?"

"Impossible!"

She almost stopped clawing the napkin in her lap to reach over to take his hand and squeeze it in gratitude for his fervor. "What if I say, 'Look, let's forget it,' right now? You couldn't forget it, could you?"

"I guess not. But listen, I need you in the business. Even if . . . whatever . . . I wouldn't fire you. Do you know how much sales have increased since you started dealing with customers?" She knew from Fay it was sixteen percent, and Fay had asked, What are you waiting for? How come you're not hitting up old man Clyde for a big fat raise? "A lot."

"I'm not some sweet young thing, you know."

"Yes you are."

"No. I'm a widow with three children and a mother to take care of."

"I can give you—"

"I don't want to be a kept woman, Clyde."

At the sound of his first name his eyes grew wide, but wary as well. The waiter approached, carrying a platter large enough to feed a Roman legion, but he waved him away. "What do you want?"

"I think . . . I want to be a junior partner."

He was about to demand, A *what*? but he could not pretend he did not understand what she meant. "It's a family-run company."

"Who runs it?"

"I do."

"So you can make it a partnership if you like. Look, I

know I'm not a Johnson. But if you give me a small piece, percent, whatever, it would still be a Johnson-run, Johnson-owned company." His chin quavered as his jaw flopped open. "I guess you think this is awfully mercenary of me. I think so too, actually, hearing myself. But I'm not doing this for me."

"I'm not sure I can do it."

"I understand. But think about this: If I were a man working in the office, you'd have been shaking my hand six months ago and saying, 'Welcome aboard, partner,' or something like that, because if you didn't I'd have gone someplace else, and you couldn't afford to lose me."

He summoned the waiter back. Without looking across the table to Sally Ann, he grabbed several slices of white cheese from the platter and gobbled them. Then two very large olives, which he gnawed nervously, one on either side of his mouth. Not so polite, but she could not help but admire the well-bred manner in which he got rid of the pits: fist to mouth, as if covering a cough, quickly, silently, without even a sign of spitting. Then he reached for a piece of celery. What was he doing? Pretending he was having lunch by himself, pretending she wasn't there! So what was she supposed to do? Get up? Go back to the office and grab the sweater off the back of her chair, pack up her teacup and saucer and leave? Oh God—

"Five," he said, putting down the celery.

"What?"

"Five percent."

Slowly, she helped herself to a slice of the cheese and took a tiny bite. Hey, it was good! "Ten."

He watched her until she finished the cheese, then he said, "Seven."

"What do you always say on the phone? 'Let's split it down the middle.' "

"All right. Seven and a half."

The business side of their partnership thus concluded, they left La Stella without even ordering an entrée.

Even though Barbara was only twelve years old when her mother's secret affair with Clyde Johnson got under way, it was no secret to her. Not that Barbara understood the amour part. It was the beginning of the Eisenhower Era. Communists were hiding under beds, and a flash of atomic light could at any moment signal the end of humanity. No matter: All girls of Barbara's age were innocent; they basked in the cheery sunshine of compulsory naïveté. Annihilation? Don't be a party pooper.

Sex? Nice girls didn't talk about it. Passion was a closed-mouth kiss on a movie screen. Doing It—where the man's thing goes inside—was only for married couples. Of course, there were tramps who maybe did do It, but they wore hoop earrings. Whatever her mother was doing, she wore pearl button earrings and was a war widow. Her husband, the man in the picture on her dresser, in a sergeant's uniform for eternity, was dead. She didn't go out with men. She explained to Barbara her lack of interest in meeting a potential father for Barbara and the twins by saying, I had one true love in my life. I'm a one-man woman.

Still, Eisenhower Era or no, Barbara was no fool. When a mother comes home from work at eight at night with her girdle and stockings stuffed into her handbag—a telltale garter sticking out near the clasp giving her away—and says I'm too pooped to pop and goes right to bed, a twelve-year-old knows something is up. When a mother comes home at nine at night smelling more of cigarettes and some kind of whiskey than of the Chanel No. 5 Mr. Johnson gave her for Christmas, which she splashed on every morning, and says, Honey, my stomach's not right and I haven't been able to eat all day but thanks a million for keeping the stew hot for me, a twelve-year-old knows there is more to the pre–Fourth of July busy season at Johnson Flag and Banner, Incorporated, than stars and stripes. When Mr. Johnson calls on a weekend and whispers, Hello, Barbara, may I speak to your mother for a moment? and a mother takes the call on the new extension phone in her bedroom and giggles and whispers for the next hour, a twelve-year-old knows something funny is running up the flagpole.

And when a mother leaves you in charge of the house and your two brothers—because your grandmother is getting so forgetful she goes out to the grocery store and winds up being escorted home by the policeman who found her wandering in Riverside Park—then a twelve-year-old knows her mother must be working on something very big.

So big that by 1955, Sally Ann would call home at least once a week and say, Barbara baby, I'm so sorry, but we're overwhelmed here and by the time I get home it'll be after midnight, so I'll just sleep over at Fay the book-keeper's house, unless you think you can't manage. But of course she could. Barbara was a responsible girl.

In 1958, Barbara Jane Freund was probably the most responsible girl in her freshman class at Barnard College. She steadied herself against the kitchen counter and rubbed her left penny loafer over the top of her right one.

"What are you doing?" Sally Ann inquired.

"Scuffing them. They're supposed to be scuffed." Her

mother smiled, amused at the fashion, not in the least censorious, the way a mother ought to be. "I promise you," Barbara said, "I won't ask for a new pair."

"I told you," Sally Ann said too patiently, exhaling a slender, patient stream of smoke, "don't worry so much about money." Her mother could take any simple declarative sentence and turn it into an insult. "Trust me. I'm good for an extra pair of loafers."

"Mom, I didn't mean—"

"I've been putting away money every single week for you and the boys ever since I've been at Johnson."

By this time, of course, Barbara knew, without ever having heard a word, that her mother and Clyde Johnson were lovers. It was unfortunate that the word could not be uttered, because, as her only knowledge of lovers came from *Anna Karenina* and gangster films, she had no clear picture of what her mother's life was like. She realized Sally Ann was not Mr. Johnson's floozy, tippy-toeing around in a froth of pink marabou, sipping champagne. She had visited the office and watched her mother sitting across the partners desk, facing Mr. Johnson, strategizing how best to pull the rug out from under Fiedler's Fine Flags by grabbing the Friendly Sons of St. Patrick account.

"Oh, before I forget," Sally Ann said, "I have the Flag Manufacturers Association convention coming up."

"Where is the convention this year?" Barbara asked.

"Palm Springs."

"That's California?" Her mother nodded. "You're going?"

Barbara's shoe scuffing, like the rest of her be-one-of-the-girls endeavors, was not going well. Her loafers still looked new, deliberately, pathetically scuffed. She knew

she would never get her appearance exactly right. Neat?
Yes. Clean? To be sure. But Barbara understood that she
had been born the sort of female saleswomen in better
stores know to ignore. Not only did she lack fashion
savvy, she looked sincere. Also, there was always slightly
too much or too little distance between her knee socks
and her pleated skirt, as if she'd deliberately tried to be
stylish but failed. Her ponytail either lay so low she
looked like a beatnik or was raised so high she might as
well have been a full-grown mare.

"Mr. Johnson needs me at the convention. Goodwill
ambassadress and all that."

But saleswomen trilled, May I help you? to Sally Ann.
Her mother didn't dress like a mother. Not like a secretary. Certainly not like a mistress either, Barbara had to
admit. No ostentatious jewelry. No mink stoles. Still, she
always looked just right. Right but rushed, forever on her
way to meet her lover, coming to breakfast fully dressed,
ready to escape the house the instant she finished her second cup of coffee. Sally Ann had stopped wearing skirts
and blouses—secretary clothes—a few years earlier. Now
she wore dresses. Fine dresses—gray wools in winter,
beige linens in summer. She didn't wear jeweled scatter
pins, such as the Barnard alumnae who had interviewed
Barbara had worn, no monkeys or frogs with sapphire
eyes leaping from chest to shoulder. Sally Ann wore
pearls. Beautiful globes of purest white that still con-
tained every color in the world; strands and strands of
them. They were big enough that the rich women who
knew real from good fakes stared at them respectfully on
the street.

Each morning at breakfast, her mother appeared fully
made up, her face so flawless it looked like a pearl itself.

She tucked a dish towel into her collar to protect the front of the dress and her pearls, then smoothed three layers of paper napkins over her skirt. The instant her coffee was gone, she would rush down the hall into her bathroom on her shiny leather pumps, gargle with Listerine, put on her Ruby Royale lipstick and, blowing kisses and calling Bye!, race out the door.

"I hope you don't mind my going to Palm Springs. It is business." Her mother looked the way she always looked when they spoke, somewhere between bored and insulted. She closed her eyes for a second. Her lashes, triple coated with mascara, made furry shadows on her pale cheeks. "It's not that I want to go."

"I know." Barbara had gone to the library and checked. In all the United States, there was no Flag Manufacturers Association.

"I work six days a week, nights sometimes, I never take a day off, never take a vacation."

"Fine," Barbara said, raising her voice. "Go. I didn't say—"

"You implied," Sally Ann shot back, even louder.

"No. You inferred, Mom." Her mother seemed to be tuning her out. She was examining her grapefruit for pits. Then she lit a cigarette and became preoccupied with watching the ash grow each time she inhaled, gazing, cross-eyed, down at the Parliament stuck in the center of her lips. Or maybe she simply didn't want to argue. Once they uttered a word, all they could express to each other was irritation. "It's just . . . I'm at Barnard now. I don't mind living home until the twins go off to college. God knows, it's close enough. But I need to be able to stay late at the library. And—don't hold your breath or anything—but what happens if a boy did ask me out? I need you here a little more. What if it's ten at night and Danny's reading or talking on the phone, or Davey's watching TV, and Grandma decides to take a walk over to Broadway in her nightgown again?"

"May I point out," Sally Ann said to the coffeepot as she poured her second cup, "that the last time she walked nearly a mile down Broadway around eleven at night when it was raining, you were right here, on the phone with one of your friends. Not even studying."

"I know. I apologized. I put her to bed and turned out the light—"

"Barbara, I'm not asking for apologies or excuses. I'm just pointing out that you don't *have* to be here every second and neither do I. As long as the boys have a sense of, you know, an adult presence. Not that they're not good boys. But they're boys. You were the one who offered. Believe me, if you wanted to live a full college life, you know I was all for it."

"But Grandma—"

"As far as Grandma goes, I've offered to make other arrangements." Sally Ann became distracted, shaking her teaspoon left and right with incredible patience and tenderness to get a perfect, level measure of sugar.

If Barbara had had a best friend, she might have said, My mother keeps looking for an excuse to stick my grandmother into a nursing home. File her away under Senile. And the friend would have said, Well, Barb, if your grandmother is peeing when you're standing in line with her at the bakery, or telling dirty jokes in Yiddish very loud in the elevator, it might not be the worst idea in the world.

Except her best friend had gone off to Goucher. And Barbara really wasn't making any new friends. Had she confided that to a Barnard classmate—or written to Moira at Goucher—they would have said, You won't meet anyone, you won't have anyone to talk to because *you're not living a regular college life*. I mean, Moira would have written back, who's going to form an I-Thou relationship in Intro to Zoology lab?

But how could she move out of the apartment and abandon her grandmother? How could she leave her brothers when they'd be applying to college next year and going off the next? Oh sure, her mother would come home most nights. She'd skim their applications, maybe even say, Hey, Davey, you need a comma between adjectives when each of them modifies the noun alone. But she wouldn't read their essays over and over, each time putting herself in the mind of a different college admissions officer. She wouldn't have time to take them down to Brooks Brothers—now that they had a little money—to buy blazers for their interviews. She certainly wouldn't need to cherish every possible second of their adolescent blabbiness before they left home forever to become men.

What if eventually she did move into the dorm? What was there for her at Barnard, besides her classes? The Columbia boys she met at the West End Café or a Friday-night fraternity party? They were invariably nice to her. Without exception, they felt comfortable with her, laughing, chatting about courses, pouring out their hearts about the girls who wouldn't have them.

She wasn't like any of those desirable girls. She watched them. She listened to them. The carefree ones at the sundial who wore circle pins and tam-o'-shanters and had sixty-four teeth and boyfriends with blond hair so straight it flopped when they walked. The sophisticated ones who sipped black coffee at Jake, who wore black tights and had boyfriends in black turtlenecks whose tragic, handsome faces were ravaged with pockmarks. Even the intellectually ferocious ones, who truly did not seem to care about makeup and clothes, or about deodorant, were having liaisons. With faculty members. Those were the students she envied most, but not for their liaisons, because most of those associate professors looked like tweed-covered toads. No, those girls were the ones who had read it all and knew it all, who on the first day of class would bring up *Poor Folk* and the role of the social novel in subversion of the existing order, while the class was trying to discuss *Crime and Punishment.* And the professors would never say, Shut your mouth, we're talking about Raskolnikov today. They'd never shake their heads, a fast, dismissive shake, as they did when Barbara ventured an opinion. They'd say, How perspicacious, Miss Frothingdale.

And so she stayed at home. Her brother Danny went to Wesleyan, and Davey went to Brown. Three years later, her Grandma Ruthie entered the Hebrew Home for the Aged, where, a month before Barbara's graduation, in 1962, she died of what would now be diagnosed as vascular dementia.

Well, Barbara told herself as she stood in line with all the other girls in their caps and gowns, I've done it. But there was no elation inside, no hint of an exclamation point. She certainly felt no desire to throw her cap in the air, or even to twirl her tassel around her index finger. She would be a teacher. That was all she'd ever wanted to be. She was graduating with a three point two average and a bachelor of arts degree in history. And she was letting her mother down.

She knew Sally Ann was in the audience, in a folding

chair, probably relieved that for a few minutes she did not have to hide her disappointment that her expensively educated daughter could not find a better place for herself. She had no man. She was not going on to graduate school. No awards. No honors. No coterie of witty friends. When you asked Barbara, What's new? the answer was invariably, Nothing much. Barbara could see the twins beside Sally Ann—tall, dark and handsome, the way American men were supposed to be. They were already pinned to girls with blond flips, and no doubt, right this second, they were twin-talking to each other, puzzling why poor Barbara—who objectively was not bad-looking at all—had not found at least a boyfriend, if not a genuine fiancé.

Buck up! she admonished herself. Be proud! You're going to be a teacher of American history! The world is your oyster! All right, so not the world. Maybe you are a little provincial. Still, you'll be doing what you want to do, standing before a class, making the Missouri Compromise *mean* something! But teaching at Far Rockaway High School in Queens? Please. Wasn't teaching viewed by modern women the way petit point had been by colonial dames, a genteel filler of time, something to do while waiting for a marriage proposal?

She looked up and down the line at her graduating class. Sure, there were a couple of girls going to medical school and law school; someone in her medieval history class had been accepted at Cambridge. But what did she, what did the rest of them, truly want? To get married. Those two about-to-be-alumnae in front of her, girls with manicures and engagement rings, were chatting about sterling-silver patterns. One was saying Grande Baroque was hardly grand and the other laughed: *Mon dieu,* wouldn't Louis Quatorze think "Baroque" amusing? Four years of higher education, to become Grand Acquisitors. But Barbara had gone on only three dates in four years of college. There seemed to be no five-piece place settings in her future.

As she stood on the verge of adulthood, Barbara Freund felt very much the way her great-grandmother Dora had when she stood at the rail of the SS *Polonia* sixty-three years earlier. Not nauseous. But scared. Uh-oh, the line was beginning to move. Her education was over, her real life was supposed to be beginning, but there was one thing she still didn't know. From sea to shining sea, where was there a place for someone like her?

# 6

Chuck Blair didn't feel like a big shot. Three years earlier, they'd come to him and asked him to run for the Wyoming State House of Representatives. They'd made it sound like the world's biggest deal because they weren't asking him to spend ten years in county office first. We need young men like you in Cheyenne, Chuck. He knew what they needed—his two names, Bryant and Blair, old valley names to put up against a newcomer, a Democrat who was looking surprisingly popular. They needed his old man's check too, that's what they needed. It was probably Willie's idea, Chuck had thought, to ease him out of the Circle B slowly. So Chuck said, No way. To be stuck in Cheyenne during ski season? To be on a committee studying tertiary treatment of wastewater? But then his mother said, Do it, Chuck. Shine in your own light. It will do you good. And do your father good too, seeing you like that. So it had been his mother's doing, his mother's money. Judy was for it too. Give you something to call your own until the Circle B comes to you, hon. So he said okay.

Chuck knew the Circle B was most likely coming to him someday. But it wasn't until Willie's surprise fiftieth-birthday party that he understood how far off someday was. Shhh! everyone began hissing when they heard his father's truck pull up. The ass-kissing constituents' calls of Chuck-Chuck-Chuck-Chuck ceased. *Shhhh!* Willie

Blair strolled through the door into the mud room off the kitchen that Thursday night, and as he was kicking off his boots and calling "Lo?" Lois flipped on the light. Fifty people crammed into the kitchen roared Surprise!

For a moment, his father's tan leather skin turned ashen. He stood so still that Chuck thought: This is it. He's going to keel over, crack his head on the coat pegs on the way down. Everyone seemed to sense it. The rowdy neighborliness of the room turned to stiff silence. All eyes were on Willie. Chuck gulped his bourbon. The ice clinked so loud against the glass he was sure everyone could hear it.

But then his father's face broke into the broadest smile Chuck had ever seen on him. Putting his arm around Lois, drawing her as close as he could, Willie griped to the crowd, "And all these years I trusted this woman!" As everybody started hooting and clapping, he added, "I should have known something was up when I smelt her Swedish meatballs."

"You think something's up?" Lois laughed.

"My age sure is. Well, I've been begging her to make those meatballs again for only, oh, ten, fifteen years." Friends and neighbors moved in on the couple, the men to shake Willie's hand or offer hearty backslaps and arm punches, the women to stand on tiptoes to kiss his cheek. Lois eased out of her husband's embrace and hurried over to the dishwasher, where Chuck was stuck listening to Dave Prouty blab on and on about diesel fuel prices; for his shitty fifty-buck campaign contribution, Prouty thought he'd bought you for your whole term. Chuck didn't realize his mother had come up beside him until she slipped her arm into his. "Go over and say something nice to your father."

"Soon as the crowd thins."

Almost as he spoke, the guests fanned out into the parlor and the dining room. Swedish meatballs were followed by olive-cheese toasts and pigs-in-blankets. Not once did his father glance his way. Platters of roast beef sandwiches were set out and a great bowl of what folks kept saying was the finest German potato salad in Jackson Hole. Chuck stood beside Doc Montgomery—Listen, Chuck boy, you got any idea what the damn Public Health expects me to do?—waiting for his father to stop flirting with Becky Gillers from the County Assessor's office and pay him some mind. Here he was, waiting in line for his old man's attention, not like the state legislator he was but like some ranch hand wanting a favor from the big boss.

The line was too long. Before he could get to his father, his mother carried in Willie's favorite, her carrot cake with cream cheese frosting. He watched his old man as he sauntered over to the cake. Did he say, Hey, Chuck, are you too much of a big-shot politician to keep me company while I blow out the candles? Of course not. But Willie did manage to grab Mary Jane over and kiss the top of her head. He didn't even bother to scan the room for his son—who was less than six feet away.

Yet to see his father was to marvel. Look at him: so goddamn robust he didn't need to take a deep breath to blow out the fifty-one candles. Whatever air happened to be in his lungs was force enough. In a room bursting with vigorous men, Willie was the most vigorous. Chuck knew Willie still ate like a horse—steak and fries once a day, cakes, pies, twice. Plus, when he got home every night, knocking back a couple of whiskeys the size of which would have stupefied any other man. It wasn't only that

Willie never gained an ounce. He also got handsomer with age. More appealing to women too. Like some older-guy movie star, he shone brighter than all other men. Technicolor Willie: bronze skin, black hair shot with a touch of silver precisely where it ought to be, at the temples, eyes the boldest blue. Sure, his father was a little dried out from being outdoors his whole life, but that did not diminish him at all. Like a piece of jerky, thought Chuck, his old man would last forever.

And here am I, Chuck said to himself. Charles Bryant Blair. A grown man with a wife and two kids. I've got my own secretary in Cheyenne, American and Wyoming flags behind my desk, my picture with Spiro Agnew up on the wall. And what do I have to show for it? I have to live in a house I don't own. Oh, my parents built it for me, all right. Made such a big production, having me and Judy sit down with that contractor to say how many bathrooms we needed and did we want a wall oven. But the title stayed in my mother's name, and there was no way she'd sign it over without my father giving her the okay. Fat chance of his seeing that kind of generosity on Willie's part, since Chuck knew nothing he did was ever right in his father's eyes.

What the hell kind of life was this? When he wasn't rushing off to Cheyenne or driving around Jackson Hole kissing asses, he was working on a ranch that should have been his. Working like a dog for his old man, who, come to think of it, treated his mangy mutt better than he treated his own son. Good going, Cloud, or Attaboy, Cloud, Willie was always saying, with a big grin. Hey, Cloud, you my best boy? Never Good anything, Chuck.

What did he get from his father? A limp handshake on election night! The handshake and that pissed-off, curling-inward thing the side of Willie's mouth did. Or if Willie did say anything, it would be: What the hell did you hire that backhoe for, Chuck? Which meant, You jerk. But wait just a minute. Talking about mutts, who the fuck did his old man think *he* was, the son of a big ugly squaw and that pipsqueak Jew. Not that Chuck hadn't been respectful to his grandparents when they'd come for visits, but he sure was relieved they were both dead and gone by the time he'd run for the House.

The worst of it was, Chuck had no one to talk to. What was a wife for? But he couldn't complain too much to Judy about his old man's fault-finding, nit-picking ways. He had to keep most of it bottled up, because he knew she would have run the Circle B exactly the way his old man and his mother did. Judy's idea of a big night was going over to his parents' for dinner—even though she knew he hated sitting at his father's table—and gabbing about frozen bull semen.

True, Judy acted like Mrs. America, bucking him up all the time—Chuck, honey, if that's how you feel, go back to your father and tell him if he gave you responsibility for that fence, then he shouldn't come crying about how the rails aren't set right after you finished it, because you have legislature matters you've got to take care of. Bucking him up, but he had to wonder: Once the ranch was his, would Judy consider it not his, but theirs? Or even hers? Would she look down her Bob Hope nose at him the same exact way his old man did?

His worst fear was that his mother would die first and bequeath the ranch to his father, and the old man would screw him every which way to Sunday. Leave it lock, stock and barrel to Mary Jane. Or have his executors sell it and give the proceeds to the Methodists. It wasn't fair. He,

Chuck, owned the Circle B name: *Charles Bryant* Blair. He wished he had the guts to ask his mother about what was in their wills. Judy told him, I'm sure it's coming to you, but you've got a right to ask, what with you giving half your life over to them. If he could be positive he was coming into money, he wouldn't be beholden to every loser who wanted a favor in Cheyenne. But he just couldn't bring himself to ask, because to ask was to kiss ass.

His worst, worst fear? Getting fucked by his own son. That his parents would skip over him and leave the place to Charlie. Seven years old Charlie was, and already asking his grandpa how much alfalfa acreage for hay, already racing across the road to his grandma's when the school bus dropped him, instead of coming home. Judy said, It's okay; he does little chores for your mom and keeps her company, and it gives me time to take Kaylea skiing. Chuck hated to admit it, but there was something about his own son, his own namesake—Charles Bryant Blair, Jr.—that gave Chuck the creeps. His own flesh and blood! He honest to God wished he didn't feel that way.

But Charlie was too much to himself. Weird quiet. You never had a clue what he was thinking. Whenever Charlie did something bad and Chuck would wallop him, the boy wouldn't make a sound. Unnatural. When he was little he'd go running to his mother. Okay, not crying. Not saying a word. Just leaning against her, unwilling to get out of physical touch, like she was Home in a game of tag. Now, of course, he didn't run to her. He was too big. He just took whatever Chuck was dishing out, then—not even giving a dirty look—walked off like nothing had happened.

No doubt about it, his son was one cold fish. Kaylea, four years old, was much easier to take. Like Judy, a big smile all the time. But like him as well, cut out to be a fine athlete. Not like Charlie. Come winter, all Charlie wanted to do was toss a football with his friends. He had the makings of a champion except the one thing it took—competitive spirit. When he strapped on a pair of skis, all he'd do was whoosh down a trail a couple of times. To Charlie, skiing wasn't about winning, or even getting good. It was just a means to an end—hot chocolate with whipped cream. Little Kaylea, on the other hand, had the killer instinct of a serious skier. She was probably not as good as he, Chuck, had been at her age, but right off the bat, from the time she was three, she was crazy about skiing. Just as the boy and Judy were crazy about the Circle B.

I'm the only one of all the Blairs, Chuck thought, slipping into the kitchen to avoid cockeyed Rocky Plunkett of Plunkett Lumber, who's not crazy for something. Well, crazy about one thing. He closed his eyes so a picture would come. Lu Anne. Jesus, what a girl! Not just beautiful. Like a ballet dancer, with her incredible long legs and swan neck, except with tits, big ones. She had character too. Being so understanding while he tried to figure a way out of his mess—out of the marriage, out from under his old man's thumb—it almost broke his heart. He wished to hell he could set her up somewhere so she could quit working in Reservations over at Jenny Lake Lodge, but Judy kept the checkbook and knew every damn nickel that came in and went out. The few bucks that folks who needed favors slipped him now and then—a hundred here, a couple of hundred there—were only enough to buy Lu Anne little presents: a gold heart on a chain instead of the diamond heart he knew she was dying for.

People who thought politicians were cleaning up had another thing coming. Most of it was penny-ante stuff—a fancy dinner, ten percent off on an Oldsmobile. Who the hell wanted an Oldsmobile? Maybe a member of the United States House of Representatives could rake in thousands, get Remington sculptures or Hawaii vacations, but not Wyoming State Representative Chuck Blair.

After Lu Anne there was Sharon, and after Sharon, Kelly, and after Kelly, Patti. Kathie came and went, then Ginger. For a time, after Ginger, there was only Judy, his wife. That period of fidelity occurred during the bitter winter of '79, when, day after day, temperatures climbed to a high of only twenty below, when the wind shrieked like a tortured animal, when his parents died.

Willie and Lois Blair died together, swerving to avoid a head-on collision with a Jeep Wagoneer driven by a Swiss chef recently hired by the owners of the new Rising Moon Lodge. Their truck hit a patch of ice on a mountain road and plunged nearly a thousand feet into a crevasse just large enough to hide a Chevy pickup for five days.

"I'd be pleased to handle the funeral arrangements," his father's creep of a lawyer, Tom Kunkel, was telling him. Chuck heard, but the words didn't sink in deep enough to generate an answer. "I could speak to the folks over at Hudson's, tell 'em you want something simple." The lawyer's eyeglasses were so thick you couldn't even see what color his eyes were. Old and ugly. And the guy was a Democrat, which showed what kind of a loser he must be. "Now, here I go, assuming you do want something not so . . . should we say elaborate? What is it they say, Chuck? When you assume, you make an ass out of you and me." They faced each other across the desk in Willie's office, Chuck in his father's chair, white-haired Kunkel opposite, in the straight-back without arms all Willie's underlings always sat in—the foreman, the men trying to sell insulation or insurance.

But now Mr. Bleeding Heart Liberal, Esquire, himself—who had never given Wyoming State Representative Chuck Blair the time of day—was sitting in it and sucking up so hard it was almost embarrassing.

Because now Chuck was the man in the big chair. Well, he did deserve some sucking up. He was getting smarter. Like doing the proper mourning thing, which, after all, he was feeling. Truly. Sure, he'd thought a lot about what would happen to the ranch after his parents were gone, prayed it would come to him so his life would be easier, but he'd never, *ever*, wished them dead. And already he was genuinely missing his mother. The sheriff had told them death must have been instantaneous, which helped a little. But now, with the lawyer here, Chuck was acting sad, but shrewd too. Not kissing Kunkel's ass to get a preview of what was in the will. Not just acting smart, but *being* smart, because he understood that since the lawyer was brown-nosing him, it meant the Circle B was definitely, completely, totally, his! "I guess you must be in a state of shock, Chuck."

"I guess. Though I had this awful feeling when they didn't show up by the next morning that something real bad—"

The door opened and there was Charlie, his son, staring at him. Big for a boy not yet fourteen, unnaturally tall, over six feet. Without words, Charlie was challenging him: Who the heck are you to be sitting in Grandpa's chair? I'll tell you who I am, Chuck thought, you little overgrown shit-head. I'm the owner of this whole fucking place now. "What is it, son?"

"Mom wants to know what you want for lunch."

"It's not even eleven o'clock."

"Should I come back later?" Standing there, face showing nothing, like the village idiot. Okay, Charlie was smart enough, but the truth was, he wasn't the son Chuck had expected, not the son he'd wanted to share his name. He'd had a dream of what his boy would be like, even before he was born. A friendly, happy kid, real outgoing. Looking sort of like him but with Judy's coloring, so he'd be an all-American blond-haired, blue-eyed boy. Not that either of them actually looked Indian or anything, but when you touched it, the black hair they both had was a little too heavy to be a white man's hair. "Dad?"

Chuck realized he must have been waiting too long to answer because Bleeding Heart Kunkel suddenly made a disgusting phlegmy sound and gurgled: "Why, you must be Chuck junior."

"Yes, sir. I'm Charlie."

"Good to meet you—"

"Son," Chuck said, giving the boy his Christmas card picture smile he was glad the lawyer was noting with an approving smile of his own, "tell Mom I'll take whatever she gives me."

"Okay," Charlie said, and closed the door.

Almost daily, but especially these last few nightmare days, Charlie felt at a loss to understand his father. Oh, his words were simple, clear enough. Chuck wasn't a fancy talker. Yet Charlie sensed that what Chuck was saying had a meaning just the slightest bit different from everybody else's English, so he never felt he was grasping what his father truly meant. It was almost like those creatures in the *Space Devils* comics, the Astrofiends, who looked and talked exactly like humans and could even have babies with them. Not that his father was an Astrofiend, a breeder of maggots that fed on energy instead of mass and when let loose would consume star after star, devouring an entire galaxy in a single year. Of course he knew it was just a story, though some nights he'd be up till one or two, sick with fear about it, afraid one was breathing silently in the darkness at the top of the staircase. He was much too old for that sort of thing. It shamed him.

Charlie's mother was waiting in the kitchen. She'd hauled out enough pots and pans from his grandma's cupboard to make Christmas dinner, even though all morning long folks had been driving up to the house, carrying in casseroles, plates of Saran-wrapped, already sliced cake, baskets of fruit, boxes of candy. Not that his mother wasn't a good mother, because she was, but he prayed she wasn't planning on overlooking all those rich-smelling, neighbor-made casseroles and whipping up something herself, because unlike his grandma, his mother was one lousy cook, except for her lime Jell-O–sour cream mold with fruit cocktail.

His Grandma Lois. Charlie leaned against the wall. At least he comprehended the weight of the word "heartache," which was in every other song on the country radio station he listened to. Charlie's heart was aching all right, a physical pain in his chest, swollen to twice its normal size from the tears he hadn't been able to cry since he heard his grandparents were missing. Whenever his grandma was baking—in the exact spot where his mother was standing now—she'd pull off a piece of cookie dough and say, Here, Charlie, test this for me. Like it wasn't a treat. Like it was a favor he was doing her, tasting that buttery, vanilla-y stuff. Sweet enough, Charlie?

"Charlie?" Pots and pans were stacked haphazardly on the stovetop, without regard to size and balance, looking as if they would crash to the floor at any moment. His mother turned to him. She looked frantic. Wisps of blond hair that had escaped from her ponytail stuck out from her head in hysterical squiggles. Her eyes were lost in dark circles that got bluer with each hour. "What did your dad say?"

"What? Oh, he said he'll have whatever you want to make." She reached for a big skillet resting on top of a double boiler. The tower of pots clattered, and as Judy jumped back, startled, Charlie raced over, preventing the pile from crashing by capturing it with his body and arms. "I think someone brought over a plate of sandwiches with stuff like tuna fish and egg salad," he said, his chin on the skillet. "That's what he'd like, Mom."

"You think so?"

"I know so," he replied, still hugging the pots. He hated lying to his mother. For all he knew, his father would take one look at those triangles of sandwiches and say, Doesn't anyone here know I hate egg salad worse than anything? How would he know what his father wanted? The man was a total mystery. Either he was off in Cheyenne or, night after night, coming home long after they were all in bed. Days, he was either at meetings in town or else on some other part of the ranch from wherever Charlie and his grandpa . . .

Shit, now the tears were clogging up the corners of his eyes. He kept himself thrust against the pile of pots so he wouldn't have to turn and face his mother. But she knew about those uncried tears, in that smug way mothers have, where you can almost hear them on the phone, telling their friends, It was the sweetest thing, Charlie trying to hold back . . .

"Oh, Charlie, I'm so sorry." He stayed where he was, because if he set the pots down and turned around, she would hug him. There came a point where a guy got too old for direct contact. All a hug did was make him want to pull away, and he knew that would hurt her feelings. "I know how much you miss them," she was saying.

"Well, I guess I do," he managed to say.

"It's okay to cry, honey." Charlie swore she must sit in front of the TV with a pad and write down every June Cleaver line.

"I know."

His Grandpa Willie. Just the Saturday before, he and Charlie had begun something they'd been planning for months: training Charlie's new dog, Jingles, as an avalanche dog for search and rescue. That first day, they'd dug a pretty deep trench in the snow. Then Grandpa told him: Hold on till I get Jingles out of sight, then hunker way down in the trench, so's the dog can't see you. Time after time, Grandpa would lead Jingles away in some direction or other before setting him off to find Charlie. That's what Charlie couldn't get out of his mind: the sight of his grandfather and his beautiful, dark-red mostly Irish setter romping through the thigh-high snow, like some big kid and his goofy puppy.

Later that day, instead of going home, he'd gone on with his grandfather to the big house and changed into a pair of his grandpa's jeans. Would you look at that! Willie had exclaimed to Charlie. You're bigger than me. If you sneeze, those jeans'll bust! A little short on you too, you

big lug. All afternoon, he'd hung out in the kitchen,
while his grandmother made oatmeal-raisin bread and his
grandpa told him about being at the battle of Midway in
World War II, how that battle had changed the course of
the whole war in the Pacific. Listen, Charlie boy, being in
a foxhole in the sand, knowing you're right in some Jap's
bombsight, if that don't make you . . . can I say piss in
your pants in front of the boy, Lois?

Monday, as soon as the machine they had at the ceme-
tery thawed out the ground and they got the graves dug,
his grandparents would be buried side by side, the way
they died. Last night, Charlie had prayed to God that
what the sheriff told his parents was the honest truth, that
they'd been killed by being thrown forward, smashing
into the dashboard and the windshield, as the truck hurtled down the mountain. Died before impact. But his
prayers hadn't eased his horror. Charlie couldn't sleep. It
was eating him up inside: Would sheriffs do that? Lie?
Take the pain of awful-but-true stories upon themselves,
where it didn't hurt so much, and make up gentler things
to tell the families? He'd heard the crunch of the tires in
the snow, looked out the window and seen the sheriff's car
drive up that night. By the time he'd come down, the
sheriff was inside and telling his parents: The doc told me
they were already gone, Judy. Chuck, believe me, they
didn't feel a thing, hardly knew what hit 'em.

"Charlie."

"What, Mom?"

"What are you thinking?"

"About Grandma and Grandpa." But had either one of
them survived the impact? Oh God. Thinking that gave
him the sickest feeling, nauseous and wildly hungry at
the same time. He couldn't get it out of his mind. Had

either lived to realize the other was dead? Lived to suffer the agony of crushed limbs, of knowing they would never get out of that icy crack in the mountain? Lived in terrible pain, to slowly freeze to death?

"Tell me what you're thinking about, Charlie."

"Just how the three of us were sitting right here last Saturday, after Grandpa and I were out training Jingles."

He was still facing the pots, but his mother came, put her arms around him anyway. Her head didn't even come up to his shoulder anymore, and he felt like a huge fool. "I know you wanted to go out looking for them the other day, with Jingles."

"I'm as strong as almost anybody in that search party, Mom. Come on! You know how I can climb!"

"It wasn't we were afraid you weren't up to it, Charlie. It was we were so shaken up." His mother sure had been shaken up, practically screaming, Where are they? That was after the sheriff came back to say they couldn't find them but knew they had to be somewhere on the mountain, because the driver of the Jeep had come forward, and besides, they could see the actual tracks where the Chevy's tires had left the road. His father had just stood there, his mouth hanging open—looking totally out of it. It was only because his mother was carrying on so loudly that Kaylea came down from her room then and started bawling without even knowing what was going on, while he, Charlie, told the sheriff, I've been giving my dog avalanche training and we could assist the search party, and the sheriff said, Thanks, Charlie, but no close relatives allowed—which Charlie knew was a load of bull—and his mother got even more hysterical, starting to shriek, You're staying right here, Charlie Blair! You're not setting one foot out that door! It was then that Chuck finally had the brains to say, Jeez, I'm worried sick, and shake his head so the sheriff wouldn't think he was . . . what Charlie knew his father really was. A family man who didn't give a good goddamn about his family.

By the time Charlie left home to major in Animal Sciences at the University of Wyoming in Laramie, his father no longer even pretended to be a family man. The house where Charlie's grandparents had lived so peaceably resounded not with his parents' fights but with the igniting roar from the engine of his father's newest car or truck, which would drown out his mother's inevitable half supplication, half pep-rally plea: Come on, Chuck, let's talk about—

About how best to ration water in the years of drought. About how to stop getting ripped off on feed bills. About the cost of Chuck's new Corvette. About the kids' birthday dinners, which Chuck never managed to show up for. About the letter Judy opened from the Internal Revenue Service: Our records indicate you have not filed your 1981 return. About driving off at eleven in the morning on Christmas Day, just to drop off a bottle at Hank Riggs's place, five miles down the road, and not getting back until two A.M. on the twenty-sixth, while the Riggses— Judy had meanwhile learned—were over at Shirley's mother's, in Grand Junction, Colorado. About items on the MasterCard bill: the Road-E-O Motel in Cheyenne; Caribou Jewelers in Dubois; the Ski Biscuit Inn in Teton Village.

Charlie, across Wyoming in college, did not even have to try not to dwell on his parents' troubles. By his senior year in college, he had taught himself that their disputes were endemic, like scours were to cattle. "No, they're not going to get a divorce," he was explaining to his sister.

Kaylea, in her first year at the University of Colorado, had developed a great sense of drama. Each individual sentence was pronounced as if it might be nominated for an Oscar. "But if Dad is you-know-whating his brains out and doesn't even try to hide it, how can Mom live with it?" When Charlie didn't answer fast enough, she threw in, "Doesn't Mom have any pride, for God's sake?"

"Sure she does, but it doesn't come out in telling him to go to hell and getting herself a lawyer." Christ, he had to study for his Advanced Beef Production and Management final. He was so close to an A. But his sister had phoned, the first time all semester, announcing, I smell trouble, Charlie! Behind her exclamation points, he could hear fear. "Look, Kaylea, her pride comes out in the way she keeps going. If she left, what would happen? They'd have to sell the ranch and divvy up the proceeds. Which would mean she'd wind up losing the only thing she really cares about—other than me and you. And she knows it's going to be my life too. Yours too, if you'd wanted it."

"What if Dad wants out?"

"What?" He was distracted by the black panties under the desk chair. His girlfriend's souvenir. An oversight, preoccupied as Lindy was with finals? An excuse to knock on the door later that night?

"What if Dad wants out?"

"He can't afford to leave," Charlie explained. "Anyway, it's a family thing. She runs the ranch and he knows it. I mean, he makes a show of playing cowboy, but you know he's too lazy to do much, plus whenever he does anything, he screws up. And he needs the bucks."

"What about being in the state house?"

"Kaylea, they earn small. He spends large." He put his hand over his *Analysis and Decision Making in Beef Production*. He had to go. "How's studying going?" he asked.

"Oh, Charlie, I'm sorry to bother you now. It's just that Mom's voice . . . I heard something in it. Like she senses something bad is going to happen."

"Well, with him it's never good news. But relax. You've got finals."

If she didn't let him off the phone, he could end up with a C for a final grade. If he'd simply gone to the library and studied, he could have pulled at least a B plus. Now Kaylea was going on and on, and then Lindy would be knocking and calling "Chaarlie." He slid over to the edge of the bed and, with his feet, searched for his socks and boots. "I've got to get to the library. Can I call you tomorrow?"

"You think I'm melodramatic, Charlie."

Of course he did. "No. I just think Mom's having a rough time. He being . . . well, what he always was and both of us being gone. Empty nest."

He knew his sister well enough to read her silences. This one meant: Okay, I'll let myself be persuaded. "Okay. Well, good luck with your finals."

"Thanks. You too."

"Oh, Charlie, how's the girlfriend? I forget this one's name."

"Lindy. She's fine."

A lousy night, but he had to study, and the panties on the floor told him Lindy was coming back. As he trudged to the library, gusts of wind whipped powdery snow into thick spiral nebulae that kept trying to engulf him before swirling onward, seeking another victim. The flesh of his face, toasted from the heat in his dorm room, from his own flashes of desire for Lindy and annoyance at his sister's theatrics, felt scalded by the cold. The skin seemed to shrivel against his bones.

Charlie rewrapped his scarf, a gift an ex-girlfriend had knitted, trying to get it to stay up around his cheeks. He felt like the shrunken head—a hideous brown rubber thing—yet another girl had given him for his sixteenth or seventeenth birthday. At the time, it had touched him to know she'd probably consulted with her friends, who had ruled she hadn't known him long enough to give him a serious gift, like aftershave or a wallet. Instead, she'd bought the head to show him she was a fun person. Not exactly truth in advertising, if he recalled. He'd probably gone out with her for a couple of months, and although he remembered her name was Marnie, the only image he could conjure up of the whole relationship was the lipless, grinning shrunken head.

Maybe that was the trouble with him. Girls. Women. Not the Knitting Girl and nice, overeager Marnie and all the rest. No, Charlie knew the trouble was him. Too many girls between Carrie Gundersen in eighth grade and Lindy. He was no—what did they call it?—satyr. That had always been his consolation: I don't use women. I'm a nice guy. I call for a date Tuesday night; Monday night if there's no football. I've never pushed myself on anyone. I never brag about conquests. I like women. I like being with them, talking to them. And in fact, Charlie had treasured each one. Thought about them, composed ardent love letters to them in his head, actually told at least half of them he loved them. He couldn't understand why guys were so petrified by those three words. Not that he ever said them lightly, without feeling or meaning, just to get laid. He'd always meant "I love you," from his heart of hearts. Each one of those girls was, for that time, his future wife. Not one wife with different faces. No, for each girl he imagined a different house, different kids, a whole different life.

Most recently, his thinking had been it was inevitable. He and Lindy would live on the Circle B, once it was his—she'd all but told him she'd love that—although she'd probably get some good job in Jackson Hole. They would hang out with his friends from high school, but Lindy was so outgoing and smart they'd probably also wind up socializing with all the arty types and millionaires who were grabbing up land in Jackson Hole like it had gold under it. Not boring insurance-selling millionaires; thoughtful, charitable, fun-loving, art-collecting millionaires. Okay, he wasn't worldly. But he was wise enough to know that he, Charlie Blair, was the real thing. He was, by birth and by nature, what all those new guys in Jackson Hole in brand-new Stetsons and ironed jeans yearned to be. They'd be fascinated by him. Their wives would think: That Lindy Blair is so *real*.

Jesus, it was freezing. Every time he raised the scarf so it wrapped around and kept his cheeks warm, his neck got an icy smack of snow. Why the hell he hadn't worn his parka he'd never know. Well, he did know: because he'd just grabbed his books and the jacket that had been thrown over the chair and raced out, wanting to be in the library when Lindy knocked on his door.

Rectangles of lamplight made the sandstone of the dorm buildings glow. Everyone was now hours further along on the road to finals than he was. When he went off to college, his mother had told him what a great opportunity it was, how he was going to find out so many new things about himself. Naturally, he'd put down the prediction to her need to make life sound like a great adventure, even when it stank. Especially when it stank. But in fact, he did discover something new: that he was damn bright, a real student, the first to show up in chem lab, the one who actually tried to get through all the assigned readings, even in lit class. When he was running one of the great ranches in Wyoming, he would have a library with leather-bound books he would read, not be a know-nothing like his father. Chuck didn't read. He didn't even listen. He was a parrot who could only squawk the party line: Iran. Contras. Polly wants a cracker. His father was a lawmaker who believed the law could be violated anytime it pissed you off.

The ranch was in trouble now because his father kept pulling out money and his mother couldn't stop him. But once Charlie was there, running things . . . With him and Lindy . . . He could picture their life. Their wedding in Casper, where she came from——in a Catholic church because her folks were real religious, but that was all right——their honeymoon in Hawaii.

Except that was what frightened Charlie: He had pictured a honeymoon in San Diego with Kristen——her majoring in zoology and all. A honeymoon mountain-climbing in Switzerland with Lisa. A honeymoon skiing in Steamboat Springs with Ricki; he would have skied with her in Switzerland, but he'd already taken Lisa there. He'd planned at least fifteen honeymoons already. What kind of man falls in love fifteen times?

At last, he reached the library. Although his ears were numb, his forehead hurt so much he had to tap some girl he knew from his Constitution class to ask if she had aspirin or anything. He wound up taking her Midol. She told him, You've come a long way, baby, and he pretended to be amused. It took him ten minutes before he could find an empty chair. Head after head was bent, shoulders raised in defensive, don't-talk-to-me posture.

Two summers earlier, Kaylea, at her peak of snottiness, had sneered, You fall in love like a teenage girl. When he asked, What the hell do you mean by that?—suppressing, You're fifteen, you bitch—she'd answered, You love love, Charlie.

But he had loved all those girls. Not as bodies. He took pleasure in talking with them, except when they went on about the most boring stuff, about past relationships or the hundred different instances of latent sexism they'd encountered that day. But to have loved so many of them? That scared him. Was he really any better than his old man? Not in matters of honor or patriotism or common decency or ethics; that much he felt confident about. But in the matter of women. Because there were a couple of cold winter nights when he'd caught his father sitting back in his recliner, watching his wife's face aglow in the light of the fire or the TV, and his old man had got the most tender expression on his face, which all but said, My Judy. My dear little wife. You are my one and only love. That was what his father's face said.

Charlie had also run across his father one summer night at the Snake River Overlook. Chuck had his arm around a girl hardly older than Kaylea. Love, true love. Yes, lust as well, but Charlie could see the way his father was lost in that girl's eyes; it was deeper, more gentle, than mere eroticism. He was so lost he didn't even see Charlie. Another time, Charlie had spotted him in a bar in Jackson, with a woman who looked like a hooker, or maybe she was just from L.A., with short shorts and long earrings. He'd stayed in the shadows and watched Chuck kissing her hand like he was a French courtier. No, that made it sound like a bullshit maneuver, and in truth, after the hand kiss, his old man had looked at the woman with love all over his face.

Back in his dorm room after the library, Charlie was surprised to find himself drifting into sleep in his own narrow, lumpy bed, Lindy's panties where she had tossed them. So tired. He barely remembered leaving the library, passing the pay phones, walking through the snow back to the dorm. He was considering reaching for his phone to say, Good night, Lindy, or I'm getting dressed and coming over with your panties. Except the next thing he knew, its ring was jarring him awake.

"Charlie?"

"Kaylea?" His stomach did a somersault. Something wasn't right. He'd just calmed her down. "Anything wrong?"

"Mom called. Don't worry. She's okay."

"Oh, good. Well, thanks for letting me know." What a pain in the butt.

"Charlie." Her voice was too cool.

"What? Is something wrong? Is it Dad? Is he—"

"Charlie."

"What? Tell me."

"Dad sold the ranch."

Naturally, after another twenty seconds of detachment, Kaylea broke down on the phone, sobbing so hard he could barely make out what she was saying. But what she was saying was not only that Chuck Blair sold the ranch but that he had told his wife about it in a phone call, probably around the time Charlie was being so reassuring that all would be fine. I'm selling the ranch, Chuck had announced, and by the way, I'm leaving you too. In a less-than-two-minute call from Cheyenne, which ended when, put off by Judy's hysterical squawks, he'd slammed down the phone. Instead of coming back to the Circle B, he was going to send Tippi, his secretary, who would fly in from Cheyenne to serve Judy with the papers and pack up his clothes and his gun collection. Charlie spent nearly an hour calming Kaylea, making her swear she'd stay in Colorado and take her finals. He'd even ended the conversation by telling her he loved her, something he had not said to his sister in his entire life.

He considered calling Lindy, but that thought left his mind as soon as it entered: He could all but hear her saying, Don't worry, Charlie. You have me.

He was relieved it was after two, too late to call his mother. He was free to get stinking, puking drunk. But the bars were closed. He prowled the halls until he found himself banging on the door of his freshman-year roommate, Vince Goodall, an alcoholic—or at least a guy with an incapacitating drinking problem—who could always be counted on to have a couple of bottles in his room. In case of a blizzard, man.

Vince, somewhere between inebriated and dead drunk, refused to allow Charlie to go off with a bottle. Instead, he swept his clothes and books off his chair, poured Charlie a beer stein full of grape-flavored vodka, which tasted like a liquid lollipop, and demanded, *Qué pasa*, man? So Charlie told him that his father had left his mother and—because that wasn't fucking the family enough—had sold her life and Charlie's future. Sold the ranch. Vince said, Aw, shit, and Charlie said, Yeah.

Talking to a man, however, was not like talking to a woman. It did not heal. Besides, Vince's room lacked the reassuring, life-can-be-sweet scent of lavender candles and lemon shampoo. It smelled of unwashed laundry and vomit. So Charlie rose and, taking the still-half-filled stein with him, said, Thanks, Vince. And Vince said, Listen, man, promise me something. What? Charlie asked. You won't blow your old man's head off. No, no, of course not, Charlie said, although the thought had not only crossed his mind, it had lingered there. Was there still. Good, Vince said, because your going away for life would be the frosting on your old lady's cake. Charlie returned to his room, finished off the vodka, awoke the next morning with a harrowing pain behind his left eye, and went to take his Advanced Beef Production and Management exam, even though he was forever banished from the land he loved.

Charlie knew that whenever Chuck came home to Jackson Hole from legislative business in Cheyenne, he held morning court in a coffee shop just off Broadway, the Grand T. Although the place's full name on the sign that swung over the door was The Grand Teton Coffee Shop, it was not a coffee shop in the modern sense. Even the most idiotically trendy tourist would die before being overheard asking for cappuccino in a true cowboy hangout like the Grand T. Plain food plus coffee, decaf and, for the ladies, tea. Lipton, none of that cranberry-mint-jasmine crap.

Built in 1922 and finished in that flush Harding era just days before the Teapot Dome scandal broke, the coffee shop was a large, square room with shoulder-height pine wainscoting. The wood was stained darker than mahogany by decades of french-fry grease droplets wafting in from the narrow kitchen directly behind. Tables were rough spruce planks on legs. The seats and backs of the chairs were covered in red oilcloth that had begun to dry and crack by the mid-1950s.

Although Mrs. Hubie, the wife of the owner and cook, came in on occasion to cover the cracks with orange duct tape—the closest match she could find to red—unsuspecting summer tourists often found the backs of their bare thighs caught in a jagged oilcloth fissure that bit their flesh with the viciousness of a rabid wolf. The cashier, Hubie's half sister, sat beneath a cuckoo clock, by a brass cash register behind a glass counter with a display of cigarettes, chewing tobacco and gum. Tourists, thinking they were seeing a splendid example of cowboy craftsmanship, often asked where they might buy a cuckoo clock like the one of black wood in the shape of a church that stood on the ledge above the cashier's head. In fact, Hubie's father had brought it back from the war in 1945, having stolen it from a rectory when his unit marched into Germany. It chimed each quarter hour. A small figure, a priest or minister—whatever Krauts have, Hubie's father used to say—emerged from the church trailed by an acolyte, a badly carved figure that resembled a banana with a nose. The two revolved twice, after which the requisite number of bongs could be heard. The tourists were merely told: Not for sale.

The Grand Teton Coffee Shop was a bit of a luncheonette, a dash of a diner, a restaurant that closed every day at three o'clock so Hubie and his mistress, Myrna, the fifty-five-year-old waitress, could have their time together before Hubie had to get home for supper. No-nonsense, artery-clogging breakfasts were served until eleven forty-five, although, truth be told, Hubie would fix up a damn good egg-white omelette with veggies, providing you were a regular—that is, if your myocardial infarction had been caused by forty-five years of the Grand T's sausage 'n' cheese egg specials. If you were a tourist, or even a new-comer, a Hollywood mega-agent with a thousand-acre ranch, you not only got solely what was on the menu; you also had to bear the slow sideways glances of the local boys before they turned back to each other, amused—not conspicuously, not cruelly. They were Wyoming men. But the slightest elevation of eyebrows—at the straight, clean edge of your fingernails, the soft, buttery leather innocence of your boots—all but said ha-ha-ha! Not that such derision kept the outsiders away. It only made the Grand T more enticing.

On those mornings when the Honorable Charles Bryant Blair was in town, doing business at the Grand T, the party faithful were the first to pay homage to their state representative. Sipping cream-laced coffee, they would finish their reports and gossip, take what orders Chuck had for them and, by five minutes to eight o'clock, slip out of their chairs. Myrna, the waitress, would then run her gray rag over their side of the table so that the more powerful ranchers, shopkeepers and restaurant and hotel owners would have a clear, albeit unsanitary, spot on which to set their plates of pancakes or steak and eggs. Before the German cuckoo clock on a ledge over the cash register chimed nine, those petitioners would be gone and Myrna would be back to remove Chuck's dishes, his egg-coated knife and fork, and to refill his cup yet again. She'd give a final swipe to coffee droplets and toast crumbs, so that when the truly powerful came by—lobbyists for mining interests, representatives of cattlemen's associa-tions and the Church of Latter-day Saints, the Republican State Committee—the table would look pristine. These were the only individuals for whom Chuck would always push up the silver slide on his string tie.

Representative Blair held forth at the third table from the door at the Grand T. He kept an index card and a pencil stub from Little Dogie Miniature Golf in his back pocket and jotted down whatever reminders were necessary. You want folks to feel free, he liked to say, and nobody feels free when assistants are around. So that December, when Charlie got home for Christmas after finals and came to a late breakfast at nine-thirty—arranged by Chuck's secretary in Cheyenne—he was surprised his father was not yet alone.

A woman. Business. A lady's skinny attaché case standing by her chair. Her back was toward the door, but she was wearing a suit. Not lawyer's or banker's gray. Red. And not a dark, holly-berry red or a hunter's red but the jolting, sun-imbued red Charlie had seen on the T-shirts of rich tourists, which heralded tropical paradises: Maui! Virgin Gorda!

"There's my boy!" he heard his father boom to the woman in his big election night voice. "Howdy, Charlie!" Chuck and the woman pushed back their chairs and stood. Charlie, who had frozen at his father's "boy," slogged toward the table as though making his way through two feet of wet snow. Chuck shook Charlie's hand with a politician's excess of vigor while grabbing his tricep. "Good to see you!"

"Hi." Charlie understood that his father needed to meet him in a public space to avoid the scene they had never had. He was prepared too. The sale of the ranch seemed to be a done deal. His mother, reiterating what Kaylea had told him, said it was signed and sealed and had to be delivered on the first of January. So there was no

point in spewing forth what he felt. Besides, he was afraid
that if he started spewing, he might never stop. He would
go on raging, like some nut screaming on a street corner
about Jesus or the CIA, not shutting up even when the
ambulance came to take him to the bin. And if he flat-out
punched his father—smash!—right in the center of
Chuck's overcologned face, so he could have the pleasure
of hearing what he could only dream about, the crunch of
the breaking bone of his nose? No; besides the small matter of Honor Thy Father and Mother, his old man was getting . . . what for the ranch? Hundreds of thousands? A
million? More? Developers were now coming in with
truckfuls of money, buying land for corporate retreats,
resorts, condos.

People were calling Jackson Hole the new Hamptons,
the new Sun Valley, the new Vail, the place where every
rich, striving jet-setter and tycoon with a checkbook had
to be. So even after alimony and whatever, his father
would still have something left to offer—or lend—to his
son. Here, Charlie, I know fifty thousand won't buy shit
around here, but you can put it down on a nice little
spread in Montana. "Charlie, I want you to meet Allison
Pugh. Ali's from Salt Lake."

"Hi, there," Allison said. "Good to meet you."

Charlie looked at her for the first time. Tall. Pretty in
an overdone way. She had a one-color white face. Her
makeup looked so thick that if she scratched her cheek,
she'd leave a furrow. Her eyes were outlined with a heavy
blue line, her lips by a narrow red one, reminding him of
how his sister had crayoned the wicked queen in *Snow
White* in her coloring book. His Grandpa Willie would
have noted: She's no spring chicken—take a look at her
neck. Probably in her mid-thirties. But she did have a

good body. A great body. Big boobs, little waist and curving hips, more like those Vargas drawings from *Playboy* than an actual woman. Her appearance of height was mostly due to the boots she was wearing. Not riding boots. The heels were so stupidly skinny and high that you couldn't help but think about porn flicks where the girls wore such boots.

"Hi," Charlie said. He waited for her to pick up her attaché case and leave, but she and his father sat back down.

"Well?" Chuck demanded. "Grab yourself a chair, Charlie! We'll talk." Charlie took a chair from the empty table in front of theirs and sat beside the woman. Better, he reasoned, because he didn't want to wind up having his eyes drawn to her boobs as if they were magnetized and have his father think he was a kid. "Ali's with Aspen Development."

"Colorado?" Charlie asked her.

"No," Allison said. "Not the town. The tree. We're a Salt Lake outfit." She didn't exactly lisp; it was more like she possessed double the normal quantity of saliva. "We're active in Utah, Colorado, Wyoming, Idaho."

"Aspen's the company that bought the ranch," Chuck explained.

"I was hoping we could talk about that."

"Sure."

"I mean . . ." He waited for Allison to say something like I'll leave you boys alone, but she stayed where she was, looking from him to his father and back again, checking the resemblances, the differences. She seemed less than fascinated, he thought. Her curiosity was on the level of someone studying billboards on a boring car trip. "I don't mean to be impolite, Dad, but I was thinking about, you know, a kind of a longer, private talk. So maybe another time—"

"Now's fine," Chuck said. "You can say anything you want in front of Ali. Listen, there's nothing about the deal she doesn't know. I mean, she was the genius who dreamed it up and put it together! And I do mean a genius! Want anything, Charlie? Bet I can convince Hubie to make you up some waffles."

"No. No, thanks. I mean, I thought we could talk about not just the ranch. About home stuff."

"I'm so sorry you all have to pack up and leave the premises so fast," Allison said in her juicy manner. Charlie wished he had one of those question-mark-shaped suctioning drains dentists used. Just hang it over her teeth, let it slurp. "But there's interior work that's got to be done on the main house this winter, and we're under terrible time pressure. Of course, we wouldn't want anyone to move at Christmastime—and I don't mean that just corporately. I have an involvement here personally. I hate the thought of *anyone* spending Christmas at a hotel. That's like the saddest thing in the world, isn't it? I wouldn't have that on my conscience, so even though the contractual date was December sixteenth and it's an Aspen property, we said Hey, put up your tree at home, share your holiday with people who are supportive. Don't even think of leaving before the new year. I don't know if you know, but we have relocators actively scouting for your mother. It's a total service. She won't have to pack a dish." The more she spoke about business, the more animated she became, smiling, fluttering her blue-mascaraed lashes, making sweeping gestures with her hands.

"'Scouting'?"

"Scouting for a place for her to live. She wants to stay

in the area." Charlie was going to say either, Where the hell else would she go?, or, Her family's been here forever. But Allison was too quick for him. "Aspen has some fabulous condo properties with the most incredible views of the Tetons and . . . Do I have to sell *you* on the beauties of this place? But she wasn't interested, and I'd be the last one to try and force something like that on anyone, especially considering the circumstances. I'm sure she takes this personally. It's only human, and believe me, I understand people's feelings of attachment to a house—to the land, in this case. Very deep, very profound. But forgetting all that, this deal was inevitable on a purely economic level. What's 'the land' to your mother or to you is also a commodity in tremendous demand."

"Charlie knows that, Ali," Chuck said.

She gave no sign that she had heard Chuck speak. "Jackson Hole is where the action is. Aspen sent me here with a blank check. They said, Make it happen."

"What about you?" Charlie somehow managed to ask his father. His own mouth was so dry he couldn't swallow. Allison had gotten not only his ranch but somehow his saliva as well.

"What *about* me?" Chuck said.

"Where are you staying?"

His father stuck out his head, narrowed his eyes angrily, as if trying to get a better look at the creep who would ask that question. Finally, he said, "At Ali's place."

"In the Rainbow Crest Condos," Allison clarified. "It's one of Aspen's finest properties. Each unit has its own deck and hot tub. Totally private."

"I didn't know," Charlie said to Chuck, amazed he could still speak.

Chuck widened his eyes and put on a smile. "Well, I

haven't told your mother yet. I mean, the where business. Where I'm staying. And who with. But I've been open and aboveboard with her. She knows I'm in love with someone else."

Chuck's eyes were glued onto his son's. Charlie understood his father was listening to some internal political stage direction: Look 'em straight in the eye. Keep smiling. Chuck's hand, however, slid halfway across the table, then stopped to search nervously, blindly, rotating at the wrist, back and forth, back and forth, for Allison's. When at last she put her hand up on the table, Chuck's seized it.

"Ow!" Allison snapped.

"Sorry, baby. Charlie, there's no need for your mother to know details yet."

"What details?" Charlie asked, exhilarated to discover—yes!—that he seemed like a regular, calm person instead of a guy whose heart was pumping out so much blood his skull might explode.

"You know," his father mumbled, a third grader's blush ruddling his cheeks. "The 'death do us part' details."

"You and Allison."

"No, me and Krystle Carrington. Of course me and Ali. I'm sorry. Maybe I shouldn't have sprung this on you first thing. But I didn't want to hold up her meeting you, because she's been dying to, Charlie. Meet you, I mean. She's been saying, 'Hey, Chuck, you can't keep CBB junior all to yourself!' Am I right, Ali?" Charlie turned in time to see the woman lower her head a bare half inch.

"That's right," she said, her wicked-queen lips parting with reluctance, as if there were mucilage in her lipstick. "I couldn't wait."

\*          \*          \*

When Charlie was graduated from the University of
Wyoming, Allison Pugh was long gone and working on a
deal for a forty-five-hundred-acre ranch south of Missoula,
Montana. Before she left Wyoming, however, she sold
Chuck what she assured him was "the best of the best," a
two-bedroom condominium in Timberline Vistas that
featured an indoor as well as an outdoor hot tub, a sauna,
walk-in closets with built-in shoe racks, and stereo speak-
ers in every room, including each of the two and a half
baths.

Chuck, bitter over paying top dollar for the sumptu-
ous lodgings he had assumed would be home to him and
his new wife, furious with his about-to-be-ex-wife and
her divorce lawyer over what he called Judy's sheer
greed—her demand for half of the two million he had
received for the Circle B—decided to draw the line on
spending. Also, because of new financial pressures—he
was involved in a new relationship, with a 34D lawyer
from the Wyoming Coal Board—he would probably
have to get a nicer apartment in Cheyenne. So his graduation gift to his son was a three-hundred-seventy-
dollar watch. His secretary signed the graduation card
Love, Dad.

Although there were agribusiness jobs to be had
around Jackson Hole, Charlie sensed he could not bear
knowing that while he was, say, attending a sale of bulls,
he would hear talk that the new owner of the Circle B,
Starr-Jaeger Pharmaceuticals, had brought in a special
crew from Vail to build a sauna and steam bath and hot
tub inside a giant pustule of winterproof glass. He didn't
want to rent a mountain bike and find out from the guy
at Big Wheel Cyclery that Starr-Jaeger had sold off a
thousand acres of his Grandpa Willie's best land to Black

Bear Associates, which was actually one guy from Boston, who had grown weary of investment banking and was building a ranch that would be called the Circle B, with parentheses saying Est. 1894, as if it had been his family who'd had the spirit to come to Wyoming for the land grant.

Spirit. The one bright spot at home was his mother's spirit. Charlie was proud of her spunk. More than spunk. Guts. No I'm-just-a-rejected-housewife-who-never-worked excuses for her. She'd typed up a résumé, presenting herself as a manager of a profitable agricultural enterprise. After only two weeks, she was a loan officer at the Teton County Bank for Savings, with a huge desk and a fountain pen. Every time Charlie walked into her new house, she'd demand, Did I give you my business card yet, Charlie? Right before handing it to him, she'd hold it up between her thumb and index finger, and she'd mouth, Judy Clendenen Blair, Assistant Vice President. A trace of a smile would remain as she waited, time and again, for him to read it. When he'd say, Great, Mom, she'd nod with a banker's perfect blend of dignity and congeniality.

But the sight of her, blonder now, her ponytail replaced with a feather cut, her rancher's blue jeans supplanted by a banker's-gray skirt, grieved him, as though she had suffered a small death.

Just turning left onto her block brought down his own spirits, until, as he walked through her door, he would feel a wave of loss he had not felt since the death of his grandparents: a weight on his chest, a sense that the air inside the place was composed of gases heavier than nitrogen and oxygen. Judy's house wasn't meant for a fifth-generation Wyoming woman. It was a lifeless place, a nonwesterner's vision of a ranch house: a log facade, a rough pine rocker on the porch. But it sloped like a Swiss chalet. Her living room, with its cone of a fireplace, could have been picked up from a Vermont ski resort and plopped down in Jackson Hole. The rooms opened wide on each other in outgoing California style. Huge, double-paned windows offered a vista of a knoll dotted with more new log houses. The mountains, the awesome perpetual presence in Charlie's vision and his life, seemed diminished from inside her house, farther than they actually were: streaks of gray shadow behind the knoll.

He didn't belong in her new home, although he knew his mother wanted him there. There was no longer any joy behind her smile. She'd become doggedly serious about being happy on her own. Gone were her old books, *Love's Tender Fury* and *Heifer Selection and Cow Culling*. Now it was *Making Your Own Miracles*; *Life! After Divorce* and *Queen James: A Bible for Christian Feminists*.

Even though his mother still ruffled his hair when she came home from the bank and said, "Charlie boy, I don't know what I'd do without you," when he installed an automatic garage door opener, he knew his home could no longer be with her. He could not shake the image of how it had been when he was fifteen or so, coming home from school, sitting at the kitchen table doing his trigonometry while his mother sat across from him, contentedly working on the ranch's books, sometimes humming along with a cassette in her Walkman, big, romantic Judy Garland or Frank Sinatra songs. Now she was too busy trying to be happy to be contented. Mind if I go, Charlie? Gotta go, Charlie. Meetings, dinners, support groups.

Of the four jobs he was offered, he wound up taking

the one farthest from Jackson Hole, at the GG Ranch, so far west in Idaho he could practically see Oregon. His first night there, his window open wide, he got nearly drunk on a June breeze that scented the air like a freshly cut peach. Dazed by his day's drive past cascading waterfalls, through majestic evergreen forests, he told himself—actually said it out loud to the dark room—"I'm going to love it here!" If the great silver Tetons that soared over the green and gold valley in which he grew up was the most beautiful sight on earth, then surely these acres in Idaho, so close to the Snake River that on still nights he could hear its splash as it flowed west, were close enough to his notion of Eden that although he was no longer home, he began to believe he had not been expelled from Paradise.

And how could he not love his job? he kept asking himself. The Graebers, the family that owned the GG Ranch, had run out of ranchers. The elder son had retired to Arizona, the younger kept polo ponies in Sun Valley. Since none of their children wanted the place except as a hunting and fishing camp, a Fourth of July picnic ground, he, twenty-two-year-old Charles Blair, Bachelor of Science, was in charge. What a spread! Just working the place made him feel prosperous. It was rich, irrigated, so that the very soil gave off a more fertile smell than the land of the Circle B. Abundant feed, fine watering holes, terrain neither too steep nor too flat. A beautiful herd of Black Baldies, a crossbreed of Herefords and Black Angus.

True, the cowboys called him "college boy" and hooted—slapping their thighs and throwing their heads back in laughter as if overacting in a silent movie—when he demonstrated how to recycle tractor tires into portable feed troughs, but the fourth time he showed up at the bar where they went drinking every Friday night, he talked about going for elk in Wyoming, and they said, Hey, ever try mule deer? Even before they went hunting they stopped calling him "college boy" and began to call him Charlie.

At first the Graebers' lawyer and accountant paid humiliatingly frequent visits, stressing that they were used to more seasoned managers. They pored over his books, demanding, Can you go through that one more time? about his marketing plans. But after a couple of months they began to say goodbye with robust handshakes and genial smiles. The accountant said he'd be pleased for Charlie to meet his daughter Jennifer when she came home from Idaho State in Pocatello. By the time winter came, Graeber the elder's calls from Scottsdale declined from twice a week to once a month.

"It really *is* beautiful," his sister, Kaylea, conceded, looking out his kitchen window. The entire landscape was white. Icicles hanging from the frosted trees were giant diamonds in the morning sun. "Now what do you want? Your ankle looks like you blew up a balloon under the skin, so I'm at your service."

"You are?"

"For the next five minutes," she said. "What'll it be, coffee or hot chocolate?"

"Are you in a good mood?"

"You want both?"

"If I can get both, I want both." He couldn't believe his sister had actually come to visit him. He'd driven home Christmas Eve but could spend only one day. Come on out, Kaylea, spend a few days with me, he'd suggested, thinking he could make a fortune putting money on her not even crossing the border into Idaho. But right after New Year's, before she had to go back to Boulder, she had driven out to stay with him.

"I told you how nice it was out here," he said.

"It's better than nice. Do you know you're shivering?" Charlie thought of the phrase "chilled to the bone," but that did not describe how cold he was. The membranes of each of his cells must be frozen stiff, the cytoplasm thick, syrupy, like vodka left in the freezer. "Keep that foot raised," Kaylea snapped. "It could be broken." She was short, like their mother, but lacked Judy's old, easy tractability. Even when she had been three and Charlie six, she'd barked out orders to him like a tiny drill sergeant: Find me my Weebles! Gimme that Oreo!

"It's not broken."

"How do you know?" she demanded. "Are you the expert on everything?" He stood and tried to stomp off to his room, but he could barely hobble. He lowered himself back into a chair and let his sister slide another chair beneath his leg. Whatever energy he had left he used to keep from grunting with pain. "I think it's broken, Charlie."

"It's not."

"Do you want me to help you take off your clothes?"

"You're still trying to see me naked."

"Believe me, Charlie, whatever you've got, I've seen bigger and better."

She was an incredible pain in the ass, he thought as he limped off, but he was so relieved she was with him, in his house on this freezing morning, that he felt himself choking up. It had snowed hard the night before. It had seemed a benevolent snow, heavy, insulating. But just before dawn, he'd been concerned that the temperature might drop. So he'd left Kaylea, who'd fallen asleep over a bag of Doritos and one of her books about environmental stuff—how herbicides were destroying plants that blue-lipped butterflies or something fed on.

He'd had to make sure that enough hay had been put down as bedding so the cattle would not be lying directly on the snow. The temperature plummeted as he drove, and by the time he got to the herd, a short distance away, he discovered that the cattle had eaten the bedding. A mean wind had whipped up, icing the snow. As he and one of the men walked back to the truck to get more hay, his right foot seemed to fly backward. He nearly recovered his balance but, in doing so, did a little jig that ended by his tripping over a snow-covered rock. He lay there, the breath momentarily knocked out of him, feeling his ankle swell against the seams of his boot. By the time he got up, he was soaked. And he still had to go and get the hay.

He returned to the kitchen dressed like an invalid, in pajamas and a University of Wyoming sweatshirt—he did not have a bathrobe. As if the rich aromas of chocolate and coffee filling the kitchen weren't dizzying enough, he was hit by the sugar scent of some Sara Lee cake he had bought, frozen and forgotten back in August.

"Danish," Kaylea announced. "Well?"

"Not broken. I told you."

"Then let's talk."

Watching the ease with which she poured coffee for them both, he realized she had either lived with a man or spent a good many overnights. It made him feel old and lonely. "How do you think Mom's doing?" he asked.

"Fine, fine," Kaylea said dismissively. "She had a date New Year's Eve with a sixty-five-year-old Austrian ski instructor named Hans. Now she's going to make him her lamb stew."

"That'll get rid of him."

"Forget about Mom. I want to talk about you."

"There's not too much to say. Still getting the feel of the place."

"Are you happy here?"

"What do you mean, 'happy'?"

She set his coffee down and sat across from him. "When anyone does that 'define your terms' shit, they're not happy."

"Stop being an asshole."

"Do you have any friends here?"

"Yes."

"Name two."

"Lay off," he said, reaching across the table for the milk and sugar. "I'm just getting my bearings. And I didn't grow up here. It's a small town."

"Please. I feel like a city slicker here. They didn't even have gel in that general store. Hair gel. Don't pretend you don't know what gel is."

"Don't the hair gel cans pollute the environment?"

"Shut up, Charlie. What do the women around here wear? Pigtails?"

"Only with their underarm hair."

"Are you seeing anyone?" He shook his head. "Any prospects?"

"Not really."

"So you're just going to go celibate?"

"No. I went to a dance at the Cattlemen's Association."

"That must have been a thrill and a half. Well? What happened? Why do you *always* make me pull teeth, Charlie?"

"Nothing happened. The two women nearest my age were sixteen and thirty. I don't want to talk about PSATs, and the old lady seemed less interested in me than I was in her, if that's humanly possible."

Kaylea took the Danish from the oven and set the aluminum tray in front of him. "You can have them all."

"Boy, do you feel guilty about bullying me."

"No, Charlie," she said, in a voice that suddenly sounded like his Grandmother Lois's. He lowered his head to sip his coffee. It wasn't that he was ashamed to cry in front of his sister; he hadn't expected gentleness, though. A couple of tears would be fine, but he was afraid he might lose control and sob. "I feel bad you're so unhappy here." Instead of arguing with her, he pulled off a square of Danish and studied the white sugar swirl on the top. "Is it the loneliness or the job?"

"Both," he said softly.

"Tell me."

"It's just me here. I go drinking with the boys, or read a bunch of USDA booklets, or go to cattlemen's meetings and listen to proposals for amending the Insecticide, Fungicide and Rodenticide Act. And I say to myself, 'I don't give a shit. It's not mine.'"

"What's not yours?"

"This place. It's not that I can't run it. Sometimes I'm surprised at how good I am. This is what I've always thought I'd be doing all my life. Everything I've ever done since I was a kid was a preparation for something just like this."

"Except not like this, because it's not yours."

"It's not mine. It's not my herd or my house. I'm a hired hand. But I didn't major in animal science because I've got a thing for cattle. I wanted to be equipped to take care of what was mine, my family's, in the best way possible. Maybe that's selfish. Who the hell knows."

"Give yourself more credit. You were preserving a trust. You would have taken care to bring the best animals to market and maybe made a decent living. But you would also have been maintaining something for folks who'd be around long after you were gone."

"It would sort of be self-interest, though, because they'd be my great-great-great-great-grandchildren."

"Maybe. That's out of your control. Maybe your kids or your kids' kids wouldn't have wanted any part of it, like here, whatever their name is."

"Graeber."

"But you'd have been doing more than just leaving a ranch to some Blairs in the twenty-second century. Look, Charlie, I know you think my environmentalism is a lot of bullshit."

"No. I probably agree with you at least half the time. I just don't like lectures on how I don't give a shit about the food chain."

"Okay. No lectures. You would have preserved the land, Charlie. There's no way you would have sold out the way Dad did."

"I know."

"Not just because you wanted to pass on a working ranch. Because you would have known that the corporations may hold it for a hunting lodge or a dude ranch for a few years and then . . . Condo City. It's gone. It will never come back. So you would have saved it because the land is worth more than the trees and the forage and the water that're on it. It has value to people who don't own it, to people who will never see it."

"You know, you give me a bad rap. I'm more conserv-

ative than liberal, but I'm not some right-wing nut who
wants the right to shoot bald eagles, for Christ's sake."

"Like Dad."

Charlie shook his head. "Grow up, Kaylea. Do you
really think he believes in any of his crap? He believes in
nothing. Trust me: A few thousand rich liberals from
New York and L.A. will decide they need full-time
authenticity instead of part-time and move to Jackson
Hole year-round. They'll register to vote and start contributing to candidates, and he'll have a conversion that
will make what's-his-name's—Saint Paul—look like kid
stuff. He'll become Wyoming's biggest Democrat. He'll
start the Jackson Hole Symphony Orchestra and demand
government funding for the arts. He'll beg for more environmental impact studies. He'll weep over a dead eaglet."

"He wouldn't go that far."

"If there was a TV reporter around?" Charlie stood,
hobbled over to the stove and poured hot chocolate into
his cup. He held the steaming cup in both hands. Its heat
brought back the serenity of his childhood, when he'd
come in from the cold: hot chocolate and fresh clothes,
warm from the dryer. "But that's history."

"He's still your father. You can't do a memoryectomy.
There are psychological—"

"I know, I know. I'm talking about Jackson Hole.
That's what's history."

"I don't understand you. How could you *not* come
back? What place in the world could be better?" She
crossed her arms over her sweater and waited. Any
minute, she would start tapping her foot. It wasn't that
she was brighter or even thought faster than he, but she
had always been able to talk better. Often, she made him
feel dumb. Throughout their childhood, his sister had

always won their arguments—except for the few times he'd socked her. "Well? The correct answer is: There's nothing better."

"I know I have to make my own way now."

"And do what?"

"I don't know."

"Nothing in agribiz?"

"I don't think so."

"But you're so good, Charlie. I mean, maybe you won't have to work someone's ranch forever."

"Then do what? Run a feedlot? Become an executive for some big beef-packaging firm, work in an office building in Omaha, pitch for the company softball team? I want . . . I don't know. Something exciting."

"Well, it's not exciting, but it's a living."

"So is being a Mafia hit man. So is being a state legislator."

"There's no job category 'Anti-Dad,' Charlie."

"What's wrong with wanting to be better than he is? Forget that he's a total jerk. You know, who else would sell the family ranch, the family future, to a Salt Lake City slut for—what?—ten, twenty percent less than he could have gotten anyplace else?"

"No shit!"

"No shit. And forget that he's a crummy human being who can't even remember to buy a Christmas card for his kids."

"But if we'd gotten the card, we would never have gotten the I-love-you-it-breaks-my-heart-not-to-be-with-you phone call Christmas Day."

"Day? Ten-thirty at night. And forget that he's dumb. You know, I used to think he wasn't dumb, just narrow. But his entire world is Wyoming. Forget the rest of the country. He has zero interest in a world beyond himself, beyond his own interests. Like, he loves Reagan. Why? It's part of his job. Do you think he ever actually listened to one of Reagan's State of the Union speeches? Knows anything about supply-side economics? And just go ahead and ask Dad about anything in the news that's not on his agenda, like the Iran-Contra business. Okay, he'd know the name Oliver North and get all red in the face and say, 'A great man, a fine American!' But if you ask him, 'What's going on with this Contra stuff, and by the way, who are the guys on the other side?' he wouldn't know shit."

"Don't you think he's just supershallow?" Kaylea asked. "Because to be perfectly honest, I don't like the implication that we're the direct descendants of someone who's seriously stupid."

"Not seriously. Probably in that dull-normal range. But what do you call somebody who—when I told him that I'd gotten a job as a ranch manager in Idaho—all he could say was, 'Huh? Why not Wyoming?' Didn't ask me about the salary. Didn't ask what part of Idaho or the size of the ranch or what kind of herd. Not a word about what the job entailed. He's like that about everything. Completely lacking in curiosity. That's my definition of what stupid is. All he wants to know about any issue is what the coal mining or tourist industry lobbyists tell him. Oh, and how big a bribe he's going to get."

"You don't really think . . . ?"

"If I tell you 'Grow up,' you'll get pissed. You know, I wish I could whip it up to feel sorry for his dumbness, but I can't," Charlie said. "Even when I thought I'd be running a ranch my whole life, I knew that wasn't going to be my whole world. I figured I'd still read, go to the movies, listen to music, watch the Sunday-morning news shows. I realized I'd be doing stuff like going to Washington, lobbying for the Cattlemen's Association. But I also had the sense I'd travel someday, get to New York, Florida, California—and not just Disneyland. Go abroad, even."

"Daring, Charlie."

"I know. I've got a wild side. But let me finish, now that I'm mouthing off. All along, I knew I'd get involved in some cause. Advise a 4-H group, work with Indian kids. I mean, we live in America. We're part of something larger than just us."

Kaylea walked over to the sink, stood beside her brother and put her hand on his arm. "Remember Grandpa Willie talking about the war?"

"I remember."

"How he was fighting with guys from all over—he did all those hysterical accents. But how for the first time in his life he understood he was part of something bigger than himself, bigger than the ranch, bigger than Wyoming. Something important?"

"I remember. It's something I always wanted to feel. But see, it's like this . . ." Charlie set his cup in the sink, as if having his hands free would allow him to concentrate. At last, he shrugged, a pumped-up shrug that dragged his shoulders up to ear level, as if to demonstrate to his sister his bafflement. "I don't know what I'm looking for. Excitement, but more than excitement. Something with some life to it."

"You want a life that means something, Charlie."

"Where the hell do I go to find it?"

\*          \*          \*

A year later, on a January night so unseasonably warm he was wearing just a sweatshirt and jeans, Charlie waited outside the Three Rivers Hospital emergency room to see whether Jimmy Brower, one of the cowboys, had spent the day moaning and clutching the right side of his belly because of chili or acute appendicitis. He finished a *Sports Illustrated* feature on Vinny Testaverde, then skipped over an article on the radical notion of decreasing the distance between the sideline and the limit line on the lacrosse field from six to five yards. He passed advertisements for jock itch powder and Gatorade and came upon a recruitment ad: "Semper Fi, Guy!" It showed a trio of marines— one a dazzling ebony and the other two burnished a pale copper from the sun—with Popeye forearms. Compared to these three, Vinny Testaverde, a couple of pages back, was a sissy. They were shown racing through a green landscape—though not so lushly green as to evoke Vietnam—toward a hovering helicopter. "Be a Marine!" the ad charged, with the unstated caveat: If you're man enough.

Charlie yawned and glanced up. It was getting close to midnight. The hospital waiting room, with its aggressive fluorescence and its badly pitched plastic seats, which tilted him so far forward that he felt any second he would lurch out and fall onto his nose, felt summer hot. A young mother and father, his age, maybe even younger, who had told him how their eighteen-month-old had swallowed the fin of a Little Mermaid doll, were clutching each other's hands. They kept looking from the closed door of the ER over to Charlie, and he was worn out from nodding reassuringly, as though somehow he possessed the knowledge that their little girl would be all right. Two seats down from him, a woman in her fifties, whose husband had severed a finger while planing a door, looked as if, for yet a fourth time, she was going to beg Charlie to explain how the heck such an accident could happen. Quickly, he lowered his head and leafed through the magazine. An ad from a dairy cooperative proclaimed: "It's not a Super Bowl without the cheese!" but Charlie didn't really notice the resplendent two-page photograph of hundreds of yellow and white squares on a humongous hero bread because he was flipping back to the Marine Corps ad.

He did not even have to think about it. He did not want to be a marine. Having grown up in the company of cowboys, internationally certified he-men, he had no need to further demonstrate his masculinity, or to possess a forty-four-inch chest and an M14. By nature, he was too easygoing to find any appeal in saluting or being saluted; in fact, the thought embarrassed him. Yet Charlie sensed that something in the photo was important, actually calling out to him. The helicopter? Well, that's where his eye was being drawn and . . . Okay, it would be a kick to go for a ride in one of those.

He closed his eyes. Could this be one of those moments when a hardly-ever-churchgoing man like himself was struck by divine intervention? God showing Charlie Blair *this* was the meaning he was looking for, that by being a helicopter pilot, he could rise closer to His light? Although Charlie knew men who routinely prayed for personal favors—Let me pass organic chemistry; Let the shadow on the X ray be a shadow; Let Debbie love me; Let the Cowboys cream the Redskins—he'd always felt this sort of begging was a shabby practice. Most of the time, he hadn't anything to say to God. When he had, it was: Thank you for this sunset, for turning the lake pink and

orange. Please have mercy on all those people in the earth-
quake. He definitely felt funny asking the Lord for voca-
tional guidance.

Nevertheless, keeping his head down against the silent
demands of the young mother and father, against yet
another What made him do that? from the middle-aged
wife, against the smell of disinfectant, Charlie studied the
ad again. What had drawn him in was not the helicopter
itself but the small red, white and blue flag on its side. On
and off, he'd been thinking about doing something for his
country. During freshman year, in those late-night "If you
could be anything you want, what would you be?" talks,
he'd said, A rancher. Or? A honky-tonk piano player—
except I can't play the piano. Well, I don't know. Maybe
like an FBI agent or something.

Where his father had been a minus—giving nothing,
grabbing whatever he could lay his hands on—Charlie
could be a plus and give back. Not become a pencil-
pushing bureaucrat counting off the ways to avoid responsibility. Not do something any functionary could do: he
couldn't see himself in the Animal and Plant Health
Inspection Service, checking out hooves or grapefruits.
The FBI? When he'd said it in the dorm, everyone agreed:
Too hokey. Work for the Forest Service or the Fish and
Wildlife Service? Become a Park Ranger? He kind of
liked the notion of living in a national park, although he
realized that instead of being in a cabin on a mountain in
Yellowstone, he could get stuck giving tours of some battle site from the Indian War of 1877. But the Smokey hat
didn't do it for him. Splendid isolation didn't do it for
him. People. He needed to work with people, to fit in
someplace, not be so damn alone all the time. Then what?

The door to the emergency room swung open. The

tiny girl who had swallowed the Little Mermaid's fin was
wheeled out, pallid but smiling. Her parents, sobbing
"Megan!" leaped from their plastic seats. Charlie smiled
at the wife whose husband had planed off his finger, and
she finally smiled back as if to say, Ten fingers, nine fingers, what's the dif?

Not the marines. Well, then, what did he care about?
Fairness. Straight shooting. Standing up for all those rules
the slick operators kept trying to undermine. Standing up
for the law. Standing up for justice. The FBI? Too hokey?

He cared about justice. Not a lawyer. Black and white
were Charlie's colors, not gray. A cop? A sheriff's deputy?
Something more. He didn't want to be like his father.
Not just in matters of morality. That went without say-
ing. He wanted to live in a world larger than a town, a
county, larger than Wyoming. He wanted the feeling his
Grandpa Willie had during World War II, that he was
joined with other Americans for the good of their country.
Not the marines. Sort of . . . What? Not might. Right.
The FBI?

Hokey? Clean-cut? The truth was, so was he. Was this
a way of trying to stick it to his father, by becoming a cog
in the vast and hated federal wheel? Maybe. But if he
couldn't live the life he'd planned, the least Charlie Blair
should do was live a life that was worth something.

# 7

If Barbara Freund had lived in the time of Solomon the Wise, she might have been Queen of Israel. Not simply because she was a fine figure of a woman: noble nose, fine shoulders, full breasts and shapely legs. The king would have gone nuts for her black eyes, lustrous as jet, sparkling with . . . Okay, not with actual genius. However, while not brilliant, she certainly would have had the quickness of mind to check out the blueprints for the Great Temple and even make a couple of constructive suggestions.

But times, alas, had changed.

"Nervous?" Nicki Lipsky asked her.

"No," Barbara told her. "I love knowing that on a singles weekend with five hundred women and four hundred and ninety-nine men, I'll be the one who has time to read *The Rise and Fall of the Roman Empire*."

Ha-ha-ha, ha-ha-ha. Nicki's voice rose, then ascended even higher. Barbara suspected she wanted to be known as a girl with a musical laugh. Laughter comes easy at twenty-two. But at age twenty-eight, Barbara herself knew meeting a man was no laughing matter. That is why, in the month of May, in the year 1969, she and her fellow teacher from Far Rockaway High School were in the Catskills.

Now a word about these mountains. Compared to the majestic Rockies, the noble Tetons—even New York's own Adirondacks—the Catskills might at first seem the work of a deity less adept than the Creator. But they have a certain grace and mystery. Washington Irving was intrigued enough to use them as the setting for "Rip Van Winkle." True, the highest peak, Slide Mountain, rises only slightly more than four thousand feet; it seems an overambitious hill compared to the nearly fourteen-thousand-foot Grand Teton. Not awesome, then, but nonetheless lovely.

And mad with color. The dainty greens of May, the melancholy greens of August, change in autumn into breathtaking hues much too wild for the West. Golds, entire rainbows of reds, browns and oranges, mesmerize with their dying beauty, like an aria sung with the soprano's last breath.

At the end of the last century, immigrant hicks, Jews from the hinterlands of Romania and the Ukraine, looked upon the Catskills and were astounded to discover such gorgeousness so close to the pushcart pandemonium and sewage stink of the Lower East Side of Manhattan. They hied themselves one hundred miles northwest to do what they had done in the old country: farm. But the land was rocky, the soil thin. Even the dairy cows they raised seemed more listless than content, as if they sensed the futility of their owners' dreams.

So early in the twentieth century, desperate farm wives began renting out a room or two to city folk yearning for nature's simplest gift—the sight of green against blue. Soon farmhouses became boardinghouses and boarding-houses hotels, and by the 1920s, the Catskills became known as the Jewish Alps, the Borscht Belt.

Here Jews could stay Jewish, eating kosher food, lis-tening to Jewish comedians, stretching with Jewish calis-

thenics coaches, dancing to Izzy Kravitz and His Jive
Five. Here, too, Jews became Americans, playing baseball, golf, tennis, fox-trotting, mamboing, trekking with
the *Guide to Eastern Birds* to become nature mavens.

They sent the next generation to the Catskills' summer
camps, and their children learned how to honor the
American flag, ride a horse, shoot a rifle, pitch a tent. But
while there may have been an Italian tenor singing out his
heart in a Catskill hotel nightclub or a Presbyterian counselor teaching archery, nearly always the Jews were—in
the word that can connote communal comfort or suspect
exclusivity—clannish.

However, there were also descendants of Eastern European Jews like Dora—Ruthie and Sally Ann and Barbara—who had never seen these mountains. While they
never denied that they were Jews, they never celebrated it
either. Unschooled in their faith, they had no knowledge
of the literature, laws, commentaries and liturgy of their
people. They were about as familiar with Jewish tradition
as American WASPs were with morris dancing.

Thus, a Jew like Jake Blaustein, a stranger in the
strange land of Wyoming, could slip into Blairdom with
ease. Within him, what was there to hold him back? He
knew the Bible was a book Tammany Hall politicians
swore upon before perjuring themselves. What did
Judaism mean to him? Why embrace the faith of his
fathers when his father had beaten and reviled him?

But by remaining in New York, with its culturally and
politically influential Jewish minority, Jake's sister, her
daughter and her daughter's daughter were able to stay—
casually, indifferently—ethnic Jews. They salted their
conversation with the occasional "kvetch" or "kibitz."
They could prepare chopped liver that might not make

Escoffier repudiate pâté but was nonetheless tasty. They stayed Jews partly through sentiment, partly through inertia and partly because they sensed that even by becoming Unitarian or Catholic or Episcopalian, they would still never be able to nullify what they were: Jews to themselves. Jews to others. The archenemy to anti-Semites.

What was Barbara Freund, that indifferent Jew, doing in these mountains? She wanted a man to love. A Jewish man, of all things. Because in some spot just beyond her consciousness, she knew that what she was had a value, whether or not she chose to redeem it. She did not wish to be held accountable for letting five thousand years of history end with her by having children who would get lost in America and cease to be Jews.

So there she stood, just inside the doorway to the vast dining room on the first night of Grossinger's Hotel's Memorial Day Singles Weekend. She and her fellow teacher Nicki Lipsky waited in a long line of the hungry and anxious unmarried. The maître d', meanwhile, was casting his eye over them all. In less time than it took him to blink, he evaluated each—the cerebral and the dopes, the Orthodox and the unaffiliated, the chic and the schlepps, the suave and the shy—and then pronounced his or her table assignment.

If that makes this Catskill hotel sound intimidating or this chubby gent judgmental, that is certainly not what its founders intended. The hotel was meant to be home away from home. It was built for warmth, with great, comfy chairs, jokey busboys, giant bowls of hot soup. Its interior was decorated in the era when it was assumed God had created forests so that man might have wall paneling; from the floor almost to the ceiling, the dining room was wood, and the wood emitted a gentle golden glow, so that all the guests appeared finer, richer.

But as everyone from a fruit fly to a high school history teacher knows, mating is serious business. The maître d' couldn't succumb to softheartedness. He had to be tough; he had a responsibility to his species. "Be with you in a minute, girls," he promised. He tried not to appear a harsh judge. His forever smiling mouth had stretched so wide over the years that he resembled a dolphin in a navy-blue suit.

Please! Barbara beseeched no one in particular. Let it be our turn. Let's get this over with. The maître d' looked near her. Not at her. Like every male eye that was glancing her way, his quickly took her in and moved on, to the lesser woman at her side. To Nicki, with the long dark hair she ironed every morning and evening. To Nicki the home economics teacher, a young woman who, after four years of higher education, could whip up a seven-layer cake in six minutes. To Nicki, who was wearing the miniest of minidresses, barely more than a ruffle of Pepto-Bismol pink. Not only had she sewn it herself; while she was at it, she'd stitched up not the then-fashionable hip belt but a raspberry-colored sash that emphasized how much smaller was her waist than her slender hips.

The sixties, Barbara decided, nervously eyeing a waiter hurrying by, bent nearly double by the weight of a tray of brisket, was not her decade. It had begun with elegant, breastless Jackie, an exquisite but ill omen. Naked, in front of her mirror, Barbara's figure might be a baroque symphony of curves, but truth be told, she knew not only history but current events. Marilyn Monroe had been dead for seven years, and the reigning queen of popular culture was Twiggy.

"Do I look as if I have any bones at all?" Barbara asked Nicki.

"What?"

"Or do I look like an amoeba in sling-backs?"

"Stop it, Barbara." Even her voice was petite. "You're just nervous."

"Give me one good reason why I should be calm."

"You think *you're* uncalm? One guess how nervous *I* am," Nicki demanded.

"So nervous you won't be able to eat a thing."

"Yes!" Nicki's mouth opened to show how dumb-founded, how delighted, she was at her fellow teacher's perspicacity. Her gape—quickly followed by a giggle even Barbara had to concede was cute—was actually designed less for her companion than to flaunt her effer-vescence, her pearly orthodonticized teeth. Barbara understood that the true audience for Nicki's performance was the two grim fellows marching back toward the maître d'—and thus toward them. The men were clearly incensed at their table assignment.

At the sight of Nicki, however, the handsomer of the two, clad in a natty sports jacket of the sort an about-to-be-wealthy radiologist might wear, parted his tight lips and, quickly, dilated his nostrils in what Barbara sup-posed was a Steve McQueen–like display of virility. By the mysterious, subliminal signals that govern human mating rituals, the man in gray slacks and a spiffy navy blazer beside him—a stockbroker? a Cadillac sales-man?—realized he had lost the prize. His eyes moved over to Barbara. After an instant, his glance told her: I will not be rude, but although the maître d' is about to seat us beside each other at one of the tables for ten—"You two girls and you gents, table forty-seven!"—and although I may be your companion at meals from this Friday-night dinner to Sunday's lunch, I am in the market for someone like Nicki, a woman who is so superior she will not even notice me. Also, for a woman who displaces less space than you do.

Barbara's fine black eyes may have grown slightly moist, of course, but she certainly did not cry at this unspoken rejection. Still, she could not completely hide her vulnerability. Thus, she let this man, his friend, the maître d' and, indeed, every man in a hundred-foot radius know that the girl next to the girl in the pink dress wasn't sure whether she was vanquished by shame or by righteous anger, but vanquished she was.

"You're not fat," Nicki reassured her later that night. Their room was among the hotel's least expensive, in one of many small outbuildings, cabins on the edge of a piney wood.

"I never said I was fat. But you can't make a case that I'm not big-boned. People come in small, medium and large. I'm large, you're small."

"Stop putting yourself down, Barb." From across the space between the twin beds in the darkened cabin room, Nicki's voice came in enchanting peeping sounds, like those of a baby chick endowed with language.

"Saying I'm large doesn't mean I'm putting myself down. But that guy in the blazer—"

"Jeff," Nicki cut in. "Did he tell you he's in his father's business? Wall coverings. They did practically every room when Justice Goldberg went to the UN."

"They did not wallpaper the UN."

"No, no. Where he *lives*, Barb." Even the first time they had met, in the teachers' room at Far Rockaway

High School, Barbara noticed that Nicki's chirpy voice rose at the end of many of her sentences, thus making her listeners feel something wonderful was about to be uttered. It endowed each subsequent sentence with a magic it never merited. "And don't tell me Jeff is small, because he's got to be at *least* five eleven, if not six feet. He went to Penn . . . University of. Not Penn State."

"But he's small-*boned*. Go, call room service, ask for a tape measure. You'll see: My thigh equals his waist."

"Stop it!" Nicki peeped. "If you think large, you'll *be* large. Think . . . Suzanne Pleshette with, uh, a little Joan Hackett around the mouth! That's *you*."

Barbara shut her eyes against the darkness. For a moment, she willed herself to be Suzanne Pleshette with a little Joan Hackett. She smiled a Pleshette-Hackett smile at the Crown Prince of Wall Coverings, watched his basset hound eyes come alive with admiration and desire. Not that she wanted him, with his establishment-pig clipped sideburns, any more than she'd wanted Harvey, the only guy who had asked her to dance at the Frugathon after dinner, Harvey of the Largest Jewish Accounting Firm in Northern New Jersey. With love beads and a goatee that looked as if he'd absconded with some old girlfriend's pubic hair. Not that she wanted any of the allegedly eligible men at the Weekend. All right, maybe Mark, a Titan whose big-knuckled hands, with black hair on the backs, hinted at a touch of the beast. He'd sat across from her at the big round table and spoken intelligently about Nixon's reescalation of the war in Vietnam and been admirably courteous to the overtaxed waiter. Yet the instant dessert was finished, he'd attached himself to Nicki, whose contribution to the entire discussion of war and peace had been "Really?" and "I never thought of that before!" He had not left Nicki's side until one A.M., and then, she'd confided to Barbara, only because he made her agree to a prebreakfast walk around the lake.

Think Suzanne Pleshette with a little Joan Hackett! Nicki was not certifiably dumb, but she was so delighted with her own life that she might as well have been. Vietnam? Terrible. The assassination of Martin Luther King, Jr., the ensuing riots? "Terrible, terrible." But to Nicki, "Terrible, terrible" carried less emotional weight than finding an all-in-one ecru body stocking and tights at *less than half price* at Lord & Taylor.

Nicki's breathing grew slower, deeper. Every suspiration seemed a sigh of contentment. Twenty-two years old, her first year of teaching. By the end of the summer, she'd have Mark's, or someone's, diamond on her slender fourth finger. After two more years, she would retire into motherhood and tennis lessons. She'd fall asleep each night and her delicate hand, with its two- or three-carat ring, would nestle on the warm hairiness of Mark's powerful chest.

How Barbara envied Nicki Lipsky! How appalled she was to discover such jealousy within herself. But here she was, twenty-eight years old, sharing an apartment with a speech therapist, a social worker and an associate editor of *Adhesives World*, all of whom, including Barbara herself, while understanding that women like Nicki diminished their own humanity in their eagerness to please men, would still cede twenty IQ points to be a Nicki.

To have been born half girl-child, half siren. To be schooled in womancraft, to be able to whip up on a Singer, for a total cost of fourteen dollars, a pants suit to wear on a blind date with a surgical resident at Columbia Presbyterian . . . then turn down all the resident's requests and pleas for further dates because he had talked about icky operations over dinner.

Over dinner! What dates Barbara did have, blind or otherwise, were movies with coffee after. Making out and coffee after. Intercourse and nothing after, except the can of Tab she retrieved from her quarter of the refrigerator when she returned to her apartment.

She even envied Nicki her work. She, Barbara, was teaching the subject she loved to students whose lips curled with disgust as she tried to lead them along the historical trail of how America got from there to here. But from the home economics room, shared laughter, from even the most hostile of students, as they carved sheet cakes to make six-pointed Hanukkah stars or triangular Christmas trees. What fun Nicki must have, explaining how to blend in egg whites or demonstrating—*Voilà*, girls!—the magical creation of a buttonhole.

Twenty-eight. Losing friend after friend, no matter how many reassurances were made that marriage would not mean an end to getting together and having—you know, Barbara—the kind of evening men just don't care about, a hold-nothing-back talk or an off-off Broadway play.

Twenty-eight. Both her younger brothers were already married; Danny's wife was pregnant. Twenty-eight. She taught all day and gave two nights a week to Young Professionals Against Racism, one night to Listening to Bach at the New School, one night to dinner with her mother. Her mother still wakened each morning thrilled at the prospect of another day as executive vice president of Johnson Flag and Banner.

When Barbara awoke each morning, the first thought

on her mind was not of One more day at Far Rockaway
High School, or even Maybe Chinese food tonight, but of
I am alone. Was there some curse on the House of . . .
whatever her grandmother's maiden name had been?
Blaustein. Had a Blaustein woman incurred God's wrath
with some egregious sin, like wishing, for even a half second, that she could check *P*—or even *C*—rather than the
box marked *J* under Religion?

Look at the family history. The women were doomed.
Her Grandma Ruthie's husband had turned out to be the
barely imaginable, a Jew Who Drank and Hit. Her own
father, shot in the heart by a Nazi. Maybe that's why her
mother had taken up with Mr. Johnson, because she
sensed that any marriage was doomed. But at least for a
time her mother and grandmother had men who loved
them enough to want to make a life with them. They'd
had a home. They'd had more than a quarter of a refrigerator. And they'd had children.

Two-thirty. Barbara was exhausted, but sleep would
not come. To waken and retire every morning and night
for the rest of her life with an empty heart was more sadness than she could bear. Except what could she do? Kill
herself? Ridiculous! All right, the thought had occurred
to her on very bad nights. Like this one. But she had never
even gotten around to imagining how. Well, she'd
rejected a few ideas. Her pill-popping friends had
extolled Seconal's gentle virtues, but on the single downer
she'd once tried, she hovered at the edge of consciousness,
heavy-limbed, nearly paralyzed, yet unable to tumble
over into oblivion. The pill had terrified her but so
zonked her out that she could not even move her tongue
to express how truly frightened she was. She could not
imagine leaving life that way. Slit her wrists? Taking a

cold metal razor blade between two fingers, then seeing the blood and—oh God—what if you changed your mind? Ditto jumping off the Empire State Building, because as you were hurtling past the fortieth floor, you might suddenly think: Uh-oh. Suicides *do* go to hell.

Talk about hell. "Come on!" some cheerful man was urging her the next morning. She did not even glance up from her seat on the cold, damp grass off to the side of the net. He had one of those hearty, life-is-a-party voices. "Volleyball!" he enthused. "Don't you want to play?"

"No, thanks." Forget that anytime a ball flew her way, her only reaction was to duck. Barbara was so fatigued and so shaken by her dark thoughts—she'd actually formed a mental image of a blade's dark shadow over the blue veins of her wrist—that she regretted giving in to Nicki's insistence that even if she didn't want to play, she should at least be a good sport and walk her friend over to the game.

"Come on!" the too-bright voice urged. To her right, from the court, Nicki was beseeching her: "Come on, Barb! It'll be fun!" The volleyball man extended his hand to pull her up from the grass on the sidelines. And if she took his hand? An image flashed through her mind: a small, slender fellow, purple-faced from strain, unable to lift her off the ground.

"Thanks," she said, "but you don't want me on your team." When he did not withdraw his hand, she glanced up. Tall, solid as a Frigidaire. So he probably could get her on her feet. But she did not want to be gotten up, especially not by one of those overexuberant, asexual men of the sort who keep trying to organize games long after even the most avid athletes decline to play. "Really. No, thank you."

"Okay." Suddenly, he was sitting beside her on the grass. "Jed Miller," he said.

"Barbara Freund." He was fair. Dark-red hair. Nice smile. Interesting face, actually. His cheeks were prominent, his eyes somewhat Asian. If Genghis Khan had married an Irish poet, they could have produced a child who looked like Jed Miller. He was not overexuberant. Not in the least asexual.

"So," he asked, "shall we?"

He was older, she realized, well into his thirties, with the deep eye crinkles of a man who had been happy all his life. His "shall we?" sounded neither smutty nor wise-ass. Still, Barbara answered cautiously, "Shall we what?"

"Get through the Where do you live? What do you do? preliminaries. I live on Nineteenth Street."

"Is that the Gramercy Park area?"

"Where I am? Only if you're a real estate agent."

"And do you tell me what you do, or do I tell you where I live?" she asked.

"What I do won't take long. I'm a high school history teacher." Of course! He couldn't be anything else but. What was it about him that made it so easy for her to tell? The gray gym shorts, the much-washed navy T-shirt with no message? Or was it the ease of his long limbs? His large frame lacked the competitive tension she could spot in lawyers even when they relaxed. The openness of his smile? None of the I-dare-you-to-please-me challenge of doctors, the aggressive jollity of salesmen.

"I'm a history teacher too," she said. She liked that he did not shake his head in TV sitcom disbelief. He simply rested his elbows on the grass, then drew up his long legs to form a comfortable inverted V. It was the posture of a man set for easy conversation. "How come our jaws aren't dropping and we're not saying '*What?* You've got to be kidding,' with seventeen exclamation points?"

"Could it be possible we look like teachers?" Jed asked.

"Sincere? Slightly unfashionable, although we're sweetly unaware of it?"

"That's it!"

Barbara smiled, despite knowing that her best feature, her dark eyes, turned into two mere dashes beneath the arcs of her brows whenever she did smile, making her look like Mr. Magoo. Jed gave her the easiest smile back, as if he'd known her forever. Lounging on the grass, listening to the grunts of the volleyball players, the clunk of palms on ball, he was enjoying her, not assessing her. No "Let's see: good skin, great tits, not much of a waist, shoulders that would look better on a running back, intelligent eyes, inexpensive sports clothes." She simply looked good to him. As he did to her.

"Now it's your turn," he told her. Direct, firm. Precisely what you'd expect from someone who five days a week faced roomfuls of fuck-this-shit antiestablishment adolescents who did not want to be taught anything, especially history. He wasn't handsome. His brownish-greenish-grayish eyes lacked size and drama and were encircled by pale lashes many shades lighter than his dark-red hair. His chin? Not weak, though a bit small for such a large face. But Barbara sensed that even if his looks were not memorable, people would recall him as nice-looking as much for his nature as for his features. That Jed Miller: *nice*-looking guy. She liked that. Tall. He must be at least six feet. She'd never gone out with anybody that tall— Stop it! No one was going out with anybody yet and— "Your turn," he repeated.

"Oh. Okay, I'm ... You didn't tell me where you teach."

"At Shorehaven High School."

"That's on Long Island?"

"Right. Now no excuses, no evasions. Unless teaching's a cover and you're CIA."

"I am. They sent me to Far Rockaway High School to propagandize against the Paris peace talks." She wished—although it wouldn't matter to him—she had put on a touch of mascara to compensate for the puffiness under her eyes. Strange, that tormented night she'd just endured seemed a secondhand story of some other woman's sad life.

"How old are you?" Jed suddenly asked.

"Twenty-eight."

"I'm thirty-eight. We're both too old to be coy. Correct?"

"Correct."

"So how about this? I like you a lot."

Barbara fought down the urge to protest, Oh, but you hardly know me. "I like you too. A lot."

"But what? You're thinking something. You have a look on your face."

"It can only go downhill from here."

"Trust me," Jed vowed, taking her hand and holding it between his. "It won't."


Ten weeks later, Barbara Freund and Jethro Miller were married in the study of a rabbi who had picketed the United Nations for the establishment of the State of Israel, waved signs to Ban the Bomb, marched with Dr. King on Selma, Alabama, and, currently, was awaiting trial in Washington on charges of impeding the lawful functions of government by blocking the steps to the State Department with a hundred other members of the clergy to protest the war in Vietnam.

After the ceremony, he asked the couple where they intended to go on their honeymoon. Jed told him Long Island. In Shorehaven. That's where I—we—teach. Barbara's the newest member of the Social Studies Department.

We're going to spend the time looking for a house, Barbara explained, still slightly stunned that such a sentence could be coming from her and be about her life.

Listen, Jed told him, I waited all my life for the girl of my dreams—

Woman of your dreams, Barbara and the rabbi simultaneously corrected him.

Right, and while I was waiting, I socked some money away, so we're going house hunting for our dream house.

And what a dream of a place it was. As Jed's mother, a woman the size of a small house herself, trumpeted—in a voice that made men quiver and dogs wince—as she walked up the brick path edged with hardy red and white impatiens and tall, proud blue salvia: All God's children should have it so good! True, it was far from a mansion. But ten thousand dollars and a twenty-nine-thousand-dollar mortgage had bought them a three-bedroom, two-bath, cedar-shingled colonial on a sixty-by-eighty-foot grass carpet whose green perfection was interrupted only by a great sycamore in front, a crab apple in back and their dream of a swing set for the children they would have.

For their first-month anniversary, Barbara brought two glasses of chilled sparkling wine outside to Jed and waited somewhat tentatively as he flicked a button on the lawn mower and—yes!—the motor ceased its roar. "I'm still a little nervous it's going to turn on me and eat my feet," he admitted. He took the glass and lifted it toward his fine house, then to his wife. "To us!"

"To us. Isn't it wonderful, Jed? We actually own a piece of America. Do you ever think what our ancestors would have given just to be allowed to own property, to belong somewhere?"

"Well, now we do. We're as American as Dick and Jane, grown up."

"Weren't they brother and sister?" Barbara asked, holding up her glass to the dappled light coming through the leaves of the sycamore, marveling at the sparkling beauty of the bubbles, at the beauty of it all.

"Okay, so how about Pocahontas and John Rolfe?"

"Good, because I like to believe they were a love story. And we definitely are."

"Can't get more definite than that."

They kissed, not caring a whit that Erica Buonaventura, a sophomore in Jed's second-period class who lived across the street, was watching and would no doubt report the kiss, with embellishment—*long* and, I swear, with tongues, plus they were drinking, and it looked like they were humping!—to the entire student body of Shorehaven High School.

The following year, they adopted a mutt with huge, triangular ears from the Animal League, bought a couch and a coffee table on sale at the Workbench and told each other, "Don't worry, it'll happen," when Barbara failed to conceive. The year after that, they put in rosebushes, spent all the money they had earmarked for bookshelves and wall-to-wall carpeting in their bedroom on a new roof—and visited a gynecologist who specialized in fertility. He told them to try for a year. They did. That year, they bought the bookshelves and a framed map of Long Island dated 1847, and they visited a fertility specialist at Mount Sinai Hospital in Manhattan. She told them mazel tov; Barbara was four weeks pregnant.

After eighteen hours of labor, with Jed by her side the entire time, Barbara gave birth to Lauren Ruth Miller, a seven-pound-eleven-ounce girl with a powerful set of lungs, soft red fuzz for hair and—surprising for an infant—black eyes as luminous as her great-great-grand-mother Dora's had been on the day when she looked upon the Statue of Liberty.

Even though she played second base on her junior high school softball team, Lauren Miller was not a true athlete. Although not tall, she had her father Jed's rangy limbs, so when Sunshine Ziegler threw in from right field with her usual maddening inaccuracy, Lauren could stretch out her arm and—whomp!—the ball would obligingly smash into her mitt. She was quick enough to tag out the too-ambitious base runner and hurl the ball with enough strength and precision that Sarah Wu, the first baseman, got it in plenty of time to complete the double play. But Lauren had also inherited her mother's tendency toward introspection. That quality, compounded with her own relentless inquisitiveness, caused her to be, in the words of her coach, Ms. Guthrie, "an undependable pain in the butt, and if you think they'll put up with your flaky crap on the Vikings, when you get to senior high, you've got another thing coming, sister."

Lauren, despite her profound respect for Ms. Guthrie's foot-tapping, tough-talking style, knew she would never be what her coach insisted she had it in her to become: a fine ballplayer. Even at age thirteen she was analytical enough to know that besides fine and gross motor coordination, athletes needed concentration. Ms. Guthrie was wrong: She was not flaky; she could concentrate. Yet her eye was lured from the ball because how could softball— how could any game—be as engaging as real life? For instance, if Cathy Foti and Diana Parker, two girls who were strictly Debating Club and therefore, by definition, totally anti-intermurals, suddenly showed up at the softball field, peering through the chain links of the batting cage, what they were looking for or at *had* to be more important than any contest between the Shorehaven Junior High Mariners and the Manhasset Indians. If Todd Rodriguez strolled over to watch their game, wasn't speculating on why he was there infinitely more engrossing than concentrating on some Manhasset asshole who had gone down swinging twice before?

And how, would someone please tell her, was she supposed to concentrate, with the Lauren Miller Fan Club sitting in the first row of benches at every single home game? Lauren knew hell was not some flaming place with guys with cloven hooves. Hell was having parents, teachers up the hill at the high school, who at three o'clock would leap into their car, drive to Walt Whitman Elementary, pick up her brother, Adam, and then come to watch her play ball. All three of them, for God's sake, even though she knew it sickened Adam to get dragged to her games. But he was in one of those eleven-year-old, ass-kissing, parent-pleasing stages, and he'd pretend to love Being a Family and give her a high five at game's end (later, he'd stick his head into her room and sneer that her batting sucked the big one).

Hell, in fact, *was* Being a Family. When they were

watching her and she'd get distracted—checking out Ms. Guthrie whispering to the coach of the Syosset team, trying to see if she was giving off any lesbian signals, a subject of much debate among the seventh and eighth graders; or noticing this or that group of boys passing by outside the ball field on their way home—and so totally miss a ball, were her parents disappointed? Sad for her? Humiliated in front of a fellow teacher that their own flesh and blood had screwed up? No. At the same precise second, her parents' heads would swing—one left, one right—like two perfectly controlled pinball flippers, so they were facing each other. Then they'd smile *knowingly*. Oh, it made her so goddamn mad! Like they *knew* she was trying to dope out if Ms. Guthrie was gay or just a feminist who didn't believe in lipstick. And they *knew* that she was not only watching Rob and Akira and Andy walking home but also had a major crush on one of them, and they *knew*, without a doubt, that it was Akira, and they *knew*, in all their teacher smugness, that she was absolutely cringing and dying from their stupid knowing looks at each other, so at the same microsecond, their heads would flip back and they'd start watching the game again.

By the time Lauren got to Shorehaven High School, her attitude toward her parents' knowing looks, their silent commentary on her adolescence, had changed. From mere anger, it escalated to fury when, soon after her fifteenth birthday, they had given each other the Look in the midst of her refusal—okay, screaming defiance—at the breakfast table to spending spring vacation at Colonial Williamsburg when she *had an invitation to stay at Janet Franzese's house and I told you her parents would be there the whole time and there's no way in hell I'm going*. Their look said: It's all right. Lauren has to ventilate. She'd taken her mother's stupid crock of orange marmalade and flung it across the room, over the sink. It broke a pot of African violets and cracked the window. Her mother had calmly risen from her chair as if she were going to take the breakfast dishes to the sink. Instead, she smacked Lauren across the face. And Lauren spent spring vacation watching some schmuck in breeches dip candlewicks.

Six months later, however, in the first semester of her junior year, she was sitting on the floor of her room with her best friend, Cleo Rubinstein. Their arms rested on the sill of a wide-open window. Even though it was an unusually raw October afternoon, they were forced to bear the cold because they were sharing a Camel Light, blowing the smoke through pursed lips so it streamed outside and dissipated in the damp, frigid wind blowing across Shorehaven from Long Island Sound. Lauren, having spent the past quarter hour moussing and gelling her red hair into the over-the-eye style of film noir doxies, was now pushing the annoying wave back from her face as she reminisced about her parents' Look. "They're so sure they know everything I think or do, even though they are, like, such innocents." Sometimes she felt her parents were young, dewy kids, hopelessly in love, and she a worldweary sensualist.

"Like, you're *positive* they don't know that you were at Joey's the night you said you were sleeping over at my house and they called and you weren't there?"

"They know I was *somewhere*—"

"Oh God," Cleo recalled. "I told your mother you were sound asleep with the worst headache in the world, that you'd actually yakked, so it was definitely a migraine. And five minutes later—"

"—my father's at the door. Please! Do we need a

remembrance of nightmares past?" Adolescence, in Lauren's opinion, was a highly overrated state. Most kids she knew were somewhere between malcontented and suicidal. So how come so many adults looked back on it with such longing? Not her parents, though, and she wanted to ask them why. Because they were teachers? Because somehow they'd retained some memory of the pain? Except to ask them anything was to feel the full power of their gale-force sincerity. Sit down, Lauren. That's a good question. Let me think about it. Oh God, their decency wiped her out.

"*Your* nightmare, Lauren? Like, how about the world's greatest trauma for me? I have him for U.S. History and I'm borderline between a B and a C. So he says, 'Are your parents home, Cleo?' So I say, even though I'm shitting a pile of bricks and totally petrified, 'They went up to Vermont at the last minute, Mr. Miller, to see the leaves changing.' Then he says, 'I want to see my daughter. *Now.*' I mean, was that not the worst moment in my life?"

"I'm not saying they totally didn't know I was with Joey—"

"I told them you were with a whole bunch of kids and—"

"They're not stupid. Right? College graduates. Master's degrees. The *Times* crossword puzzle. But they didn't know what was going on with Joey, because I took my mother aside and did this big mother-daughter confiding scene. Weeping buckets. I told her I was racked with guilt because I'd let Joey touch me on top but not below the waist—" Lauren shook her head in sadness at her parents' gullibility. Cleo chuckled compassionately. "And she believed me." Had she really, though? Her mother was a teacher, for God sakes. She should know kids better.

Was she a fool, believing a story like that? Or was she just pretending not to know, taking the easy way out? "What can I tell you? They think they're sophisticated because they listen to MacNeil-Lehrer—"

"Who?"

"News guys on public television. Anyway, they're incredibly naive. My parents, not MacNeil-Lehrer. They lead such constricted little civil servant lives, but they need to feel a sense of mastery. You know what I mean? So they try to convince themselves they're onto everything I'm doing."

"Then how come your mother gave you that speech about condoms?"

"Just, you know, from some teacher-education seminar. Not because she knew about me and Joey."

But at her high school graduation, when Lauren stood at the podium to receive the Shorehaven Veterans of Foreign Wars plaque and three hundred dollars for her prizewinning essay, "Korea: Remembering the Forgotten War"—after also having won the Belle Harding Pappas Memorial Award for Excellence in English and the Nassau County Coalition Against Domestic Violence's Citation of Distinction for her volunteer work—she began saying, "I'd like to thank the Veterans of Foreign Wars . . ." As she searched for her ex-boyfriend Joey in the turbulent blue sea of caps and gowns, she spotted her mother and father. Giving each other the Look. An instant later, they turned back to look at her. Tears of pride were streaming down both their faces, and Lauren Miller got so choked up with love for them and for their goodness that despite having drafted a gracious yet economical twenty-four-word acceptance, the only thing she could say was "Thank you."

*    *    *

Even when she was a toddler, Lauren's favorite question, indeed her only question, was "Why?" She genuinely wanted to know. As a pigtailed child, she'd say, "What's going on here?" True, for a couple of years of her adolescence she was too sullen to actually pose questions to adults, but throughout she remained infernally curious. She read, she listened, she watched. That was her nature. And so she became a reporter.

A newspaper reporter—although she was insightful enough to sense that it wasn't the shrewdest career choice. In her senior year at Columbia College, when she was a member of the editorial board of the *Spectator*, she told her boyfriend of three years, Jon Nathan, "Sometimes I worry that the end of journalism as we know it is coming. I have all the glib answers, but what I really want to understand is *why* it's come to this."

Jon smiled slightly. She could tell what he was thinking: Lauren is babbling again. He was the cool one, the comp lit student. He was always acting Europeanly, amused by any show of emotion that was not chilled by intellect before being served up. But Lauren believed that all his Continental cool was simply a sophisticated form of the midwestern-German-Jewish low-key style he'd been born to. She, the woman, the New Yorker, the student of history and political science, was the Designated Emotional One of the two: good old Lauren, always carrying on over some issue or other. "'The end of journalism as we know it,'" Jon repeated. "How Edward R. Murrowesque. What does it mean?"

"The end of newspapers. More than that, even. The end of the printed word. I'll be washed up. A dinosaur with a notebook. Watch: At some point in the twenty-first century, we'll fall into a state of permanent semiliteracy. A picture really will be worth a thousand words."

"Who's the 'we'?"

"Americans. And because of our cultural dominance, the world will follow."

"I see." With his black, curling hair, full, kissable mouth and irresistibility to women, Jon resembled Lord Byron so closely that all he was missing was the cape—and the passion. Lauren understood cool people often derived enough heat and light from anxious partners that they had no need to emit any of their own. Still this knowledge didn't stop her from trying, desperately, to break through his ice and locate the ninety-eight-and-six-tenths-degree heart she was convinced beat within. Because if she couldn't get there first, and find it and lay claim to it, Jon could sell tickets to all the women eager to take up the quest themselves.

But with Jon, it was always more a matter of mind than of heart, and Lauren knew he felt she was over-endowed in the heart department and less than gifted in the mind. His disengaged "I see"s to her contentions made her wildly eager to prove she really was serious enough to be worthy of such a brainy boyfriend. Inevitably, she'd start jabbering. "You *will* see, Jon. Nobody's going to read a block of print longer than a paragraph at any one sitting." Know when to shut up, she admonished herself. As a *Spectator* reporter, she had already learned the value of self-restraint, how a calm, anticipatory expression—a cocked head, a raised eyebrow—made all but the most worldly subjects release a torrent of words. But as always with Jon, her own words surged, each shoving the one before it out of the way in its eagerness to impress and ingratiate. "You're the one studying literature. Doesn't it make you nervous that it's almost always our parents' generation saying the book is *much* better than the movie? How often do you hear that sentence from people our age?"

"You're wrong. Everybody loves Shakespeare." He pointed to the dome of night sky that arched over West 100th Street. Up on the roof of his off-campus apartment, the air was soft. The geraniums someone had planted gave off an alluring-repulsive scent, part flower, part skunk. Lauren wasn't sure if by gesturing toward the heavens Jon was saying it was getting late and chilly and they ought to get started messing around if they wanted romance under the stars, or he was on the verge of quoting one of those lengthy "goddess of the night" passages he was given to. At the beginning of these recitations, she was invariably bewitched—oh, the exquisiteness of the language—but by the time he finally got around to rosy-fingered dawn, her mind would have drifted to the reading she hadn't done for her Elites in Twentieth-Century America class or to how great a bowl of Raisin Bran would be before she went to sleep, especially since, after her Everyday Life in Postwar America class, she'd stopped at a really good fruit stand on Broadway and bought a perfect peach.

She replied, "The reason everyone's so crazy about Shakespeare is because they don't have to read Shakespeare anymore. Shakespeare's a movie."

"Maybe," Jon said, stretching out on the blanket he'd brought up, making clear this was not a discussion that interested him. But for the first few long kisses, even as his hand drifted to her breast, she kept on making her point, albeit in her head: Magazines were mimicking the jump and jazz of MTV. Newspapers were mimicking magazines: sidebars in sidebars, paragraphs tossed out for bar graphs. Lauren could feel her future shrinking. There would be many, many more journalists than there were jobs.

Not television jobs: plenty of those, for the entire world was tuned in. Even Lauren herself would turn to TV for information, and she'd felt the familiar comfort of having that information instantly analyzed. Americans were leading the world in showing that full attention was necessary only for the one hundred eighty seconds it took to report any single event—although admittedly, if that story concerned a plane crash, a cataclysmic meteorological event or the murder of an American white child, the audience would stay with the coverage till their eyeballs dried to dust.

As that night gave way to morning, as more nights made way for more days, as Lauren dropped by the placement office week after week, she learned that her intuition was correct: with newspapers folding or downsizing, there were fewer jobs. Too bad. People like her needed not only to track down the facts but also to write about them in order that she—and everyone else—might understand what was truly going on. She was not, as the placement officer delicately explained, in an expanding market situation.

Which was why, three months after that night on the roof, two months after she was graduated from Columbia with, admittedly, a grade-point average that would not knock the socks off the Human Resources Department at the *Houston Chronicle* (and one month after Jon wrote to her from the University of Barcelona, where he was studying medieval Spanish literature on a summer fellowship, to explain that he had fallen in love at first sight with a

Torres Naharro scholar named Elena and—"I wish I could find a way to say this without hurting you"—had made her Señora Nathan), Lauren took the only job offered to her, as a reporter for the *Brandywine Blade,* a new weekly in suburban Wilmington, Delaware.

The *Blade* had taken over the lease of a long-gone Aamco Transmission franchise, and the office reeked of ancient grease. But she was too young to yearn for the stink of ink, and besides, she was ecstatic. A real reporter! She threw herself into covering school board skirmishes, fire district feuds and the metamorphosis of Gigi's Hair and Nail Salon into the Serenity Day Spa. But the *Blade* was a small paper. Some weeks, Lauren made up her own assignments just to keep occupied. Those times when she did bring in a good story, it would often be chopped in half or dropped entirely if a last-minute ad came in—or a photo from the editor's next-door neighbor's church's Strawberry Festival. Although she tried to keep busy, there were weeks when she finished all her work in six hours.

She made peppy calls to her parents—"God, I haven't had a second to myself! I haven't shaved my legs in *eons.* I look like Chewbacca." But in fact, Cardwell's Funeral Home down the street was livelier than the *Blade.* Forget all those thrilling forties movies, Lauren counseled herself: Not a single gum-cracking reporter or delightfully demented photog was hanging around this city room, a space so cavernous that its two computer terminals looked like dollhouse furniture. Her editor, the much-put-upon president of the local orchid society, communicated mostly by phone and fax from her greenhouse.

For the first time in her life, she felt not merely lonely but bereft. She joined an aerobics class and a book discussion group at the library, hoping to meet some women her age. She took a course in basic auto repair, called What's Under the Hood?; volunteered at the hospital and led story hour in the pediatrics ward; and, dutifully, put in an hour on Tuesdays and Fridays at an eighteenth-century alehouse said to be Wilmington's favorite bar for clever twenty-somethings. While she did overhear some lively conversations, she was never asked for her two cents. Once, when she threw in her two cents anyway, the looks she got were clear: We don't need your two cents. She never made a single friend. Not even a warm acquaintance.

After eighteen months, Lauren moved on, to a South Carolina daily, the *Greenville Journal-Times,* where she had two beats: business ("Leroy Lovecroft of Palmetto Awning and Canopy met with officials of the Small Business Administration last Thursday . . .") and petty crime ("After last week's plague of graffiti at the Ravenswood Mall, Detective Nelson J. Wylie announced . . ."). She started dating a botanist she'd met when covering a Southern Soybean Growers convention. He looked like Bono. However, he was obsessed with writing a textbook, the response, he explained darkly, to sinister misrepresentations in *Basic Soybean Strategies*, and after seven Saturday-night dates, he told her he was sorry, he wished he could be a more balanced person, but he had to choose between writing and sex. When they parted, he shook her hand.

Baseball season sustained her. Every night the Greenville Braves were in town, she headed to the municipal stadium. As the day's heat rose, making the infield shimmer, she watched the home team play the Chattanooga Lookouts or the Birmingham Barons. Her first game only made her long for home, not just for her father, master of meaningless sports statistics, guardian of the old Brooklyn Dodgers flame, but for the New York mishmash of fans at Shea Stadium. Glancing around her in Greenville, she saw only two colors of faces, white and black. And bad sportswear, as if every ugly shirt in America had migrated to that particular ballpark in South Carolina.

But as the season progressed, Lauren grew less harsh in her judgment. She became familiar with the players—with the right fielder's emotional fragility, the catcher's worrisome metacarpus—and got to know the other regular fans as well. In Delaware, she'd learned that a hello, how are you, from a stranger was not, as in New York, a sign of psychosis and had learned to respond politely to such a greeting: I'm fine, thanks. How are you? Still, she viewed these salutations as somehow impolite. In New York, a nice passerby left other passersby alone.

New York etiquette was slightly different for seated strangers. Another fan at Shea Stadium might respectfully say, "Isn't that John Franco something?" and she would respond, "I should be that cool under pressure." A conversation about relief pitchers might ensue. Likewise, a person sitting beside her on the subway might speak about some neutral, weatherlike topic or even disclose a personal calamity such as a philandering spouse or a sick child: cheap talk therapy for the cost of a token, and the stranger could rest assured that the conversation and the relationship would end at West Thirty-fourth Street. Lauren, in fact, received far more than her fair share of these confidences. She did not know if it was some inner sympathy she projected or that she simply looked like a reporter—a person who expected to hear sad stories—but she wound up listening to numerous

tales of vile landlords, cruel bosses and perfidious significant others.

However, all these encounters had left her unprepared
for the irresistibility of the southern charm of intimate
strangers: Why, hello there! Hi! I'm Randi Lee Brinker-
hoff! It's you, back again and looking fresh as a daisy! Hi!
My name's Sonny Dobbins. Good to see you again! Why,
hello! Didn't you just want to stagger with that heat
today? Hi! That's a real pretty barrette you got in your
hair. Might I ask where you bought it? Oh my, New
York! No wonder it's so fashionable! . . . How could she
keep her cool in the face of that? So while she was scoring
close to zip with men, and not much higher with her
peers, she developed a circle of baseball friends: George in
electric bulbs, Yancy the chicken fryer, Nola the secretary,
Bobby and Bobbi, the brother and sister dental hygien-
ists. Why, hi, Lauren! Look, Nola, it's Lauren! Here, Lauren, have some peanuts.

None of her group ever discussed why they never
missed a home game; the accepted truth was that they
were the Braves' best fans and that was that. Why they
never stayed home a single night when the Braves were at
home, what they did during the Braves' road trips, why
they never saw each other outside the ballpark, why they
never mentioned any other friends, was nobody's business, perhaps not even their own. Each knew what the
others did for a living, although Lauren suspected that
Sonny's claim of owning a textile mill was an exaggeration. She knew she could find out the truth with one
phone call, but the truth did not matter. Sonny's compan-
ionship and his knowledge of AA ball did.

"Oh my! Oh my!" he was declaring, rising from his
seat on the aisle. He was a large man, given to large jew-

elry. A heavy gold cross on a thick gold-link chain hung in the V of his open shirt, and a gold ring with a great sparkler that could have been diamond or zircon glittered beneath the night lights. "Oh my!" As he rose, so did all the other fans. With two men on base, one of the Braves had smashed what looked like a line drive to center field. There was an enormous intake of air as the entire stadium held its breath. Going, going—

Lauren was on her feet in the row behind Sonny, her eye on the ball. One eye, because the other one detected a slight movement in the area of Sonny's back pocket. Perhaps if she'd been a South Carolinian, her full attention would have been focused on the Braves, but she was not, and so caught a fast flash of some metal that was not gold.

"Sonny!" she called, but the fans were howling their anguish as the hated Carolina Mudcats' center fielder, a human pogo stick, jumped up and cheated the Braves out of three runs. Sonny did not hear her. His right rear pocket flapped down over his buttock, having been slashed by a razor, his wallet removed.

In not more time than it took for the razor to flash, Lauren was out of her seat, handing off her purse to Bobbi, pushing past Bobby, moving to the aisle. Who? Where? No one was racing off, but a slim young man in neat khakis and a plaid button-down shirt was casually mounting the stairs, hands in his pockets, as if going to get himself a cold beer.

He glanced behind him and saw her. His head was shaped like an eggplant, bulbous on top, tapering down to his chin; his neck looked too thin a stem to hold such weight. She kept climbing. "Excuse me," she said, moving past him. She sensed him doing a once-over for the instant they were on the same step: no purse/money and credit card must be in pocket/jeans too tight/forget about it. Going faster, rushing now, she finally saw a security guard, a man in his late fifties who moved as if he had eaten too many free hot dogs.

"That guy in the plaid shirt," she said, knowing to slow her New York speech enough so it would be intelligible to him. "Over there. Just picked a pocket. Be careful, he has a razor." The presumptive pickpocket sensed something, because as he turned and ambled past a men's room, his stroll turned into a jog, then a run. The guard, meanwhile, flicked on a walkie-talkie and muttered something so southern she could not make out what it was. Come *on,* she thought, The guy's probably in New Jersey by now.

As if hearing her unspoken criticism, the guard took off as if all the hot dogs were merely fuel for his jets. Whoosh! Away! The pickpocket ran faster. So did the guard, his hand over the gun in his holster. Lauren was right behind him, trying to keep up. Down the ramp, around, toward the exit. And out? No. Three guards waiting there, guns drawn. The pickpocket looked left, looked right, then, slowing down, raised up his hands over his head. One hand was bandaged. Oh God, what if she'd made a mistake? She moved toward him.

"Drop the razor," the first guard shouted.

"It's—" The man tried to speak. Lauren was now standing beside him.

"Drop it!" a guard shouted. "Get away, ma'am!"

"It's taped to his hand," Lauren called out. "The razor. See it? There it is. Don't shoot him. Let him untape it."

"Get back, ma'am!"

"I'm with the *Journal-Times.*" Though this disclosure did not appear to wow the guards, they let Lauren remain near the pickpocket while he nervously picked at the adhesive tape that circled around and around his hand, looking for an edge to pull. Finally, as droplets of sweat dripped into his palm, he found one. "Listen," Lauren said to him, "I'd like to get your story. No, not now. I know now isn't good. But I can come down to the jail later, listen to what you have to say." The tape was thick and tightly wound, so that he looked like a mummy undoing his own wrapping. "Unfortunately," she went on, "I saw you do it. Well, I saw the razor slash the pocket of the man with the gold jewelry. And I see that bulge in your pocket, which I guess is his wallet. I thought you guys worked in pairs, to pass it off. I'd like to hear why you work alone." He was nearing the end of his tape and, Lauren surmised, his rope. "I can't help you in any way except to tell your story. Where you learned to do what you do, what kind of world you came from, what kind of family. I can tell by looking at you—"

"Ma'am," the guard snapped, "I've been patient, but you got to stand back."

"—that you're not a two-bit petty criminal like they're going to try to make you out to be." She felt the guard's hand clunk onto her shoulder, draw her away. "See you later," she called to the pickpocket as the razor dropped to the ground and handcuffs were snapped on.

She returned to her seat to give her companions the news of the loss of Sonny's wallet and its recovery. Then she raced to the parking lot and sped to the jail in time to give an encouraging wave to the pickpocket before he was escorted through the heavy door. The next afternoon, she interviewed him. The following morning, her "The Life and Times of L. Fred Bleiber, Pickpocket" ran on page one. It was enough to get her to Ohio.

At the *Columbus Star*, Lauren got to cover the criminal courts. Here, at last, were reporters to drink with, to talk with, to jog with. She became pals with the paper's restaurant reviewer and ate frequent cilantro-sprinkled dinners. She went out with two men: the administrative assistant to the lieutenant governor, an exuberant fellow with a handlebar mustache, who took her pub crawling, and an assistant professor of electrical engineering at Ohio State, a more placid soul, with whom she began a bird-watching log. Her city editor became so enraptured with her coverage of the Torkelson murders that he gave her fifteen hundred words in the Sunday edition for a review of the case. But by that time she missed New York so much, missed her friends and her family and her family's beagle, Lucy, so dreadfully, that it was a rare night she did not begin to weep when she was brushing her teeth. When she confided this to her kid brother, Adam, he said, So, Lauren, cut the shit and come home.

She mailed out ninety-six résumés, to the *New York Times*, the *Newark Star-Ledger* and *Newsday*, to *Women's Wear Daily*, the *New York Law Journal* and *Crain's New York Business*—as well as to the only paper in the New York tri-state area that turned out to have an opening, the *Jewish News*. So what if her knowledge of her roots was limited to her mother's chicken soup and her father's penchant for obscure Jewish sports celebrities: Red Holzman, sure, Lauren, easy, everybody knows him, but betcha a buck you can't name me the sport Ken Holtzman played.

Jews? Jews. What did she care? She was going home.

# The
# Americans

# 8

From the parking lot, the First Christian Church and Bible School just outside the little town of McBride, Wyoming, had seemed foreign to Charlie, though perhaps that was because the cross sat atop a steeple that looked like the Eiffel Tower painted white. Yet once he'd walked downstairs, he knew it. He had been in a thousand such basements. Its dreary Masonite walls sealed in deoxygenated, Lysol-scented, overcaffeinated air. The place had seen too many election days. Too many Alcoholics and Overeaters Anonymouses and Stamp Clubs and Tickled Pink Quilting Bees had paid twenty bucks for a roof and squeaky bridge chairs.

Now it was Wrath's turn. His, too, because the purpose of Special Agent Charlie Blair's going undercover was to get some sense if this indeed was the group behind the fizzle of a bomb in Mike Pearlstein's Big Elk Video store in Jackson Hole. The FBI's informant, Russ Dillard, had sworn it was. If so, was the crime a one-shot act of lunacy or swagger that could end in the leader's or leaders' conviction for violating a fellow citizen's civil rights? Or was this act just the tip of an iceberg that would loom larger and more dangerous the closer to it he came?

Charlie sat in the metal chair and rubbed his hands together. Not from eagerness. Not from nervousness: He was so jumpy, mere hand rubbing would be pointless. No, he was fighting the nearly irresistible urge to stroke the new beard the FBI had made him grow: Hey, Blair, we're not going to let you anywhere near a location you grew up in without some sort of disguise. He'd thought they were kidding. "I'm going to be way the hell in the sticks, forty, fifty miles away. And I haven't been there in years, except for a quick visit every now and then. Besides, I used to have a nice nose and now it's mashed all over my face. Who's going to . . . ?" "A beard." In three weeks, it had come in surprisingly lush, as if it had been waiting for years for permission to break through. Black, although here and there in the bush were a few gray hairs. Clean-shaven, he had to admit, he looked like who he was—a guy who'd been in the FBI for ten years. Now the unsmiling face he saw in the mirror each morning appeared somewhere between pissed off and slightly deranged.

The man standing at the front of the basement did not look the least bit deranged. "Let's look at the three races," he suggested to his audience. "There are some men of God—fine, upstanding men—who will swear on a stack of Bibles"—Vernon Ostergard, the leader of Wrath, allowed himself a small smile—"that members of the yellow race and the black race don't have souls." He massaged his chin with the first three fingers of his hand. "Just like animals have no souls."

Vernon Ostergard wasn't at all wrathful as he spoke. And though he had the clear, expensive voice of an announcer in a Buick commercial, he did not seem to be trying to sell anything to his meager audience. On the contrary, Charlie Blair noticed, the man's excellent voice was actually muted. There was even a hint of a stammer in "Just like animals," as if Ostergard was still hoping against hope that someone else could come up to where he was standing and take over the burden of telling people what was really going on in America.

God is supposed to be everywhere, Charlie thought, but He's not spending a minute more than He has to down here. Not that the basement of the First Christian felt evil. It was just gloomy beyond redemption. The windows, barely a foot below the ceiling, had gone unwashed so long that even the harsh sodium vapor light from the parking lot could not penetrate their murk. Nonetheless, he had to admit, Vernon Ostergard seemed to outshine the place.

Strolling back and forth and back again over four feet of asphalt-tile floor, thumbs hooked into the pockets of his nicely laundered gray corduroys, the head of Wrath was less orator than Mr. Average American. There hadn't been much in Ostergard's file, but whatever was in the printouts had made him seem to Charlie like a run-of-the-mill Militia Christian Identity White Supremacist Posse Comitatus lunatic, leadership division. One arrest for arms violation, one for breach of the peace, one for fraud by check. Trial on the check charge, hung jury, case dropped. Yet as closely as he looked, Charlie could not detect a nut. No, Vernon Ostergard was coming across sound as a dollar to his audience, the way a respected uncle would—decent, kind, but pulling no punches.

"When these folks preach about the yellow and the black, they keep giving the same example: 'You can love your dog. Man's best friend and all. You could say your dog's got a personality, even. But who's going to stand up and declare God gave Rover a soul?'"

The rancid-smelling man to Charlie's left, confused by the rhetorical question, began to raise his hand until, realizing he was the only one voting, he pulled his arm tight

against his body. Trying to appear casual, he took to
scraping out the greenish-black crescents from under the
long nails of his left hand with the scraggly nail of his
right pinkie. Dumb and dirty. Precisely what Charlie had
expected to find at a Wrath meeting.

Talking about dirty, if not dumb, where was Russ Dillard, the bureau's crack informant, the Gulf War muni-
tions expert, the guy who allegedly—when pressured to
plant a bomb in the Jewish guy's video store—rigged it
deliberately so it wouldn't blow? Charlie had memorized
Dillard's face, studying mug shots from his arrests on
counts of drug dealing, felonious assault and the botched
bank robbery that had brought him to the FBI's attention. With beard, without beard, long hair, short hair,
Dillard's face was memorable, an elongated oval, like an
egg from a constipated chicken, with as much chin as
forehead. Unmistakable. Unmistakably not in the room.

Ostergard was the surprise, because Dillard had
described him as crazy. Well, if that was true, it was crazy
lite. Not an obvious nutcase, but a guy who had no interests beyond his own bigotry, who had walked out on a
wife and three kids, telling them there were just so many
hours in a day. But here he was, not four feet from Charlie, and not a sign of wackiness. Neat almost to the point
of fastidiousness, a well-pressed red-checked shirt tucked
smoothly into his cords, cuffs buttoned, a man remarkable for his regular-guyness. Neither tall nor short.
Around forty, with the melting jawline of middle age and
a nose that took up a bit too much room on his face.

To Charlie, Ostergard seemed the sort of ordinary guy
you'd spot at six o'clock at a Kentucky Fried in any small
city in America, picking up a bucket of extra-crispy to
bring home to the family. Pleasant. Order a bombing?

This guy? No way. You'd probably even talk to him: about the rain, or how the Nuggets were doing. His thinning brown hair, parted and combed casually over to the side, was neither shaved into the buzz cut of some sicko stockpiling M16s and Dinty Moore's Beef Stew in preparation for Armageddon nor Brylcreemed flat into Hitler hair. Scary? Not in the least. Hysterical? There wasn't a glint of psycho shine in Ostergard's gentle gray eyes. In fact, those eyes were his most remarkable feature. More than gentle, they were downright loving Christian eyes. You wanted them to look upon you.

"And some of you have heard certain ministers saying the black race isn't human, that they're beasts created prior to man," he was saying, a little sadly. "Or that blacks are cohorts of Satan. Now listen, folks. I'm no preacher. I'm just . . . Vern."

Ostergard, Charlie could see, did not lay it on too thick. No showy shake of the head, no tsk-tsk leading you to understand he believed these preachers were misguided. Nevertheless—so subtly that although Charlie tried, he could not pick up a gesture, not even a blink—the man was somehow able to communicate he disapproved of this kind of talk but was simply too righteous to come out and accuse men of the cloth of being, well, a little nuts. He also made you feel that he, Vernon Ostergard—and not those wrongheaded ministers—was the man to listen to when you wanted to know the truth about race.

Charlie rested his chin on the pedestal of his hand and glanced to his right. Besides the stinky guy on his left, the audience was mainly losers—regular losers plus a couple of skinhead losers. One of the skinheads had a blue lightning bolt tattooed on his scalp over his ear—in case he changed his mind and decided to be an accountant. The other was scarily skinny. On a below-zero night, all he wore were jeans, boots and a leather vest over his bare skin. A large iron cross hung to his sternum, so his ribs appeared to radiate from its center.

The oldest of the regular losers, a man at the end of his forties, wore a dark-brown sports jacket and tan slacks. His tie was unknotted, his white shirt open two buttons' worth, but despite the attempt at looking casual, he sat with the arms-tight-to-the-body posture of the deeply pissed, galled that he had guessed wrong about white supremacist fashion. The others, like Charlie, looked like workingmen, or men looking for work. One of them was heavy, with the greasy face of a chronic potato chip eater. Another, small, had the cute, snub-nosed face you'd see on a boy baby doll. His clothes were oddly baggy, as if he'd lost weight or was wearing some full-sized guy's things. Charlie thought the other two were probably ranch hands, except they had the unfocused look of men who hadn't worked for a while. One was blonder than blond, the other so dark-skinned Charlie couldn't see how he'd passed the Wrath whiteness test.

From his quick glance at the license plates on the cars and trucks in the lot, he'd noted nearly all of them were local vehicles from Teton County, although none bore the low numbers of old-time residents. Of all the men, only two looked as if they woke at the same time each day, shaved, ate breakfast and went off to work. Unlike Ostergard, however, these two did not seem like average Joes. They were far too alert. While their bodies faced front, their heads swiveled slightly. Charlie could feel their eyes working, like lizards' on the lookout for insects. Clearly they were Ostergard's men, scrutinizing the audience, checking out each man's reactions. Filling a couple of the empty seats, too, while they were at it. And acting as bodyguards. One looked so boyishly soft he was almost girlish. The other was short and compact, with the sloping shoulders and tree-trunk neck of a serious bodybuilder.

Except for those two, the rest of the listeners reminded him of guys he'd gone to Jackson High with. Not his buddies. His friends had fallen into two groups: the jocks and the diligent guys who worked a job or two after school to help their families or save for college. No, Wrath was pulling in the losers, the boys who never once knew the answer in class, the boys who, at best, could dig up one fellow loser to have lunch with, the boys who dropped out after junior year. Here they were now, aged nineteen or forty-nine, undereducated, under- or unemployed.

But not Vernon Ostergard. He was no loser. True, not a bright, shiny winner. But a nice guy with a kindly, bigtoothed smile. A good neighbor who'd help you retile your shower, who'd remember to ask how that cold of yours was coming along. He seemed genuinely decent.

But if that was true, how come he was up there, talking such shit?

"Well, let them sermonize about the blacks and the yellows. You know and I know they're not the big issue. I'm here tonight to talk to you about the white race—and sure, we *do* spell it with a capital *W*. How come? Because we're special. God created us last for a reason. He had special plans for us. Now, what does that mean to me and you?" He was looking directly at Charlie.

Easy, Charlie warned himself. It's okay. He's never laid eyes on me before. Maybe all these other guys drive over to McBride once a week for free coffee and doughnuts, and I'm the only new face. He's going to check me out and he's going to wonder—because if the size of this audience here is any indication, Wrath's not packing them in. Still, as Vernon's gentle eyes studied his, Charlie was torn between wanting those eyes on him and wanting to look away to avoid their straight-to-the-soul search. Lord, don't let me sweat. He was afraid of what those gray eyes would find in his own blue ones. They probed so deep, as if Ostergard could see through the openings of the pupils right into Charlie's head.

Suddenly, Charlie felt such an explosion of adrenaline it made him queasy. If he'd been edgy before, he now became almost uncontrollably jittery, primed for action. His legs ached for want of movement. His body was ready for trouble, set to spring, the way it always got when he was about to move in and make an arrest. Except there was nothing to do now, so all that adrenaline kept swirling inside him like a goddamn tornado, making him want to puke. He forced himself to stare back at Ostergard, right into *his* pupils—although Charlie could see nothing beyond two tiny black circles.

"It means," Ostergard was instructing Charlie, as if they were the only ones in that basement, "God created *us* in every single way superior to the other two races. Do you know what His plan is for us?" Charlie felt himself swallow, grateful the beard was just full enough to hide his Adam's apple's nervous bobbing up and down. He found himself shaking his head: No, I don't know what His plan is. Tell me, Vern. "We are the leaders and teachers for the blacks and the yellows."

He is good, Charlie realized. Better than good, because by talking right to me he's making me feel I'm worthy of his attention, that I'm a big shot. And the awful thing was, for a second, basking in the comfort of Ostergard's gentle gray gaze, he did feel a flash of manly pride, as though he'd only tried out for reserves but was told he was so fine he'd made varsity. Damn, I'm *white*!

The next second, he thought about Dick Alexander, his buddy since the Academy, the guy who worked night and day to save Charlie's ass after his screwup in that bank robbery case, the guy who had managed to keep a letter of censure out of Charlie's file, the guy who was godfather to Morning, the guy who was, yes, blacker than the ace of spades. And Charlie felt like the world's biggest shit. What was inside him that even for a second he was capable of such arrogant, dumb-ass prejudice? This wasn't the subtle bigotry you pick up in a country where race matters; this I'm-white stuff was low-class, stupid shit.

As Ostergard withdrew his attention—with apparent reluctance—Charlie watched him go on to gaze just as deeply into each man's eyes, one loser after another, as he explained to every man in the audience his innate superiority. And Charlie saw how each head lifted, proud, how each pair of nostrils flared at the awesome thought that God had chosen its possessor to be white.

"But how do whites come off in the Jew-owned, Jew-controlled media?" Ostergard shook his head in sadness, and Charlie marveled at how untheatrical, how genuine, this heavyhearted shake of the head seemed. He could sense the men around him inching forward in their seats. They all yearned to stand and give this fine, troubled man, their Vern, a reassuring pat on his shoulder: Don't despair, Vern. I'm with you. "All of you watch TV. What do you see? A racially mixed couple. Pillars of the community. Not just accepted. *Liked*. Everyone wants to be friends with them, don't they? And the same goes for a black college professor or judge or doctor. Or how about a sensitive and gifted homosexual? A wonderful guy—right?—who only wants the same thing all of us want: a home, a family. Or—this is the latest wrinkle—the poor but honest and hardworking illegal alien from Mexico. Ever ask yourself, Where does all this stuff come from?"

Now, once more, Ostergard was looking directly at him. Charlie did what his instincts told him to do, which fortunately coincided with what the psychologist at Quantico had suggested. You know how they tell women to play hard to get? the shrink had asked. Well, that's the ticket with these types. Don't be too easy. So, unlike the men on either side of him, Charlie did not bob his head up and down, saying, Yes! Come on! Tell us, Vern!

Jesus,. why couldn't he stop pumping adrenaline? What a jerk he'd been! Desperate for a ticket home. It had seemed a piece of cake back there in Cheyenne: Hey, I'll go undercover. High as a kite after passing the psychological tests for an undercover agent. Exhilarated by the training. How come it had stopped being a piece of cake so fast? They'd warned him, Charlie, your nuts aren't made of iron. You're going to feel afraid. So soon, though?

Objectively, the worst danger here would come from overconfidence. He was at a public meeting. Real danger would come later. Later, if and when they accepted him in Wrath, because he knew these guys were governed by different laws. We might all live in the USA, but theirs was an alternate America in which the FBI was part of the army of occupation. Ostergard was one of a new breed: not the old-time crazies who thought they could see under the bed the boogeyman that the government had missed. No, he and all these new-time crazies thought the government itself was the boogeyman.

Admittedly, Vernon Ostergard did look like good old Uncle Normal, but what kind of normal guy devoted his life to being white? (What do you do for a living, friend? Oh, I'm white.) Spent day after day, year after year, griping about Jews controlling TV, getting irate that blacks are portrayed as educated on situation comedies?

"On the other hand," Ostergard was saying, "a white racist—who, really, is any racially conscious white person upset by the off-the-charts rise in miscegenation, who worries about the darkening racial situation in America—is shown *at best* as a bigot, despised by the other characters. At worst? You know: a dangerous psychopath." Ostergard chuckled, a sad, knowing chuckle. "And obsessed with firearms. Isn't the white racist 'gun nut' the biggest stereotype on TV and in movies these days?"

Smello, the guy next to Charlie, chuckled back. They all did, but as the evening grew longer and Ostergard lectured on, Charlie, although still amazed at the man's sheer likability, became increasingly restless. His adrenaline ebbed and receded. His ass grew sore. His left leg tingled, then fell asleep altogether. "The Jewish control of the mass media is the single most important threat we face today. Not just in America. In the world." Charlie clenched his teeth to curb a yawn. He sensed Ostergard was onto him, actually observing his jaw tightening. Well, that could work for him. Knowing he had to be careful not to seem too thrilled too fast, what better way to say "It's your job to thrill me" than to get a little glassy-eyed? And who the hell wouldn't, after an hour and a half of hearing about Sumner Redstone and

Katharine Meyer Graham and Joseph Lelyveld, name after name of Jews and Jewesses—Ostergard seemed to love saying "Jewesses"—who controlled the media?

Could this be the guy who ordered Russ Dillard to set a bomb? Charlie kept asking himself to keep awake. But no one with half a brain could keep awake listening to this because it didn't add up. If the Jews were so powerful, how come they couldn't swat a fly like Vernon Ostergard, shut him up permanently? Where was their international conspiracy when they needed it? Couldn't the guys who invented the Uzi take out a dozen assholes in Wyoming?

But if all the white, Jew, black crap was numbing him, another part of Charlie remained hyperalert. It wasn't just that they had ordered a bomb set in a video store. He, Charlie Blair, was walking a fine line. Sure, he looked like one of them, because, in truth, he was. Wyoming born, Wyoming bred. Whiter than white. Well, a little Indian, a little Jew, mixed in generations back, but white enough to be Wrath's poster boy. He belonged. But unlike Smello and the others in the audience, Charlie was not a loser—and he knew this was what drew Ostergard's attention. Maybe even his suspicion.

The collation after Ostergard's talk reminded Charlie of the ultimate nightmare sixth-grade party, where boys and girls stand on opposite sides of a punch bowl of Kool-Aid, frozen, by the awareness of their own lack of cool, paralyzed by having absolutely nothing to say. No, this was even worse than sixth grade. The silence in the First Christian Church and Bible School basement was so overwhelming you could hear the scrape of plastic spoons stirring sugar inside Styrofoam cups. Standing, the losers in the audience looked sorrier than they had sitting. Even judged by loser standards, these guys didn't make it: Pustules instead of pimples. Flabby-assed. Pigeon-toed. Wall-eyed. Charlie moved far from Smello, who was sprinkling doughnut crumbs and splotching coffee onto the stains on his gray sweatshirt.

The only person anyone spoke to was Ostergard. In the silence, Charlie could overhear every mutter and mumble. "Liked what you said tonight, Vern," one said. "Too bad there ain't more like you, Vern," another remarked when the warmth of Ostergard's handshake was still with him. "Too gol-durn bad." To one at a time, the head of Wrath bestowed his gifts: a fast but not discourteous smile, a few words of elaboration: "The Jewish leaders are planning to use the other races to destroy the white race." And "ZOG isn't coming, Hank. It's *here*."

Charlie observed a miniature Ostergard and Smello reflected in the shining metal of the coffee urn. It was not an old, beat-up electric perk with a dent and a cruddy spout, the kind that belonged in a church basement. No, Wrath had a great, shiny, domed machine, such as you'd see at a wedding with a fancy caterer. Smello kept moving in, Ostergard kept backing up; in their silvery reflection in the urn, each of their steps looked like the beginning of a dance that never got under way.

After Smello, Charlie realized that Ostergard was moving through the group with the ease of a seasoned politician, winning them over and getting rid of them with speedy efficiency. He shook each man's hand, seeming sad to let it go yet giving them no choice but to say goodbye and leave the basement. The two associates, Charlie realized, had slipped away. Suddenly, the leader was shaking his next-to-last hand. Then he and Charlie were alone.

"Howdy. I'm Vernon Ostergard."

"Howdy," Charlie said. "Darrell Frederickson." He felt his hand in the grip of a perfect shake: firm but not crushing, not too damp, not too dry. His "Frederickson" had come out gravelly, although he'd practiced saying his new name on and off during the four-hundred-mile drive from Cheyenne.

"Haven't met you before, have I?" Ostergard inquired.

"No."

"You from around here, Darrell?"

"Riverton."

"You know Greg Fleming?"

"Can't say I do." Most likely, Charlie figured, there was no Greg Fleming.

"What are you doing in Jackson Hole, if I can ask?"

Charlie decided that at this rate, playing hard to get would take him another year, so he offered Ostergard a friendly smile. "Found a job. Can't beat that."

"No, you can't. What is it you do?"

"Mechanic. Auto mechanic." Four days earlier, he'd cruised service stations asking about work and finally found a job at a Chevron twenty-five miles east of Jackson, on the road to McBride. The owner, a man named Bill, had inquired about his last garage job. It was a while back, Charlie told him. Me and the boss had words, so no use you calling for a reference. Bill replied, What did you do after that, Darrell? Wanted to get away some, Charlie explained. Drove a cab over in Lincoln, Nebraska. But being a mechanic . . . it's kind of in your blood.

From the time in high school when he got his first car, a 1968 Dodge Dart, Charlie understood what was happening under the hood. He'd fixed machinery on the ranch, so there wasn't much to learning to do his own repairs. He'd always been a pretty fair amateur mechanic. Yet he realized that if he had to do anything more than simple jobs for Bill—minor tune-ups, changing front brake pads—he could be up shit's creek without a paddle. However, he needed a cover, and he couldn't risk doing what he did well—ranch work. In that world he might be recognized. Or it might stir up too much inside him, and he couldn't afford to get distracted by anger or sorrow. Okay, Bill finally responded, after a long, Wyoming silence. Tell you what: I'll give you, say, half pay for a month— Two weeks, Charlie interrupted. All right, Bill replied. Two weeks as a trial period. If you work out, then full pay.

"Well, Darrell, what did you think?" Ostergard asked Charlie.

"About your talk?" Ostergard nodded. "I guess I'd say"— Charlie paused, pretending to search for the word he'd already chosen—"interesting."

"That's not very good," Ostergard said with a good-natured smile. "'Interesting' puts folks to sleep. I want to wake them up."

"Look, Mr. Ostergard—"

"Vern."

"Okay. It's not that you don't speak real good. It's that I came expecting something else."

"Like what?" Charlie barely felt the touch, but Ostergard's hand was on his shoulder blade, steering him out of the basement, up the stairs.

"That paper that was on my truck, about the meeting. It said something about how government is taking over our lives."

"And that's something you feel, Darrell?"

"Every damn day, to tell you the truth. Probably every

damn hour. But—tell me if I'm wrong—you seemed to be onto something else. About blacks and Jews and stuff. I don't care that much about them. They stay out of my way, I stay out of theirs."

They stood before the door to the parking lot. Ostergard put his hand on the metal bar used to push open the door but then stood still. Slowly, sadly, he shook his head. "But it isn't something else. It's the same thing."

Charlie shrugged. "Sorry, Vern. I guess I just don't get it."

"Who controls the government, Darrell?"

"I guess you wouldn't say Clinton."

"I guess not. It's the Jews. Jews crawling all over the cabinet, that's bad enough. But there's more. When I was talking about them controlling the media, did you really understand what I meant?" Beyond the door, Charlie could hear footsteps—three or four guys—a truck idling, but Ostergard seemed oblivious to their presence. All right, Charlie could understand that if a man got so taken with the sound of his own voice nothing could distract him. But Ostergard didn't seem involved in himself so much as in Charlie, striving to comprehend his doubts, struggling to help Charlie see the beauty in his truth. "By letting the Jews control our news and our entertainment, we're not just letting them steer our politics in the direction they want it to go." He spoke slowly but not at all condescendingly. "We've basically handed over to them control of our government." Charlie nodded: Yes, I'm listening. "They're running the show. The whole show."

"What show is that?"

"The big one. 'Ladies and gentlemen, we bring you the United States of America!' We've given ourselves over to them. But you know and I know nothing's ever enough for them. They've got to have it all. And to get it, they've seized control of the minds and souls of our children so there'll be no one left to fight them, no one left to realize what's happened." He looked sick, but whether from disgust or grief, Charlie couldn't tell. "You have any children, Darrell?"

"A daughter. Good girl. But she's living with my ex. In Colorado. Hardly see her."

"Well, that good girl of yours . . . Did you ever stop and think her attitudes and ideas are being shaped more by Jewish television and Jewish movies than by you or her mother, her teachers, her pastor or any other influence? How old is she?"

"Twelve."

"That's an impressionable age, as I'm sure you know. And what is she learning about the world? It's bad enough the Jew-controlled entertainment media have *already* convinced a whole generation that homosexuality is okay. Quote gays unquote make great neighbors! And while you're at it, what's wrong with white women dating or marrying black men, or with white men marrying Asiatic women? That's what they've got most people believing, that it's okay if we all become brown. Is that what you want for your daughter?"

"No!" Charlie snapped. "Of course not."

"Do you want her taught that all races are equal in ability? In character?"

"That *is* what they're teaching," Charlie said.

"Who is 'they,' Darrell?"

"The schools."

"Who runs the schools?"

"The government," Charlie replied.

"And who runs the government that's taken over our lives?"

"The Jews?"

"ZOG!" Ostergard trumpeted. "It's ZOG, Darrell. Zionist Occupation Government." And as he pushed open the door to leave, he assured Charlie: "We'll talk some more."

There was a gap between the sash and the weatherboard of the single window in Charlie's furnished room, and a thin stream of frigid air blew in, freezing the upper half of his already icy pillow. Each time he slipped into sleep, he'd yank down the thin, pilled quilt protecting the top of his head in order to wrap up his ice-cold feet, so he'd waken from a near-frostbitten ear. The same indraft of ice-cold air made an unceasing *shhhhhh!* sound, as if someone were trying to stop him before he shamed himself by crying out all the misery he felt.

For starters, the shame of his own fear. Because that's what it had been at the meeting. That big quease, those uncontrollable jitters? Pure unadulterated scared shitlessness. For Christ's sake, he'd been an agent for over ten years, been in a couple of really ugly situations. Sure, he'd pumped adrenaline like a wild man those times, but that was when the going was tough. An experienced agent should not be getting that fight-or-flight response the very first day of an assignment that might take months, a year. And what had set him off? No particular threat. Just his own dread.

Next? His stupidity in coming home to Jackson Hole. Oh, there had been that momentary elation, his heart rising like a rocket, lifted off by bliss, as he'd reached Towogote's Path, saw that staggering view, new each time, as if he were the first man ever to see the valley. As he descended, he spotted a raven and rolled down his window to hear the harsh beauty of its laryngitic caw. For a second, the bird dipped down, as if acknowledging his return. Welcome home, Charlie!

Home. Charlie had nearly shouted it aloud to the raven. Hooooome! And then he'd actually laughed, because what popped into his mind was an image of E.T. Not a scene from the movie but what it must have been like for that little guy afterward, when he got back to his own planet. Finally, E.T. felt . . . right. That was exactly how Charlie was feeling in that moment of homecoming: right. Like that cute brown wrinkled guy. Breathing his kind of air, seeing his land, his sky.

Except here he was in this crappy freezer of a room, all someone on half a mechanic's salary would be able to afford. The only place that would take him without some kind of reference, thanks to his jerk-off FBI cover. Listen . . . what's your name? Darrell. Listen, Darrell, a guy from Domestic Terrorism had explained to him, we want 'em to think you've got a past you don't want anyone looking into. You're down on your luck, searching for something—a cause—to latch onto. Know what I mean? We're thinking of giving you a record. What do you want, criminal possession of a firearm? Nah, wait a sec. You're going to Wyoming . . . How about . . . Aggravated assault on a peace officer sound good to you?

This ten-by-twelve freezing hellhole was now his home. This, and Bill's Auto. From the minute he stepped into that church basement and sat down at the Wrath meeting, he couldn't risk going to see his mother or his sister. Couldn't even tell them he was in the area.

His father? No way. Charlie spoke to him, at most,

twice a year. Chuck liked to shoot off his mouth: My son went and became an effing FBI agent. My own flesh and blood sucking on the government tit, an agent for the Fat Boy's Institute. Luckily, the state legislature was in session. Chuck would be in Cheyenne. Or, weekends, holed up with Marissa, his new wife—twenty-four years old— and their new baby in their new house. Charlie had never seen the baby. Probably never would. His own half sister, Demi. Not like half. Named for the actress. D'*mee* Blair. Jesus H. Christ. But who was he to roll his eyes at names, when he'd gone along with his wife, Stacey, in naming their daughter Morning?

They'd been in bed the night he agreed, the place in which, in the early years of their marriage, he'd never been able to deny Stacey anything. She'd been so hot then, even in her ninth month. That throaty voice in the dark, her breasts enormous, like some pagan love goddess. If it was a boy he would be William, for his grandfather, but they were still stuck on If it's a girl. He wanted Lois, for his grandmother. Stacey would have none of it. Charlie, she said, Morning is *the* most beautiful name. He said, It sounds like Mourning. As in bereaved. What are you going to do, Stacey, put her in black Pampers? Charlie baby, she murmured—and with her rough, sexy voice she could get away with calling him baby without sounding phony—it's unique. Morning Blair. Like Tuesday Weld. Nobody will ever forget it. Maybe they'll just call her Morning, like Cher and Madonna. He'd said, far too lightly, Great, but what if she's just a regular girl, not a star? What if she wants to be a nurse? I can *feel* it, Stacey answered him, hugging her belly. It's the most amazing thing. I *know* this baby is going to do something great. Maybe not acting or singing, but something. Before he knew what was happening, she was kissing him, taking his hand and putting it on her hot, love-goddess breast, and as one thing led to another, without another word he had somehow agreed to have a daughter who not only was called Morning but also had an appointment with destiny.

Each weekend that he drove to Colorado Springs to see Morning, it broke his heart. Beside the balloon of a woman his wife had become, his daughter was two-dimensional, a stick figure. Four feet nine inches, eighty-five pounds! As if Stacey, once again, had begun eating for the two of them. But Morning was twelve, for God's sake. She should be on her way to becoming a woman.

No! Don't give me that crap about her being petite, he'd shouted at Stacey in one of their Saturday-night fights. I'm tall, you're five six. You're *always* so damn negative about her, Charlie! I am not! I love her. She's a great kid. But she's not a world-class athlete, and you're pushing her— You can go to hell, Charlie, always making me out to be the worst kind of stage mother! Listen to me, Stace: Morning is not great. She's just good. And we both know that on the ice, good isn't good enough. Stacey shouted back: Coach says she's Olympic material! And Charlie, red-faced, fists clenched, blasted at her: That son of a bitch isn't going to tear up his meal ticket, is he? *Is* he? Except theirs were whispered shouts, because neither had the heart to waken the child who had come home from the rink with legs quivering with fatigue, lips chalk white. Their star.

He'd stayed over one Sunday night in January and taken Morning out to the House of Pancakes after her six A.M. lesson. She'd had three sips of juice and the top of a bran muffin. Through her bloodless skin, which saw no light of day, Charlie could make out the separate convexities of the radius and ulna of her forearm. Right from the restaurant, he'd taken her to a doctor, who said, Well, yes, she's on the small side. But not malnourished. Right, he'd shouted at the doctor. No whispering this time. He really roared. In this damn town, not one of these little girls is being starved to death! They're all going to be Tara fucking Lipinski, God help them. The doctor banged his fist on his desk: Get a grip! Behind the examining room door, Charlie heard Morning sobbing. When she got dressed and came out, she would not meet his eye but kept her head down, although he couldn't miss the rosy blotches of hysteria on her cheeks. In his car, all she said to him was: I don't care how you try to sabotage me! Where did you get that word? he blurted out, so loud she shuddered. I didn't mean to yell, honey. I'm sor— She cut him off: I'm going to skate, Daddy. Nothing you do can stop me.

Oh sweet Jesus, he was so cold! And there was no warmth he could look forward to once this case was wrapped up. No wife—no big, cuddly fat one; no hot, slim sexy one—waiting in a cozy house with a fire going in the den and a kettle of soup on the stove: Oh, Charlie, I was so worried! No kid bouncing downstairs and saying Hi Daddy I'm glad you're back you've got to help me with my science project boy you look so tired are you okay Daddy? He knew they would never come back to Cheyenne.

He really wanted a dog again. Instead of going out to lunch, he could go home, take it for a run. Maybe a coonhound. Go hunting on weekends. Have it sit in the passenger seat, windows rolled down, its great black ears flying in the wind.

Sooner or later, he and Stacey would have to make their

peace. But the truth was, he was in no rush. He didn't want to face parting, whether it turned out to be ugly or just unpleasant. He'd be officially alone then. Single. And he'd have to date, sit through drinks and dinner and hear about each one's life, starting when she was a zygote, then have to go through his life story and—two dates after that—start having to answer for why the relationship wasn't working. In fact, the sexual part of him had died, or at least was in a coma. Maybe an irreversible coma. He didn't care. He hardly ever thought about it anymore, hardly ever wanted it. When he did want it, he could do it himself in two minutes. Better than getting stuck listening to why some woman's mother hadn't been there for her.

He had become a loner. Probably worse, even. A loser. A college education, a decent job, not bad to look at. And for all those advantages, how was he in any way superior to those guys at the Wrath meeting? All right, he didn't believe all that crap. But wasn't he pretty damn close to Darrell Frederickson, the half-pay, half-assed class-B mechanic? Alone. In an icy room where the quilt smelled of some other guy's aftershave. Home but not home, a stranger in a town in which he was not allowed to know anyone. Desperate for warmth.

What could be in store for him? After death, everyone knew the greatest danger to an agent in an undercover operation was getting so comfortable in the world he was investigating that he became part of it. The Behavioral guy had warned him about this, but it was common knowledge. There were FBI agents who never fully came back from being wiseguys, revolutionaries, Klansmen. For the rest of their lives, trapped between two worlds. Homeless men. He wished the cup of coffee from that big

shiny pot hadn't felt so warm in his hands, that the child-
ish sweetness of the powdery sugar on the doughnut
hadn't comforted him so. He'd licked it from the sides of
his mouth, off his fingers. He wished he hadn't felt so
gratified that Ostergard had let his men wait, the truck
idle, while he explained just how America had gotten
stolen from them all.

Maybe this was part of the process. He had to allow
himself to be snookered a little in order to be believable,
believed. Instead, he sensed he had been snookered a lot.
And hearing that bigoted shit? He'd been turned off, not
really repulsed the way he should have been. Bored, not
enraged. Had he thought of Good Dick Alexander out of
duty more than decency?

Here were these government-hating crazies, wanting
to tear down just about everything he had sworn so
gravely to uphold. Charlie Blair loved his country. Yet
what was Wrath representing to him this lonely, frigid
night? The only thing he had to look forward to—to get
him through this terrible coldness—was three days from
now. The next time he would get to see Vern.

# 9

Yes, Lauren Miller had done her homework, and sure, she knew Jackson Hole was becoming the new Vail, the next Squaw Valley, the spot for all seasons, where people came to ski and hike and hunt and ride, where private jets flew in daily from Los Angeles and New York, discharging people in thousand-dollar cowboy boots yearning for authenticity. However, she also knew that the total permanent population of the town of Jackson was five thousand.

It was this Pop. 5,000 that stuck in Lauren's mind. A cute numeral. She'd pictured setting down on a bumpy landing strip, then walking into a rinky-dink shack with a ceiling fan, an amalgam of *Stagecoach* and *Casablanca*.

Consequently, she was so taken aback at the hordes of alpine-sweatered skiers this late into winter, lined up before brightly lit Avis and Alamo and Budget car-rental counters, so startled by the timbered, touristy cowboy-ness of the place, so overwhelmed at the profusion of brochures touting dog sledding and ballooning and Indian jewelry and horse-drawn sleigh rides and Old West cookouts, that she was five minutes into her ride toward Jackson before she noticed the Grand Tetons in her rearview mirror.

She pulled over to the side of the road, got out of the car and looked back. Late afternoon had begun bleaching the color out of the March day, but the whiteness of the clouds was still accentuated by the muted blue of the sky. The clouds themselves were lovely enough; with the sun behind them, they had the iridescence of good pearls. Yet they grayed beside the brilliant white of the snow-covered mountains.

In their frosted mystery, the Tetons deserved to be viewed in their own silence, Lauren thought. The slushy whoosh of pickup trucks and SUVs rushing along the highway was a desecration. She got back into the car, but before she could shut the door, a howl echoed off South Teton across the flatland. Coyote! Her upper arms got goose bumps at the wild cry (although this particular sound actually came from a park ranger's husky demanding its dinner).

After the beauty of the mountains, the coarseness of the streetlamps and flashy signs along Jackson's ugliest commercial strip was almost hurtful. Still, they were not glaring enough to diminish the looming awesomeness of the sky as night descended. It arched over the land, more dark and portentous than any sky Lauren had ever seen. The stars did not twinkle in this sky; they were frozen points of light.

She pulled up to the Buckin' Bronc. The motel stood on the hem of the outskirts of Jackson, between an auto parts store featuring shearling covers for car seats and a closed-for-the-season bike rental shop. Even before she registered, Lauren understood that for fifty-five dollars a night she was not going to be thrilled. However, room 116 was more dreadful than she'd feared. Just outside her door, a vending machine with ancient peanuts and suspiciously dusty trail mix growled without cessation. Inside, in her bathroom, the nearly overpowering scent of pine room deodorizer made her wary of breathing too deeply, for fear she would discover whatever smell the pine was masking. Dispirited, she flopped onto the bed, but the clammy coldness of the plasticized coating on its dark-green spread made her rebound.

She peered out the weather-smeared window into darkness. Whomp! She was hit by the nightfall blues. Lauren's old nemesis, sneaking up on her when the workday was done, all during her years of reporting in Delaware, South Carolina and Ohio. She hadn't even considered that the blues would trail her west—hadn't thought about them at all—because she'd been so high about finally getting the assignment she'd been fighting for. Besides, she was safe, a New Yorker once again. This was no more than a business trip. But go tell the blues that.

They hung on, not easily allayed, certainly not by a chat with the desk clerk about how to get to Big Elk Video—although he was more than professionally cheery. He smiled and called her ma'am, as if he were Jimmy Stewart in *The Man Who Shot Liberty Valance,* and muttered, Muh neme's Stan, whistling his *S*. She smiled back, but it was a reflexive gesture made by the muscles of her mouth. How she wished she could be made of rougher stuff. Did Christiane Amanpour feel weepy when night fell on Bosnia? Lauren realized she must be emitting vulnerability waves, because, as if to hearten her, Stan pulled out enough maps to mollify the general of an invading army, patiently delineating alternate routes to the store in orange and purple highlighter.

From experience, Lauren knew a drink, even three drinks, would not make her view night in a rosier light. Nor would a call to her friends in New York, hearing about a brilliant Chinese art film, a hot new jazz club, a cool bistro, an eligible man who would no doubt be married by the time she finessed her way out of *JewNew* and her parents' house into an apartment in Manhattan. Only eight hours had elapsed since her plane left JFK, but already she felt permanently cut off, as if she'd died.

Even from her family. Her family? Oh God, a call to her parents or to Adam at law school? The worst. Hearing those comforting voices say Lauren! Hi! would only induce a lump in her throat—which not only would they discern but would make them insist, in voices fraught with italics, *Something is wrong.* No, no, don't tell me "nothing." True, her brother would be a hell of a lot more laid back, but with or without words, Adam also would demand, *What is it?* Recognizing that she was being drawn back to her room, perhaps to succumb to tears or to feeding three quarters into the vending machine for revolting peanuts, she waved goodbye to Stan and drove to Big Elk Video.

It was six-thirty, and while there were still a few customers browsing, she sensed that she had gotten to the store during the dinner hour lull. Or perhaps having some nut plant a bomb on the shelf beside *Schindler's List* was bad for business—although the man behind the counter did not look as if he was agonizing over imminent bankruptcy. In fact, he looked pretty calm, checking out one customer's choice and, it seemed, chatting with her about her selection. Was the man Mike Pearlstein, the owner?

She'd assumed it would be a snap to find a Pearlstein in a crowd of Wyoming WASPs. But among the locals she'd espied so far, this man would not stand out. Tall. But then, everyone in the West seemed tall. At five feet four, Lauren had always considered herself average, but walking through the Denver airport to change planes, she'd felt like a refugee from a land of pipsqueaks.

Possibly-Pearlstein was in his mid-thirties. Clean-shaven, short-sideburned. In-control Republican hair rather than tousled Democratic hair. A long face with temporal bones slightly indented around eyebrow level, as though the obstetrician had been a little heavy-handed with the forceps. He wore jeans with a green and red plaid shirt. Now that she thought about it, from the second she'd gotten off the plane in Jackson Hole, everything not timbered or blue-jeaned came in dark green, dark red or some combination of the two. Her red Geo Metro, the green rug in the halls of the Buckin' Bronc and the spread on her bed, the cranberry-colored Shetland sweater on the woman at the register at the front of the video store. Maybe it was some quirky Wyoming Christmas fixation. Or maybe green and red were the only Certified Nonsissy cowboy colors. In her black slacks and gray ribbed turtle-neck, Lauren felt small and somber, like a countertop black-and-white TV in a store display of forty-inch color models. Except for her red hair. She'd taken it out of a ponytail and was wearing it loose, with a headband, on the theory that many men talked more freely to women with unserious hair, a sad truth she had come upon as a reporter at the *Greenville Journal-Times* when her barrette broke during an interview with the CEO of FiberMaid Mills.

"Hi!" Possibly-Pearlstein called out. "Looking for anything special?" He was a sandy sort of man, one basic color all over, his hair between gold and brown, the ruddiness of his suntan or windburn dulled by an undertone of yellow. With his coloring and indented head, he looked like Mr. Peanut.

Lauren strolled up to the counter, smiling. "Hi!" she responded in the lively manner she had cultivated on the *Brandywine Blade,* her first job, when she discovered her *Columbia Spectator* cool and Gen-X ironic detachment were consistently being mistaken for either disdain or clinical depression. "I'm Lauren Miller—"

"Good to meet you, Lauren!" In the manner of a naturally shy person who has read many self-help books, he shook hands with extravagant congeniality. His voice resounded. His smile was a semicircle of teeth. "I'm Mike Pearlstein."

"Great! You're the man I wanted to meet." Before he could ponder the possibilities, she added: "I'm a reporter with the *News.* In New York." The night before had been nearly sleepless as she pondered the practicality and the ethics of dropping "Jewish" from the paper's name. She did not want to risk coming so far, only to find that no member of Wrath would speak to a reporter from the *Jewish News,* although she did concede there was a chance one would—to boost an ego, to evoke hurt or outrage. However, if she divulged the *JewNew* connection to even a single person, word could get back to Wrath and she might have to return to New York having proved her editor, Eli, right. Give them the lead, not the whole story, she concluded. If someone asks, Is the *News* the full name of your paper? then go from half to whole truth.

"The bomb thing is history," Pearlstein said. "I don't want to—"

"How do you know it's history?" Lauren asked. "Oh, is it okay if I call you Mike?"

"Sure."

"*Is* it over?" she asked, sounding concerned for him. "I

mean, did the police and the FBI assure you it wouldn't happen again?"

Pearlstein's upheld hand—Stop, please—and his shake of the head were sadly familiar television gestures. No doubt about it: Over the years, he and the rest of his pals in the global village had watched heads of state and celebrities giving those same signals to journalists: No comment! Lauren knew how to handle it. She held back. There was no follow-up question. Instead, she peered at him a little anxiously. Like many reporters, she understood instinctively that most people perceive silence as a sickening void that needs to be filled. "They didn't *guarantee* it wouldn't happen again," he said. "I mean, not in so many words. But whatever point these people were trying to make"— he smoothed down the front of his already smooth hair— "they made it. I'm honestly surprised you heard about it in the Big Apple. It didn't get all that much attention."

"Well, someone claiming the bombing called Denny Rettig, that right-wing guy with a syndicated radio show."

"Do you New Yorkers ever think maybe people call the right 'right' because they are?" Pearlstein asked pleasantly, trying to change the topic. Lauren always found it hard to believe that when a Jew started talking like a conservative Republican he was not necessarily acting out *Dumb and Dumber;* he might actually be a conservative Republican. When it quacks like a duck, her editor in South Carolina had advised her, first thang you look for is webbed feet. "Not that I ever got the chance to listen to this Rettig," he went on. "But from what they told me the caller said to him, putting the bomb in my place was obviously a mistake. The message was something about foreign elements."

"And?" Lauren asked. Pearlstein glanced toward a customer checking out the New Releases shelves, as if by sheer will he could teleport him over to disrupt the conversation. "Are you suggesting that by 'foreign elements' the caller was talking about Indonesians in Wyoming? Bulgarians?"

"I don't know."

"Mike," she said, lifting an eyebrow.

"Who can say for sure?" he mumbled, looking down at a basket of returned cassettes.

"Are you from this area originally?" He shook his head and picked up a copy of *Star Wars* as if he had never seen one before. "Where are you from?"

"Ohio."

"Where in Ohio?"

"Cincinnati."

"No kidding! I used to be court reporter for the *Columbus Star*."

"You're so young," he said, with a diffident smile that was more natural to him than the great toothy one he'd been flashing earlier.

"How long have you lived in Jackson Hole?" she asked.

"Six years."

"And you're how old?"

"Thirty-nine," he said.

"That's a real thirty-nine? Not a permanent state of affairs?" He looked mystified for a moment, but finally, realizing she was kidding, he smiled. Now that they were friends again, Lauren asked, "Are you Jewish?"

"Uh, yes," he answered, not knowing quite what to do with his smile. "I mean, I'm not religious, but—"

"Many other Jews here in the Jackson Hole area?"

"Some. It's not New York. Not Cincinnati either."

"Most of them come in recent years?"

Pearlstein put down *Star Wars*. "You're jumping to the wrong conclusion about the 'foreign elements' thing."

"Maybe. But this Denny Rettig regularly has people on his show who talk about how 'international bankers' are responsible for people out West losing their farms and ranches. Are 'international bankers' Bulgarian too? Or is it just another code word for Jews, like 'foreign elements'?"

"I don't know."

"Let's forget that call to the radio station," Lauren said, sensing she was about to lose his goodwill. "Did the cops or FBI give you any idea who they suspected?"

"They didn't say anything."

"Well, you seem like a smart guy." That was more than hyperbole but short of a blatant lie. "Try to figure this out with me. Did they ask you a hundred thousand questions about your associates, like who might want to plant a bomb on one of your shelves—next to a movie about the Holocaust? Or did they just ask a few routine questions, because their hunch is it really wasn't connected with you, except that your last name is Pearlstein?"

"They just asked, you know, like 'Do you have anybody who's really angry at you or who's threatened you?'"

"And what did you tell them?"

"Are you taping this?"

"No. Of course not. And I didn't write it down yet, because I got the feeling you weren't comfortable talking about the whole subject. I didn't want to make you any more ill at ease."

"Thanks."

"You're welcome. Is it okay if I just jot down a couple

of things now? I have a good memory, but I don't want to test it." He shrugged, so Lauren reached into her pocket and drew out her pad and pen. "Did they show you any photographs?"

"A bunch. Took more than two hours."

"Do you know who showed them to you?"

"I don't get what you mean, 'who showed them'?"

"The local cops from Jackson? The Teton County sheriff's office? The Wyoming Division of Criminal Investigation? The FBI?"

"Oh. Gee, I forget. He was wearing a suit, so it couldn't have been anyone local. I mean"—Pearlstein chuckled—"if they're not in uniform, they sure in heck wouldn't be wearing suits."

"Did you recognize anyone in their photos?"

"I couldn't be a hundred percent sure. Some of them looked, you know, so average. I mean, of course I know my regular customers. I'm even getting to know the out-of-staters who have places here. But gosh, we get so many tourists."

"When you say average, are you talking about white men?"

"Right. No blacks, nobody who looked Jewish." She wasn't certain—beyond anti-Semitic caricatures of the liver-lipped and hook-nosed, which usually resembled Yasir Arafat—what that phrase meant. Was looking Jewish the style of Streisand or the publicly acknowledged religiosity of Streisand or the liberal politics of Streisand or the Brooklyn accent of Streisand or the nose of Streisand? To Lauren, there were a fair number of people about whom she could say: They look Jewish. Yet Strom Thurmond looked like someone's Jewish grandpa. Winona Ryder and Alicia Silverstone looked like Episcopal bishops' daughters. Pearlstein, to Lauren's eye, merely looked tall and sandy. She? In South Carolina, no one had assumed she was a Jew. Yet when it had come up, one of her baseball friends said, Heavens, you don't look it! and her editor said, Kind of thought you might be.

"Would you like a cup of coffee?" Pearlstein asked.

"No thanks. I'd love a glass of water, though." A reporter learns early in her career to decline beverages brewed in police stations and the backs of stores.

While he was gone, Lauren scribbled notes of what he had said and drew a rough sketch of the store's layout. Earlier, she had spotted one copy of *Schindler's List* on a shelf with a sign that proclaimed: *Academy Award Winning Films*. When Pearlstein returned, she asked, "Did they take anything from your store as evidence?"

"A couple of cassettes that may have gotten some stuff on them when the bomb did whatever it did."

"What *did* the bomb do?"

"Not much," he declared cheerfully. "Hardly anything."

"You weren't here when it happened?"

"No, it was the middle of the night. We were closed."

"How did you learn what happened?"

"When I got in, there was a real strong smell. Like, you know, when you're trying to light a campfire and all the matches almost catch but don't? I looked around and there it was."

"The bomb?"

"Yes. The police took it—and a couple of cassettes. The shelf too. I had to put up another one."

"They took *Schindler's List*?"

"And *The Silence of the Lambs*. That was on the other side of the bomb."

"Getting back to the photos they showed you: Were they all what you'd call mug shots?"

"Most. Not all. Some were like"—Pearlstein chewed his lip—"group shots."

"Could they be surveillance photos? Pictures taken with a telephoto lens?"

"You think so?" he asked, intrigued.

"I don't know. I haven't seen them, and you have."

"Well, now that you mention it, I guess they could have been. Just a few. Men standing around in the middle of nowhere. Just men talking."

"Did they look like they were from around here, Mike? Or did they look like . . . I don't know. New Yorkers?"

"I don't think so."

"Foreigners? Like Bulgarian international bankers with yarmulkes?"

"No."

"A bunch of white guys from Ohio here to go fly-fishing?"

"They could have been."

"Mike, does your gut say Ohio?" He shrugged. "Come on. What does your gut tell you?"

"Wyoming."

Even though Lauren was dubious about large slabs of red meat, a bias left from her college vegetarian days, she pulled into Sal & Hal's Grubsteak. She'd gone from hungry to ravenous, and having passed a couple of architecturally interesting restaurants with expensive-sounding names like Le Cowboy and Coriander, she pulled into the parking lot of Sal & Hal's simply because other cars were there. The building was a cube with a roof, a place where, out of New York, she might get away with ten bucks for dinner. By the time she gave her order to the waitress for turkey 'n' trimmings, at seven ninety-five, the rest of the customers were finishing their desserts or paying their checks. By the time an oval dinner plate the size of a meat platter was set before her, she was the only customer left.

"Anything else I can get you?" the waitress asked. She was a middle-aged woman, so short and florid and roly-poly Lauren half expected her to sing "We'd like to welcome you to Munchkin Land."

"I'm fine, thanks."

"Come here to ski?"

"No, I'm working." The waitress wasn't precisely hovering. Lauren wasn't sure whether chitchat came with the entreé or the woman felt sorry for her because she was alone. Either way, the waitress was waiting, so she explained. "I'm a reporter. I'm covering that attempted bombing over at Big Elk Video. Have you heard about it?"

"Sure. Mike—he owns the place—comes here."

The waitress was so short that even standing, she was almost at Lauren's eye level. Still, Lauren figured that by eight at night, the woman must be feeling her feet. "I'd love it if . . . Are you allowed to sit down?" Lauren asked.

"Allowed?" The waitress quickly slid into the chair across from Lauren's. "I'm Sal, of Sal & Hal's. Sal Montgomery."

"Lauren Miller." She nearly asked where Hal was but suddenly held back, afraid there might be some horrific story about a very short man and a cauldron of hot fat.

"If you want to know where Hal is, he *was* in the kitchen, but he had to skedaddle over to the library before it closed, because they're putting on an exhibition of his old mail-order catalogs. He collects them. Paid three hundred and sixty dollars for a Sears, Roebuck from 1927 two years ago! I told him, 'Do that one more time and you can take the "Sal" off the sign!' If you're here next week, you can see it. The exhibition. Go ahead, eat your supper before it gets cold."

"It's great." Actually, it wasn't merely not bad. Although the turkey fought back a little, it was tasty, with a blanket of dark giblet gravy, candied yams and a stuffing so intoxicatingly buttery Lauren knew it was going to be a thousand-calorie evening. "What do you make of that bomb at Mike's store?"

"You talked to Mike?"

"Sure. He seems like a decent guy. I bet this is upsetting him more than he's letting on." Lauren wanted Sal to know she'd spoken with Mike. In any journalistic inquiry, she'd discovered, once a person knows someone else has already talked to a reporter, he or she will be more likely to blab big time. She guessed it was because that second person was thereby relieved of the moral burden of protecting privacy. Also, she believed people needed to talk: "No comment" was rarely no comment. On or off the record, nearly everyone she had ever tried to interview had, ultimately, been willing to speak. She surmised much of it had to do with the simple, human desire to try and make sense of whatever out-of-the-ordinary event had attracted a reporter's attention in the first place. What better way to understand than to talk it through with an objective outsider? Or maybe, in this mediaphilic age, every person on earth had a fantasy about being interviewed. "So who would want to do a thing like that to a nice guy like Mike?"

"Some loony, I guess."

"Are you from around here originally, Sal?"

"Born in Idaho Falls. Hal's from here."

"Do you think the bomber was a lone loony or a loony who's part of a group?" Lauren had worried that the locals might be sympathetic to the mysterious bomber, or afraid to speak. She was relieved that Sal didn't stiffen, didn't suddenly decide she had to leap up and refill ketchup bottles. In fact, the waitress looked as if she was seriously considering the question.

"How can you tell?" Sal finally asked. "I mean, take that Ted."

"Ted?"

"The Unabomber. He wrote that long story about what he believed in. Remember, some of the papers published it? He said in there he was part of a group. He wasn't, though, was he? He was a hermit."

"You're right. You know, I forgot about that."

"Well, he wasn't from Wyoming anyway," Sal commented. "Montana."

"They have 'The Paranoid-Schizophrenic State' on their license plates?"

"Go on," Sal said. "Laugh all you want—"

"I didn't mean to be patronizing. I'm sorry."

"No offense, no apologies. Now . . . Is it Laura?"

"Lauren."

"Okay, Lauren, what I was getting at is, they got those Freemen up there in Montana. Right?"

"Right."

"And those folks who think the UN is busy getting troops together across the border in Canada to invade the U.S. And then they got the Jew-haters and the ones who want to round up blacks and stick them all in one state— same with the Orientals and Jews too, I guess, but they'd get put in different states. And even though it's where I come from, they got pretty much the same types of loonies over in Idaho. You don't really see them here."

"Why not? Wyoming's a fairly conservative state. You don't like the federal government interfering in your lives."

"But that's not loony, although maybe you being from— You're from the East?"

"Yes, I am. But I'm not saying conservative equals loony. I just want to know how is Wyoming different from its neighbors?"

Reflecting, Sal picked up the salt shaker and wiped its top with the bottom of her apron, then did the same with the pepper shaker. "Maybe because there's not that many of us. Hard to get a group of loonies together when the nearest loony is fifty miles down a bad road."

"Montana isn't what you'd call densely populated."

"I guess you're right about that. Well, maybe . . . Darned if I know. We're called the Equality State. First to give the vote to women, first to elect a woman governor. Maybe we're more—I don't know—tolerant."

"Do you think a person or a group tried to bomb Big Elk Video because Mike Pearlstein is a Jew?"

"I wouldn't be surprised."

"Is there a lot of anti-Jewish feeling around?" Lauren asked offhandedly.

"No." Lauren waited. "Well . . . I think it's like this: We've got a lot of out-of-state people coming in, buying up everything in sight. Prices go up, folks who've been here for generations say, Well, I guess I can make a killing. Except once they do, what have they got?"

"Money?"

"But they've lost their home, right?"

"They *sold* their home," Lauren said.

"Right, but they really can't afford a new one, because property values are sky-high. They find the killing they made doesn't go that far. They can't afford a home in their hometown."

"So they blame it on Jewish bankers or something?"

"No, no, nothing like that. It's that some of them see a lot of New Yorkers and folks from L.A. coming in, and first thing that comes to mind is . . ."

"Jews."

"Right. Truth is, we got all kinds from New York and L.A. Like you, for instance. But to some folks, they're all Jews. They've got money, they're not shy about spending it, so that makes them Jews."

"Does Mike have money?"

Sal shook her head. "No. Now don't go thinking that's how I feel. You asked. I told. With Mike, now, he came here for a vacation, from the Midwest somewhere. Fell in love with Jackson Hole, like so many folks do. He moved out, worked as a ski instructor in winter, hunting guide in summer, for—I don't know—five, six years. Maybe more. Saved up to open a small business for himself. He'll make a go of it, but I can tell you right now—ten years down the road, he'll still be coming in for our Monday chopped steak special."

"He'll never be rich."

"He'll never be rich and he'll never be a loudmouth. He'll never be all the things the loonies say the Jews are." Sal lowered her voice. "You know how Jews are supposed to be so smart?"

"Not Mike?"

Sal shook her head a little sadly. "Not Mike. Sweet as sugar, but Albert Einstein isn't turning over in his grave, worrying about the competition."

*       *       *

An investigative reporter begins at the edges of a story, Lauren knew, gaining knowledge, gathering leads, slowly, inexorably moving inward toward the center, toward the truth. So before she could get near the men responsible for putting a bomb in Big Elk Video, she had to learn as much about them and their world as she could. She had to gather the intelligence to understand the deeper *why* beneath the bombers' explanation and the bare facts of the police blotter. Working the circumference of a story, circling it, was the way to begin. It could be dangerous to jump right into the center—especially in a state in which people carried guns the way New Yorkers carried cell phones.

That night and the next day, she visited three different bars, two supermarkets and the offices of two local cab companies, and she stopped in at all the other stores on the Big Elk Video block. She had lunch with a reporter from the *Jackson Hole Guide,* dinner with one from the *Jackson Hole Daily*. She set up a box at the post office in the name of L. Miller, both to receive any mail she didn't want coming across the Buckin' Bronc's front desk and because she'd heard the post office was the place to meet.

At midnight, as she lowered the cover of her laptop, she realized she had gotten past twilight without once thinking of home. What's more, she couldn't wait till the next morning.

Don Vultaggio may have been the chief of police of a town with a permanent population of five thousand, but when Lauren phoned to set up an interview, he'd sounded as media savvy as his counterpart in a town of five million. Bringing a photographer with you? he'd inquired. All she could come up with was, Well, outside New York we use freelancers, so it all depends if I can reach someone in time.

The chief turned out to be photogenic, she had to admit, although not in the way she'd anticipated. Indulging in some stereotyping herself, she'd been picturing Chazz Palminteri in a cowboy hat. Behind his giant rectangle of a desk, Don Vultaggio looked as if the closest he or his forebears had ever gotten to Italy was a slice of pizza—and even that was dubious. His skin, after close to fifty years of rough western weather, had the approximate texture and color of her brown leather backpack. The bones beneath it were splendid but not Italian, the kind a Norse rather than a Roman god would have had. He had a wide brow, a tiny triangle of an upturned nose, and cheekbones that jutted straight out, then came careening back into his face at a near-forty-five-degree angle.

To allay his not unpredictable cop response to a reporter—at best a pain in the ass, at worst the enemy— Lauren inquired about his background in law enforcement, adhering to the journalistic axiom that to put a public official at ease, start with his favorite topic: himself. This was proving to be true, but New York time was faster than Wyoming time. Thus, a biography that would have been related in one hundred eighty seconds back home was now in its twenty-second minute.

However, Chief Vultaggio's recounting of his story was such a detached recitation of facts and events that he might have been reading aloud from a colleague's résumé. He addressed her tape recorder, not her. He never once smiled, never once checked to see if Lauren was suitably impressed with his accomplishments. Talk about a cool dude, she thought, realizing that this cool dude's ploy would be to keep talking and, at the end of a half hour, cut off the interview. She'd object, of course, saying she hadn't gotten enough information, and he'd respond with something like, Well, ma'am, you had your thirty minutes.

"How do you feel about the FBI coming in?" she asked.

"What makes you think the FBI's involved?"

Because one of the local reporters told me they were. "Look, Chief Vultaggio, I've done my homework. But you know I can't tell you who helped me with it."

"Maybe nobody told you. Maybe you're just blowing smoke in my direction."

"Maybe you think I'm a slick New York reporter who'd do that kind of thing. I can only tell you I'm not. But look at what everybody knows: The FBI's Domestic Terrorism group got beefed up after Oklahoma City"— Lauren had no idea if this was true, but she thought it ought to be—"and Jackson Hole is too prominent a place to ignore a bomb, even if it didn't go off. And there's a possible civil rights violation here too, with Mike Pearlstein being Jewish. So how do you feel about the FBI being on the case?"

"I don't mind."

"Who's leading the investigation? You or the feds?"

"We're cooperating."

"Come on, Chief." She smiled. Ordinarily, reporters interrogate cops the way cops interrogate criminals, using charm so that the object of said charm will come to think of the charmer as a great pal. But charm was not working. Lauren could not tell if Vultaggio was cool beyond words or if he did not like reporters, or New York reporters, or simply not her. She would have preferred someone with such fine cheekbones to have thought well of her. However, she had to get past it. The question was how. Well, she couldn't come off tough; he would laugh her out of his office. And she didn't have an intimidating amount of inside information with which to pressure him. So she decided to talk fast.

"This person who called Denny Rettig's show said he was from a group called Free America."

"Correct."

"Did you ever hear about that group before that call?"

"No."

"Did you get information about them from any of the other law enforcement agencies after the call?"

"No."

"I've heard from several sources that there's another group moved down from the northern part of Wyoming to this area, to a tiny town called McBride."

"My jurisdiction is the town of Jackson."

"I thought you were cooperating with other agencies. Did they tell you about this group?"

"Yes."

"It's called Wrath. They have public meetings. They go around to parking lots, putting flyers under people's windshields."

"Correct." Vultaggio did not make any of the minuscule moves that signal surprise: no blink, no sudden intake of breath. Still, Lauren thought he seemed . . . not stunned—the man was not stunnable—but slightly stirred that she knew about Wrath. Admittedly, she had no objective evidence on which to base this assumption, as he was sitting motionless as a sculpture in his old-fashioned wooden office chair. But she went with it. "What other radical groups beside Wrath are active in this area?"

"What do you call radical?"

"Any organization that believes the federal government is the enemy, that it's involved in secret machinations to take away citizens' guns or their land or their freedom. I'd probably also define radical as any organization that wants to curtail the rights of particular groups of their fellow citizens. So what other organizations are there like that around here?"

"None to my knowledge."

"Wrath is the only game in town?"

"That I can't say."

"Could Wrath and Free America be one and the same?"

"I don't know." For an instant, his eyes slipped to a manila folder near his left elbow. So he did know! Wrath and Free America were somehow tied to each other. She knew it in her gut. Unfortunately, she also knew she could not use as a lead "Don Vultaggio, the chief of police of the resort town of Jackson, Wyoming, shifted his eyes to the left last Wednesday and, by doing so, signaled that a bomb placed in Mike Pearlstein's Big Elk Video store was put there by a virulently anti-Semitic group called Wrath."

"Who's the head guy in Wrath?"

"Fellow named Vernon Ostergard."

"What does he do for a living?" The chief's shoulders rose about a tenth of an inch. "Is that an 'I don't know'?"

"No."

"So what does he do?" She got no response. "Why won't you tell me? Is he in law enforcement? Related to someone important in town? Your first cousin?"

"No."

"So?" His coldness was chilling to her. Lauren knew several women, talented reporters, who went to pieces when someone gave them the freeze in a professional situation. They didn't cry, didn't have an anxiety attack. They simply lost their ability to function at top speed because they were shaken to their core by the not-liking—and got sidetracked by trying to remedy the situation and be more likable. Well, not her. "You know," she told him, "it's one thing to protect your investigation. But I get the impression you're trying to protect Vernon Ostergard or Wrath. Why?"

Vultaggio glanced down at Lauren's tape recorder on his desk. "I'm not protecting them. I guess I'm trying to protect you. Nothing personal, but you may not be up to this. These are dangerous people."

"I appreciate your concern," she said, noting absolutely none at all. "But this is my job and I've got to do it. Believe me, I'll be careful."

"They take target practice in the hills outside of McBride."

"Have they ever used a reporter as a target?"

"Not yet."

"Good. What does Ostergard do for a living?"

"TV repairman."

"In McBride?"

"Yes."

"Is he doing a big business fixing TVs?"

"Can't really tell." He gestured to the tape recorder. Lauren turned it off. "Off the record," he said.

"Off the record," she concurred.

"They came south from Sheridan, because they're ambitious. They want a bigger arena. They're looking for people who fear what they fear. This valley, Jackson

Hole, has gone from being a ranching community with a tourist sideline to becoming a mecca for the whole country. Everybody's grabbing a piece of it. Rich folks come, buy a thousand acres, build a ten-thousand-square-foot house and wind up living in it maybe three, four weeks a year . . . while local folks can't find a decent place they can afford anywhere in the valley. A lot of the people who were born here, who work here, have to go over the border to Idaho to find a place to live. So there may be some here who are willing to listen to a man who's talking about getting rid of outsiders. Frankly," he added, "I'd have thought they'd be doing better business than they are."

"Wrath?"

"Yes."

"Why do you think they aren't?"

"Maybe people get nervous about that kind of anti-government talk after Oklahoma City."

"Who else figures in Wrath besides Vernon Ostergard?"

"His two . . . I guess you'd call them lieutenants. Kyle McIntyre and Gus Lang." She asked him to spell the last names, and he did.

"Do any of them have criminal records?"

"Ostergard for weapons violations, bad-check charge. I forget what else. Lang has a pretty ugly juvenile record. Property destruction, robbery, aggravated assault and battery. Was in the State Boys School. Nothing concrete on the other one." He reached across his desk and turned the recorder back on. "You know, Miss Miller, there's safety in numbers. You're alone. A television reporter goes up to McBride with a cameraman, maybe a sound-man, and the more the merrier. Well, once in a while something not so merry happens, like when those folks from CBS or ABC got held up in Montana. But usually, with a group, you can bet things will turn out okay. Can't say I'd place the same bet on you."

"Hey, Lauren," Adam Miller said, in a voice so light-hearted his sister realized how hard he was working to hide his concern. "Have you talked to any of them yet?"

"The loonies? That's what one of the women I talked to calls them." New M&M's had appeared in the vending machine that afternoon, as if in response to her dissatisfaction, so Lauren decided to fight temptation with a daily orange. Cradling the phone between shoulder and ear, she peeled the fruit. "No, haven't even seen any of them yet. Tomorrow I'm driving up to the town where they've settled—about forty or fifty miles from here—but just to check it out. See if there's a diner or a bar where the locals hang out. Adam—" Lauren interrupted herself. "Don't get nervous. I'm not going to bars where guys with swastika tattoos pummel Jews. Relax."

"Who said I wasn't relaxed?" The summer before, after his first year of law school, Adam had interned at the Manhattan DA's office. By the end of August, he considered himself unshockable.

"You're relaxed? Give me a break."

"Laur, you know how great I think you are. You're smart. You've got guts. But these people are dangerous. They don't respect the law. They don't even believe in it. And they might not even fear its power. You can't ignore that."

"I'm not. Do you think I'm going to approach them the same way I'd go to interview Wolfie Nudelman, the low-fat-pastrami king? Look, I can't tell you to switch off your fraternal instinct. But trust my judgment. I'm a pro."

"I know. Don't I read everything you write?"

"Yes. So maybe you can understand that I've got to do this story, and not just to get the leverage to get the hell out of *JewNew*. This needs to be written about. I mean, if we shrug our shoulders at political violence or at potential political violence, aren't we collaborators in the process of destroying ourselves? You majored in history too. Tell me one time putting your head in the sand has worked."

"Never," he conceded. "As far as I know. I'm not saying not to report the story, Laur. I'm saying to do it . . . from a respectful distance. Not respectful of them. Fuck them. I mean respectful of your own safety."

"Did Mom and Dad put you up to this?"

"No! I swear to God."

"I promise you I'll be careful."

"How can you be careful when they'll know you're a Jew?"

"How will they know?"

"The name of your paper."

"The *News*?"

"Holy shit! You're not telling them?"

"Not if I can avoid it."

"What if they ask if you are?"

"I'll sing 'Jesus Loves Me.'" Lauren peeled off an orange segment and put it in her mouth. The juice was surprisingly sweet.

"Get wise-ass like that, and they'll know for sure."

On her drive to McBride three days later, Lauren kept envisioning a wasteland of a town. The majestic mountain landscape she was driving through would vanish.

McBride would be grotesquely, fascistically flat, like one of Hitler's architectural renderings. She was heading toward hell on earth: sagebrush blowing across dusty streets, *Invasion of the Body Snatchers* townspeople passing each other without glances or words. Now and then a sulfurous pit worked itself into her imaginings, and so, for a moment, did gutters running with raw sewage.

In fact, McBride was a pretty little town nestled in a teacup of land with the base of a mountain as its saucer. The midday sun shone down on the great firs that served as a stately green backdrop. The stores and houses, all of pine, came in every shade of wood, from gold to almost black. Smoke curled out of chimneys that rose above snow-covered roofs. True, up close some of the houses looked unloved or, at least, unindulged. She noticed broken railings on porches, windowpanes boarded up, rotted-out steps with holes large enough to engulf a foot.

The business district was seven stores. Lauren parked in front of the grocery. Its window was mostly empty. One of the cans in a small, sad tomato sauce pyramid was so swollen it looked ready to explode and spread botulism within a hundred-foot radius. The only other items on display were two boxes of SOS, one on top of the other.

She took a quick breath. There it was, Vern's TV Repair. Across the street, just three stores down. Its sign looked new—the near-ubiquitous buck-and-rail cowboy script, brown letters on a white background—but its filthy display window and off-the-hinge storm door gave it the look of a doomed venture, the upshot of the myriad miscalculations that How to Start Your Own Business books caution against.

Except just then she noticed a great satellite dish behind the store. One of those outmoded ones that took up half a backyard. She edged forward to get a better look, pretending to search for something on the dashboard. Not an old satellite dish, she'd bet on it. Shit, she wished one of her techno-smart friends were with her. Why would Ostergard want such equipment? To steal *Baywatch* signals bouncing off some government-owned satellite? Or was the thing an uplink antenna so Wrath could broadcast its message? And if so, where did the loonies in this depressed town, headquartered in this loser of a store, get the money for such expensive stuff?

Lauren's rented car had Wyoming plates. Still, she knew she could not sit in it all day watching Ostergard's store and go unnoticed. If her little red Geo didn't stand out in a part of the country that seemed enamored of red cars, she herself would stand out—for the simple reason that she did not live in this small town. Further, if a key trait of the radical right mentality was paranoia, it was not a stellar idea to hang around here, watching. Still, what was the alternative? Even though she knew the headquarters of Wrath was in Ostergard's shop, right across the street, she wasn't yet ready to walk the fifty feet, knock on the broken-hinged door and say Hi, my name's Lauren Miller, and I'm a reporter with the *News*.

She got out of the car anyway. As she stood, her knee made a cracking sound. Her legs felt wobbly. An urge to get back in and drive—to Long Island—nearly overcame her. Instead, she reached into her coat pocket, past her pen and notebook to the small can of pepper spray her father had insisted she buy once she got to Wyoming. It's illegal in New York, he told her, but they probably have it there. They did. She walked into the grocery store.

She could feel it: She'd be met by a pierced-nose, tattooed skinhead, like the one she had seen beside Ostergard in a two-year-old newspaper photo she had come across in her research at the Jackson Hole library. He would say, Get the fuck out of town, kike. Her heart wasn't beating fast, just frighteningly hard.

"Help you?" a voice growled. Lauren let out a humiliating "Nyah" of surprise.

"Oh, sorry." The voice, abraded by at least six decades of cigarettes, came from a stout, red-cheeked man in a green thermal shirt sitting on a low chair behind the counter. He looked like the sort whom everyone in town would call Gramps, although for all she knew, he could be called *Hauptsturmführer*.

"What can I get for you?"

"Do you have any fat-free pretzels?" she managed to ask, her heart refusing to stop pounding inside her chest.

"Don't know about that," the man said. The four words took about a minute and a half, Lauren figured. Then he did his follow-up: "I'll go see." His walk was the dragging limp of someone who has had a stroke, and she felt terrible making him look for something she was virtually certain was not on the shelves. She almost couldn't bear to watch him. Glancing away, she caught a glimpse of movement across the street.

"I'll be right back," she called out. "I left my wallet in the car." She slipped out the door but stood close by it, although it was still near enough to noon that there were no shadows to hide her. Still, the two men across the street coming out of Vern's TV Repair, deep in conversation, did not look her way.

There was a youngish man—or maybe he was an older teenager—in a short army-green jacket that reached to his waist, military style, like the one in a photograph of her Grandpa Marty in his World War II uniform. A middle-aged man was beside him. Was it . . . ? No. Yes! Vernon Ostergard! Was it really he? He looked so ordinary. They headed away from her, toward a big pickup truck coming down the street, its brakes squealing as it overshot the repair shop.

Usually when Lauren was working, standing back, observing, she became so much a part of what she would write that she almost ceased to exist. She entered her story. For that moment, she had been walking step by step with Ostergard—yes, it was Ostergard—and the young man. She'd gone with them across the buckled strip of pavement that was the sidewalk, over a foot-high bank of packed snow—so real she could feel its coldness in the soles of her own boots—out onto the street where the truck's big tires were. . . . But suddenly she was pulled out of the story.

A cute guy. On her side of the street, right at the corner, in front of the drugstore. Tall. Green workman's pants. Some kind of dark sweater. Down vest that looked as if it had seen a lot of Wyoming winters. What kind of idiocy was this, being distracted by a guy. Just one more second. He was wonderful-looking, really. Fabulous black beard. Strong features. Short dark hair. What color were his eyes?

It wasn't only his looks, though, but the way he carried himself. Not in the routinely attractive, athletic way of the men around Jackson Hole, nearly all of whom looked as if they could ski up mountains. This one looked strong too, but it was as much an intrinsic as an acquired strength, as if he had grown out of the earth. She loved the way he stood, feet slightly apart, hands stuck into his back pockets. Her heart stopped its fearful pounding. It stopped altogether. She was transported out of McBride, out of Wyoming, to another world entirely, where there was only herself and this man. Oh God, he was better than good. He was splendid!

Hell! He'd seen her staring at him. Okay, so big deal. But she felt a red flush spreading from the roots of her hair, into her cheeks, down her neck. Hey, maybe she should smile at him. Then who knows? He could walk over. And she could see his eyes up close. Not that she would stay and talk or anything. Just smile, and if he said hi, she'd say, Sorry, gotta go. But to have the memory of him walking toward—

He was looking away now. But not before giving her an angry look. Why? She felt hurt. No, stricken. Then ashamed. This was so incredibly stupid.

Oh God, had he seen her checking out Ostergard? Could he think she was a Wrath groupie? Lauren might have speculated more, but just then the man stepped away from the drugstore, into the street. He called out, "Hey, Vern!" And there was happiness in his voice. Respect. As he crossed the street, she picked up a slight holding back. Was he thinking twice? He was not. There was no mistaking what that hesitation was. Deference.

Ostergard called out, "Well, howdy, Darrell!" The man nearly flew the rest of the way, as if he couldn't wait to get there.

Lauren slipped back into the grocery. A year had passed, it seemed, since she'd been inside. In that time, not only had she walked with Ostergard. She had fallen for the wrong guy. How the hell could her instincts have been so wrong? A white-trash anti-Semitic loony with a schmucky name like Darrell.

Inside, Gramps was still dragging his foot down the

grocery store aisle, toward the shelf with the pretzels. Whatever he brought her—buffalo-flavored faux-blue-cheese pretzels—she knew she'd walk out with two bags. She'd probably finish them both before she got back to Jackson.

# 10

She really wasn't pretty, Charlie told himself. One of those heart-shaped faces you saw all the time in old photographs, the kind of face that seemed to disappear soon after the Civil War. Great hair, though, a ton of dark-red curls pulled off her face by her earmuffs, then falling onto her shoulders. Almost the same shade as the mostly Irish setter he'd had as a kid, Jingles. God, he'd been so crazy about that dog. Not that her hair was limp like dog hair. It was so alive: Each ray of sun that hit it refracted into different reds or golds, so just standing there, she gave off glints of copper and bronze and blond. Couldn't tell what her body was like, because she was in one of those coats with toggle closings that make everybody look like a rectangle.

How come he'd turned her way? A sense: Someone was watching him. Not an FBI sense. No feeling of danger, not from her. A man's sense. He could feel her checking him out in a major way. When he caught her doing it, she'd blushed. Okay, he couldn't really see her turning red, but he knew she had to be. Just like he knew that if he wanted her, he could have her.

Wait! Stop! What a jerk he was, going off into some fuck-her-standing-up teenage fantasy just because a girl had looked his way. Getting distracted like this while right before his eyes, who was coming out of Vern's TV but Ostergard himself, with Babyface, that guy who'd been sitting in the audience at the first Wrath meeting four days ago! Hustling out of the shop to the curb to meet a blue Chevy C-3500 that had come to a squealing stop. The driver was someone who didn't know his ass from a hole in the ground about how to handle a truck that size.

But even as this pig of a pickup was coming to a halt, what was once again spinning around Charlie Blair's head? Was he thinking about the bomb: Who ordered it to be set? Was someone going to try again? No, his brain had been seized by that girl. He was thinking how he was touched by her. More. How much he wanted to take her small chin in his hand, study her face. In that fraction of a second, he actually pictured doing it, he was almost overcome by gladness at being able to gaze into her eyes. Green. He was positive they must be green, that soft, dreamy green of new moss. But the picture was clouded by sadness too, because he knew that this moment with her was going to be the slenderest slice of time, set apart from the rest of his life. . . .

Charlie let her go. Stepping into the street, he called out, "Hey, Vern!"

Ostergard's glance moved from the truck over to Charlie, and the prune-faced, pissed-off expression Charlie had seen vanished. "Well, howdy Darrell!"

The man alongside Ostergard, Babyface, turned toward Charlie too, although no change whatsoever registered in his face. Charlie restrained himself, walking across the street leisurely: a man in awe of Vernon Ostergard but desperately trying to be cool. He mumbled, "You said to drop by, and I got my lunch break, so I thought—"

"Glad you did!" And Ostergard did sound glad, although when he turned to the driver getting out of the cab of the pickup, he looked a lot less glad. "I told you, Gus, you don't got to slam on the brakes like it's some old hunk of tin." The driver was the other Wrath stooge who'd been sitting at that first meeting, the one who looked like King Kong's kid brother. Short, a thick-muscled bodybuilder type. Must have a nineteen-inch neck—not that there was much of it: His bowling ball of a head seemed plopped right onto his shoulders.

"Sorry, Vern," Gus muttered.

From the file photos he'd memorized before leaving Cheyenne, Charlie knew this Gus was William Gustave Lang, aged twenty-two, who'd spent most of his teen years in the Wyoming State Boys School. Just as he was trying to come up with Babyface's name, and getting nowhere fast, Ostergard made an introduction: "This here's Darrell Frederickson. He's come to the last two meetings. Darrell, Gus and Kyle."

Right. Kyle McIntyre, aged thirty-four. No record. He didn't look thirty-four, Charlie thought. Not at all. McIntyre had a puffy-cheeked, beardless choirboy face, the kind that people call ageless. Almost good-looking, like those calendar reproductions of boy Jesus paintings Charlie remembered tacked up on the bulletin board of his Sunday school class. Kyle had pink and white Jesus skin and round eyes so liquid and sparkling they made it seem like he was seeing beyond the person he was looking at and staring right into the eyes of God. But whatever claim to good looks McIntyre could have made was ruined by his mouth. It was small, all puckered up. Not as if for a kiss, but open, lips thrust forward, like that of a baby desperate to suck a nipple.

A memory popped up in Charlie's mind of the day they'd brought Morning home from the hospital. He was

holding the baby up to his face while Stacey unbuttoned
her shirt to nurse. He remembered staring into the baby's
eyes—the most extraordinary blue, the exact color of wild
columbine—saying, Hi, sweetheart, I'm your daddy, and
how amazed he'd been when her tiny puckered-up mouth
had glommed onto his nose and started sucking something fierce. Such power, such determination in that tiny
little thing.

"Howdy," Gus was saying.

"Howdy," Charlie replied. "Nice truck."

"It's Vern's." Gus's speech sounded thick, as if the
words had to get through a mouthful of oatmeal.

"Chevy makes a good truck," Charlie remarked, going
up to it, running his hand along the side of the flatbed.
"Got a Ford myself. A one fifty." He shook his head, as if
regretting the temporary insanity that had caused him to
make that choice.

"The Chev does what a truck should do." Ostergard
spoke in the overly modest manner of a man trying not to
lord his prosperity over someone less fortunate.

It was a hell of a piece of equipment, Charlie thought.
Probably thirty thousand dollars' worth. If the bureau
couldn't get these bastards for the bombing, his instincts
told him the IRS might make a net-worth case, have a
shot at a tax evasion conviction. The pickup, the coffee
urn, the damn satellite dish in the back, which could
probably transmit Ostergard's bullshit to Alpha Cen-
tauri: Could they have come from a few hundred bucks a
week in TV repairs? He squatted down to peer under the
chassis. "Neat," he commented. The truck had dualies,
dual wheels, in the rear. Plus an extended cab that could
seat five men, six in a pinch. Who the hell needed a truck
like this to haul TV sets? A vehicle like this would be

used for towing heavy stuff: horse trailers—or military equipment. With six big tires on the road, the Chevy could handle tremendous weight.

Following the others into Vern's TV Repair, Charlie saw no sign of weapons, at least not in the front room. A man in denim overalls was working on a television. Watching it, actually, enraptured; he could be looking at the last quarter of a tight Super Bowl game, except all that was playing was static and snow. Ostergard acted as if the repairman wasn't there at all, except for telling him to turn down the sound. When he failed to oblige, Ostergard tapped him on the shoulder. The man flinched, said, Sorry, real sorry, Vern, and lowered the volume until the staticky crackle stopped.

Gus Lang, in military boots heavy enough to fight a war in Antarctica, tramped into the back of the shop. Kyle McIntyre, however, remained beside Ostergard. Charlie tried not to look at his sucky mouth, but his eyes kept being drawn back to it. The awful thing was, he knew McIntyre was self-conscious about it and was furious at Charlie for noticing it. So he tried to concentrate solely on Ostergard, except Ostergard was off on the same thing he'd been talking about for over two hours at the second Wrath meeting—mixed use of public lands and how the rights of ranchers to graze their herds were being trampled by Washington bureaucrats who knew nothing about raising cattle. This was something Charlie knew about. Something he actually agreed with. He should be listening with both ears.

But then, from that reasonable premise, Ostergard took a couple of leaps of logic so enormous they could no longer be classified as logical. They defied not just reason but common sense. Somehow he was back to the Jews

again, going on about how they were using the Bureau of
Land Management in their manipulations to ruin the
ranchers so they could buy up the land cheap, build show-
place houses with huge hot tubs and have sex in them
with white women. Blond, blue-eyed white women.

Ostergard signaled he was finished by breathing an
exhausted sigh and leaning against the worktable.
"They're following me," he said quietly to Charlie. Kyle
McIntyre leaned beside his leader, almost touching him, a
silent witness to the persecution.

"Jews are following you?" Charlie asked.

"Their agents," Ostergard replied. "Government
agents."

"Like . . . ?"

"Probably FBI or ATF."

"Why?" Charlie asked, knowing his shock had to look
genuine.

"Some trouble around here. They're trying to lay it at
my door."

"What trouble?"

"You hear about a bomb that didn't go off over in Jackson?" Charlie nodded. "Well, just because they know the
power of my message, they're all over me. Wherever I go,
they follow." The guy *is* nuts, Charlie thought. With him
being undercover, no federal agency was going anywhere
near Ostergard, for fear of tipping him off that he was
important enough to be the subject of an investigation. "I
go to get gas, they're behind me." The county sheriff?
Charlie wondered. The town police? Would they be
dumb enough to tail Ostergard in an unmarked car on a
rural road where two cars were heavy traffic? Dubious.
The locals knew what they were dealing with better than
the feds. "I go to the hardware store, there's their car. Go

out for a drink, and guess who's with me? They're driving past the bar. I can't lose them." Charlie shook his head in commiseration. Ostergard seemed grateful. Kyle McIntyre, however, continued to behave as if Charlie weren't there. His eyes remained wide, never varying in expression, like a cat's eyes. It didn't matter whether he was looking at the Wrath leader, the repairman watching static on TV or a couple of small square circuit boards on the worktable. Anything or nothing at all could be read into those round brown eyes. "I wish I could just . . ." Ostergard paused. "Darrell, let me ask you something. You're a mechanic?"

"Right."

"If, say, while I was, like, at a gun show—you know, being followed, spied on—and one of my friends kind of slipped out, is there a way . . . ?" His voice subsided. He glanced down, as if overcome with shyness.

"A way to make their car not start?"

"Right."

"You could pull one of the leads going to the ignition coil. The car won't spark, so it won't start." Again, Charlie had to give Ostergard credit for subtlety. No what-a-crappy-idea expression came over his face, no uh-uh shake of the head. Still, the man was somehow communicating that this high school trick wasn't the solution he was looking for. "Of course," Charlie pressed on, "anyone who knows about cars could pick that up in two seconds flat."

"What would you do, Darrell?" A casual question: just curious.

"You mean, like, so someone wouldn't be able to figure it out?" Ostergard nodded slowly. "Probably pull one of the wires going to the starter motor. That's under the car.

They'd probably be looking under the hood for an hour, saying, 'What the heck is wrong?' and never find it. It's a bundle of wires, a little hard to reach, so you'd probably have to get down and get to it with one of those, you know, extended-tip screwdrivers. On your Chevy"—he hesitated, trying to picture the photo they'd shown him in Quantico—"the wire you're looking for would most likely be brown or that light-purple thing . . . violet, but it can change from truck to truck, car to car." Charlie felt bad thinking some poor bastard parked to go to a gun show with a common car, like a Taurus, was going to have a dead vehicle on his hands because this asshole was convinced that particular model was the official car of the Federal Bureau of Investigation. "If I can ever do you a good turn, Vern, I'd be glad to."

"You mean . . . ?" Ostergard made a twisting screwdriver gesture. Charlie Blair nodded. He felt a blaze of excitement: I'm getting there! He's starting to trust me, starting to— And Kyle McIntyre, only two inches from Ostergard anyway, put his sucky mouth right up against his leader's ear and said something so low Charlie couldn't even hear the hiss of a whisper. "Well, Darrell," Ostergard said, "if and when I need some doing done, I'll know who to call."

Charlie had been dreading the suit's arrival. She'd wear fur-lined boots and look so out of place she might as well flash her FBI credentials to everyone in Jackson Hole. No, worse. She'd be one of those overhearty, I'm-just-one-of-the-boys female agents, and she'd punch him in the biceps and ask, How the hell are you, big guy? But Jeanette S. Wagner, the suit from Washington, the control agent the bureau sent not only to debrief Charlie but to make sure he was alive, sane and in no immediate peril, was not wearing a suit. In fact, her heavy black slacks and green parka were well worn, her boots crisscrossed with powder-white lines from a hundred different snows, to make her look as if she belonged.

Her manner seemed right too: Despite the cold, she wasn't jumping around like an East Coast ninny, hugging herself, clapping her gloved hands together to keep warm. Her clear-eyed, clean looks were western too. She was tall, close to six feet, in her mid-forties, with the clear, shiny skin of a woman who either is a year-round athlete or has figured out the no-makeup-looking makeup equivalent.

As arranged, she had made a small puncture in her right front tire, then called Bill's Auto from a cell phone a few minutes after one, when Charlie was back from lunch and Bill was just going off. If he'd seen her first, he wouldn't have suggested a flat; she looked like someone who could not only change her own tire but rebuild an entire engine. But here he was with the tow truck. He'd driven the four miles to where she'd pulled off on the side of the road once her tire got low enough. As he chocked the wheel, he asked, "You from around here originally?"

She shook her head, then gave him a Department of Justice Official Business smile. "Hate to be a bureaucrat, but just in case anyone's watching you . . ." The temperature was below zero. Her breath barely made it past her lips before it froze.

"We can talk. There's not another car on the road." Charlie saw he was sounding defensive, desperate. What the hell: He was lonely. He wanted to talk to a regular person. Even though they'd told him fifty different ways during training, he hadn't been prepared for how isolated he felt. At least if you were infiltrating the Cosa Nostra you'd get spaghetti and meatballs and could talk sports or women. Mafiosi might be extortionists and killers, but they were still guys. With Wrath, all you got to do was listen to Ostergard lecture on how whites were getting fucked over, or listen to the other clowns give Ostergard their wish lists of ammo for the Final Battle, as if he were Santa Claus. No meatballs: The only food he was ever offered was the leftovers from their meetings, failed doughnut experiments—caramel-cherry or some pukey, crunchy thing that tasted like blueberry-polyurethane. To support his cover, he'd brought some Wrath pamphlets into work: "The Coming Race War" and "Us and Them—How to Take Back America," and he muttered about ZOG and race mixing. Just as he would have, Bill and the other mechanic, Paul, behaved as if he was slightly off. They were friendly enough not to seem unfriendly, but they weren't issuing any invitations for an after-work beer.

"I'm sorry," Jeanette said. "I have to go by the book. We can't risk looking like we're socializing."

"If you were getting your tire fixed, wouldn't you shoot the breeze with the guy who's fixing it?"

"This has to look strictly business." She was very determined. He sensed she might have a lot riding on this case, just as he did. She turned, so she was facing away from the road, looking at the car.

"Ostergard thinks he's being tailed," he said.

Jeanette turned to look at him. "As in tailed by a law enforcement agency?" Charlie nodded. "I guess that's why they call these guys paranoid," she observed. "Did you see anyone in either of the Wrath meetings you went to who might be Russell Dillard?"

"No," he said, loosening the lug nuts on her wheel. He'd grabbed a cup of coffee before he left, and his gloves were probably back on top of the Mr. Coffee. The wrench was so cold Charlie glanced down at the palms of his hands, expecting to see frozen, dead flesh. It was barely red. "And I didn't see anyone remotely resembling Dillard in Vern's store either. The only one new to me there was a guy in coveralls, the repairman, about sixty. He's got brown teeth. Makes you want to keep the conversation serious, because the last thing you want him to do is smile. Not that anyone says anything that calls for a smile." Jeanette Wagner appeared to be on the verge of reminding Charlie that as much as she'd like to talk, they might be under observation. By who? he wanted to ask her. Wrath sociopaths in snowdrifts, watching them through telescopic sights? He was embarrassed—no, ticked off—that she saw him as being so lonely she had to distance herself from him. He got back to business: "No reports of Dillard anywhere else?"

"No," she said.

"What's your best guess?"

"Officially, he's missing. My guess? He skipped town." Now that Jeanette had gone and done something so totally un-Washington—offering a personal opinion—he liked her a little better.

"Could they have killed him?" Charlie didn't know where that thought came from and was surprised when he heard himself express it.

"Killed him? They could have," she said coolly. He wished he could feel her calm at the notion of Dillard's being iced. All he felt was the coffee he'd had fifteen minutes earlier, rising inside him like mercury in a thermometer. "If Wrath wanted a big blast and he didn't give it to them, they might have killed him—out of pique, or to set an example for others. But we don't know that. Think about this too: If the fizzle was deliberate, whose idea was it? Ostergard's or Russ Dillard's?"

"Do you think Dillard had the guts to stand up to Ostergard?" he asked.

"Well, he was an informant. He knew we had his number. Did he have the guts? He robbed a bank, held a gun on three tellers and eight customers. That's guts or stupidity. You pick."

"Just one more question." Charlie started jacking up the car. "Ultimately, who was Dillard more afraid of? The FBI or Vernon Ostergard? Ostergard and his boys were Dillard's whole world. Could he just pick up and leave? He was the one who risked so much for them. He robbed a bank—"

"And got caught," Jeanette reminded him, "and was forced to inform, so he probably felt . . ." He sensed that the word she wanted was "guilty," but he knew it was too wimpy and psychological a word for an agent to use. ". . . bad. So I think he cut and ran."

"You know," Charlie said, "I had this idea the other day." He hoped she didn't think he was getting back into some love-me, need-me, talk-to-me mode. "Maybe Ostergard told him to blow Pearlstein to kingdom come and he screwed up and was afraid to go back. Ostergard doesn't lose his temper, but when he's even a little ticked off, he can make people feel worthless without a single word. That's his true gift, silent communication. Even if we had a million listening devices in his shop, his house, wherever, we might never get anything, because he has a way of conveying things that's amazing. I mean, he could just raise an eyebrow, and somehow one of his men will *know* that means 'Nuke Washington.' Of course, most of them are such losers they'd screw up and bomb Cleveland. Not Kyle McIntyre, though. At least I'm not ready to write him off. When someone is as unreadable as he is, you tend to believe he's brilliant, or at least smart. For all I know, he could have a sixty-five IQ."

As he changed the tire, Jeanette asked Charlie how he thought he was doing. He recognized it was one of those open-ended questions designed not only to elicit intelligence but also to test whether he was still sound of mind or had slipped over the edge.

Throughout his career, long before he volunteered to go undercover, Charlie had understood that being a bureaucracy, the bureau was not comfortable with uncertainties. An undercover operation, by its very volatility, was a danger to both the life of the agent in place and the careers of his superiors. Until he was spewing spectacular amounts of information, thus making the operation indispensable, his assignment could be canceled at a moment's notice. In fact, Washington would probably be relieved—no, delighted—to call it off. So to demonstrate that he was not only not nuts but a fount of information that must be kept spouting at all costs, Charlie kept talking until the spare tire was on and the car down on all four wheels. He reported on the meetings, on Gus Lang, Kyle McIntyre and Ostergard. No tic, no offhand remark, was too insignificant to mention.

"Do I still qualify as sane?" he asked, as he wrote up a bill.

"You're doing all right," she said, reaching into her handbag for her wallet. He waited for her to call him Charlie, but she was counting out dollar bills. There was probably some regulation that prohibited the control agent from calling the undercover guy by his real name; maybe a panel of shrinks at Quantico had submitted a report saying it might trigger anxiety—or make the guy feel so warm and fuzzy he'd let down his guard. Still, even if she wasn't calling him Charlie, he didn't want her to go.

"Listen, they're not comfortable with me yet."

"I've got to get a move on," Jeanette said.

"Ostergard likes me, I think. But my guess is, Kyle McIntyre is dripping poison in his ear. He's probably saying: Who is this guy, coming out of nowhere . . . so soon after the bomb business? So it's going to take time. You know you've got to be patient."

"There's a reason for policy, why we need undercover agents to report often. It's not some whim of Washington. If you're not becoming so ho-hum to them that they don't have a single doubt about talking in front of you, about asking for your help, then you're in danger—to say nothing of the operation."

"It could take months."

"You have months if they show signs of accepting you. If they don't, you have weeks. You knew that going in."

"But they could set off another bomb anytime."

"No grandstand plays. You can't afford to attract their attention."

"I've *got* to attract their attention. At least get Ostergard one hundred percent on my side so he'll stop listening to McIntyre."

"Oh, by the way." Jeanette stood by the car door. "About Kyle McIntyre."

"What about him?"

"There was talk his wife didn't want him leaving Sheridan, coming down here."

"I didn't know he was married."

"He's not. She was found dead a week and a half before he left." She opened her car door. "Fell off their back deck—down fifty feet into a gully. Broken neck. The sheriff up there was suspicious but couldn't find a thing. Neither could the Wyoming DCI lab, and they're good. Who knows. I'd keep an eye out for him if I were you."

"Sounds like he might have a nasty temper," Charlie said.

In the mysteries and spy stories Charlie read, bad bars stank of stale beer and piss. The Eagle, however, merely smelled of cigarette smoke and sweaty men at the end of a workday. To him, it looked as though it were trying to be not tough, just ugly. No neon signs from breweries colored the room, no gleaming display of bottles called forth a thirst. It was dark, darker than most bars, in part because bulbs that blew were rarely replaced but left in sockets, lightless, blackened. The Eagle lacked the raunch, the tough seediness, to attract desperadoes with big thirsts and deep pockets. It was just plain crummy.

Gus Lang hung his jacket and hat on a hook and came up to the bar. He was one of those men who were so massive, so mean and stupid-looking, that other men simply stepped out of his way. "How's it going, Darrell?" he asked.

"Not bad." Charlie did not step out of his way. "How's it going with you?"

"Not bad."

"Vern coming?"

"He's outside."

"You drive him, Gus?" After appearing to consider the question, Gus Lang nodded. With the black five o'clock

shadow that looked painted on his face, he looked like
Bluto in *Popeye*. A bully, a man who liked to crush things.
That was his value to Ostergard. Charlie did not think he
was stupid, though. Just slow, a human slug: It took Gus
longer than most people to process data, to brake a
pickup, to put down a heavy crate once he'd lifted it. "I
like that truck of Vern's," Charlie remarked. "Heavy,
though. How's the pickup on hills?"

"Real good."

Gus ordered a beer. The two fell into silence. Charlie
knew, of course, not to ask Gus or any of the men around
Ostergard a direct question. It wasn't simply that any
inquiry would make them suspicious. It was that no one
in Wrath seemed to talk much except to Ostergard himself. Here they were, two guys having a beer on a Thursday night, and there was no "What are you doing this
weekend?" No "What do you think of those red beers?"
Nothing. Like him and Gus, the rest of the dozen or so
men in the bar—Vern's Boys, Charlie had come to think
of them—had almost nothing to say either. They were
there to wait.

The older guy who had come to the Wrath meeting in
a tie and jacket was now in bib overalls—like the old
Mormon cowboys who used to work at his grandfather's
ranch. With his stick-up-the-ass posture, he looked
uncomfortable in them, as if he'd dressed for a Halloween
party to which no one else wore a costume. A couple of
others from the meeting were also at the bar. The big,
greasy-faced guy. One of the two men who had looked to
him like ranch hands: not the dark-skinned one, but the
other. His white-blond hair looked as though it had been
cut by the cereal-bowl method, but it was foolishly boy-
ish on a pockmarked face with a hatchet-shaped nose.

The Eagle, for Christ's sake. It ought to be a federal violation to put the name of the national bird up on a crap-house like this, built like the final project of someone about to flunk out of carpentry school. Hairy bits of insulation stuck out from the inch-wide gap between walls and ceiling tiles. The bar was hardly more than a thick wooden plank, with sharp ninety-degree corners instead of silky, rounded edges. Forget the traditional brass rail; a cheesy aluminum tube under Charlie's foot felt as if it might give way under the boot of any radical weighing more than one fifty. He glanced around. The booths were ... Jesus, Charlie still couldn't get over them. He had never seen anything so awful. All-in-one molds, a bench-table-bench prefabricated in gray-beige plastic. Where the hell had they come from? A Bureau of Prisons prototype for a mess hall of the future, rejected on the grounds that they violated the Eighth Amendment's ban on cruel and unusual punishment?

Ostergard came through the door. The howling wind was putting up a fight, as if it were desperate and was willing to brave this dump just to get in out of the cold. Ostergard and Kyle McIntyre had to press their shoulders hard against the door and walk it closed. "Bet it goes down to twenty below tonight," Ostergard said, to no one in particular. Still, all the men in the place as well as the bartender murmured agreement: Bet it does. Real cold, Vern. Right, Vern. They edged toward him, as though he were a woodstove radiating heat.

All Ostergard seemed to be radiating was anger. Not that he shouted or banged his fist against the bar. His voice remained subdued, the same Mr. Normal American voice Charlie had heard at the first Wrath meeting. Still, as he talked about what he had been talking about hours earlier, about how the United States attorney in Montana had violated the rights of the Freemen, no one in the Eagle could escape the force of Ostergard's wrath. Or his sorrow. Charlie sensed the power of the man, how everyone in that big room wanted to soothe him, console him. Even Charlie himself. Although there were no fireworks, there was something threatening about Ostergard's displeasure. You would do almost anything to calm him down, yet were afraid to interrupt him to try.

A half hour of wrath and sorrow. Forty-five minutes. Almost eight o'clock now. Since the first meeting, Charlie had taken to turning around his watch. With the face on the underside of his wrist, he could lift a glass of beer or scratch his nose and check how long the diatribe had gone on, place bets with himself as to when it would be over. What was it? Some kind of weird dictator thing? Like Hitler, Castro, ranting on for hours?

"It's not that I go with the Freemen down the line on everything," he was telling them. Fifty minutes. "You know that."

Time crawled. Boredom beat out fear. Charlie flaked out. Since the first Wrath meeting, he had rediscovered a talent he'd barely tapped in his Physiology of Ruminant Digestion class: listening to every word, able to repeat every word if necessary, yet simultaneously living another existence. He began to have second thoughts about having pressured Jeanette Wagner into pushing his acceptance by Wrath further and faster. In the here and now, he did what all the men were doing: nodding his agreement to what Ostergard was saying. I get what you mean, Vern. Never thought about that before. Tell me more.

"Their hearts are in the right place—there's no denying that, is there? Know what I call the Freemen? Our brothers in arms. But they get hung up on legal stuff—jurisdiction, commercial liens for canceling debt. They lose sight of what this fight is all about." He stopped, and when he spoke again his voice was hushed, like a prayer. "We're fighting for the survival of the white race."

Three minutes past nine. Ostergard had drunk only half his beer. Charlie didn't see how the Eagle made any money. Except for Kyle McIntyre, none of them really drank. Vern's Boys could all nurse their beers for an hour. McIntyre was a different story. He drank whiskey neat, placing his puckered mouth almost over the shot glass, taking a large sip—as if he planned on gargling with it. He swished it around a couple of times, then kept it in his mouth, taking small swallows every few seconds, until he was finished and ready for more. Besides being repulsive, his full-mouth method put a damper on conversation. Of course, being that Kyle McIntyre didn't converse, there was no problem. Drunkenness didn't seem to be a problem for him either. The bartender, a tomato-faced guy and the deceptively friendly name of Timmy, kept pouring. McIntyre kept drinking. He never nodded off or rambled on, never got belligerent, never got that vacant, stupid look. Naturally, he never acted happy.

Nine-fifteen. Unlike every other joint in the valley, there was neither horseshoe nor spur up on the Eagle's walls. It could have been a bar in North Carolina or North Dakota. Wherever, there was no doubt what it was. The writing was on the wall. Someone had stuck up a couple of bumper stickers— "White Makes Right" and "Sure you can take away my gun. Bullets first." The stickers flanked a giant Confederate flag. That was all there was at the Eagle. No television above the bar. No jukebox, no

dartboard, no pool table, no women. This was a place for
white guys who didn't have time for fun.

Not a place, Charlie knew, for a black man. His friend
Dick Alexander once told him about how, being black,
he'd developed a sixth sense about unfriendly venues.
There were spots where a black man was so rare all conversation would stop when one walked in. However,
such a place, although uncomfortable, was not necessarily dangerous. There were other places—bars, gas stations, even burger joints—where trouble was in the air.
Sometimes it just stayed in the air, Dick had conceded.
But do I want to risk it? he'd asked. Me against three or
four rednecks? Sure, I'm an agent, I've had hand-to-hand
combat training, close-quarters weapon control. The
question is, do I want to test my proficiency on a Saturday afternoon when all I'm looking for is a Coke or a can
of STP? Or do I just say to hell with it? Get out while
the getting's good.

Nine thirty-five. Finally, Ostergard said, See you,
boys, and walked out with Gus Lang on one side, Kyle
McIntyre on the other. Charlie counted out one hundred
twenty seconds to himself and followed outside. The
three men from Wrath were just standing beside the
front grille of a Range Rover, staring at the two men
who had just gotten out. One was a black man. Dressed
like a tourist, in tight black ski pants and one of those
new, thin jackets that fit like a second skin and are supposed to keep you warm to thirty below. It was pale yellow with black racing stripes, and in this bitch of a
wind, he did not look cold. He looked sleek. He looked
rich. A few feet from the front passenger door there was
a white guy, in a hat with a pom-pom, for God's sake.
Confronted by three men without pom-poms. Charlie

made four. "You don't want to go in here," Ostergard was saying. Charlie positioned himself beside Gus Lang. Four against two.

If this black man had any of Dick Alexander's sixth sense, he was not showing it. He wore a bright expression, interested, slightly amused, as if listening to an outrageous caller on talk radio. "They got Coors on tap in there?" the black man asked. His friend chuckled.

"Get back into that car and get out of here," Ostergard told him.

"Don't give me any shit, man. I'm just going in for a beer," the black man said, louder. He had a deep voice. A ghetto accent.

"Stand back, guys," his white friend said. "Come on."

Ostergard raised his voice. "You don't belong here. Get out." The black man turned and looked over at Ostergard. Then he turned to his friend and shook his head, as if to demand, Can you believe this moron?

Charlie sensed that Gus, beside him, was processing the information that this (a) black(!) man had (b) just disregarded Vernon Ostergard's command and (c) was going to try to go into the Eagle and get a Coors. Kyle took a step closer to the newcomers. With that, Charlie took two fast strides over to the men. He grabbed the black man by the neck of his high-priced jacket and half dragged, half shoved him to the driver's door. "You heard what the man said. Get out of here, nigger." For what seemed like an almost comically long moment, the black guy stared at him, not comprehending. Then he punched Charlie hard, in the gut.

Exactly as planned. He'll hit you below the solar plexus, Jeanette had advised Charlie. Pretend to double over for a second. Pretend? Then go to it. Don't try to injure him, obviously, but don't hold back. He's had special training for this.

Charlie was still groaning from the punch. He was shocked at how much it hurt. Though he wanted to bend over, embrace his torso, he punched the man in the face, hitting his upper lip and cheek. While the man put his hand to his mouth to feel for blood and teeth, Charlie belted him in the gut. The guy's abs felt like concrete. Nevertheless, grunting, he doubled over. Charlie kicked his leg out from under him and the man crashed to the ground. Charlie followed him down on his knees so he could draw back his arm and hit him again. This time, the man screamed such a horrible cry Charlie almost screamed himself. "I'm leaving!" he cried to Charlie. "Joe!" he called out for his friend. "I'm going," he vowed to Charlie. Charlie could hear scuffling behind him, but he didn't turn. Instead, he stood, and as the man tried to pull himself up, Charlie kicked him flat yet again. Not hard. The guy knew how to make noise, how to fall.

Charlie stood over him, fists clenched, panting. *Sorry*. He was dying to whisper that, but he'd been warned against it. He knows you're doing what you have to do, Jeanette had said. He knows you're going to call him nigger. He knows you may have to hurt him. He's not a draftee. He's a volunteer. Just remember the moves and let him take it from there. Charlie was dying to say it, though: *I'm so sorry*. Sorry to call you that. Sorry you have to go through this.

The man managed to get up on all fours but seemed afraid to rise, afraid Charlie would kick him again. Charlie grabbed the neck of his jacket and pulled him to his feet. "When someone tells you to get going, nigger, you get out. Understand?" The man barely nodded, as if terrified of making any gesture that might displease Charlie. "Do you understand?" Charlie roared in the man's face.

"I understand," the man said, his voice shaking.

Still gripping the jacket, Charlie pulled the man to the door of the car, opened it and pushed him inside. His white friend was already in the passenger seat. The automatic door locks clicked, and the black man, his mouth open wide in shock, patted his jacket, searching for his key. Finally, he found it and started the car.

McIntyre pulled Ostergard aside as though sensing the man might use the vehicle as a weapon. "You shouldn't have let them get into the car, Darrell. You should have finished the job. You should—"

"Kyle," was all Ostergard said. McIntyre fell silent.

Charlie turned toward his truck. He walked gingerly, as if feeling the pain in his gut for the first time. Well, it did hurt like hell. But nothing like what that other agent must be feeling. A bruising fight, a real-enough fight. No one watching it could think it was staged.

Silence. Suddenly, Ostergard was beside him, his arm around him gently, as if he himself could feel the pain from the punch in his own gut, the nausea that was coming on fast. Ostergard's soft gray eyes were more luminous than they'd ever been. They appeared lit with nothing so mean-spirited as blood lust. No, with simple joy. "Darrell," he said tenderly, almost lovingly, "you are a truly righteous man."

# 11

Three strikes, you're out, toots. That's what her father would call when he was pitching to her in the backyard. Even when Lauren was six or seven, Jed Miller cut her no slack; when she whiffed three times, he'd bawl, Yer outta here! and would not let her hit again until she actually threw down the bat and walked away from the old rocking chair cushion they used as home plate. She concluded later that being a teacher, he'd probably meant it as some larger life lesson: Play by the rules, or Seize the moment, because life does not offer infinite opportunity. But at six or seven, she could not discern his grand design, and she grew up compelled to get a task accomplished by the third try: diving under a wave, getting a boy to notice her, writing the lead to a story.

This was day three for her in McBride, Wyoming. All she'd done was gotten on a first-name basis with Dick, the owner of the grocery store, who'd said, Don't quote me, honey, but there's cars and trucks driving up to that Vern's day and night. Dollars'll get you doughnuts it's not TV fix-it business going on over there.

Day one had been a scouting expedition, the day she'd seen that guy and become all fluttery and thought for a moment: This is *him*! Every one of her normally sound instincts must have deserted her then, because that Marlboro Man without the Marlboro, that all-man, all-American dude, turned out to be a Nazi fuck-head named Darrell.

On the morning of day two, before leaving Jackson, she'd run into Chief Vultaggio's receptionist in The Grand Teton Coffee Shop, chatted her up, gone halves on an English muffin and learned—Cross your heart you won't say where you got this, Lauren, because we haven't made it public—that after giving a sermon denouncing the people who had planted a bomb in Mike Pearlstein's store as anti-Christian as well as anti-Semitic, the minister of the Pine Street Church of Christ began receiving bomb threats himself. Six phone calls so far, around two in the morning, again around four—just to make sure he couldn't get a good night's sleep. Lauren careened over an unplowed road to reach the minister, Harlan Washburn. He told her, Sorry, no comment. I've given a lot of thought to it, and I don't want to spread this kind of fear. She said, This won't see the light of day in Jackson Hole. It's strictly a New York story. So he told her, and his voice shook. Besides the bomb threats, the muffled-voiced caller had informed him, "We're turning on the oven for you and your Jew friends."

It was nearly noon of that second day when Lauren reached McBride. She stood in front of the grocery store eating Cracker Jacks, one at a time. Looking across the street to Vern's TV Repair, she commanded herself, Just do it! Instead, she'd gone back inside and bought a can of Mountain Dew and a Reese's Peanut Butter Cup, not unaware she might be harboring a wish to lapse into a diabetic coma and be flown back to New York.

When she awakened that third morning, she knew: Three strikes, you're out. She had to go. Could she hide her fear, walking into that place? She'd say something

like, Hi, I'm Lauren Miller of the *News,* from New York.
Her heart would be hammering so hard her eardrums
would throb to the rhythm.

Except here she was at Vern's TV Repair, pulling off
her earmuffs, yanking open the storm door, listening to
the screech of its broken hinge and feeling . . . Nothing.
Was it a terror so transcending normal fear that her nervous system had collapsed under the strain, rendering her
numb? Or was it simply this: She was a pro who had
weighed the risks before she left New York and determined that they were worth taking.

"Vernon Ostergard?" Four men were in the shop. An
older man at a worktable stood apart from the others,
massaging his chin, meditating on what looked like a
miniature stereo speaker and some TV guts as if he were
assembling a collage. Ostergard? Not him.

Yes! There he was, between two other men on molded
white plastic chairs pulled into the center of the room in
a tight triangle. No other furniture in the room, no
phone, nothing, not even a Styrofoam coffee cup. Just the
two men and Vernon Ostergard, on the cheapest of cheap
plastic indoor-outdoor chairs that would never biode-
grade, but would be ugly till the end of time. He looked
just as he had in that news shot she'd dug up at the
library: as bland in living color as in black and white.
With his thinning mouse-color hair, doughy skin and
narrow shoulders, he looked like the archetypal nonentity.

"What do you want?" he demanded.

"Mr. Ostergard, my name is Lauren Miller. I'm a
reporter—"

The man to his right, in a camouflage T-shirt, spat out,
"A *reporter,*" as if he could not decide whether to be sickened or enraged. He looked short but was so muscular

that he gave the impression of being as wide as he was high, a cube of muscles with a small head, like an action figure from a comic book.

"—with the *News*. We're a newspaper in New York."

The cube, predictably, was about to sneer "New York." But Ostergard put a restraining hand on the man's forearm. The forearm, she could see, was so pumped it looked inflated. In his case, however, there was no making out the muscle definition. Unlike those of most bodybuilder types, his arms were not bare but covered by a coat of hair so thick it looked like fur. With his small eyes, his face reminded her of the face of the stuffed bear she had seen in a bar in Jackson the night before. He even had a squished, upturned bear nose, so you could peer straight into his nostrils if you wanted to. She did not want to.

"I don't talk to reporters," Ostergard said. "Get out." The man on Ostergard's other side was not bad-looking. . . . No, wait. Something wasn't right about him. Pink and white baby skin. A too-tight tan sweater that revealed a ruffle of fat above his belt. Sexless, but not in a young, innocent way. Like a castrato. Some essential element was missing. Not his balls, necessarily. He wasn't manly and he wasn't effeminate. Gender did not apply to him. Glancing into his brown eyes so unnerved her that Lauren immediately turned back to Ostergard. If Ostergard looked beleaguered, troubled by her presence, if the muscle guy looked flustered, as if he couldn't decide whether to strangle her to please Ostergard or to ask her out, the castrato looked wrong, as if some crucial bit of DNA had been dropped in the microsecond before the merge that made him.

"You do talk to reporters, Mr. Ostergard." Lauren didn't smile, but she used an old reporter's trick, saying

"Pleasant" to herself to help compose her features. "You gave a long interview to the *Sheridan Press*—"

"I don't have anything to say to anybody in New York."

Still, he hadn't thrown her out yet, so she went on. "You know, people back east are taught that diversity is a good thing. You've been going around saying it's just the opposite, that the races shouldn't be mixing and mingling. You're saying a lot of thought-provoking stuff that our readers don't get to hear about."

"I don't give a damn about them."

"You might not, but when you speak out in New York, you're not just talking to New Yorkers. You're reaching a wider audience. It's the media capital of the world. If I were you, I'd view this as an opportunity."

His hand remained on the muscle guy's hairy arm. She got the sense, which she supposed was what Ostergard intended, that if he took his hand away, muscle guy would rise up and hurt her. "You're not me," he told her.

She repressed a small sigh of satisfaction; he had responded precisely as she'd hoped he would. "I know I'm not. What I am is a good, objective reporter who wants to understand what you're trying to say."

"You won't understand."

"I don't think that's accurate. I may or may not agree with you, but if you're as good a speaker as I've been led to believe, you can make me understand what your views are. And while it's not my job to endorse you or condemn you, I can get your ideas across."

"I want to know: Do you endorse us or condemn us?"

"What I believe doesn't matter," Lauren told him. "It's your views I'd be writing about, not mine." He looked so ordinary sitting there. The median American.

Well, he could be thinking "Pleasant" too. He had no frown furrows, no downturned mouth. Pleasant. Maybe she had been expecting some grotesquerie that would signify an evil nature, like Hitler with his bizarre little mustache, or Mussolini with his bald bullet head. But then she recalled the first photo she'd seen of Pol Pot, who had caused the slaughter of over a million Cambodians, and how she had been astounded by the sweetness of his smile. "Whatever your message is, is it only as big as Wyoming?"

"You think I'm going to fall for that?"

Well, sometimes it worked. "I'm not trying to flatter you. It wasn't meant as a compliment. It was meant as a question. How big, how national, are the issues you're raising?"

"How about: as important as the survival of the white race." He said it fast, angrily, as though she'd forced it out of him. But she sensed he was inventing the coercion, to save face with the other men. Having declared he did not talk to reporters, he didn't want to be seen as being so easily seducible by one of them.

Well, if he was in a pickle in regard to his followers, why the hell should she make it easy for him? Because the story was more important than her feelings about him. "I'm white," she said. "I don't feel my survival is being threatened."

"Then you're stupid."

"No. I'm not at all stupid." The shop wasn't overheated, but Lauren was beginning to poach inside her heavy coat. "I may be ignorant. Let's assume I am. Tell me what I don't know." She felt a drop of sweat leave her neck, meander down between her breasts and torso and glue her sweater to her skin.

Ostergard looked to the castrato. He might have agreed or disagreed, but there was no change in expression, although the pink tinge in his rounded cheeks deepened until the color was closer to red.

"We are threatened," Ostergard said. Abruptly, he looked away from Lauren and toward the repairman. "Mickey," he boomed, "did you forget that RCA in the back?" When there was no response, he said it again, even louder; the man looked up, said, Hokay, Vern, and left. "What we're trying to do," Ostergard went on, "is save our race. You media people make us out to be stupid bigots. We're not." He sounded calm, reasonable, not protesting too much. "When we call ourselves white supremacists, we're not saying we're better or worse than other races. All we're saying is we're different."

"In what way?"

"God created the white race last—for a purpose. We were made to rule the other races."

"Why do they need ruling?"

Ostergard shook his head in fatigue and annoyance. The muscle guy simply shook his head. "Because"—he paused for a moment, done in at having to explain yet again—"that's the God-given order of things. Whites rule. It's not a question of superiority or inferiority."

"Doesn't the word 'supremacist' imply superiority?"

"No. It just says, This is how God wanted it to be. Well, some say it's true that in certain areas whites are quote superior unquote."

"What areas?" She was about to put her hand into her pocket when she noticed the muscle guy's eyes on her. He might think she was going for a gun and not her pad and pen. "Is it okay if I write down what you say? I'd like to be able to quote you accurately."

Ostergard nodded, one small move of the head. "You have a tape recorder?" he asked.

"Yes. It would be great if I could tape the interview. Probably be easier for both of us."

Slowly, she reached into her other pocket and pulled out her recorder. Ostergard signaled to hand it over. When she did, he gave it to the castrato, who pressed the Play button. She voiced a silent thank-you for having remembered to put in a fresh tape. Her last interview, the day before, had been with the Reverend Washburn. His voice had broken as he tried to subdue his fear and fury. Removing the tape, the castrato scrutinized the recorder's mechanism. When he finished with that examination, he strode over to the worktable, adjusted the light to shine on it, then probed it with a tiny screwdriver. At last, he reinserted the tape and handed the recorder back to Ostergard. He returned it to Lauren.

"Is there a table or an extra chair I can put this on?" she asked.

"Get up, Gus." The muscle guy stood with surprising agility for someone so massive. He was short, barely taller than Lauren—far shorter than the stuffed bear in the bar. After checking the tape, she set the recorder on the plastic chair, turned it on and moved back from the men. "Where was I?" Ostergard asked.

"In some areas—I guess you were saying in some areas of endeavor—people might say whites are superior." She pulled out her pad and pen. Gus walked around her, looking her up and down, then stood at muscular attention by the door. She wasn't sure what he was guarding against: entering or leaving.

"Why do you need to write it too?" Ostergard demanded.

"It's not just what you say; it's how you say it. When I'm writing my story, I want to be able to see you saying the words on the tape. Now, in what areas are whites superior?"

"To the black race? Intelligence." SOS, she thought: Same Old Shit. "Law-abidingness." He stopped, as if waiting for her to put up an East Coast argument he could then refute. But she knew what her job was. She kept her mouth shut, her pen poised. "Superior in sexual restraint. School performance. Resistance to disease." The phrases slid out with such ease she knew that despite his one-second pauses to demonstrate that he was reflecting, this was a performance, one he'd given many times. "What I'm saying is this: I'm not judging superior or inferior, but I think it's fair to say most people think whites can be considered quote superior unquote to blacks. Maybe not in sports performance, because of their build, but in all those other ways. Now, on the other hand, take North Asians. I'd be the first to tell you that in some of those areas, North Asians are quote superior unquote to whites. Does that make them yellow supremacists?"

"If Asians are superior, why shouldn't they rule?"

"Because that's not how God meant it to be."

"Tell me what God meant."

Men in the West, Lauren thought, were generally deferential to women. Call it sexism, call it courtesy, but they were perpetually sweeping off hats, holding doors, offering chairs. Ostergard and the castrato, both seated, were content to have her stand. She was so hot. Her feet felt awash inside her wool socks and her boots. Still, she made no move to open her coat, not only because they might think she was going for a weapon but because she did not want to show them that they were able to make her uncomfortable.

"You've heard of God's chosen people?" Ostergard waited until she nodded. "Who are they?"

"The Jews?"

"No, no, no. At least not who you people in New York think of as Jews. That's what *they* want you to think, that God chose them." He chuckled and shook his head at this sad, cruel hoax. She knew without looking that the muscle man behind her by the door was shaking his head as well. "No, it's *white* people who are the only descendants of Adam. *They're* the chosen descendants of Abraham. Now you're going to ask me, where does the Jew fit into this?"

"Aren't most Jews white?"

"No." He sounded tired but patient, like a parent who has too often corrected a dull-witted child. "They are not white, except the ones who've bred with whites can be said to have part-white offspring. Now, as to what they are: Some good men will tell you that they're the children of Cain. Others call them the 'serpent seed.' Have you heard of that?"

"I may have heard the term." No, hold on. That was *Demon Seed,* a movie about a computer wanting to take over the world. Maybe it was a Jewish computer. "I don't know what it means."

"Eve and Satan had sex." He had to be kidding. Except he wasn't. "Eve gave birth to Cain. Now what would that have done?"

"Tell me."

"It would have started a line of half-devil people."

"And what line is that?"

"What most people today call quote Jews unquote.

But they're not. The *real* Jews, the lost tribe of Israel, are the white people, people of British and German and Scandinavian blood. Not people who can pass as white."

"What are you?" another voice asked her. It was breathy, almost Marilyn Monroe-ish, although quite deep. It took Lauren an instant to realize it belonged to the castrato. Stupid, she thought, to expect a soprano. "I said—"

"What am I?" She looked to Ostergard. Now that the question that had not occurred to him had been asked, he looked anxious for an answer. "Look, this interview isn't about me or my pedigree. It's about Mr. Ostergard and Wrath. By the way," she asked the castrato, "what's your name?"

"None of your business."

"It's my business if you're involved in Wrath. I'd like to have the names of the people with Mr. Ostergard when I interviewed him."

"I said, None of your business."

"Then I have to wonder what reasons you have for not giving me your name."

Because the castrato and Ostergard were seated so close together, she could not tell if there was telepathy or a subtle pressure of knee against knee, but suddenly the man said, "Kyle McIntyre." After getting him to spell it, she turned to the door and asked for Gus's last name.

"L-a-n-g," Gus said to the floor. The one the chief said had a long juvenile record.

"How come you're hiding what you are? Because you're a Jew?" Because of McIntyre's deep, whispery voice, he sounded like an inept drag queen mimicking Monroe. It wasn't amusing, though: not the question; not the man. Lauren knew no one in her right mind would laugh at this guy. She hadn't a single doubt that all that was keeping him from getting rid of her was that Ostergard wanted the one thing she could offer him—ink. The question was, how would McIntyre define getting rid of her? Tossing her out? Killing her? Criminal record or no criminal record, he was infinitely more dangerous than muscle-bound Gus at the door. She fought the urge to reach into her pocket and grab hold of her pepper spray.

"Why do you ask if I'm Jewish? Because I'm from New York?" Who was speaking? Some bolder, more clearheaded version of herself? She didn't think she had ever met this woman before. "The answer is, Mr. McIntyre, all you have to know about me is that I'm a reporter. Take it or leave it." She glanced down at her notes, then looked to Ostergard. "You were telling me some good men would call Jews half-devils. If I decide to expand my piece, maybe I will interview some of those men. But I'm here because I want to focus on you. I need to know what *you've* got to say."

Ostergard still had not digested her response. He was eyeing her closely, as if by squinting slightly he could see inside her and discern the truth. Jew? If she had to guess, he was in the final stages of concluding No, white: not from any objective evidence but because he did not want to admit to himself or his followers that he hadn't known one the instant he saw one.

"What do *I* say?" he asked. "I say, In all honesty, I can't tell you where the people who call themselves Jews came from." Humility. That's what he was communicating now. Lauren noticed the slightest rise of those narrow shoulders into a shrug, the infinitesimal tilt of the beginning-to-bald head. He was showing her: I'm not

an egomaniac like my competition. I don't make pro-
nouncements I can't prove. I'm just a decent man trying
to talk some sense. "They may or may not be the actual
spawn of Satan," he said softly. "But as a race, don't they
have all the sly qualities of a serpent?" Lauren wrote, *d ty
hv al sly qal of serp?* and waited while Ostergard waited
for her answer. At last, he went on. "They never work by
the sweat of their brow, do they? They grow fat from the
labor of others." She could see he was getting excited.
He wanted to rise from his chair, move about. Not orate;
that wasn't his style. But play his role to the fullest. He
did not have ABC and CBS. All he had was her. Still, she
could be his dress rehearsal, his lead to the big time
although he could not perform for her; he had already
strayed too far from I don't talk to reporters. He spoke
quietly: "Jews don't build. They plunder. They have a
three-thousand-year history of nation wrecking, from
ancient Egypt to Russia."

"What did they do to ancient Egypt?"

"Brought it down."

"Wasn't it God working through Moses—who I guess
you would call a white-person Jew—who brought it
down? Isn't that what the Bible says?"

"I can quote the entire Bible chapter and verse."

"Are you a minister?"

"No, I'm just an ordinary workingman." Ostergard
was very far from a buffoon, she was realizing. His gift
was certainly not deductive reasoning. But it was pre-
sentation. He chose the right words, accompanied by the
subtlest gestures, which led his listeners to precisely
what he wanted them to think. Both the words themselves and the gentle style of his "an ordinary workingman" put one notion—bingo!—right in her mind:

Jesus, a carpenter. An ordinary workingman, just like Ostergard. Some equation!

Behind her, the door opened. "Hey, Darrell," she heard Gus say.

She turned around. An ordinary workingman in grease-stained jeans. Under an old down vest, he wore a shabby flannel shirt, frayed at the collar, translucently thin at the elbow, shrunken so that the knobs of his wrists stuck out from the sleeves. The man she had seen two days before. For a moment, Lauren's composure deserted her. She must have flashed him a look—hatred, or maybe just plain loathing—because he took a step back and almost banged into Gus. But he recovered quickly and said to Ostergard, "Didn't mean to break in on you."

"She's a reporter. From New York." The voice was polite but held enough chill to say, You don't belong.

"I'll catch you tonight, then, Vern," the man replied.

"Fine, Darrell."

As he turned to open the door, Lauren said, "What's your last name?"

"What?"

"Your last name."

Apparently another signal was sent by Ostergard, because the man muttered "Frederickson." Before she could ask him to spell it, he was gone.

"One of our new members," Ostergard said.

"How many new members have joined up since you came to Jackson Hole?"

"I don't give numbers."

"One or five hundred?"

"I don't give numbers."

"All right, then let's get back to what you were telling me, about Jews being responsible for the decline of civilization. How did they bring down Russia?"

"Did you ever hear of Karl Marx? Marxism?"

"But the Jews didn't run the Soviet Union. It was Lenin, Stalin . . . I can't remember all of them. Khrushchev, Brezhnev, Andropov, Gorbachev. None of them were Jews."

"Jews ran the country *through* them. Just as they're running things here. Now you're going to say, do I think Bill Clinton and Al Gore are Jews? No, they're not. But they're tools for the Zionist Occupation Government. ZOG. Ever hear of it?"

ZOG. Of course she'd heard about it; people like him had spread their garbage all over the Web. "I've done my homework," she told him.

Monster manipulators, running the country, running the world, for there were always those who needed to believe that history did not unfold naturally but was controlled by malignant, unseen forces. Half the audience of the oh-so-cool, oh-so-asinine *X-Files* probably believed such a conspiracy existed. In the eighteenth and nineteenth centuries, Americans of this stripe suspected the country was being run by other sinister powers—the Freemasons, the Roman Catholic Church.

This time, though, in McBride and throughout the radical right, it was once again that no-brainer scapegoat: Blame the Jews. Blame the Jews for the Black Plague, blame the Jews for Germany's failures, blame the Jews for the failure of your farm, the failure of your business, the failure of you. The difference was, Lauren thought, that way back when, scapegoats like the Masons went about their business, and today people were amused at the notion that members of some fraternal order had ever been branded "engines of Satan" plotting to take over the country. They chuckled at the absurdity of the old rumors about the war that would be waged by Catholics—during which they would mutilate and exterminate American Protestants and take over the United States. Now Catholics had assimilated to such a degree that the Ku Klux Klan, which had once reviled them, accepted them as members. That was then. The belief in a ZOG was then and now and she prayed not forever.

"They've taken over our government," Ostergard declared. "They dominate the financial world. The media. They run the education of our children."

"Assuming you're right, what's in it for them?"

"Isn't that obvious?"

"I'd like to hear what you have to say." Lauren felt light-headed. The heat, she thought. No, yesterday's Cracker Jacks and Mountain Dew and Reese's Peanut Butter Cup. She was incredibly thirsty. She moved her feet so they were farther apart, giving her a firmer footing.

"What's in it for them?" He crossed his arms and leaned his head back, as if trying to come up with the best way to express it. While he was gifted at communicating what he wanted you to think or feel, she saw his gift was not one he could completely control. His pretenses came through clearly as well, so she could see his deep thought was as real as a three-dollar bill. He knew precisely what he believed and what he wanted to say. No deep thought was necessary. Given a few more press interviews, of course, he might get a little slicker. "Of course, they want to live off the fat of the land, but that's not what's driving them. What's driving them is greater than just pure greed. They want dominion over the entire world. Now, you ask, how are they going to get it?"

"Okay, how?"

"By being in league with Satan, some might say."

"I'm not writing about 'some,' Mr. Ostergard. I'm writing about you."

"All right. I say wherever they're getting their orders from—from Satan himself or from their own masterminds—it comes down to the same thing. They want to defy God Himself. They want to destroy His Chosen People, the white race. And they're already doing that by—"

The tape machine clicked off. They all peered at the small black rectangle on the white plastic chair. "Should I turn it over?" Lauren asked. She did not want to get too close to them. She did not want them to see the rivulets of sweat that were meandering from her forehead and temples, down her jaw. "Or would you rather handle it?" Without waiting for a signal from Ostergard, Kyle McIntyre picked up the recorder, turned the tape over and started it again. "How are the Jews destroying the white race?" she asked.

"By using the other races against us. By encouraging them to breed—to produce waves and waves of them in an attempt to . . . to overwhelm us by sheer numbers. But when they saw our resistance, our strength, they began an even shrewder scheme."

"Which is what?"

"Miscegenation. Encouraging the mixing of the races. Play the old song: We're all brothers and sisters under the skin, all alike in the eyes of God."

"Isn't that what Jesus said?"

"No, that is *not* what Jesus said. Read John, chapter fifteen, twelve and thirteen. He says: 'This is my commandment, That ye love one another, as I have loved you. Greater love hath no man than this, that a man lay down his life'—now listen—'*for his friends.*' The quote Jew unquote is not a friend. He is the *enemy*. Who killed Christ Himself? The quote Jew unquote. You know, if it wasn't so tragic it would be hysterically funny. They talk about genocide. But they're the ones working to destroy the white race."

The instant he said "genocide," she felt that tingle that she knew from the flu, the body awareness that you are sick and—get to the bathroom fast—you are going to vomit. But she stood still, taking notes, letting the tape roll, while Ostergard talked on and on about Jewish domination of the media, of finance and the monetary system, of education. He named names. Names she knew, names she had never heard of, names of people she knew to be Christian. Then he began reeling off names of governmental agencies and corporations and their Jews. Then the names of the white traitors, the white dupes, who deceived themselves into thinking they were powerful but were mere tools in the hands of the Zionists.

A violent cramp seized her calf, knotting the muscle into a small, hard ball of pain. It was so bad it took her breath away, but he kept talking, so she stood still, resisting the nearly irresistible urge to bend over and knead the muscle. Minutes stretched and minutes compressed until time lost its meaning. Finally, after an hour and a quarter, the tape came to an end. Ostergard gave no sign of noticing the terminating click. He kept talking, and she kept writing. She began to understand why no one had ever heard of Vernon Ostergard before.

Ultimately, he was boring. He could not stop himself. While part of the power of his message was the pervasiveness of the Zionist conspiracy, only the most loyal or the most passive or the most moronic could sit through a recitation that began with Greenspan and Rubin and

ended with such a long list of people she had never heard
of that it seemed he must be reading from the Tel Aviv
telephone directory. Without pausing for breath or effect,
he returned to the media. The names of every newspaper
and magazine owned by the Newhouse family came trip-
pingly off the tongue: *"The New Yorker, Mademoiselle,
Glamour, Vogue, Vanity Fair, Bride's—"*

"How is *Bride's* magazine contributing to the destruction of the white race?" Lauren asked.

"I'm letting you interview me, so let me finish. *Gentlemen's Quarterly, Self, House & Garden.* You bring me an
issue and I'll show you. Blacks and whites socializing,
black and white and yellow children cavorting. Black and
white couples, arm in arm. Those are the pictures you see,
like that's the normal course of events. Like God meant
for there to be homosexuals in the ministry."

Lauren was about to ask him how he made the transi-
tion from black and white couples to gays, but he was
already going on about Jews being responsible for the
spread of homosexuality and AIDS. She could tell by the
shuffle of Gus Lang's boots behind her that even he was
growing weary. "I want to see where you're getting," she
told Ostergard, sensing he was about to name more
names, list homosexuals, or Jewish homosexuals. Her legs
were so weak they were doing an involuntary shimmy.
"All the things you object to—big government, mixing
of the races, the decline in the power of the white man—
can be laid at the door of the Jews."

"Correct."

"You seem like someone who's given a lot of thought
to this, who has done a lot of reading." He nodded cautiously, not certain if she was complimenting him or setting him up. "So it won't come as any shock to you if I

bring up that some of the so-called experts on groups like yours"——Ostergard put up his hand, protesting the "groups like yours" designation, but since the pain in her legs was now shooting north to her backside, she did not let him speak but kept going——"say that people who believe that world events are being controlled by some hidden, manipulative force are not political leaders but——"

"Paranoids."

"Paranoid schizophrenics is the term I've come across."

"Well, do I look crazy?" He crossed his arms over his chest, relaxed, unafraid of whatever she might say.

"Is that question your whole answer?"

For the first time during the interview, Kyle McIntyre moved. His hands pressed down hard on the seat of his chair. He was about to vault himself over to her, when Ostergard put his hand over McIntyre's. It seemed to have not so much a calming effect as a controlling one, like a sergeant barking, At ease! McIntyre sat back. But what if Ostergard signaled, Do it. She regretted having laughed off her own paranoia, not mentioning to Stan, the desk clerk, where she was going, so the authorities could look for her, or her body. Although she had her doubts about how hard they would search. Probably stand in the middle of the street in McBride, look left, look right, say Shucks and go home.

"You know," Ostergard warned, "you can take this journalistic objectivity thing too far."

"I told you, I'm not your advocate or your enemy. I just want your story."

"All right. Here it is: I consider myself as sane as anyone. A lot saner, because I don't deceive myself about what's happening in this country. And of course they're going to try and stick some sort of label on me, paint me as a psycho."

"'They' being the Jews."

He nodded. She was getting it. "Or their agents. They try and make people believe that the truth I'm telling is the product of a sick mind." He smiled. "Do you want to hear about my unhappy childhood? Because I didn't have one."

"No, but I'd like to hear about where you think all this will lead."

There was no dramatic sigh, just a sad exhalation of air. "To war."

"Tell me about it."

"It will be a race war. Us against the Jews and their armies."

"Who are their armies?"

"Not them. They don't fight. The other races. The blacks and the yellows. Read Revelations. It's all there."

"You're talking about Armageddon, the battle at the end of the world?"

"I'm not saying it's coming right away." He shook his head hard, as if trying to get rid of a bad idea. "I take that back. The truth is, I have no way of knowing when it will come."

"But as you see it, it's inevitable?"

"It's in the Bible."

"Are you arming for it?"

"No comment."

"Wouldn't it make your enemies think twice if they knew you had, say, machine guns?"

A hint of a smile crossed his face, like that of an adult hearing the question of a naive child. "No comment."

"What do you do for a living, Mr. Ostergard?" He

flicked his wrist in the direction of the television parts on the repair table. "You do the work or own the store?"

"Both."

"And you, Mr. McIntyre?"

"TV repair," McIntyre said.

She turned. Gus Lang was looking at her, but he seemed surprised when she asked him the same question, as if it were the first he'd heard of it. "I work for Vern."

"Doing what?"

"He does what I do." Ostergard did not snap at her, but his gentle voice was replaced with a curt and wary one.

"TV repair?"

"That's right. You got a problem with it?"

"No. The other man who came by works on TVs too?"

"No, he's a car mechanic. Believe me, we have men from all walks of life."

"It's just I'm a little surprised that a shop like this in a small town can support four men—the three of you and the older man who went to the back."

"Well, it can."

"And pay for what looks like some pretty expensive equipment."

"Where do you see expensive anything?"

"The uplink satellite behind your store." She waited for him to say no, it's just a regular satellite so we can monitor the Jewish influence on Budweiser commercials. But he did not.

"It's from contributions."

"From whom?"

"No comment."

"A lot of small contributors or one big one?"

"I said, No comment."

In any interview, there is a point of diminishing returns, where the subject grows weary or begins to resent the reporter's continuing questions, for they signal that the reporter may still have doubts about their version of reality. Ostergard had reached that point and gone beyond. When he was not doing what he was good at—communicating his decency, his rationality, explaining how the world really worked—he became suspicious, testy, ill at ease. He wriggled in his chair, unable to find a comfortable position. Instead of allowing his words to flow, he spit each one out. The "No" of "No comment" sounded almost like a shout, and the final *t* was hard and absolute.

Lauren knew she had no more than one last question. "Did you or any member of your group have anything to do with the bomb that was found in Big Elk Video, the store owned by a man named Mike Pearlstein?"

"No comment."

"I find that interesting. Most people—even if they were implicated in something like that—would give a flat-out denial. How come you're—" Lauren heard the door open behind her. An instant later, she saw Gus Lang's large, hairy hand reaching out to grab her arm. "Hold your horses," she told him, and walked over to the white plastic chair. She picked up her tape recorder. "I'll call you in a couple of days, Mr. Ostergard," she said. Up close, she could see a circle of enlarged pores between his eyes, as though he'd ripped out hairs with a bad tweezer.

"Don't," Kyle McIntyre told her. He and Ostergard were leaning toward each other, their shoulders touching, as if they had become one person. "We don't want to hear from you again." McIntyre's breathy man-woman voice was so disturbing that instead of turning and leaving, Lauren began backing out.

"Just in case you have something to add, Mr. Oster-gard." As she neared the door, Gus Lang was about to grab for her arm again. "No!" she said quietly. His hand fell back to his side. His huge, bear-nosed face registered surprise, or hurt. Lauren shoved open the door and rushed out into the sweet embrace of the bitter mountain wind.

# 12

It made sense to Charlie that she was from New York. No western girl would wear a coat like that, wool and halfway down to her knees, so it looked like she came in a navy-blue box. It wasn't something a person could wear to hike or ski or even walk down the street on a ten-below day. The hood wouldn't protect her from anything more than a spring drizzle. It was a coat for a New England campus. He could picture her running after a Frisbee on an intensely green lawn in front of ivy-covered buildings, her hood with its plaid lining tossed back, her beautiful hair flowing behind her. Instead of her catching it, somebody's mutt would jump up and grab it and she would throw back her head and laugh, thinking it was hilarious she had been outjocked by a dog.

Check the radiator. They said the car had been overheating. It had been towed into Bill's Auto early, an Escort with Nevada plates, a hunk of junk to begin with. By eleven the night before, the temperature had gone down to fifteen below, a challenge to a lot of antifreezes. Charlie lifted the hood to check the coolant.

Except she wasn't a college kid. She was a reporter. Holy shit, he'd walked in and there was Gus allegedly guarding the door—Gus, who obviously had such a hard-on for her that it didn't even register that someone had walked right past him. And there she was, making notes on a spiral-bound pad. That freak Kyle sitting in the middle of the shop, practically in Ostergard's lap—although maybe it was vice versa. Charlie couldn't get out of his mind how she'd turned around and stared at him. So much hatred. He was staggered. Never, not during any interrogation, not during any arrest, had someone looked at him that way.

No, as far as he could tell, the water pump looked all right. He wanted to get this right because—wasn't this crazy?—he loved his job. Not special agent. Mechanic. He loved going out with the tow truck and boosting some tourist's battery and the tourist saying, Thank you, thank you, as if he'd performed successful neurosurgery. And he loved diagnosis, talking over with Bill or the other mechanic, Paul, what could be wrong and then going in and fixing it. Except he'd been driving up to McBride during his lunch hour and coming back late too often. Bill got pissed, and how could Charlie blame him?

Maybe the look she gave him wasn't meant for him at all. Being a reporter and from New York, most likely she was a real liberal. But at the same time, still a pro. There was something about the way she handled herself that said, This is the real thing. Even though she was young, early to midtwenties, she wasn't some phony playing at journalism. He bet she didn't have a phony bone in her body—not that he could see it, with that coat. Being a real journalist, she couldn't glare at Ostergard as though she wished he would drop dead on the spot. And any girl in her right mind would keep her eye off Kyle, he was so fucking spooky. And naturally she wasn't going to turn around in the middle of an interview to give Gus Lang a hateful look, even if he was a Neanderthal who was looking at her like he wanted to drag her off by her hair.

Instead, she had turned all her fury and disgust on Charlie.

The radiator? Shit, he didn't know. He was really pulling this out of his ass. Cooling systems were pretty much a mystery to him. If the coolant froze overnight, then that freeze-out plug should have popped. Except it was in.

But if he'd been forced to swear, he would have put his hand on the Bible and taken an oath that she remembered him from seeing him on the street two days before. They'd had one of those weird moments out of time: A man and a woman exchange looks and it's as if they flirted, started going out, became crazy about each other, fucked their brains out, fell deeply in love and then split up, all within twenty seconds.

"What you doing in there so long, Darrell?" Bill asked. "Searching for gold?"

"Don't think I'll find any in an Escort."

"You're right about that!"

"Checking out the radiator," Charlie told him. And waiting for noon so he could get out and make a call.

What was troubling him—one of the five thousand things that were troubling him, only four thousand of which had anything to do with Wrath—was that he used to be so good with girls. Women. They'd always seemed to be naturally drawn to him. When they weren't, he'd smile or do his goofy-doofus routine: Jeez, I can't for the life of me figure out how these new bindings work. After that, they were his, usually for as long as he wanted them.

But ever since the time he'd fallen for Stacey—tripping over his own dick in the process—his magic had deserted him. Not that women gagged or went screaming from his presence. No, they still found him good-looking. That he knew. But not . . . What was the right word? Compelling. Maybe it had something to do with being married, some monogamous wavelength he was emitting that made him unexciting. Maybe it was that he was getting old, although he'd never thought of thirty-four as the last stop before death.

When he'd gone to Washington for his training in undercover techniques, they made him remove his wedding ring right off the bat, because his cover was a guy who'd been divorced over a year; they didn't want a deep dent in his finger. He'd felt naked at first. His finger looked pathetic, all puckered and white. He'd felt disloyal. He wanted to tell the two girls in front of him in the cafeteria who were joking around with him about FBI egg salad: I'm married. But one night in his motel in Virginia, watching the Wizards play the Bulls, he found himself massaging that finger with such uninhibited pleasure he half expected it to ejaculate. Taking the ring off changed something: Suddenly, female agents and secretaries and just regular women in the street who never even looked down at his hand were eyeing him with real interest again.

Then he flew back to Cheyenne and drove to Colorado Springs for the weekend. He was mentally and physically exhausted from the training, keyed up about going to Jackson Hole. But he was also determined to make this a good weekend. Except Morning had done one of her Hi, Daddy, Bye, Daddy routines and been gone nearly the whole time, at a sleep-over party for one of the other skaters' birthdays. So it was just him and Stacey. Who knows why—maybe because he had been tempted so often during those two weeks in Washington—but he felt he had to get back to thinking like a married man in a real marriage, not the bad joke they'd been living in. Stacey wasn't making any moves, so it was up to him to reach across the abyss separating them. He had to admit he wasn't doing it solely not to feel like a scumbag; he wanted something more for a sex life than watching adult movies on pay-per-view. But it wasn't just about sex. What he wanted, too, was what men were not supposed to care about: wanting to hold a woman, wanting to be held. He'd just start with the holding thing. That would be nice for a while. Then he'd work up to the good stuff.

That very first night, coming out of the restaurant, he took her hand, kissed the center of her palm, told her it had been a long couple of weeks, not just because of the intensity of the training but because he was almost a continent away from her. I missed you, Stace. I wanted you. Out of the formidably sized, middle-aged-looking woman came the hot, husky voice that used to make him crazy with desire: I know you can't stand it that I've gained weight. Stacey, don't say that. I *do* want you. Charlie, do you honestly think if you start up again it's going to make me forget about everything? I mean, the first thing you said to me this weekend is, Did you look at the checking account balance, Stacey? You're being so damn cheap and then nasty—really, *really* nasty—about the new costumes she's got to have.

The bed in the Colorado Springs house was a double but sank down in the middle, where Stacey slept alone. That night and the following one, they stayed on either side of the bed, fighting the gravity that pulled them toward the center. They did not want to meet in the middle and touch. They did want to sleep but hardly could, and each knew, despite the absolute silence, that the other was awake.

What the hell else could the problem be? A crack in the radiator itself? He couldn't see anything, but then again, he wasn't a hundred percent sure what he was looking for. The last thing he wanted to say was, Hey, Bill, I can't find what's wrong.

Oh God, the way that girl had looked at him, like he was the worst racist, an animal, an imbecile. Maybe a psychopath. Someone so beneath her contempt . . . No, eminently worthy of her contempt.

Look at that. A little bit of a crack in the housing of the water pump. You could hardly see it.

He didn't get out of the garage for lunch until nearly one o'clock, and he was praying Jeanette Wagner was still by the phone. Yes! "Okay," she said. "That red Geo you saw yesterday. It was rented from Avis at the Jackson Hole airport by a Lauren Miller of Shorehaven, New York." He found himself grinning. Lauren Miller was such a great name! "Are you there?"

"Where is Shorehaven?"

"Long Island."

"Anything on her?"

"No criminal record under that name. Twenty-seven years old. Preliminary check says she probably is what she says she is. Want us to go further?"

Saying yes would seem odd. A personal thing, or just pigheadedness. They'd think he was cracking under the pressure, and it would give them an excuse to pull him out. She looked younger than twenty-seven. "No. Just wanted to make sure she wasn't a factor." He'd have to do the going-further himself. Great, like he had so much free time between fixing cars and being a Jew-hating white

supremacist. Well, he'd have to tear out all the hotel and
dude ranch listings from Bill's yellow pages and start calling.

What if she'd gotten all the material she needed and
already gone back to New York?

No. Shit, what if she was a journalist, but her paper
was the *White Light* or something and she was a dyed-in-
the-wool Wrath groupie and she'd fallen for Ostergard
or—Jesus Christ!—Kyle McIntyre. No, because then
why would she have given him such a ferocious look?
Wouldn't he just be one of the boys? Maybe she'd looked
at him that way because he'd seen her across the street
watching the store and now she was ashamed, knowing
he'd picked up that she was stalking Ostergard or McIntyre.

Maybe she hated him because she could tell he had
Indian blood. Jewish blood.

Maybe the bureau was right, making undercover
agents see their contact once a week. This was reaching
new levels of craziness. What could he be thinking? That
he could go and knock on the door of her room and say,
Hi, I'm really Charlie, not Darrell, and I don't believe in
any of this crap, it's sick, it's un-American, I'm just
undercover, and sure, go ahead, make that the headline on
your story, and would you like to have supper with me
someplace and talk and too bad I'm having to spend so
much time being a neo-Nazi because I'd really like to get
to know you, show you all the places around here I grew
up loving.

Charlie knew this was twisted. Yet when he left Bill's,
he'd stuffed a wad of yellow pages in his pocket, more
hotels, motels, dude ranches, bed-and-breakfasts—ten,
twenty times more—than there had been when he last

lived in the valley. In the shower, as he was scrubbing with Lava to get the grease off the undersides of his forearms, he was wondering how many calls he had time to make before he had to show at the Eagle, and then, if he found out where Lauren was, whether he'd have time after to—

Crazy. Even before he dried himself off, he took the yellow pages out of his jeans, tore them up and flushed them away. As he watched their counterclockwise swirl and disappearance, he realized that if his hand had been small enough, he would have reached down the pipe and grabbed them back.

*Wake up America! Who owns your farms and*
*ranches now?*

*Wake up America! Where is the wealth that*
*used to be yours?*

*Wake up America! Whose got the job that*
*used to be yours?*

*Wake up America! What has happened to your borders?*

*Wake up America! Where have your women gone?*

*Wake up America! What are your children*
*learning in school?*

*Wake up at the Wrath open meeting Tuesday, 7 P.M.,*
*First Christian Church and Bible School basement, McBride.*

The supermarket parking lot in the town of Jackson was filled with the cars and SUVs and trucks of people stopping by on their way home, so Gus Lang and Charlie had their work cut out for them. "One under every wiper. Vern says, 'The one you miss is the one we would've had.'"

"He's right," Charlie agreed, sticking a circular advertising Wrath's next meeting under a Ram's wiper, pleased that almost immediately the heavy, wet snowflakes that had started to fall were gluing it to the windshield, so the driver would be pissed as hell. "You usually do this alone?"

"Usually with Kyle." Clearly they had a standard operating procedure. Gus directed him to the line of cars parallel to his. When each of them finished, they would meet at the end of the line, Gus would hand him more flyers, and they would go off again.

"Where's Kyle tonight?"

"With Vern." Since everybody in Wrath said next to nothing, Charlie fell back into his customary wordlessness. His back ached from hanging over car engines all day. His stomach was still black and blue where the agent had punched him in the staged fight in the Eagle's parking lot. "They got to be there," Gus told him, at the end of the next line.

"Vern and Kyle, you mean? At the shop?"

"No. Another place. They got to be there to pick up something." Gus winked. "A present."

Charlie's heart thudded. He stuck a circular under a Subaru Outback's wiper and held his breath, waiting for Gus to keep talking. But Gus simply moved on to the next line of cars. Charlie followed along his line until he realized Gus was not going anywhere. A shopper, a woman, peeling the flyer off the window of her Voyager, waving the wet paper, was shouting, red-faced, at Gus.

"You dumb-fuck asshole, you put your filth on my car again, I'll rip your nuts off with my bare hands!" She brought her fist up and waved it at him. "You hear me?" Slowly, Gus began walking toward her. Instead of bounding into her minivan, she shoved her groceries onto the seat, then held up both hands and wiggled the fingers of her sheepskin gloves. "Come on, asshole! I'm ready to rip!" Holy shit, Charlie thought. He was going to have to pull Gus away from her. He'd say, Listen, Gus, I just saw a police car cruising around, and in case they pass here—

Gus turned away from her and, shaking his head, ambled over to Charlie. "Crazy bitch. Vern always says, 'Stay away from crazies.'"

"Guess that's right." The woman was standing there, sticking up her middle finger and arcing it through the air. "So Kyle's with Vern tonight." Charlie tried to sound playful. "Bet the present they're picking up isn't a toy tractor."

Gus grinned. "Bet it's not." He shuffled uneasily. The woman was still beside her car. Every few seconds, she would give them the finger again, swooping it high. "Maybe we should get a cup of coffee or something. She'll be gone by the time we get back."

When they settled themselves in his pickup, Charlie asked, "How come you're not driving Vern's truck tonight?"

"They needed it." Gus stretched his arms in front of him, cracking his knuckles outward, the comfortable gesture of a man who has just won a fight with a man bigger than he, not run from one with a woman. "To haul the presents. The stuff from Santa Claus."

"Right," Charlie said slowly. "Bet there are a lot of toys there I'd like."

"Could be," Gus said playfully. Like a child pretending to hunt, he sighted down an imaginary rifle. But instead of one click of a make-believe trigger, he held down his trigger and sprayed an almost endless round of pretend ammunition.

"Great!" Charlie told him. "It makes me, you know, glad knowing they're . . . they're not just talking about the final battle. They're getting ready."

Charlie drove to a take-out place at the edge of town, gave Gus a couple of bucks and told him to get the coffee. Gus was a born underling, he realized. He did what he was told—if not cheerfully, at least without resentment. He would buy coffee. He would probably kill.

"You wanted regular?" Gus asked when he got back.

"Right."

"That's how I take it."

"How does Kyle like it?"

"I don't know. I don't get coffee with him."

"Well, I can understand that. I don't see him as"—Charlie held up his cup—"a regular guy. He doesn't say anything. But maybe that's because I'm new."

"He pretty much just talks to Vern." Gus was burrowing in the paper bag and brought out his coffee as well as an enormous muffin.

"I guess you were with them up in Sheridan." Half the muffin was in Gus's mouth, so all Charlie got was a nod. "I'd have liked to have been up there with you guys."

Gus said what sounded like Vuh, although Charlie assumed he was saying it was fun.

"Bet it was fun." The muffin was studded with something dark. Jumbo raisins? Giant chocolate chips. Gus was holding it tight, as if concerned Charlie would try and grab it away. "What made you come down here?"

"Opportunity."

"I guess there's that."

"Kyle said, Up here we can't make our mark."

"You mean, people wouldn't hear about Wrath if you stayed in Sheridan."

"Yeah, so he said to Vern, We got to go down to Jackson Hole."

"What's here?"

"Big money. Pissed people off. Big Jew money."

"Right."

"And money for us. If we make waves, we get more . . ."

"Contributions."

"Right." He stuffed the other half muffin into his mouth, leaned against the headrest and chewed slowly, stuffing back the crumbs that slipped out with his index and middle finger. A chocolate chip stuck on his chin.

"So coming down here was Kyle's idea?"

Gus nodded. "Vern was worried. He said, We'll lose members if we leave. Lose a lot of goodwill. People will think we're getting too big for our britches. But Kyle said, Trust me. It'll be worth it, Vern."

"Is it, so far?"

"I don't know." His tongue was roving around his gums, searching for morsels. "I shouldn't be talking about this."

"Okay. Look, I didn't mean to—"

"Kyle thinks it could be better."

"How?"

"Well, you know, if we got . . . I forget what word he used. When you beat the shit out of the agents of ZOG. Or sometimes only make trouble. Marching. Making phone calls to scare the shit out of people."

"Being aggressive?"

"I guess that's it. He's telling Vern, We can't worry about offending people. This is a race war. Nice guys don't win."

"He likes action."

"Kyle? Yeah. Kyle likes action, all right. Well, we'd better get back."

"Finish the rest of the flyers."

"Damn, yes. I forgot about them."

Charlie pulled his pickup into the street. "Vern seems to like it here. Opened a nice shop. I guess Kyle and you help him."

"Right."

"How do you like it?"

"Pretty good. Lot of places to eat around here. Expensive, though."

"Sure is."

"Lot of pussy here. Did you see those girls in the lot, with those ski pants? You could see the crack in their ass. You check that out, Darrell? Get a little closer and I bet you could see their whole slit."

"Bet you could."

"See that reporter yesterday? The redhead?" Charlie nodded. "She's from New York. Her name's Lorn. Lorn Miller. I'd like to get a piece of her."

"I don't know. I don't think reporters mess around with people they're doing stories on."

"Can't hurt to find out."

"Do you know where to find her?"

"Well, I'll just get the yellow pages. Start calling motels and asking for Miss Lorn Miller. And maybe when I find her I'll drop by one night and knock on her door and say, Hello, Lorn."

\*        \*        \*

The secure cell phone they'd given him in Washington had such a silly ring that even though he was wide awake, even though it was three-twenty in the morning and utterly silent, even though the phone was right there on the bare floor beside his bed, even though he knew he would be getting only important calls on it, it took a minute for him to identify what it was. Each ring sounded like a sick lamb: eh-heh-heh-heh-heh. Between the time he heard the ring and picked up the phone, his hands became so shaky that it took another ring for him to pull down the mouthpiece. "Hello."

"Johnny, hi, it's Christie." It was Jeanette Wagner.

"This isn't Johnny, honey pie." "Honey pie" signaled it was Charlie who had picked up and that no one else was with him. If he added, "My name is Darrell," they'd know he was in danger. Every day during training he'd rehearsed the codes so they would come reflexively if he was under duress.

"Another bomb."

"Fuck! Anyone hurt?"

"One dead."

"Christ." God, let it not be Lauren. "Who?"

"A housekeeper. She worked for a Hollywood director who has a ranch just south of here. A guy named Jack Frohman."

"Never heard of him. Anything happen to him?"

"Nothing. He had to go to L.A. two days ago, some crisis with a movie he's supposed to start in a couple of weeks. He's flying back first thing this morning. He's not going to find a house, poor guy."

"That bad?"

"Worse."

"Anyone claiming it?"

"The Free America Cadre. That's the name we're sure Ostergard or whomever used to call in the last one."

"I know! Jesus."

"His dogs died too. He had two something . . . Some kind of French hunting dogs."

"Any word on the bomb itself?"

"Not yet. We need this like a hole in the head." This was a major embarrassment. Embarrassment: an embarrassing word to use in such an awful situation, Charlie thought, but there it was. Everyone in Jackson Hole on alert since the bomb at Big Elk Video, the valley crawling with FBI agents, Wyoming DCI cops, Jackson Hole sheriff's deputies and town of Jackson police, and boom! Right in their faces. "You didn't get any sense this was going to happen?" Terrific; now they'd try and make it his fault for not having stopped it.

"Just what I reported to you tonight after I dropped off my buddy. The two big guys were off someplace, obviously hauling in a shipment of arms in that big Chevy. Speaking of the Chevy, I stuck the transponder under it a couple of days ago, just like I was supposed to. You should be able to find out where they went."

"Your buddy didn't seem unusually tense last night?"

"Loose as a goose. Not too loose, like he was putting on an act. He's not a total moron, but I don't think he's capable of playing a game like that."

"Any unusual tension with the other two?"

"They're harder to read. I didn't even know there was any disagreement between them till tonight. The leader wanted to stay in Sheridan, but the other guy pushed him to come down here."

"I wish we knew more."

"Well," Charlie said, trying to sound casual, "you're

the one who keeps telling me there's no instant gratification. But I think I made a dent with my buddy tonight. He's a muscle-bound jerk, but he's still pretty much a kid. I think he needs someone to talk to. No one up there talks besides the leader. I'd always assumed the leader and number two talked. What I didn't know is that they let my buddy listen."

"Any sense that they have a cell structure? Groups around the town they're in or elsewhere the other groups don't know about?"

He knew Jeanette knew the answer even before he said, "They're not about to tell me."

"I know. Damn."

"But listen, I think if the leader and Suckface aren't as lovey-dovey as I thought, maybe I can take advantage of it. Be the leader's big-ass buddy."

"I want you to remember something," Jeanette said. "Quantico says the leader is probably a paranoid schiz and that Suckface is probably—"

"A sociopath. Will kill anything that gets in his way."

"That's right, so be careful."

Charlie had to smile. Her "be careful" reminded him of his mother. Whenever he would leave to go anywhere, even if just out to the barn, she'd call out, "Be careful, Charlie." And he'd always answer with a silent: No, Mom, I'll be careless. "What about my buddy? Any psych profile on him?"

"Not that I know of. But I wouldn't assume that beneath that rough exterior lies a gentle soul."

"That's what I figured."

"You better get back to sleep."

"Right." He didn't want to break off contact. "Who

did Free America send its message to? The same guy, that Denny Rettig?"

"No. To the *Rocky Mountain News*. Call came from a pay phone outside a gas station just south of Jackson, so he or they probably hit it coming north from the ranch. We're checking the prints on it. So far nothing. Oh, a different message this time. No 'foreign elements.' This one said, 'This is the beginning of the end of the Zionist Occupation Government.'"

"Shit. This will get them the press they didn't have the last time around. The valley will be crawling with reporters by tomorrow." He was just going to block Lauren from his mind. Except here he was, thinking about her.

"Wait till you hear the kicker," Jeanette said.

"What?"

"Jack Frohman? Not a Jew. Father's a Lutheran minister."

# 13

She hadn't felt this lighthearted since her plane lifted off from LaGuardia.

As Lauren was checking out *Beyond Ethnicity,* one of the librarians, by now a familiar face, had inquired, Do you ski? The tone of the question was dubious, and sure enough, the woman did not seem surprised to hear no. Snowshoe? she asked hopefully. In the seconds it took Lauren to envision such an activity, the librarian, Jackie, a woman not much older than Lauren herself, was jotting down directions to a meeting place.

That same afternoon, from four until darkness, they snowshoed over pristine snow on a mountainside dotted with spruce. They stood watch as a buffalo on the far side of a plain swung its head back and forth like a snowplow to clear a patch of range grass for its dinner. They'd gone out for their own dinner and, in the superficial intimacy of women getting to know each other, related life stories. Lauren suspected that the sum of her disclosures sounded, to twice-divorced Jackie, more like a prologue than an actual tale.

Still, the walk and the wine, the animated talk about books and men and politics, the recollection of the ascending moon spreading gold light along the horizon, made her feel, if not euphoric, pretty damned high. She was back in her room at the Buckin' Bronc, humming "Surrey with the Fringe on Top," heading into the shower, when the phone rang. Grabbing a towel, she leaped across the room—a veritable gazelle, she proclaimed to herself—and dove across the bed to answer it.

"Lauren Miller?" She'd heard the voice before. Wyoming, making sure to give each syllable of her name plenty of room.

"Yes." She stretched the cord so she could reach her pad and pen.

"Chief Vultaggio."

"Oh. Hi, how are you?"

"Fine." Did his blood have to do a complete circulation before he could say the next word? "We've had certain information . . ."

"Uh-huh," she said encouragingly.

". . . that you may have attracted the wrong kind of attention."

Amazing, how fast exuberance can take flight, leaving a hollow swiftly filled with dread. "What kind of attention is that?" she asked.

"Can't say for sure. If I were you—"

"Did the threat come from Wrath?"

"I can't tell you that."

"You have to tell me. If I've been threatened, I have a right to know the nature of the threat and who made it."

"Let's put it this way, Ms. Miller." She waited. "If any of your friends from McBride come calling, you might not want to set out the welcome mat." She waited some more. "If I were you, I'd keep my door bolted." Papers rustled. "Anybody knocks, make sure you know who it is before you open the door." That he was not riveted by their conversation did not surprise Lauren, but the shuffling she heard from his end disconcerted her—the sound of someone cleaning out a desk drawer, or pinning up Most Wanted posters.

"I'd like to know what's waiting for me on the other side of the door."

"No need to panic."

"Do I sound as if I'm panicking?" Stupid to give him that opening. "All right, I'll bolt my door. Is the threat just here, at the motel? Am I okay once I'm outside?"

"I remember telling you these are dangerous people. I'll stand by that statement." He did not say goodbye.

Lauren wrapped the towel tighter around her. What should I do? How should I know what to do? Maybe just . . . She raced to the door and put on the chain. I'll call Adam, in case they find my body or I'm missing or— No, I'll E-mail him their names. Great: just what he needs. Could they really be out to get me? Did Ostergard decide he made a mistake talking? Could it be one of the other two, acting on his own? Could they have sent someone else? That Darrell?

Maybe they bugged the phone or put a listening device in the room. No, too James Bond. Except they're operating that satellite, and if they know what to do with teeny TV parts, they'd probably have the technical expertise to—

Trying not to think about *Psycho,* Lauren took a fast shower and packed her gear. Slowly, with the chain still on the door, she peered into the hall. No one. The only noise was the heartless growl of the vending machine. Am I being hysterical? she asked herself. He said bolt the door. He didn't say don't go out. Okay, he did tell me they were dangerous. Why did he make that call? Think. All right: He heard something and was morally or legally or politically obligated to pass it on. But who is that link between Wrath and the chief of police? An informant? Or could Vultaggio be a Wrath sympathizer, or even one of them, and want to scare me? No, that's over the top. Besides, if he wanted to scare me, he would have told me, Get out of town; maybe even added, Fast.

Realizing she could still be standing in the same spot, trying to figure out Don Vultaggio's place in the cosmos, at midnight, she yanked open the door and hustled with her duffel bag, backpack, new end-of-the-season-sale snowshoes and laptop, all the way to the front desk. "Stan," she said, a little breathless.

"You're not leaving us?" It touched her that he seemed genuinely hurt. "Is there something we could do we haven't done?"

"Oh no! It's a wonderful place," Lauren assured him. "And you've been terrific. Really, you're the world's greatest direction giver." He looked almost persuaded, so she added, "Without you, I'd be driving around in circles somewhere in the Canadian Rockies. But listen, Stan . . ." She took a deep breath. "You know I'm a reporter covering a story here." He nodded. "Well, sometimes reporters can put a nose or two out of joint. I think I'd be better off someplace else, where I wasn't registered under my own name."

"We could give you any name you want, ma'am."

"Thank you. But they may already know I'm staying here. I don't know if I'm being melodramatic. I probably am."

"You're still on that Big Elk Video story?"

"Yes."

"I guess you can't be too careful, then."

The cold spell had broken that afternoon, and the temperature had gone up to what had sounded like a tropical twenty. But during Lauren's three-minute drive to the ATM, the wind howled like a sound effect in *Dracula*. An ill-tempered mix of sleet and hail smacked at her windshield. Abandoning what she had to admit was a demented plan to hide in her car across the street from the Buckin' Bronc and watch to see if Ostergard or McIntyre or Lang came calling, she drove past two motels and pulled in at a third, the Sagebrush.

She registered as Frances Perkins, feeling mildly depraved at paying cash in advance for her room. The desk clerk was no Stan but a golden jock, one of the corps of the well-muscled and good-looking who came to Jackson Hole to work in the tourist industry in order to finance expensive athletic habits. He, like so many of them, seemed extravagantly cheerful. Perhaps they thought solemnity rude. Possibly they were simply happy because they believed they would emerge from these tedious jobs at age thirty not merely marvelously fit but somehow famous and rich as well. One glance, however, seemed to have told him Lauren could not advance his cause. He offered his lowest-wattage smile and proffered a plastic key card.

Punchy now from the fresh air and exercise, dopey from wine, depleted by roller-coastering between fright and the shame of overreaction, Lauren slept deeply until just before dawn. She wakened in a panic, which only deepened for the minute she could not recall where she was or why she was so terrified. By six-thirty, however, she was standing at the Avis counter at the airport, exchanging her red Geo for a green one, on the theory that if anyone from Wrath had watched her as she left Vern's TV Repair, he would have seen her get into the red car parked directly across the street and might even have noted the license plate.

"I guess you haven't heard about it yet," the Avis man observed.

"About what?" She hurriedly signed her name and initialed everything he said to initial without looking at what she was initialing.

"About the bomb."

"The bomb at the video store?" Lauren unzipped her backpack to put away her credit card and license.

"Not that one. Another one just went off. Couple of hours ago." Her backpack clunked to the floor. "Not even on the radio yet," he reported, his chin rising a self-satisfied inch.

"Where did you hear about it?"

"My sister-in-law."

"What does your sister-in-law do?"

"She knits a lot."

"I mean, how did she hear about a bomb?"

"She got one of those police scanner radios for Christmas, from her brother down in Santa Fe."

"Did you hear anything else from her?"

"Like what?"

"Like, did the same group claim responsibility?"

"Now that you mention it"——he made a great show of swooshing a mouthful of air from cheek to cheek——"I think she said it was the same group. Can't remember what they call themselves, though."

"Where did the bomb go off?" Lauren demanded, then offered him a fast smile as an apology for her snappishness.

After due consideration, he accepted it. "At this Hollywood fella's ranch. Jack Frohman? The director? Ever hear of him?"

"I'm not sure."

"He's very famous. House is gone."

"Any casualties?"

"His gun dogs. He had two. And a lady who lived there. Housekeeper."

"Could you show me exactly where the ranch is on a map?"

But for the weather, the JF Ranch would have looked like the aftermath of so many disasters Lauren had seen on television: bombings, hurricanes, tornadoes, earthquakes. A mound of rubble rising from a field of scattered debris. But snow had already softened the scene, coating a fractured window frame, a toilet bowl and strands of electrical wiring, the only identifiable objects. It was like viewing a nightmare through a window frosted for Christmas, except in this instance there was no glass to protect the onlooker from the stench of chemicals and scorched wood.

A sheriff's deputy stood just behind the crime scene tape, chatting with a woman Lauren assumed must be a reporter for one of the local papers. Either the woman had a great memory or the cop was just passing the time of day, because although her pad was out, she wasn't taking notes. She did keep nodding a great deal.

Lauren strolled around and said good morning to a couple of the other deputies guarding the scene, already red-faced and runny-nosed from the cold. She offered to go get them coffee. Their response was a wary "We just had some." Nevertheless, after a fifteen-minute investment of time listening to the younger of them describe bombed dog parts in bet-I-can-make-you-barf detail, she elicited an acknowledgment that yes, come to think of it, somebody claiming something had called in to some newspaper.

"Same group as the last time, at Mike Pearlstein's store?" she inquired, trying to sound as local as possible.

"It's not up to me to talk about the case. You know that." He was trying to sound like an old hand, so inured to journalists he knew all their sly ways. But his too-blinky eyes and needlessly graphic description of one of the dead dogs' snouts told her he was still a kid spouting grown-up lines he'd been taught at the academy.

"That's okay," she reassured him. "I think I heard something about it anyway. The Free America Cadre again."

"That's the one."

"Same message?"

"You know I can't give you that information."

"Come on," she said, "give me a break."

He hesitated. She knew not to smile, which would only make him feel he was being manipulated. "Something about Zionists," he said softly.

"Like what?"

"I forget."

"That ZOG business?" she asked casually. "Zionist Occupation Government."

Even though all he would tell her was, "Could be," she knew she had it.


The first building between the ranch and the town of Jackson was Feeny's Fine Feed. By now, Lauren was familiar enough with western ways to assume she would not be denied use of a phone, and she was right. Except when she lifted the receiver, she suddenly realized she had no one to call. What could *JewNew* do with a hot item? Oh, a description of what she had seen at Frohman's ranch would probably be her lead for the story she would write, but *JewNew* wouldn't be going to press until the following Wednesday. She called it in anyway, and Eli Bloom, her editor, demanded, "So what do you want me to do? Put out a special edition and shout 'Extra, Extra' in Times Square?"

What was she going to do? Her years on dailies had taught her to get it fast, get it factual, and get it first. She entertained a half-second fantasy of calling in the story to the *Times,* any *Times*—Los Angeles, New York, Seattle—but that evaporated when she realized that within another three or four hours, an Associated Press reporter from whichever was the nearest city—Bozeman, Montana, or Salt Lake—would be using the phone or the bathroom at Feeny's; she wasn't needed.

Lauren glanced around the place, expecting to see stacks of gigantic Cow Chow bags. But no feed. All she saw was a desk, a filing cabinet and the manager, eyeing her and his phone in her hand. His arms were crossed, making an X over his chest; his thumbs were hooked anticipatorily under his arms. She was a reporter. When was she going to report? All right, she could do it. She could call anyone . . . CNN. Offer them a beeper, an on-phone portrait of what she'd seen.

What exactly is the Free America Cadre, Lauren? the anchor would ask. Picturing a shot of a map, or maybe even file footage of the JF Ranch, with *Lauren Miller reporting from Jackson Hole* superimposed, she would respond: Before the first bomb was discovered near here in the town of Jackson, Donna, one that luckily did not go off, no one I spoke to—folks from Jackson Hole, people in law enforcement, experts on the radical right—had heard of the Free America Cadre. However, there is a group called Wrath and . . .

True, she would be going over to the enemy, TV news. But just temporarily. And she would be breaking a story! Leaning against a wall, her back to a Pamela Anderson calendar, she called Information for the area code of Atlanta. What could be so hard? There would be no camera. No one would see how her hair had frizzed in last night's sleet. All she'd have to do was close her eyes to concentrate and write aloud, describing the upside-down toilet, the window frame without its glass, how everyone around the crime scene kept mentioning the death of Frohman's two dogs, Maverick and Buddy, before that of his housekeeper, Eileen Hogan.

Flying high on her own gas: That's what she was doing. Buoyed by the thought of everyone she knew seeing her name on television, she let herself be thrilled with CNN's imagined offer to fly her to Atlanta to "have a talk." Then she puffed up with righteousness, because she was telling CNN, Sorry, TV's just not my medium. It was only when she replaced the receiver that she realized she had forgotten the area code for Atlanta. But there was the feed store manager, in jeans, a denim shirt and a denim vest, tapping his foot slowly but expectantly, waiting for his show business debut.

What was going on in his head? Lauren wondered. How was she imagining it? CNN or NBC? Her saying: I'm standing here at Feeny's Feed with Joe Schmoe, the manager. Joe knows these parts better than I do, so let me put him on the phone to give you some background. She turned to the man she was about to let down and murmured something about having to return to the crime scene to check out a rumor. Instead, she headed north, back to Jackson.

A winter's worth of plowed snow stood on either side

of the road, high walls that formed a gorge for traffic, cutting off the rest of the world. Like everybody else, Lauren thought about Warhol's fifteen minutes of fame, but she knew it had become just another fatuous truism. While it worked to her advantage, the prevalence of interview-ready Americans disconcerted her. Journalists talked about it all the time, how not just witnesses and bystanders to some crime or catastrophe who happened to be in the neighborhood of a microphone, but mothers and fathers, husbands and wives, children of victims, would meet the press while the body was still warm. Sometimes, it was true, they broke down and sobbed before the cameras, but not so much they couldn't get a few words in edgewise. People no longer seemed able to push away a mike or a tape recorder. Was there no one who suffered in silence anymore?

News was becoming entertainment, and everyone wanted to be in show business. Joe Schmoe at the feed store. She'd heard of teachers elbowing aside students to get to reporters after a schoolyard shooting. Neighbors behind police barriers stepped on each other's feet, cursed each other in the crush to get closer to the press to comment on the local serial killer or bank defrauder or rape victim they barely knew. Days, months, even years later, long after journalists had forgotten them and their dead, or their wreck of a house, or their cat who miraculously survived the big flood, the self-styled "survivors" and "victims" were still phoning in to newsrooms and TV and radio stations, pressing to be interviewed whenever a similar cataclysm occurred. Were they simply looking for the world to comprehend and acknowledge how calamitous their loss was? Or were they trying to be important in the only way that counted anymore, by being validated by the press, by being a celebrity?

Lauren knew that in the cruel arithmetic of the media, the bombing was a lucky break. But it wasn't her story. Driving back to town, the little Geo bumping and rattling over every stone, every chunk of ice, Lauren, watching a near traffic jam of cars and trucks heading in the opposite direction, toward the JF Ranch, recognized what her story was: that Eileen Hogan—aged forty-six, a housekeeper, a divorcée who had a son majoring in theater at the University of Utah, a Catholic who sang alto in her church choir and had a collection of over a hundred Barbie dolls—and two Brittany spaniels had been the first victims of this latest war against the Jews.

By nine o'clock, the rest of the customers were gone from Sal & Hal's Grubsteak, and the owners invited Lauren to join them in their nightly ritual, diving into all the desserts that wouldn't be fresh enough for the next day's customers.

"I know this sounds lame," Lauren told Sal and Hal, gazing down into a bowl of bread pudding, "but if you ever come to New York, I'll make you dinner."

"I reckon that'll keep me in Jackson," Hal muttered. He tasted a piece of his own lemon meringue pie, then nodded with serious pleasure, as if he were chief judge in a bake-off and was indicating to the lesser judges that, yes, this pie here wins first prize. Hal even looked the part; his cloud of white hair was pulled back loosely into a ponytail, so it resembled a British jurist's wig.

"That's real nice of you, Lauren," Sal said. "If I get a little money together, I might do that. Leave him home."

"What do you think you'd like to do in New York?"

"Try on mink coats at some real posh store. Bloomingdale's?"

"Sure, Bloomingdale's."

"Go see *The Lion King.* Maybe look at a couple of museums." Sal broke off an edge of brownie, tasted it, then shook her head wearily at her husband. "You're sneaking coffee into them again, and then you have the nerve to wonder how come you have three-quarters of the pan left over."

"How's your story coming, Laurie?" Hal inquired, grabbing the rest of the brownie from his wife's plate, stuffing it into his mouth and saying "Delicious" through a mouthful of chocolate and walnuts.

"Not bad." Had she been in New York or Washington or even Columbus, she would have kept her work secret. But after yet another long night and day of reading Christian Identity tracts on the Internet and reviewing her notes on Wrath, she'd gotten so low that she needed to hear some reassuring voice say: That's terrible! My God! They actually believe that stuff?! She needed more than that, she admitted to herself. A call to either of her parents would have offered not just a That's terrible! but also an attempt to put such dangerous claptrap into historical context. What she needed to calm her own growing paranoia—This is what they all think secretly—was to see shock and repugnance registered by a disinterested party. A non-Jewish party who would speak freely, not knowing Lauren's affiliation. For all Hal and Sal Montgomery knew, they were three Presbyterians sitting around a lemon meringue pie.

"Dig up anything new on our old friend Vern?" Hal inquired.

"Listen to this," Lauren said. "Vern is renting his house

and his store up in McBride, so not much hot financial news there. *But* I got my brother to do some digging. He's in law school and gets to use Lexis-Nexis for free. That's a huge, expensive database law firms and rich newspapers access. I had him check all kinds of records in Wyoming. Guess what?"

"What?" Sal asked.

"Well, there are records of two businesses Ostergard's been in that were dissolved while he was still in Sheridan. One was his TV shop up there. Gonzo. Closed. Another was a corporation called Learn from Vern; that was dissolved in '96. Near as I can make out—" She laughed. "God, did you hear me just then? 'Near as I can make out'? I sound like I'm from Wyoming."

"Don't bet the ranch on it," Hal advised her.

"It's a good thing I'm waiting for tomorrow's applesauce cake, or you wouldn't have a prayer. Anyhow, Learn from Vern seems to have been a setup to distribute audio- and videotapes. The year it was dissolved was the same year his divorce was granted, so maybe he closed it down for some legal reason. Who knows? Maybe it plain went bust. But I'll tell you what he does have up there. A single-family residence valued at a hundred thirteen thousand dollars with a mortgage of ninety-three thousand. Now, he bought that house after their divorce, because Louise Ostergard, his ex, got their old house. That one was worth eighty-nine thou free and clear. So there's a fair amount of money around, but no clear source of income."

"I don't get it," Sal said. "What kind of bank is going to give a mortgage to a TV repairman whose TV business was dissolved, whose other business went down?"

"He might own other property," Hal interjected, snatching another brownie and eating it ostentatiously.

"No. No other real estate that my brother could find. Now, I know a hundred and thirteen thousand dollars won't buy a palace in the New York suburbs, but what about in Wyoming?"

"Once you get out of Jackson Hole," Sal mused, "where prices have nothing to do with reality? That could buy a nice place, better than average."

"And he's got to have some cash," Lauren thought out loud, "or at least some credit, what with that jazzy pickup truck of his, and his satellite. So now I'm trying to find out something about a company he still has that didn't fold: Aid to Indigent Westerners."

"A company? Or a charity?" Hal asked.

"That's the weird thing. It sounds like a charity, doesn't it? Except it's listed as a corporation, with shares. Charities don't have shares outstanding, do they?"

"Not that I ever heard of," Hal told her.

"And the guy I told you about who looks like a grizzly bear, that Gus? He's listed as president. Ostergard is vice president." She shook her head and pushed back the bread pudding. "I'm so bad at this."

"No you're not!" Sal declared. "Bad at what?"

"Following a money trail. Not just where it leads: figuring out what it means. And I can't find anything on Wrath itself. It isn't even listed, not as a corporation or a charity or foundation. I can call reporter friends for help, but all they could give me is general guidelines on how to look. I'm not an investigative reporter. Well, I guess I am now, but I don't have the business knowledge. And I have no money to spend on this. Zero. If I stay after Sunday, my paper won't even pay for my motel anymore."

"Stay with us!" Sal and Hal offered in unison. Lauren didn't know how to respond. It was an extraordinary offer, yet the kind of extraordinary offer ordinary people routinely extended. Like her parents: Oh, Lauren, baby, would you mind giving up your room for a week and sleeping on the Hide-A-Bed, because we've invited an exchange teacher from Wales to stay here instead of that motel on Northern Boulevard, and it wouldn't be right for him to have to sleep in the den.

"Thank you so much. Let me see how it goes," she told them. "I have a little money I've saved up. Anyway, if you knew what crazy hours I keep, you wouldn't be so generous."

"Oh, stop it," Sal said.

"I wish there were another way of saying thank you besides thank you."

Back at the Sagebrush, Lauren's thoughts zinged and zapped like lightning. How *did* Wrath get its money? Where did Ostergard get his? He wasn't supporting himself, his ex-wife and children, Kyle McIntyre and Gus Lang, by replacing burned-out TV tubes. Did the bucks come from legitimate donations from supporters with deep pockets? Some more devious route? Oh God, she was so tired. She wished she could sleep. Was an individual or a foundation passing money to Aid to Indigent Westerners? Even though it was a corporation, Lauren sensed AIW had to have been set up to deceive—to sound like a charity. A foundation could list it in its books; what auditor would question such an entry?

But who would want to give Ostergard money? There was always the possibility of a rich nut who loved the idea of banishing all blacks to some hellish section of Alabama, or annihilating ZOG and restoring white men to their proper place. Who else might contribute? If you didn't stick around Vernon Ostergard too long, before he bored you so stiff you'd pray that ZOG existed so their agents could come in and, with one round from a semi-automatic, shut him up, he might seem a good prospect to some special-interest group. His government-is-evil conspiracy theory embraced many causes—grazing rights on government-owned land, mineral rights, gunning down the assault weapons ban. Might an arms manufacturer, might a group like the National Rifle Association, ever slip kindred spirits a little something—ten or twenty thousand—to keep Ostergard shooting off his mouth?

And what about Ostergard? What was he doing, this night after the second bombing? Lying back smug, daring the locals and the feds to prove he had something to do with Eileen Hogan's murder and the destruction of the JF ranch house? Was he sleepless, fearful because he'd turned himself into the focus of what would be a massive law enforcement and media search? Before dinner, when Lauren had called Stan at the Buckin' Bronc for her messages, he told her that reporters were starting to pour into town. Sooner rather than later, they would find the same likely possibility she had found, the link between the mythical Free America Cadre and Wrath. They would find Vernon Ostergard.

All right, calm down, she told herself. She started her relaxation exercise, relaxing her toes, her ankles. By the time she got to her knees, she was thinking: There's *got* to be more. Maybe she could find something—as long as her money and her editor's patience would hold out. What else could she do? Pack up and go home? Okay, possible, because even at this juncture she had the makings of a good story. Good enough for Eli Bloom. But not good enough for Lauren Miller—even if she had to dip into the savings account meant to launch her from Long Island into Manhattan, to get herself an apartment with a bed, a table and chairs. She'd worry about a couch next year.

She'd worry about getting out of *JewNew* next year too. She'd be twenty-eight then, not much older than twenty-seven but so close to thirty she might as well get depressed now.

Would next year be another one like this? Blind dates with guys who were occasionally nice, rarely more than? Regular dates with slicked-back-hair, double-breasted-suit guys she'd meet at bars, or with sweet guys who were friends of friends of friends—friendly guys, so friendly they made her congenitally friendly beagle, Lucy, seem frosty? Dates with grim guys who hated their jobs or who, at age thirty-two, were going back to school for an M.B.A. or a J.D. or an M.D. because life wasn't meaningful? With guys who hated their mothers or their ex-wives or ex-live-ins, for whom the average date was a four-hour opportunity to vent that hatred? Another year like this one? Shit. She couldn't remember the last time she'd been really attracted to a man.

She could. Him. Darrell. That she was thinking of him humiliated her. Was she becoming like the Charlotte Rampling character in *The Night Porter,* that schlocky, exploitive pièce de dreck? Was she like a woman who could collaborate in her own debasement with a Nazi? Darrell Frederickson. The mere thought of him diminished her. That was it. No more. He's history.

He stopped being history shortly before noon the next day, shortly after Lauren had a wholly unsatisfactory interview with the Teton County sheriff.

Unlike Chief Vultaggio, Sheriff Bart Grady was all toothy smiles and thundering cheer, like a square-dance caller who wants to see everyone out on the floor: Gosh, Lauren, I wish to hell and gone I could tell you if we're looking at Wrath or not on this thing, but darn it all, if I say where we're looking or not looking, it would compromise the investigation, now wouldn't it, and it was awful nice of you to drop by and I want you to feel free to call if you have any more questions.

Sitting in the parking lot, trying to think of what to do next, she noticed a deputy bringing in a man in handcuffs, a gawky man with black-framed glasses and a giant Adam's apple. Child molestation, she thought, or performing heinous acts in graveyards. There was simply something wrong about the prisoner: an odd side-to-side gait as if he limped on both legs. His expression seemed more appropriate to speculating if it would rain next Tuesday than to being hauled in to the slammer. Not that a person's appearance could always be relied on. Who was more engaging than O. J. Simpson? For that matter, who was more pleasant, average American Man–looking than Vernon Ostergard? Still, she mused, most people tended to be somewhat readable: not specifically what they were thinking, but whether they were innately belligerent or sweet-natured, whether they were nuts or normal. Most people could and did read others, and they trusted their instincts with good reason. Only the more gifted psychopaths, she decided, the Ostergards, the Simpsons, could fly under that extrasensory radar.

Which was when Lauren thought of him again. Darrell. There was something about him that didn't add up, and the reason for that—she started her car and pulled out of the parking lot—was that there was nothing wrong with him. His eyes, for instance. Not just beautiful eyes. Intelligent eyes. Even if he went around saying "Duh" all day, his eyes would seem intelligent. And although he obviously was a workingman, he didn't have the demeanor of someone desperate and angry, barely making ends meet, or of a congenital loser eating his guts out in silent rage over abuses by some remote power—the federal government or Jews or the Sierra Club. So what had brought a guy like him to his first Wrath meeting?

After her dessert debauchery of the previous night, she picked up a yogurt for lunch and took it back to her room at the Sagebrush. What had Darrell Frederickson found at Wrath that made him keep going back? The first time she'd seen him, he'd been on her side of the street, and when Ostergard came out of his store, he'd called out "Vern!" That had been about now: twelve-fifteen or so. The second time, when she'd been conducting the interview, he'd walked in . . . she couldn't be certain, but probably somewhere around noon. So say he had his lunch hour from twelve to one.

If he was working in the town of Jackson itself, he couldn't make it up to McBride and back in an hour, much less hang with Vern and the boys. So he was probably no more than, let's see, fifteen minutes away. Stretching out the yogurt by taking tiny dabs on the plastic spoon, she found herself leafing through the Yellow Pages. Service stations. Why the hell was she doing this? This was so twisted.

No, not twisted. A legitimate line of inquiry. Darrell Frederickson hadn't been one of the guys who came down with Ostergard from Sheridan. He was a new member. What had made him join? Wouldn't it be interesting if . . . if she could what? Examine why a relatively normal man would join such a movement? Discover that any relatively normal man had better things to do and that normal did not apply to Darrell? See him again?

Opening one of the maps Stan had given her, Lauren made a circle around McBride with a radius of about fifteen miles. She brought the map back to the bed and picked up her yogurt and the phone. What the hell was she doing? She did not dare stop to consider her answer. Okay, not lucky three, but she hit pay dirt on the fourth. "I'm calling about one of your employees, Darrell Frederickson," she said.

"Uh-huh."

"Are you the Bill of Bill's Auto?"

"Yes."

"This is Betty Ann Jensen from Rocky Mountain Savings and Loan. Hope you're having a nice day."

"Fine."

"Good! I'm calling to verify employment. Is Darrell Frederickson employed full time?"

"Yes."

"Do you know what his previous job happened to be, sir?"

"Uh, driving a cab. Over in Nebraska."

"Would you happen to know where in—"

"Lincoln."

"If I can ask you, do you happen to know if Mr. . . . um . . . Frederickson is from Lincoln, Nebraska, originally?"

"I think he's from—if I remember right—Riverton."

"That's in Nebraska?"

"Wyoming."

*This* was what made being a reporter fun: The secretary at Riverton High School confirmed that Darrell Frederickson had been a student but had transferred in 1980. Where to? After a minute of You'll have to call back/Really, I don't mind holding, Lauren was jotting down *Cowan H.S., Muncie, Ind.* The office at Cowan was less accommodating: We require a written request on your letterhead. A call to an old colleague at the *Columbus Star* got Lauren the name of a reporter on the *Indianapolis Free Press* who gave her the name of a reporter on the *Muncie Herald* who said Hey, slow day, no problem. He searched the name in the paper's morgue and called back: Your Darrell Frederickson. Born May 31, 1965. Student at Cowan High. Died on January 22, 1982. Car he was driving got slammed by a train on the C and O tracks.

It's hard to be a neo-Nazi when you're dead, she told herself. Okay, then, who would become Darrell Frederickson? Who wants a false identity? Criminals. All the time. But why would a criminal want to infiltrate Wrath? To steal a lousy pickup truck? Granted, pickup trucks had a deeper resonance in Wyoming than they did on Long Island, but it seemed a little excessive anywhere to go to that much trouble, even for a vehicle as shiny and big and blue as Ostergard's. Unless there were big bucks somewhere. Or a cache of weapons worth risking a life for. Possible.

On the other hand . . . What? On the other hand, she did not want Darrell Frederickson or whoever he was to be a criminal any more than she wanted him to be a racist, an anti-Semite, a sore loser in the game of life. She liked his stance, feet apart, hands in back pockets. Not the posture of a criminal.

On the third hand, he could be . . . What? Although she could get no confirmation, Lauren had heard rumors of Jewish organizations sending in volunteers—both

Jews and Christians—to join radical groups to see if they could dope out a group's goals, its structure, its potential for danger. And naturally she'd heard of law enforcement undercover operations.

Why in God's name was she doing this?

Because she was curious, she explained to herself. Because—okay—she was in much more desperate emotional straits than she had realized and anything over six feet tall with hands in its pockets looked good. Because the alternative was sitting down at her computer and beginning her article. Because she was a reporter, and she had to find out who this man Darrell Frederickson was.

# 14

Vernon Ostergard was not weeping and wailing about being a suspect in the bombing of Jack Frohman's ranch house. Still, the minute Charlie walked through the door of Vern's TV Repair, he could see that Ostergard was at least wrought up. Sitting crossed-legged on a white plastic chair beside Kyle McIntyre, he was chewing on the knuckle of his index finger. The harder Charlie looked, the more troubled the leader of Wrath appeared; his back, normally straight, kept curling until he was so hunched over it looked as if he had a bellyache.

Well, from the look of the block-long business district of McBride, a bellyache was the right response. Two two-man squad cars from the sheriff's office sat in front of the repair shop, and a gray Chevy Lumina, which even the least paranoid citizen of the United States of America would make as an unmarked police car, was parked right across the street, in front of the grocery. The guy leaning down talking to the driver couldn't be anything but FBI, which had finally shared its intelligence from Russell Dillard with the local authorities. The bureau's spirit of cooperation did not, however, extend to confiding it had an agent currently in place within Wrath.

"Darrell." Ostergard acknowledged his presence, although it was evident that merely speaking a name took tremendous effort. Charlie had expected to find him exhilarated. A conspiracy theorist's dream come true:

squad cars, knocks on doors in the middle of the night, lawmen in and out of uniform. What could be better? All that was missing was a black helicopter hovering overhead. Instead, he appeared, if not defeated, certainly diminished. Definitely nervous.

"Vern!" Charlie said, trying to sound upbeat. He nodded to Kyle McIntyre, except McIntyre was in one of his I-don't-see-you-I'm-looking-at-God states and did not acknowledge that a third person had just entered the shop. With its suck-mouth, little-boy nose and wide, round God-focused eyes, McIntyre's face seemed to Charlie like a drawing made by a disturbed child; while all the features were composed of innocent circles, the total effect was sinister. "I parked my truck half a mile beyond here," Charlie told Ostergard. "Walked back. Figured they didn't need to know my license plate."

"Good thinking." Ostergard expired the words as a sigh. He went back to chewing his knuckle but took it from his mouth long enough to put his finger up to his lips: Shhh! Just before he reinserted the knuckle, his eyes swept the walls and ceiling of the repair shop, signaling there were hidden ears—government ears, ZOG ears—listening in. Well, Charlie thought, eight, nine hours since the bomb blew? Assuming the Teton County sheriff didn't have his head up his ass, he'd have a warrant by now. Assuming, too, that he could get his hands on some jazzy equipment, a long-range mike could, at that very moment, be picking up the sounds of Ostergard slurping his knuckle.

Charlie hunkered down beside the leader, but before he could get in a word, Kyle McIntyre sprang from his seat, walked to the door and pointed at it with a fast jab of his thumb: Get the fuck out of here, it said. No I'm-

looking-at-God expression now. His eyes were entirely on
Charlie. Out! he mouthed. Charlie checked Ostergard.
Okay. Pretending to be above it all or too flaked out to
notice. Still, this time, McIntyre apparently was not
speaking for anyone but himself. "Vern," Charlie whispered, "sorry about all this."

"Can you believe this?" Ostergard demanded. "Did
you see them out in front?"

"Want to walk out back, get some air?"

Out! McIntyre was still shouting silently to Charlie,
now tapping his extended thumb against the front door.
Charlie stayed where he was, at Ostergard's side. McIntyre's eyes clouded over, although whether that was
caused by some internal storm or just a trick of the fluo-
rescent lights was hard to tell. Out! Out! That mouth was
like one on a just-landed trout—outraged, frenzied. It
would have been comical, or pathetic, except Charlie had
to admit a trout usually did not have a Ruger semiautomatic tucked into its belt. Out! It might have been a
standoff—McIntyre at the door, repeatedly ordering him
to leave, Charlie remaining in a squat beside Ostergard's
chair—but just then Ostergard rose and, without a glance
at either of them, headed toward the back room. Charlie
followed into the room that had been off-limits. After a
second, so did McIntyre.

If the deceptively narrow, low-ceilinged back area had
ever been Wrath's arsenal, weapons were no longer in evidence. Now it was little more than an oversize corridor
lined with shelves that were divided into boxes. Each
shelf was deep, at least as long as the average shotgun, but
all were empty, not only of weapons but of any television
sets or TV parts.

Ostergard accelerated through the room as if he were

jet-propelled, blasting out of the back door into the freezing air of the yard. Outside, there was only the satellite dish, nothing more. All was whiter than white. The late-winter sky was thick with clouds, the land covered with snow that had melted, then refrozen to the mirrored, milky surface of an unused skating rink.

Ostergard walked cautiously until he was twenty feet or so from the house. "The bomb—" he began in a whisper, still not confident there was enough distance between him and the government microphones.

McIntyre cut him off. "Vern!" As he spoke—so fast the name sounded like Fern—he tried to insinuate himself between Ostergard and Charlie, but the footing was so slippery he gave up and stayed in place.

But the leader of Wrath did not wish to be cut off. "The bomb," he repeated, leaning forward to get as close to Charlie's ear as he could. "Did you hear about what happened? At that ranch?"

"On the radio." Charlie kept his voice low.

"It wasn't . . ." Despite his nervous manner, Ostergard's face appeared content, carefree. No matter what, Charlie realized, he always looked pleasant. Some are born smart, some are born strong. Vernon Ostergard's gift was having been born looking kindly. Whether he was quoting Revelations about the end of the world, decrying the corruption of children by homosexuals, raging against affirmative action or fulminating against the castration of the white man by the Zionists, the corners of his mouth and eyes were forever smiling, lifted with the slightest upward slant, which could not be offset by disposition, age or gravity. Still, no one would mistake his mood for good humor. Each time he fell silent, his knuckles would be drawn to his mouth and his lips would begin to bubble with the saliva produced by the gnawing. "We had nothing to do with the bomb!" he insisted.

"Guess the law doesn't want to hear that," Charlie replied.

"First thing we knew about it was when the phone rang last night. God-awful hour. It was—"

"Vern!" McIntyre spat it out, as if hoping his harsh tone would serve as a slap in the face, stop the mealy-mouthed protestations of innocence or the naming of names.

Ostergard neither told McIntyre to keep out of it nor tried to stare him down. Instead, he spoke softly to Charlie, as if addressing a Wrath meeting with Charlie as the entire audience. "It was one of our friends—supporters, I guess you'd say. He said, Vern, did you hear about it? And Kyle— He was listening. Sometimes he monitors my calls. Kyle said, Hear about *what*? Then he—this supporter—told us what happened down at that director's place, that some woman had been killed, blown to pieces. It would be a murder charge and—" This time, Ostergard cut himself off. "Darrell, you have my word of honor—"

"Vern," McIntyre said, "Darrell hasn't been with us that long." The very breathiness of his words was almost comical, yet tiny hairs on the back of Charlie's neck and on his arms lifted up. "It's too cold out here, Vern. We should go inside." McIntyre managed to sound both solicitous and menacing, although whether the threat was to Charlie alone or included Ostergard was unclear. *"Let's go inside."*

Slowly, Ostergard extracted his knuckle. He looked in McIntyre's direction, Charlie thought, yet could not look directly at him. "If you can't take it out here, Kyle, *you* go inside. I'm talking to Darrell."

"You know you shouldn't be talking, Vernon," McIntyre said, and pivoted away from Ostergard and Charlie. He took a stride toward the back door, then another. Too long a stride. McIntyre's right foot slid forward on the ice, his left skidded back. Suddenly, his legs were splayed in a split. His crotch hovered a few inches above the ice. He grunted a couple of times: Huh! Huh! Then, seeming to recognize how girlish the sounds coming from him were, he stifled his pain and mortification. For a long moment, his trunk swayed above his outspread legs.

Ostergard took a step toward him and reached out his hand. Ignoring it, McIntyre fought to stand on his own. He could not get enough purchase, however, not even to bring his legs together so he could get up onto his knees. Four or five times he nearly succeeded, only to slide back into the split. At last, he could do nothing except grab onto Ostergard's forearm and his belt and haul himself up. Without a word or a glance back, he walked and slid to the shop.

Whatever had gone on between the two men seemed to upset Ostergard's momentary control. No knuckles anymore; he wrung his hands, now red from the raw cold. As his teeth started chattering, Charlie saw he was pulled to follow McIntyre as iron filings are drawn to a magnet. He said, "Guess Kyle's pretty upset, Vern." Ostergard nodded, bringing his hand toward his mouth once again. Catching himself at the last moment, he rested both hands against his neck, lowering his chin to keep them warm. "You were trying to say, back there . . ." Charlie reminded him. "About the bomb that blew up the director's house . . ."

At first there was nothing but silence. Then "Does anyone believe we had nothing to do with it?" came out like a sob.

"I believe you. Of course I believe you. But how come Kyle didn't want you to say you had nothing to do with the bomb?"

"I don't know." Charlie waited. "He thinks it can work for us," Ostergard finally said, trying for a bright tone. "Because we didn't do it. So how can they trace it to us? But people will *think* we did, and that's good PR. Not really 'we.' Not Wrath. But the Free America Cadre . . . What they're saying sounds like our message, doesn't it? It will show everybody that folks like us mean business."

"Shit, Vern."

"What, Darrell? *What?*"

"Do you think it's good PR that some churchgoing white woman was killed?"

"That was an accident," Ostergard muttered. "An unfortunate accident."

"Forget about PR, then. Do you think ZOG's going to leave you alone now that they have a chance to get you? Do you?"

"But they *can't* get us. That's Kyle's point. There won't be any evidence, because we had nothing to do with it!"

"You know how they work better than I do, Vern." Ostergard nodded in agreement. "But didn't you ever hear of people getting railroaded?"

"What?"

"Wouldn't they plant evidence? I mean, they know what a threat you are to them, right?" Ostergard's head bobbed up and down: Yes, yes, of course I know. "Is there anything they can trace—"

"Nothing!"

"Explosives or blasting caps or anything like that?"

"Absolutely not! I'm sure . . . I'm ninety-nine percent sure." His momentary optimism began to dissolve, and Charlie could see him sinking back into knuckle-gnawing anxiety. "I mean, look, Darrell, we've been storing, you know, supplies."

"Supplies? You mean guns? Sure. I figured as much."

"All kinds of firepower. Ammo. Not that we're planning anything. But we have to be ready when the time comes. I know what we have, but I don't always . . ." He took a deep breath. "I don't actually go and take inventory every day. Impossible. If I did that, I wouldn't do much else, would I? I do the buying, though. Not the checking in of deliveries every time. Sometimes not even the buying, if it's a small transaction. For all I know, Kyle could have bought some supplies like that. Explosives or something. He's very . . . He sees the big picture. Very few do, and I trust him with . . . everything. *Maybe* there could be a case where he thought, well, we might need this or that, and went out and bought a few things and forgot to tell me. But I don't think so. That's not like him. We work as a team."

"Gus?"

"Gus helps. He's a foot soldier. Not a general. Kyle's my general." Ostergard blew on his hands. "It is *cold*. You've got on a warm vest. I don't." Having just spoken of McIntyre, his general, Ostergard seemed to want to go back to him. He rotated away from Charlie, taking small, careful steps, until he was directly opposite the door, gazing at it.

Charlie unzipped his down vest and handed it to Ostergard. "Vern, listen." He waited until Ostergard's eyes were on him. "I'm no genius, but this looks like bad trouble to me. Those sheriff's cars are the least of it. This is a murder case, and that director—"

"He's not even a Jew!"

"But the guy who made that phone call saying he was Free America or whatever, he thought the director was a Jew. You know what the media—their media, like you're always saying—you know what they're going to say about this." He slipped his vest out of Ostergard's hand and draped it around the man's shoulders. "They'll say, 'Drag 'im in, hang 'im high.' Except this time you're the 'him,' Vern."

Ostergard said nothing, as if waiting for a solution to present itself to him. Finally, he looked at Charlie. "What the hell am I supposed to do?"

"If you'll pardon my French, Vern? Save your own ass."

Ostergard grasped Charlie's upper arm with both his hands and held on tight. "How? If they're out to get me, and believe me, they are."

"It's not for me to say." Charlie sensed Ostergard's grip loosening, so he added, "Give them someone else."

"Who?"

"I don't know. Could anyone . . . I don't know how to say this the right way, Vern, so I'll just out and say it: Could anyone be wanting to challenge your, uh, leadership? Trying to make a point that the war against ZOG isn't a war of words but a real war? With real bombs?"

Ostergard shrugged. His eyes moved toward his shop. "It *is* a real war." He took a deep breath. "What so many good people—our brothers-in-arms, so to speak—don't understand is that to win you need the support of the people. Now, you can get that through sheer power—political power *and* firepower. Okay, we don't have anywhere near that yet. I'm the first to admit it. But you can also get it by making more and more converts to your cause. Except you *can't* get their support if people think you're crazy and dangerous and will make their lives worse instead of better. We have to fight on their territory. Be reasonable. Be clean. Keep the skinheads away from the cameras. And you've got to talk softly. You can't say 'Hitler was right.' You never say 'nigger.' You don't shout. You can make them believe anything if you say it nice and polite. Not everyone agrees with me. Some people say, No, Vern, you *should* scare them."

"Could one of those people be trying to set you up?"

"Can't be. Worst case would be we're brothers who may not see eye to eye. But we're all one family."

"Okay. I didn't mean to—"

"How would I know if I'm being set up?" He spoke so quietly Charlie could barely hear the words. "Would the man doing the setting up tell me?"

"The last thing I want to do is try and get between you and any of your friends, but, well, if I didn't bring it up . . ."

"I appreciate it, Darrell. I just don't know where to go from here."

"Another thought, Vern. I guess my head's been spinning ever since I heard the radio. Hate to add to your burdens, though."

"No, no. I appreciate your interest."

"Could it be someone in Wrath, or who came to the meetings, who might be—what the hell's that word?—a renegade? Going off on his own?"

"Christ almighty! I hate to admit it, but I've had that notion too." Ostergard was still gripping Charlie's arm with both hands. "I mean, not that I know anything about that bomb that fizzled out in that Jew's video store over in Jackson. But it's a distinct possibility someone among us was waiting for the next bomb to blow after that first one. *That* one made its point quietly. Maybe didn't get as much media attention as it should have, but I thought it was pretty darned effective."

"But if they were waiting for a second bomb," Charlie suggested.

"It didn't come. There are some within the group who I sense feel my methods are too tame. But I've built this organization up from nothing. *From nothing!*" He looked toward the huge satellite dish as if to say, See what I've done! Look where I'm going! But the satellite dish was not broadcasting, and Ostergard needed an audience. He'd found one, and Charlie knew he might go on for hours, especially now that Ostergard had the vest on his shoulders and the audience in his grasp. "I know what I'm doing." He looked to the shop. "And every time I don't trust my own good instincts . . . I don't mean to toot my own horn, Darrell, but—"

"Vern, you deserve a brass band!"

"Thank you. And you're right. You can't just go out there and blow things up, no matter how just your cause. It's not just good PR or bad PR. They're devious. That's the only way they know. We've got to be devious too. We made some strides, coming down here from Sheridan, but we might have attracted a little too much attention."

"I hear you, Vern."

"One small scare, then another, then another. Keep them off balance. Keep them frightened but not panicked. Small is the key. Subtle. Anything big will get them sympathy. We need them unsettled, so they're not at peak efficiency. They have to be thinking all the time: When will it happen again? Where? Will the next one be the big one? Will it happen to me? Drain their energies. That's how to do it."

"That's how," Charlie echoed.

"It's not that I can't understand the man who wants to strike out. There's so much provocation. But I say this all the time: Before we get to a war of weapons, it will be a war of wits. Some folks can't see that. We don't have the numbers yet. We don't have the firepower yet, not to take on the armies of ZOG. I try so hard to make my brothers understand—"

"You may be too sympathetic, Vern."

"What do you mean?"

"I mean, someone or some group took the action against your advice, against your leadership. Against you. How can you talk about making them understand, when it's you who'll take the blame?"

Once more, Ostergard glanced over to his shop. He seemed to sense McIntyre's eyes on him, to hear a silent, irresistible *Vern!* His speechmaking gave way to four stilted words: "What would you do?"

"Look, I don't want to get on Kyle's bad side, though I guess I'm already there. But between you and me: I'd want to know who's responsible. As a kind of loyalty-check thing. And in case you have to make a trade—them for you. If you want me to check up on anybody in the group, or if you have any ideas you need looking into in a quiet sort of way, I'm just a phone call away. Hell, I'd quit my job in a minute for you, Vern. You know that."

"Thank you, Darrell." He pulled the vest tighter around him. "Don't stop dropping by—if you're not afraid of meeting a few deputies."

"They don't scare me." Kyle, on the other hand, scares the shit out of me. "And if you got any thoughts about how to look into this, or poking around you want done to get the quote law unquote off your back, well, Vern, you know what they say in the marines: I await your orders."

This time, Jeanette Wagner waited on the side of the road in a Toyota Corolla with a dead battery. Another agent was with her; he looked like he was from Miami, with a lifelong, inch-deep tan. He wore a stupid-looking cowboy hat with a too-small brim and a feather that must have been plucked from a parakeet. Charlie guessed he was playing her husband; in any case, he was stomping up and down alongside the road, pretending to be pissed off about the battery. Banging his fist theatrically into the palm of his hand, then giving a bark he must have thought was a happy cowboy yelp when Charlie pulled off the road, he needed acting lessons. He told Miami to get in the car and pretend to try to start up the engine.

He wanted to get this over with. It was almost one o'clock, and this would make the fourth time he'd be late getting back to the gas station after his lunch hour. He wasn't a shirker, and he hated to look like one, especially to Bill. The truth was, he was coming to think of his work in the garage as his actual job. The rest of it was some bizarre extracurricular assignment he'd somehow gotten stuck with.

As he pulled the jumper cables from behind his seat and opened the hood of his truck, he reported to Jeanette on his conversation with Ostergard. She kept saying, No kidding! No kidding! as he told her it was clear Ostergard could not, with a hundred percent certainty, swear the bomber wasn't his boy Kyle, directly challenging his leadership. Or that the bomber wasn't a Wrath member or sympathizer, inspired by the first bomb, disgruntled by the lack of a second. "Who do you think he suspects?" Jeanette asked.

"Can't say for sure. Or even not for sure."

"Could this whole thing be a fake? I mean, could Ostergard be putting on a 'What am I going to do?' act for you, to cover up that he's the one who did it or had it done?"

"If he's acting, he's a damn sight better than your husband over there. And if he did it, why would he still be here, waiting for us or the State of Wyoming to grab him? Why not head for the hills somewhere?"

"Let's stay with the acting for a minute," Jeanette said. "Could he be acting in order to draw you out because he suspects something's not right with you?"

Like he hadn't considered that before. Just one more in a corral of happy thoughts that kept him awake every damn night. Could all Ostergard's cordial "Darrell!"s be a cover while he and McIntyre figured out who Darrell was and what to do with him? Or were they the real thing, a welcome from a leader who badly wanted a follower who was not a nut, not a loser, but the sort of white man who could claim to be Chosen without others snickering at the presumption?

"I don't know, Jeanette."

"Fair enough. Another question: I guess I could look at a map, but I have you. Could their arsenal be in Sheridan, wherever Sheridan is? Maybe they never moved their stuff."

"Maybe, but say you were moving your whole company to Jackson Hole, and your company's business was preparing for Armageddon. Would you leave your weapons more than three hundred miles away—or would you put them in a safe place not too far from your new headquarters?" Charlie was amazed she was sticking around so long. But she'd wanted to debrief him in person right after his lunch hour at Ostergard's and not wait to speak to him after work. He clamped the cables onto the batteries and signaled Miami to turn on the ignition. "What happened with the transponder I stuck on the bottom of his truck?" he asked. "If it was driving somewhere to pick up weapons, it had to drop them off somewhere else. Don't you know where it went?" Jeanette glanced heavenward. He knew what it meant. "Not working?"

"No. Sorry. But listen, we don't want you to risk taking it off. It's small and so well hidden it's highly unlikely they'll find it. Even if they do, they'll think it was put there after the second bombing."

"Hope so. By the way, want my latest nightmare?" Charlie inquired.

"Go ahead."

The car started. Miami stuck his hand out the window and gave him a thumbs-up sign. "That it's not Kyle McIntyre. Not one of the creeps who've come to the meetings. That it's Russ Dillard." The possibility of an FBI informant slipping out of the bureau's control, then putting his expertise to lethal use, had been on Charlie's mind since the middle of the night, when Jeanette had called him about the bomb.

"Don't even think that," she said, shuddering. "No. It can't be him."

"Why not?" Charlie asked, taking off the cables. "Because you don't want it to be him?"

"No. Completely different type of bomb this time. The first was a single tube with a minimal amount of smokeless gunpowder. Some sort of an electronic timing device. It was made not to do any damage, and it was . . . well, let's say not unsophisticated. About what you'd expect from a Russ Dillard." She went for her wallet, but this time, since he had stopped in his own truck and not the tow truck, he told her no. Obviously, she did not get the distinction, but then, she was from the East. Naturally, the word "East" made him think of Lauren Miller. He had been bowled over when she turned to face him and he saw that her eyes weren't green. So dark. Not even brown. Black. For that one second he'd looked into them, he couldn't distinguish pupil and iris. "This bomb, at Frohman's ranch," Jeanette was saying. "Want to hear my nightmare? The recipe for that bomb is no secret. For God's sake, it's out there, on the Web. Fragmentation grenade, they call it. Grenade? It's a weapon made for mass destruction. *Mass*. Available to one and all. Whoever made this one made it really mean: probably five, six pounds of nails in it. Meant for max damage. We have to wait for preliminary lab results, but it looks like he used a regular lantern battery and one of those little alarm clocks you can buy at any drugstore—the kind of cheap stuff Rudolph used in the Atlanta Olympic bombing. Simple ingredients, easy recipe."

"What did he use as explosive?" Charlie asked.

"Dynamite. You know what?"

"What?"

"My little guy's in eighth grade. Good in science, not great. But if he had a bad grudge and a free afternoon and access to a construction site and didn't mind fifty-fifty odds it would blow up in his face . . ."

"Boom?"

"Boom," she said.

\*        \*        \*

Charlie felt sorry for the woman who had pulled into
Bill's Auto. She had one of the lousiest cars on wheels, a
Plymouth Reliant, and even after he explained that the
problems she was having were probably caused by the
choke sticking and went through the whole thing with
her, how when it closes up it makes the car run with a
richer mix and that fouls the spark plugs, and he invited
her to come over and take a look and then he'd show her
how to clean the plugs, she still was babbling away
about Ooh, this car is driving me crazy—get it? *driving
me*—and her babble was California girl talk, cute, high-
pitched. But if she was from California, it must have
been horse country. She had a long face and prominent
teeth that, unfortunately, were closer to yellow than
white. Not the worst face in the world, but her kind of
looks required a certain dignified way of speaking, like
Mister Ed, and here she was going on about her
Reliant—El Lemon, she kept calling it—in the style of
someone five foot three, with a thong bikini. *Those*
things are the spark plugs? she was asking, and sure, he
knew she was flirting with him and was nervous about
it, knowing she was not good at it, and he felt sorry for
her and was trying to find an opening to say something
like, My wife had the same problem with her car, to put
an end to her discomfort, to say nothing of his, except
she wouldn't let him get a word in edgewise. They don't
*look* so yucky, she was telling him, hanging over the
engine more than was necessary to show her butt,
which—he hated to be cruel, but he'd had only two
hours' sleep—would have looked better on a mare.

He wished Bill and Paul would get back from lunch so
they could see how patient he was with customers and
how much they liked him. Except they'd probably waited

around till one-fifteen or so for him to come back and got disgusted and finally left. He'd put twenty bucks of his own money into the cash register so he could tell them how, when he'd stopped to boost a battery on company time, he'd gotten paid for it.

He was just about to tell her, You know, my wife . . . , when he noticed a car across the road. A Geo Metro. Green. She had a red one. Lauren.

Someone was in the car. Nobody just sat around like that way out here. With all the scenery in the valley, who would sit and stare at a Chevron station? Too far off for him to get a visual, and the guy was wearing a baseball hat pulled low over his face. Looked too small for Kyle McIntyre, but he couldn't be sure. Could it be someone from the bureau, watching out for him? They had better cars than that, and they wouldn't just be sitting out there in plain sight. *Could* it be Kyle?

There was a gun in the office, on a hidden shelf under the cash register. A Glock, like his service weapon. He finally cut into the woman's babble, saying, "Right, well, you know, my wife was having the same problem with the carburetor on her car, and she wound up getting rid of it." Sure enough, she was out of there a minute later. A couple of seconds after that, Charlie was in the office, slipping the gun in his pocket. He stayed inside and waited.

The Geo was moving now, pulling into the road. Crossing over. Definitely not McIntyre. Okay, but if McIntyre was certifiably nuts, or feeling threatened enough to want to get rid of Darrell, or if he discovered some misstep the man who was calling himself Darrell had made, could he have gotten somebody else to do the job for him so quickly? Why not? How many guys in Wrath had a full calendar?

Maybe it was just some jerk in a Geo. For all he knew, it could be a private eye tailing Horseface. Okay, not that, but there might be a perfectly innocent explanation for why someone was sitting across from the gas station watching and waiting till Charlie was alone. Well, he wasn't going to stroll out of the office and give the guy in the car a nice, slow-moving target. He waited, his hand in his pocket, the gun in his hand. The car pulled up to the pump, but on the far side, so the pumps blocked his view. He tried to remember which side of a Geo the gas tank door was on, but he couldn't.

Charlie felt the cold that goes from the inside out. The driver's door was opening. Oh, for Christ's sake! A girl in a white Polartec anorak and— She took off the baseball cap and shook out her hair and walked right up to the office.

"I'd like to talk to you," Lauren Miller said.

"What?" He sounded like a moron. Okay, he was supposed to be a moron. He was Darrell Frederickson.

"I'm the reporter who was with Vernon Ostergard the other day when you came in. My name is Lauren Miller."

"Do you need gas?" he asked. Well, if he'd tried he might have said something dumber, but the thing of it was, he hadn't tried.

"No. I'm here to talk to you. I have a couple of questions—"

"Get out." He didn't know what to look at first, her hair or her eyes, and the rest of her was good too. A nice face. A sweet face, although she did not seem the kind of girl—woman—who would want to be called sweet. Without that stupid coat, she had a good body, what he could see of it through layers of anorak and sweaters, but he didn't want to get caught looking at her body.

"Vernon Ostergard mentioned that you were one of the newer members of Wrath, that you'd joined——"

"Didn't you hear me?"

"I heard you."

"Then get the hell out."

"Not so fast." Was she nuts, talking like that to a guy who might be some kind of a maniac, alone in a service station, in the middle of a road that stretched miles? "Let me tell you about Darrell Frederickson," she said. "Born May 31, 1965. About your age, right?" Charlie stared. Her eyes were so sparkly. She didn't have the accent, but the way she talked—fast, confident—told you she was from New York. "He transferred out of Riverton High to a school in Muncie, Indiana." Don't worry, they'd told him during those two weeks in Washington. Your identity will hold up. They never check that deep, and even if they do, they'll find out you're what you say you are. Unless the "they" is a reporter. "But Darrell never graduated from the school in Muncie. He was killed when his car crossed some railroad tracks and a train hit it. January 22, 1982. So what I want to know is——"

He pulled out the gun and held it on her. "Get out." She went white for a second, staring at the gun like she'd never seen one before, which was what he expected. He hoped she wasn't going to faint, though then he could catch her. Which would be great when the guys got back from lunch and saw him with an unconscious customer in his arms, holding a gun. "Now."

"So if you're not Darrell Frederickson, you're either a criminal . . ." He couldn't believe she was still standing there, talking. Staring at the gun, true, but talking. ". . . or you're in law enforcement. I vote law enforcement."

"I vote you get out of here."

"I vote you put that thing away. What if it went off by mistake? I mean, even if you are a criminal, you don't want to face a murder rap, do you? The worst a criminal would probably do is hit me over the head with the gun butt—the handle thing."

"But if all I do is hit you on the head, you'll wake up. And the next day or the day after, you'll reveal some personal information I don't want revealed. So maybe I'll take you someplace and put a bullet through your head. Get rid of your car later. They'll never find it. They'll never find you."

She was frightened. He could feel it. See it in the way she was forcing herself to meet his glance. It would be nice if someday he could go to New York, look her up and say, Hey, Lauren, didn't mean to scare you that time at the Chevron station, but— "You're not scaring me," she told him.

"Then you're not as smart as you should be."

"Listen: I think we can help each other. I mean, I'm assuming you're on the right side of the law. You'll have to show me some ID and then I'll do some checking, but we could trade information."

He set the gun back on the shelf, then grabbed her arm to lead her back to her car. She looked up at him and smiled. "So what's your name?"

# 15

Oh, that one terrible instant when she was staring down the barrel of his gun, into its darkness. Lauren knew he was slanting it that way deliberately to terrify her, let her check out what eternal nothingness looks like. A thought suddenly occurred to her: What if he's not a good guy? Paralysis seized her, the freeze that comes just before the sweats, the loosening of the bowels. Wait! she would have cried if, for once, she hadn't been wordless. It *has* all been prologue. The story's just begun.

What happened then to let her body know—thank God, thank God—that it did not have to humiliate itself in its final flash of life? An infinitesimal movement of his wrist, which lowered the gun, so Lauren was no longer looking down the hole at her own death? Her mind rejecting all possibility of extinction because it could not accept its own arrogant miscalculation? Whatever, when she raised her head to look at him again, she knew not only that he was not going to pull the trigger but that he was not a bad guy. Okay, she couldn't swear without reservation that he stood on the right side of the law, but he was not wicked.

"You're not scaring me," she told him, but she could see he knew she'd been scared nearly shitless. "Listen," she went on, "I think we can help each other." He shook his head once: Don't even think about it. "When I say help each other, I'm assuming you're not a gunrunner or a serial killer."

Years earlier, when she was twelve or thirteen, her mother had said: Trust your gut, sweetie. You've got a good gut. "Of course, you'll have to show me some ID, and then I'll do some checking." As if to prove her mother was right, he slung the gun under the cash register. Her sigh of relief, unfortunately, was not a feminine release of pent-up breath but the sound of a frog croaking Oy!

Now that he had disarmed himself, she expected a declaration: I'm with the Wyoming Division of Criminal Intelligence. He'd whip out his badge, she'd glance down and see his name, which was— No name. No badge. Instead, he grabbed her arm and began to haul her toward the door. What the hell was he doing? Dragging her back to her car? God, could he pull! She remembered, from a book about the civil rights movement, how demonstrators were trained not to fight the police but to let themselves go limp so they'd be a load and a half, harder to move. Except she didn't want him to think she weighed a ton, and instead of resisting, she just looked up at him and smiled and asked, "So what's your name?"

The smile was obviously less than winsome, because he sounded angry. "Darrell Frederickson." He was wonderful to look at. That great beard. She wished she could touch it. Tall, broad-shouldered, with a mostly handsome face that could shift to homely with a change of the light. An excellent head. Black hair, though much too short. She hoped that was his Wrath cover, looking like a militia moron. But it was not his striking looks that had quieted her fears. His eyes were not merely beautiful but good.

"Do we have to go through this Darrell business again?" she asked.

"Maybe there's a dead guy with my name somewhere, but that's not me. Now I want you the hell out of here!"

"Stop yelling. Hey, how about letting go of my arm? Can't we talk?"

"Here's talk: One, my boss will be coming back any minute. Two, I've got nothing to say to you."

"I definitely do not have the wrong Darrell Frederickson. You—whoever you are—left a trail. People do. You told your boss you were from Riverton."

Maybe she shouldn't have mentioned his boss. His grip tightened like a blood pressure cuff. She tried to pry open his fingers but got nowhere. "What were you talking to my boss about?"

"Nothing. Relax. I made up . . . that I was somebody—"

"Who?"

She didn't want him to rethink the gun, so she spoke quickly: "I said I was from Rocky Mountain Savings and Loan. Checking an application. Let go of my arm, damn it!" They were out the door now, almost at her car, yet she could not transcend her own stupid vanity and let herself go limp so she'd drag like dead weight. "Look, I know you must be upset about me blowing your cover, but you have my word. I would never do that." He opened her car door and pulled down on her arm, twisting it back slightly so there was nothing she could do but get in. "Just hear me out!"

"There's nothing you can say I want to hear."

He was waiting for her to shut the car door and take out her key. She leaned back against the seat and headrest and placed her hands lightly on the wheel. "This is the deal, formerly-known-as-Darrell. I don't expect to get official secrets out of you. And for my part, I'm not going to give up any of my material a law enforcement agency has no need to know. But whether you've heard about it or not, cops and journalists trade information all the time. If you don't believe me, ask your superiors." She saw this last remark was not the way to his heart. "Excuse me: As you well know, reporters and cops scratch each other's backs, metaphorically"—sensing it would be unwise to stop to see if he knew what "metaphorically" meant, she continued—"and all I'm asking is that you listen to what I have to propose." He grasped the top of the car door and was about to slam it shut when a tow truck with two men inside pulled into the station. Its horn tooted in greeting as it pulled over to the garage. Formerly-known-as-Darrell waved to the men. As he did, Lauren slipped out of the car and leaned against the pump. "Ten bucks' worth of regular," she told him.

"Self-service," he said coldly, turning toward the office.

Lauren knew she had crossed the line and he was now finding her a pain in the ass. That was the last thing she wanted. Well, maybe not the last thing. Would his wink, his smile, be worth her missing a chance to learn more about Wrath than she ever could on her own? "If one of those guys getting out of the tow truck is your boss," she said, "wouldn't he want to see you helping a tourist in a rented car who's a lame-o from New York and can't work a gas pump, instead of turning your back on her?"

As he yanked out the pump nozzle, he asked, "What do you think this is going to get you?"

"A full tank and time enough to tell you we have to talk. I'll meet you in a restaurant in Jackson called Sal & Hal's Grubsteak. Eight-thirty tonight."

"We don't *do* dinner around here."

"I'm not inviting you to have dinner with me. I want to meet you in a public place where I can feel safe talking, until I'm confident about who you are."

"Not there," he said.

Lauren tried to read something on his face but couldn't find anything. "Okay. Let me think. You know a bar north of Jackson, the Grizzly?" He didn't say yes, but neither did he say no. "Same time, then. Eight-thirty." She crossed behind him, stepped over the hose and climbed into the car for her backpack. While she rooted around for her credit card, he stared at the cash readout. When she offered the card, he snatched it without looking at her, and when he brought it back with the charge slip and waited for her to sign, he stared down the road at nothing. "I'm sorry," Lauren told him, as she got into the Geo. "I'm sure this has been a tough assignment for you. I guess I'm only adding to your troubles." He turned his back on her and headed for the garage. She watched him in her rearview mirror. She had never seen a man walk better.

She called Visa, reported her card lost while she was cross-country skiing, which, while untrue, made her feel quite robust. Then she mailed it to herself on Long Island, along with a note saying that since she'd rubbed the card hard against her sleeve, the only two people's prints on it should be hers and those of the man she believed to be a cop who had infiltrated the radical group Wrath. Hope I'm not wrong about him, but just in case, he's going by the name Darrell Frederickson and working at Bill's Auto, a Chevron station on the road to McBride. Mom, Dad, Adam, remember I love(d) you with all my heart. Don't worry, I'm okay.

Having sent her qualm home, Lauren sat in her car

outside the post office, thinking about formerly-known-as-Darrell. For a moment, she named him Joe, then decided it would be better not to call him anything, so she wouldn't be disappointed if he turned out to be a Dwayne.

His handsome-homely combo was a guaranteed heart-melter, she knew. Plain, ordinary news-anchor handsomeness—symmetrical features, oversize eyes, predictable chin clefts—was of interest only to prepubescent girls and women without imaginations. But take a fine feature or two—in his case, blue eyes pure as the sky beyond her windshield, a generous-lipped mouth—and add to them a nose, probably too big to begin with, that had doubtless been broken and Dumbo ears, and you came up with one irresistibly interesting face. Yet that was not his sum total. There were also splendid parts: broad shoulders, big hands, flat ass, long legs. Not-to-be-sneezed-at attributes: guts, self-control, the graceful walk, the presumptive knowledge of where to put transmission fluid. Pretty likely gifted in bed, probably intelligent, perhaps kind.

He was so fine she wanted to call her friends and speak of him for hours, so fine she wouldn't know where to start. Well, better to save herself the humiliation when it turned out he'd been hired by Hamas to infiltrate Wrath and steal their cache of sarin.

She grew so moony sitting in her car, tracing in memory the veins on the backs of his hands, that by the time she walked over to the town hall for the press conference, forty reporters had already gathered. Journalists, familiar with the loneliness of new towns, alert to the possibilities of the inadvertent dropping of a crucial detail by a colleague, tend to be a sociable group. And so they were, trading fleabag-motel stories and political gossip, passing around tortilla chips. This time, though, she just responded to Hi, Janis Traven, *Denver Post,* and to Mark Linsey, Fox News, with a nod and a curt Lauren Miller and moved on, leaving Janis and Mark, and then Carrie and Dick and Bernice and Warren and Mel and Marion and Big Al from Chicago to bond with one another. She knew too much to become pals with those far behind her.

More reporters crammed in. Camera crews, with their equipment and elbows, added to the crush. By the time Chief Vultaggio, Sheriff Grady and the head of the FBI's Denver office, a man named O'Donnell, walked out on the stage, nearly one hundred members of the press, most of them suitably dressed for polar exploration, sweated and murmured discontentedly through the officials' terse opening statements. During the question and answer period, they sneered openly at the three officials' guarded responses, demanding: Why won't you tell us whether the bomb fragments were sent to the state police in Cheyenne or to the FBI lab? What do you say to charges that a piece of the timing device that was supposedly logged in at the sheriff's office is missing, and can you give us the names of people who had access to it? Why not? How long was Jack Frohman questioned and by which organization and why can't we know what he said and where he is now? Is he in protective custody? Is he in any way being considered a suspect or an accessory? Do any of you have anything to say to the bomber?

Smart questions, idiot questions. But Lauren's favorite trio was now Vultaggio, Grady and O'Donnell, for never once did they utter the name Wrath or even mention that such an organization existed. Outside afterward, with the frosty air cooling her cheeks, she leafed through her notes and folded over the only page with information that was new to her: The second bomb was different in composition and design from the one that fizzled at Big Elk Video—more amateurish, definitely more deadly.

All right, then, Lauren mused: What did she have going for her? So far, she was probably the only member of the press who had made the trip to McBride, who knew about Wrath, who had interviewed Vernon Ostergard. So far, except for the staff of the two Jackson Hole dailies, she was the only journalist who wasn't going to spend the afternoon trying to get the lay of the land. What better time to start her article? Return to the Sagebrush, sit at her laptop and go through her usual process—type and delete leads, visit the soda machine, check her E-mail. With luck, she'd wind up with a table littered with gum wrappers, a couple of pages written and time for a nap and a bite to eat before going to the Grizzly to wait for formerly-known-as-Darrell.

What would really happen if she went back to the motel? She'd wind up getting nothing more than computer-googly eyes and no first sentence because she'd keep thinking about him. Not useful, intelligent thoughts, preparing questions, like, What made you become a con artist and how in God's name are you able to convey that air of integrity? Or, if he was a good guy, Is your undercover assignment a response to the first bombing and what made your law enforcement organization decide that Wrath was the group to penetrate? No, she'd luxuriate in turning over in her mind possibilities about who he could be, about where he came from. She'd end up creating fifty different biographies for him. Yet each one of those histories would be cut short by a single fantasy: how his body would feel against hers, the texture, the heat of it, in the first moment of their coming together.

Which would mean a total waste of an afternoon. Plus it disturbed her that she was putting so much energy—strike "energy"—so much passion, into daydreaming about him. What was with her? Was it because half her friends were married or engaged and the other half seemed perfectly content with being single? Was it that her own life was on hold, as she worked at a job she didn't want, lived in her parents' house, in her old bedroom, with her old quilt, her old Monet reproduction, her old books, from *Madeline* to *All the President's Men*? Was she the only twenty-seven-year-old wondering whether "For every Jack there is a Jill" was a vicious hoax, whether people like her—the ones most desirous of giving and receiving love—were doomed to go through life alone? At what age do you stop hoping and start researching artificial insemination and single-parent adoptions? Twenty-seven and a half?

She strolled through Jackson for nearly a half hour, past stores selling camouflage clothing and big-game-hunting videos, boots and chaps, Navajo sand paintings and Apache baskets, sweatshirts with grinning elk, skirts with suede fringe, as if she were an acquisitive tourist on her inaugural shopping expedition. She was on the verge of buying an utterly unnecessary computer mouse painted like a moose, when a sign in the window of a log-sided store across the street stopped her: *Paradise on Earth for Sale! We Custom-Build Your Dream Log Cabin!* She walked over and opened the log door.

"Hi!" Lauren smiled at a man whose unsmiling glance told her he did not believe she could afford paradise on earth. "I'm one of the eight thousand reporters racing around town," she explained. "I just have a quick question about construction." She waited until his head dropped a quarter of an inch, which she took to mean go ahead. Fishing the afternoon's press release from her pocket, she asked, "Do you know what six-d galvanized wire nails are?"

"Sixpenny nails," he muttered, although he did not find it necessary to expend any excess effort and move his lips.

"What do they look like?"

"Two inches."

"Two inches long?" He nodded. "Are they used a lot?" Another nod. "If someone went to a building-supply store and asked for five or six pounds of nails, would that be unusual?" This time, a shake of the head. No. "Okay, I won't waste your time asking you where these places are. Can I use your phone book?" Another nod. He reached under his desk and flopped the phone across to her. "You wouldn't know which of these places do the highest volume of business, would you?" she inquired, allowing more than a touch of skepticism to creep into her voice, showing how dubious she was that he would have the answer. As she figured, he needed to prove to her he did.

Lauren struck out at Valley Supply and Little Falls Building Suppliers, although the man at Little Falls did tell her two FBI agents had been around just before closing time the day before, asking about purchases of nails. But at Plunkett Lumber, Scott told her to check with Kent, who told her no, not me, go over to Len. Len, an elderly man whose face seemed to be a repository for all the wrinkles in Wyoming, knew something, although he wasn't about to tell her what it was. "Not that I don't want to help you," he roared above a high-pitched grinding sound—more metal against metal than metal against wood. He did not appear hostile, or even sullen, although it was clear he had nothing more to say to her. He went back to counting long, flat strips of wood, and his lips formed seven, eight and nine.

"You mean the FBI said something about keeping it under your hat?" she shouted.

"Nope."

"They haven't been here yet?"

"Not that I know of," he boomed.

"Any other law enforcement organization? One of Bart Grady's deputies?"

"You know Bart?"

The grinding stopped as she was bellowing, "Sure." She lowered her voice. "I spent some time with him. Really nice guy. Very helpful." Although not to me. "Sir, just hear me out." Lauren had learned to say "sir" and "ma'am" in South Carolina. It had a soothing, civilizing effect on her, helping to negate the don't-have-time-for-a-lot-of-politesse-shit New York style into which she often found herself lapsing. It also worked well with people over sixty-five, even in the heart of Times Square. "I'm not racing after a hot news item. I didn't just get here yesterday. I've been in Jackson Hole for ages, researching a major article. And believe me, it won't get written today. So you won't be telling me anything that is going to turn into a big headline tomorrow and compromise the investigation in any way."

"Sorry, ma'am, but—"

"I understand. Just a general question, then: Is it common for someone to come in and buy five or six pounds of sixpenny nails?"

"Good-sized job, you'd need that many," he said reluctantly. "Maybe more."

"Did anyone besides the contractors you usually deal with come in and buy that amount?"

"I told you, I don't think I should say."

"Was it the guy with the nose . . . ?" she asked, pushing up her nose into a slight upward tilt, figuring that covered at least seventy percent of the population of Wyoming.

"That's him," Len said at last.

"That's what I figured. How tall would you say he was? I've heard conflicting stories, although one of the people only saw him when he was sitting down."

"Small. For a man. Taller than you."

"I'm five four."

"Well, maybe five six. Not much more."

"Blue eyes?"

"I think so. Like I told the deputy, hard to recall."

"And what color hair?"

"Brown, 's far as I remember."

"Has the sheriff's office asked you to come in to look at mug shots, or have they come back to show you any?"

He set the strips of wood he'd been counting down on the floor. "Nope. Said they'd come get me if they needed me."

"Did the deputy mention his name was"—she picked the first name that came to mind—"Darrell?"

"Didn't say his name."

"If you had to guess, would you say he was in his late twenties or early thirties—or some other age?"

"Are you trying to snooker me, young lady?"

"No. Just giving you options."

"'Options.'" He shook his head, not angrily but amiably. "Well, thank you for your options."

"You're welcome, sir. About how old?"

"Early to midthirties, I would guess. Hard to tell, when you get to be my age."

"Did he pay cash?"

"Cash, and didn't ask for a receipt. Which kind of struck me."

"How come?"

"Said he was with Red Dog Construction. Never heard of it, but folks are coming in these days from all over, buying up every acre they can get their hands on, throwing up houses. But no matter what construction outfit you're with, who doesn't need a receipt?"

"Maybe the owner," Lauren suggested.

"This . . . Darrell, you said?"

"Who knows? Maybe Darrell, maybe Joe. A lot of different names floating around."

"In your head."

Lauren laughed. "That's true."

"Well, whoever this Darrell-Joe fella was, he didn't look like he owned anything."

"What do you mean?"

"Well, now that I'm getting what they call a mental picture, there was something about him. Needed a haircut. Clothes didn't fit right."

"Too short? Too long? Too loose? Too tight?"

"Too big. Like a boy putting on his daddy's clothes, but not quite. And ratty-looking. The clothes. Not honest, worn-out work clothes. Kind of dirty. Button missing on his shirt. At first I thought he was trying to look like he was from someplace, you know, what they call cool, where the men open their shirts to show what they got, which ain't ever anything to write home about. But then I saw: Nope, button's just popped off. Come to think of it, it wasn't only his clothes. Even his money was ratty-looking. Some of it was dirty and crumpled-up-looking. I didn't think it then, but I'm thinking it now. Not businesslike. You know what I'm saying? Nothing dead wrong with him or anything like that. Just wrong enough not to be right."

Len insisted on seeing her out, guiding her past Paints, around Power & Hand Tools, to the door. "Sir," she said, just as he was about to haul open the door, "let's say I wanted to get my hands on some dynamite without too much of a hassle."

"That's not a very good idea," Len said, amused. "Might muss up that pretty hair of yours."

"Supposing I was willing to take the risk. Could I steal it from a construction site?"

"You?" When he smiled, his wrinkles folded like a fan. "Well, now, I'd say most contractors are pretty careful with dynamite these days. It's a lot dearer than a few pounds of nails, and you don't want to have to go crying to Bart Grady, 'Boo-hoo, Sheriff, some varmint made off with my dynamite.' There's a fair amount of dynamite around these parts, but then, we got a lot of rock. But why would you have to steal it?"

"Well, assuming I don't have some sort of a permit—"

"Permit, did you say? You don't need a permit."

"You don't?" Why was she surprised? This was Wyoming. You could probably have your own neutron bomb.

"Just need to show you're an adult, sign for it. Maybe need some photo ID, your driver's license. Couldn't say for sure. Over a certain amount—I forget how much—you've got to prove you have storage."

"Where would I go if I wanted to buy twenty, thirty, forty sticks and didn't want to show a license or didn't want to bother about details like proving I had storage space?"

"Do I look as if I'd know something like that?"

"You look as if you're smart, observant—"

"You know what they say about flattery?"

"That it will get me everywhere? I hope so. Anyway, besides being smart and observant, you've been around for a while. Look, whatever you tell me, I'm not going to quote you, not going to bring in your name or the name of the lumberyard in any way. I give you my word."

"Gil Curry Excavation. No sign, just looks like one of those big gray warehouses, except shrunk way down." His hands marked off a cube about the size of a doll-house.

"Thank you!"

He shook his head unhappily. "Your folks know you're doing this sort of thing?"

Lauren was sick of herself. She had brushed on and tissued off her mascara twice, and here she was, filmy-eyed from mascara remover oil, seeing herself in the mirror as a blur, like an aging fifties sex goddess in a made-for-TV movie. The mascara wand was still in her hand, and once more she was staging a great internal debate. Not of the Lincoln-Douglas caliber. No, she was being torn in two by Should I or should I not do my lower lashes?

At last, she put away the mascara, blinking a few times to clear her vision so she wouldn't wind up driving into a stray elk. She reached for the blush she had already applied and admonished herself: This is beyond idiocy. First of all, there was barely enough light in the Grizzly to distinguish between the stuffed bear and the taller guys. Second, if she didn't get her ass in gear, formerly-

known-as-Darrell would be there before she was. Without the home-field advantage, she might as well be
meeting him at the far end of one of those spooky,
closed-for-winter roads that wound around the mountains.

Ready: Out of the bathroom. No, she would not waste
one more second, would not change from the blue sweater
into the pink shirt, which, when worn with her Wonderbra and opened three buttons' worth, made her want to
say "voluptuous" out loud. Set: The two pens, pad,
recorder, pepper spray, in her right coat pocket; motel key,
car key, Tic Tacs, in her left. Go.

Step out into the hall and— Oh shit! Here he was, giving her shoulder enough of a shove to make her stumble
back inside the room. "Don't be afraid," he was saying as
she tripped over her own boot and fell. "Take it easy.
Don't scream." He closed the door behind him. The only
thing preventing her from shrieking was her own hand,
clapped over her mouth in horror. He was hunkering
down beside her, flipping open something—a badge—
but by the time she realized what it was, she was already
trying to punch him in the face, except he ducked. "Calm
down," he said as he stood.

"Son of a bitch!"

"Sorry I had to do it this way. Give me a minute and
I'll explain—"

"You don't have a minute." She pointed to the door.

He stood but, instead of leaving, took her outpointed
arm and pulled her gently to her feet. "I pushed you back
in because I didn't want you yelling in the hall," he said
reasonably, holding up the badge beside his face so she
could see that the man in the photo ID—a man without
a beard—and he were the same.

"If you didn't want me to scream, you could have met me at the Grizzly." They stood in the minuscule vestibule by the door. It was so tight she could not place enough distance between them to stand back and see his face. Yet she wasn't ready to give up the security of being near the knob. "Why couldn't you have met me there?"

"Couldn't risk it."

"How did you find me?"

"Not easily." She held out her hand for his identification. A gold badge. A raised FBI seal in the center. That surprised her, because he seemed as if he was a Wyoming kind of guy. His name: definite non-Dwayne. Charles Bryant Blair, Jr. His ID number. "Called a few places," he was relating, "asked for you. Then a few more. Finally figured you must be under some other name."

"And? You divined the name I was using?"

"One of the agents went around, flashed . . ." He pointed to the ID. "Described you. Lucky he tried the motels before the bed-and-breakfasts, or we'd still be looking."

She studied his credentials, examining the gold badge, looking from the photograph to the man and back again. In the picture, whenever it had been taken, his hair wasn't much longer, yet he looked much younger. Handsome, really handsome, without the beard. But he also looked infinitely less appealing. His image was the bland, self-righteous cop face she'd gotten to know so well when she was covering the criminal courts in Columbus, the complacent face of yet another young man who has no unanswered questions. Yet as she looked at it harder, she saw a hint of unsureness, the eyes a bit too wide, whether from nervousness at the importance of the step he was taking or because he knew his eyes to be his best feature. . . . She was staring at the photo much too long and hoped he'd think she was being cautious. "Well," Lauren finally said, handing him back his identification, "where would you feel comfortable talking?"

"No place."

"We're past that." She was pleased by how tough she sounded, not at all like the moony adolescent she'd been ever since she turned and saw him on that street in McBride. "Where else?"

"Here. I realize you may not feel comfortable having a man in your room, so if you'd rather go sit in your car or something—"

"Please," she said dismissively, and led him the foot and a half into her room. Once she got there, however, she realized there was only one chair. "Have a seat."

"That's okay. You . . ." He gestured to the chair.

Of course, like a jerk, she didn't take a seat. No, instead she said, Please, you, and then he said I'm fine standing and she said It's no problem, I'm more comfortable on the bed, which must have sounded as whorish to him as it did to her, because once he was in the chair, he looked away from the bed as though afraid she'd contort herself into such a position that he'd be gazing at her pudendum. She eased off her boots and sat Indian-style, her back against the headboard, hoping to look prim, but her wool sweater slid down the headboard's slick veneer, so a second later it did look as if she was about to go into a pudendum pose. Quickly, nervously, she placed her coat beside her, the pocket with her pad and the pepper spray easily reachable. There. Better. Except then she suggested, Why don't you take off your jacket? and it came out in too provocative a tone, sounding like an invitation that would immediately be followed by: And your pants.

"Okay," Lauren snapped, "what's the deal?"

"The deal? The deal is, you tell me what you think you have that's so valuable."

"And what do I get for it?"

"The thanks of your government."

"That and a nickel will get me a ride on the IRT." His face did not change expression. "One of my grandmother's old sayings," she explained.

"What's the IRT?"

"One of the three subway lines in New York."

"Keep going. I've heard of the place."

"And a nickel used to be the fare."

"That's some saying. You've got a real sharp grandmother." The moment he said it, he seemed to regret it. His feet performed an awkward box step. "I didn't mean any disrespect. My grandpa used to say"—he looked up, as if waiting for a cue—"'I never met a horse that felt sorry for itself.'"

"Words to live by," Lauren replied. Wonderful to look at, easy to be with. It made her uncomfortable. Part of the pleasure of fantasy was the comfort of knowing it was all there could be, because the reality would likely be dreadful. Yet here he was, so likable, so smart, so manly a presence, that he was better than her imaginings. "What were we talking about?"

"How you were going to give me the information you picked up—"

"And how you're going to thank me on behalf of a grateful government. What do they call you, by the way? Charles? Chuck?"

"No. Charlie."

"Okay, Charlie—" What a good name! "This is my

deal. I have some interesting leads about Ostergard's financing—"

"From where?"

"Can I please finish?"

"If it's Lexis-Nexis newspaper reporter stuff . . . Is it okay if I call you Lauren?"

"Sure."

"Well, Lauren, if it's that sort of stuff, thanks, but we already have it."

"I wouldn't try to give you something you have," she retorted. She sensed he knew she was bluffing, because a small smile crept over his mouth, a half smile in which the right side of his face expressed amusement, while the left remained strictly business. "And I have a good description of a suspicious-looking man who bought around five pounds of nails."

"We have that too."

"I don't think so. Even if you do, it's not as detailed as I was able to get."

"Anything else?"

"I also think I know the likely place where he got the dynamite." This was news to him. She could tell by the way he tried to shrug it off.

"Don't you think it's your obligation as a citizen—"

"I don't need my moral compass adjusted by the FBI. There is nothing I would like better than to see this guy caught. And while we're at it, if I could give you something to hang Ostergard and his creeps, I'd do it in a second."

"I didn't mean you're not a good citizen. But the bomber himself is a ticking bomb. If we don't get him fast, he's going to do it again."

"Charlie."

"What?"

"The paper I work for: It's in New York. You know what the name of it is?"

"The *Jewish News*. We had to check up on you before I could speak to you. We figured you probably wouldn't blow my cover. You'd know if you did, Jews could get killed."

"That's a cheap shot."

"No it's not. Most reporters will go for the headlines. That's the way it is."

"Most reporters are as ethical as FBI agents, which may not be saying much for either group. But just so you know, I'm not doing what I'm doing out of parochial interest. This is about Jews, sure, but it's about something bigger too."

"I know," he said quietly. "Look, let's agree we're both decent people."

"Okay."

"You know, I had a great-grandfather or a great-great who was Jewish."

"Where was he from?"

She was surprised to feel let down by Charlie's shrug. "I don't know." A Jew. An interesting fact that obviously meant next to nothing to him. "My great-grandmother or something was an Indian."

"What tribe?"

"No one knows for sure. Cheyenne, maybe. Or Arapaho."

All the lost tribes. Was it inevitable, dissolving into the melting pot? Was that the only way to become truly American, to lose what you were? In her family, practically all that was left of a brilliant religious, cultural and intellectual heritage was a recipe for chicken soup and the knowledge that Sid Luckman of the Chicago Bears was the first quarterback to use the T-formation.

Charlie looked at Lauren and shook his head. "Did Ostergard know what paper you write for?"

"I guess I forgot to mention it."

"Are you . . . ?"

"Yes, I am." She waited for either a "No kidding" or a "That's what I figured." Neither came. "Have you ever met one?"

"Yes, I've met one," he said.

"One?"

"A couple, actually. I'm a real worldly guy."

"Where?"

"Where did I meet them? One of my professors in college. One of the guys in the bureau down in Atlanta, where I used to be."

She smiled. "You're right. Very worldly. Now let me tell you what I'd like from you, besides the thanks of my government."

"Shoot."

"I want to make this the best article I've ever written. I need background on these guys. Any details on their criminal records. Whatever you found out about them in Sheridan."

"We might be able to help you there."

"I want your thoughts on Ostergard, McIntyre, Gus Lang and the guys who hang out with them."

"I can't give you anything that might sound like it came from the inside."

"Can you tell me what goes on at their public meetings? I tried to go to one when I first got here, but they wouldn't let me in. Some goon in a camouflage outfit said it was only for men. Whatever you'd tell me would be what a hundred other people know, so it wouldn't compromise you."

"A hundred people? In Ostergard's dreams."

"No kidding!" Lauren breathed. "How many, then?"

"About a dozen. Fifteen on a good night. Does that surprise you?"

"I thought there would be more."

"Why? This is Wyoming. Do you think we march around carrying torches?"

"Is your Wyoming 'we' a real 'we'?" she asked. "Or a Darrell 'we'?"

"Both. I was born right around here. Saint John's Hospital, here in town. Grew up on a ranch twenty miles south, went to the University of Wyoming in Laramie. I guess no one's calling us the Knee-jerk Liberal State. But there's a big difference between being conservative and being a racist, anti-Jewish goon in camouflage."

"I know that."

"I'm not sure. You people—"

"Music to my ears," Lauren said.

"What?"

"The 'you people' business."

"I meant reporters, for Christ's sake. You *reporters* write like half the West is holed up in the Rockies somewhere, waiting for UN forces to invade. And the other half are sympathizers."

"Do you have any actual numbers?"

"On Wrath? That I've seen, a total of fifteen, twenty guys who show up at one meeting or another or at a bar Ostergard goes to. I haven't seen any evidence of a cell structure yet. That's telling you more than I probably should, but there might be others, who are careful not to associate with Ostergard. There could be a hard-core group left in Sheridan, although I doubt that, at least as far as Ostergard and Wrath go. Sounds like whatever support he had up there evaporated or found something else when he left."

"I've seen a couple of estimates of numbers nationally for these kinds of groups. What have you heard?"

"Actual members, or supporters? Between ten and forty thousand."

"That's what I've heard."

"Now let me tell you another thing you people don't get." Charlie smiled, a megawatt smile. Lauren, smiling back, found herself not merely being charmed but seduced. Was he doing it intentionally or did it just happen? Here she was, tilting her head so her hair just happened to fall over one eye, running her thumb over the ridges in the bedspread in response. She pulled out her pad and pen. "Numbers don't matter," Charlie told her. He seemed intent, serious, so she guessed charm just seeped out, no matter what he was doing or talking about.

"I think numbers do matter," she responded. "There were four million Ku Klux Klansmen in the late 1920s. That was a big growth time for them. You know why? Because a Catholic was running for President. Four million schmucks in sheets. It's not just that those numbers would have scared the hell out of me if I'd seen them marching down Main Street. It's that those numbers translated into political power long after Alfred E. Smith. They helped keep Jim Crow alive for forty more years."

Charlie leaned forward. "When I say numbers don't matter, I'm talking about a different kind of arithmetic. How many people do you think it takes to burn down a black church or blow up an abortion clinic or Jack

Frohman's house? How many geniuses did it take to bring down the Federal Building in Oklahoma City?"

"So what can we do?"

"The FBI? What we're doing. We had reason to believe a person or persons in Wrath violated a federal law, and so we were able to start an investigation. I couldn't have gone in there if all they were doing was saying Jews are Satan's seed and we're going to have to have it out with them come Armageddon. Short of inciting to riot or advocating the overthrow of the government by force, they can say anything they damn well please. You want your First Amendment, this is the price you pay."

"What about hate speech, making it a crime? Not you, FBI guy. Just you, Charlie Blair."

"Sounds like a can of worms to me," he said.

"To me too, although I'm sure something must be wrong if you and I share a political opinion." She was realizing he was more intense than his loose-limbed style suggested. When he listened, he did not miss a nuance. When amused, he seemed delighted to his soul. "What about a beer?" she asked.

"Sounds good."

Over beer and a plate of nachos she set between them, at the foot of the bed, Charlie gave her a rundown of what had gone on at the Wrath meetings he'd attended. It was the same and more of what Lauren had heard from Ostergard himself: the near-endless naming of names, most of which Charlie couldn't remember, the intricate analysis of how ZOG was taking over the world, and ZOG's schemes for using the other, inferior races, as well as homosexuals, to subvert God's will, which was the hegemony of the white man.

"How crazy are they?" Lauren asked.

"Hard to say. Ostergard doesn't seem nuts, although the shrink I talked to in Quantico said he's a paranoid schiz. This is what they tell me: It's like a pyramid or a triangle. At the top there's the paranoid like Vern, who believes the world is being manipulated by a huge conspiracy. He starts with his own delusion, reads the work of other paranoids, forms a conspiracy theory. Guys like him can be persuasive to people who feel the world is working against them. Blame everything on one group. It has to be an all-powerful group, because otherwise you'd be a wuss for not taking it on. This way, you're a freedom fighter. The enemy can be Jews, it can be the gun control lobby—"

"Or Jews manipulating the gun control lobby. That's what we're taught to do at ZOG meetings."

"Could you sneak me into one?" Charlie asked.

"As what? A specimen? Anyway, who's under the paranoid schizophrenic?"

"The sociopath, aka psychopath, aka Kyle McIntyre. Antisocial, wants to inflict pain and suffering, uses the movement as a vehicle. Kyle's a smart guy, though."

"What do you think his relationship is with Ostergard?"

"What do you mean?" Charlie said.

"You know what I mean."

"Are they gay or something? Beats the hell out of me, but I don't think so. Gay would be understandable. But there's some weird connection between them. My guess is that it's beyond sex. Maybe a sex substitute like power—"

"Like guns."

"Don't tell me you really believe that."

"How do I know? Guns aren't part of my culture. I

mean, there's some duck hunting on Long Island, but most of the men I know are into work, sports, politics— a little art on the side. They don't hunt. And I cannot see any fun in killing animals."

"It's shooting."

"You only wound them? Come on."

"We only shoot what we eat."

"Really?"

"No."

"What were we going on about?" Lauren asked.

"Before your Bambi speech? Vern Ostergard and Kyle." She wished she could spend the night on Bambi, teasing him, talking to him. "This is what we know. Ostergard divorced his wife, left his kids. Doesn't see them. They're all still in Sheridan. She works for the phone company. Seeing some guy who used to be in Wrath. She and the new guy have no criminal record of any kind. Now what do you know about Kyle?"

"Not much."

"Try this. His wife didn't want to make the move to Jackson Hole. Next thing you know, she's fifty feet down a gully behind their house with a broken neck."

"Oh my God!"

"Lots of suspicions, but nobody can prove anything. Case closed. Aren't you glad you didn't piss him off?"

"I think I *did*, but I'm out of there." She offered him another beer. He declined, so she opened it for herself. "You're not out of there, Charlie."

"No," he said, and looked at his watch. Lauren glanced at hers. Nearly midnight. "This is the first time I've been able to be a human being," he said. "It's not bad at the garage. They're nice guys. But I made one speech too many about how the federal government is run by the

Jews. That's what I was supposed to do to establish my cover. They pretty much steer clear of me. I spend most lunch hours with Ostergard. Most nights too, at that hell-hole of a bar they go to. Or at a Wrath meeting. Or Oster-gard gives me garbage to read, then quizzes me on it next time he sees me." Lauren set aside her beer and her pad and pen. "I meet my control agent once a week, although since the bombing I've seen her twice. But it's totally pro-fessional. I report. She checks to make sure I haven't become a fascist or anything and then goodbye. Nothing personal: She won't even call me Charlie."

"I don't see how you do it."

"I don't either, to tell you the truth. I just do it."

"What made you volunteer? I assume they didn't force you into it?"

"No. I raised my hand. Thought it would be a good change."

"A day at the beach is a good change."

"Thought I'd be a natural, fit right in. And I do—unless my buddy Kyle has something nasty planned I don't know about."

Suddenly, Lauren could barely bring herself to speak. She was so filled with fear, her voice squeaked. "Are the two of you on the outs?"

"Not on the ins," Charlie replied, closing his eyes, tak-ing a deep breath.

Getting himself ready to go, she sensed. "Isn't your family worried about you?"

"My mother lives ten minutes from here. My sister's about a half hour away. When I said I'll do it, I thought: Won't it be great to be near them again, great to be *here* again. There's no more beautiful place on earth, no matter how much they try and mess it up. But of course I can't see my mother and sister, can't call them. I have to avoid all places they might be. That's why I couldn't meet you at Sal & Hal's. They've known my family forever." He shook his head. "They might even recognize me, though it's been years." He examined the toes of his boots, then looked back at Lauren. "I live in Cheyenne. I'm married. I have a twelve-year-old daughter. She and my wife have been living down in Colorado Springs for almost three years, but before I came here I drove down to see them every other week."

She swallowed hard. She herself had no idea what to say, but the reporter took over. "If this place means so much to you, why did you leave it in the first place?"

"Oh," Charlie said, "that's a long story."

"'Once upon a time . . .'"

"I've got to be at the garage at six-thirty." He clasped his hands behind his head and stretched out his legs. "Once upon a time . . ." he began.

# 16

"Once upon a time . . ."

Here he was, in a puny motel chair with its arms hugging him, looking over at this woman he hardly knew, talking so much, going into so much detail, he felt the telling of his life could take as long as the actual living of it. Not just stuff like, And when I was three my sister, Kaylea, was born and my mom couldn't get back from the hospital because there was a blizzard and they didn't get the roads open for four days so I was stuck in the house with my old man. No, Charlie found himself looking for the words to bring Lauren back there with him. He wanted so badly for her to hear the wind's moan, oscillating in some mysterious way so it was like a voice saying something just beyond understanding, the way downstairs grown-up talk sounded from his room. He wanted Lauren to look outside, to see how the whiteness obliterated his grandparents' house, the mailbox, the fir trees along the road.

Then, for some crazy reason, he proclaimed, Hold your horses! You've got to know this about fir trees. He gave her the old mnemonic device: *fir, flat*, needles *friendly; spruce sharp*, needles *square; pine*, needles in *packages*. Enchanted, she repeated it, wanting to know if it would work with New York trees, announcing she couldn't wait for daylight to see for herself. And her grin! He felt as if he'd given her a fabulous, expensive present.

But then she admonished, Hey, Charlie, don't get sidetracked. I want to know what it was like being there alone with your father. He knew—he just knew—her wanting to hear more was no act. No exaggeration either, the way some women magnify vague interest into rapture at your every word. Lauren was truly hooked on his history.

So he remembered for her that the power had gone out. By that time, his old man had had a few to celebrate his new daughter and was so smashed he couldn't remember how to start the backup generator. The house grew colder and colder. Charlie got into his jacket but didn't know how to button it. The pipes froze. He put on his mittens. His teeth would not stop chattering. He recalled the sweet stink of bourbon that lingered in a room, even after his father left it, and how, after four days, with every window shut against the cold, the big old house reeked of it. Years later, in high school and college biology, he would get nauseous breathing formalin, because for some reason it brought back that smell of bourbon.

His father slept a lot of the time, his snoring loud and wet. Charlie was hungry, but since he was three, he could reach only the bottom bins and the lower shelves of the refrigerator. Not that he was starving to death or anything, he explained. His father opened a can of Spaghetti-Os for them and made cheese sandwiches. But then Chuck got bored playing picnic. No TV, no phone, no lights. Just a three-year-old kid for company. He got angry too, saying, Shit! Shit!, dumping over the Chutes and Ladders board because he couldn't get the generator to go. He'd have another drink or two and fall asleep again. Charlie got colder and hungrier. He ate bottom things: an apple with a brown mush spot, orange Jell-O, raw bacon. He couldn't understand why he hadn't had the brains to drag over a chair to get to the good stuff, the peanut butter and Velveeta and grape juice, on higher shelves. To this day, he said, whenever he thought about it, he could almost feel the griping stomach pains that came with the diarrhea.

What was so incredible about Lauren was that she didn't do what you'd think a New Yorker would do. None of that "Well, maybe subconsciously you wanted to get sick, to let your mother know how terrible she was for abandoning you to your father." Instead, her hands clasped against her chest, right over her heart, she announced, I swear to God, I'd like to borrow your rifle and shoot the bastard. You wouldn't *not* have a rifle, would you, Charlie? He laughed and said, A couple, then added, I'll get you an NRA membership—he almost said "For Christmas"—for a present. She got a little smile right after "present." She knew he'd caught himself.

That second, looking at her sitting on the bed, her hair tumbling onto the shoulders of her brilliant blue sweater, he pictured her as she had been when he walked in on her interview. Standing before Ostergard and McIntyre, with Gus Lang hulking at the door. Her hair had been cradled in the hood of her coat. She was writing down all the terrible things Ostergard must have been spouting about Jews. What struck Charlie at the time was her professionalism—attentive, in control, she acted not the least bit fearful or as if she wanted to slit Ostergard's throat. She'd even had the presence of mind to ask for Darrell's last name.

He stopped for a breather sometime after one o'clock. She told him, Charlie, you know what? You make me feel like the king in *Scheherazade*. Remember that story? Actually, he did. Okay, she commanded, I'm the king. Tell me more. If he weren't afraid it would sound like the world's stalest line, he would have said, You make *me* feel like a king.

For a while, he convinced Lauren it was her turn to talk. She spoke about her schoolteacher parents, her brother in law school, her beagle, the quince tree she planted in her backyard for her first Earth Day. Even the sophisticated New York way she spoke—quickly, lightly, as if afraid someone was going to accuse her of being dull—couldn't hide the out-and-out love she felt for her family. Yet she confessed she was ashamed of that love's power over her—so strong she hadn't been able to establish a life for herself in the cities where she'd worked. When she couldn't bear the lack of love anymore, she'd gone running home to Long Island. Come on, Charlie. There's nothing more. You've heard it all. You're the guy with the story. Keep going.

So he continued. It was so satisfying, observing her eloquent features—brows drawn together in anger, mouth agape with shock, an occasional gentle smile—express his own feelings. He was handing his life over to Lauren so she could live it too, from the dogs and horses in his life to his grandparents' sudden death to how, when he was sixteen, he got thrown and the horse toppled on him and he wound up with his leg broken in three places. And how his dad got suckered by the bimbo from Salt Lake City and sold the Circle B.

As the night moved on, her mesmerized silence and the low golden lamplight seemed to turn his telling into some sort of ceremony. Not quite peyote and visions from the Great Spirit; Dos Equis and a vision of his life not as a series of episodes but as a whole, the way he'd never been able to view it before.

It was so damn late. He really had to go. He watched Lauren draw up her knees, rest her arms on them and lay down her head, ready to hear more. Then a horrible thought popped into Charlie's head: What if this whole thing is some journalistic technique to make me talk, and I'm making a horse's ass of myself? He could almost hear his Grandpa Willie saying, There's more horses' asses than there are horses.

As if she, too, had heard a competing voice, Lauren chose that instant to leave the headboard and move toward him, letting her legs dangle over the edge of the bed. Their knees were only inches apart now. She must have realized something was up, because two minutes earlier he'd been yammering nonstop. Or maybe yammering was just background noise to her. Maybe she was used to New York men who babbled about stuff like their feminine aspect and what they felt the first time they ever saw a rosebud.

Hey, Charlie, she said. He loved hearing her say his name. You don't owe me any more than you want to say. She'd eaten off her lipstick with the nachos, and her face was so luminous she looked like an angel in one of those Italian paintings. Her blue sweater was no white robe, though. Not obviously clinging, but it managed to highlight what he wanted to see, except he knew he had to keep his eyes away. Except he couldn't.

You don't owe me any more than you want to say. What she really was telling him was "You don't have to talk about your wife." No big fuss. No "Aren't I being noble?" She said it straight. Charlie wasn't sure if the precise word for her was graceful or gracious, but her thoughtfulness was instinctive. No parent—not even the best schoolteacher parent—could teach the decency Lauren had been born with.

He didn't owe her, she said. Nevertheless, he told her how he'd met Stacey Barrows. At the time, he'd assured himself, their coming together was fate, because she was in town only three days, a bridesmaid at a college friend's wedding. She literally bumped into him on a street corner and started apologizing in that husky voice and tantalizing southern accent: Ah aim so sorreh! The next thing he knew, he was buying a ticket to fly down to Athens, Georgia, to try and ingratiate himself with Stacey's parents, Dr. and Mrs. Otolaryngologist. He never pulled it off, because of their unwavering conviction that their Stacey had fallen victim to some hex Charlie had put on her. However, they were cautiously optimistic, praying she'd snap out of it and realize how much better she could do. Just before Stacey and her father took their first step down the aisle, Dr. O told her, Honey, you can still walk out of here a free woman—a remark she recounted to Charlie during their first dance as husband and wife. During the ceremony itself, when the minister inquired if anyone knew any reason why these two should not be joined in holy matrimony, Charlie heard a rustle in the first pew. Stacey's mother, he figured, being restrained. Although, in truth, it might have been his own mother or sister. A week before the wedding, Kaylea took him on a hike, on the trail they used to go up as kids, sat him down on a rock and said, Charlie, I don't know how to word this, but Stacey's not nice. Screw off, Kaylea. She responded, Don't think Mom feels any different. What do you mean, she's not nice? he demanded. Not a nice person, Kaylea replied. She comes from a good family, he countered.

Charlie was not entirely unaware that his own "good" meant "well off," just as he sensed that Kaylea's "not nice" was Wyoming for "slut." But lust and sense are natural enemies, and his lust was unbeatable.

He'd imagined a honeymoon in Paris, because that was the most sensuous city in the world. Drinking at a sidewalk café, leaving a hundred- or thousand-franc note on the table—he didn't know what francs were worth, but some extravagant amount—and rushing back to their room, dying for each other. Or maybe Venice. He pictured them kissing in a gondola, getting so aroused that the slow ride back to their hotel was agony. But Stacey wanted to rent a house on the beach in Jamaica: It comes with servants, Charlie. Whatever, he said.

Whatever. Save for sex, their marriage was a slow downhill slide from blind lust to infatuation to disappointment to anger to indifference. At the beginning, all they needed was their passion. He and Stacey might go out to dinner and speak to each other coldly, like tight-lipped partners in a small, failing business: Could you please explain to me *why* we're getting electric bills like this? How can you *possibly* ask me to trust your judgment after last Saturday night? Yet the minute they got home, they were the lovingest couple in town.

With Morning's birth, Stacey began losing her erotic edge, as if childbirth had given her a breather and she'd decided she didn't want to bother with passion anymore. Too much volatility. Too messy. And Charlie Blair just wasn't worth it. Her enthusiasm waned slowly, however, so he didn't consciously realize his loss until one morning when he found himself listening to a marriage counselor on the *Today* show, who had written a book advising Americans how to put the oomph back into their oomph-less marriages. Charlie was stunned by the segment, as though instead of hearing a dork in a bow tie, he was listening to the Word of God.

When Morning was six, Stacey took her to a skating rink and watched the little girl take to it as if she'd been born with blades on her feet. That was the beginning of the end. The end itself was when Dr. and Mrs. Otolaryngologist bought a house in Colorado Springs so their granddaughter's ice life would not end with her father's humiliation and demotion to Cheyenne. I'll take care of food and shelter, Dr. O told Charlie, implying that the upscale version of these basics was beyond Charlie's limited means—which in fact it was. You just pay for the lessons and Morning's little costumes.

Presenting his entire life to Lauren hadn't just been easy, it had been necessary. Once he'd begun, he felt as if he would go on talking forever. But now here he was— holy shit, he couldn't believe the time!—sitting on the edge of the chair, with nothing left to give her. His story was finished, and he was knee-to-knee with a redheaded New York woman in a sexy blue sweater and jeans. All he wanted was to be magically transported out of her room. Or dead. Dead would be okay. He wouldn't have to face saying goodbye.

He got up slowly, like an old man. "Hey, do you know what time it is?"

"Five."

"Listen, I'll have someone get back to you with the specifics on Ostergard's and Gus Lang's criminal records. And I'll see if there's anything else I can get for you that won't get me strung up. But before I go, I need—"

"The dynamite place. Gil Curry Excavation. It's supposed to look like one of those big warehouses, except shrunk down. Gray. There isn't any sign. You have the description of the guy?"

"Short. Five five or six. Light eyes, probably. Slight build, probably. Brown hair, probably. Early thirties, probably."

"Shabby clothes, kind of dirty," Lauren added. "Button missing on his shirt. Looked like he was dressed in his father's clothes."

Charlie closed his eyes, trying to recall the first Wrath meeting. Yes, someone like that. Not the smelly guy; he was too tall. "I might have seen him at a meeting."

"Can you remember anything?"

"I have to let it percolate," he told her. Not a brush-off, but not an I'll-call-you either.

All through the night, he had been looking into her eyes. He'd have thought, their being so dark, truly black, they would be unreadable. But in fact, when she wasn't being a reporter, they reflected everything you could possibly want to know about her and then some. Except right now. He wasn't sure if they were glistening because she was overtired or because she was going to cry at his going away.

"This is awkward," Charlie finally observed. "Isn't it?"

"No. It's painful."

He waited for her to cry. Once she started, he could put his arms around her and go pat, pat, or say there, there, and maybe kiss her on the head. Then he'd be out like a shot. So where were the tears? Why was she not saying anything?

Sweet Jesus, this was the stupidest thing he had ever done, babbling on and on about such private stuff as if he were one of those creeps on a daytime talk show. Not that he was blaming Lauren for his humiliation. She hadn't manipulated him into revealing every single thought that had ever passed through his head. She was simply one of those people other people feel comfortable talking to. Besides her brains, that quality was probably what made her a good reporter. And he had been pathetically vulnerable to the lure of a good listener, stuck as he was in this current hell of an existence and, before that, in the mini-hell of his marriage.

As for Lauren, of course she'd want to hear him run off at the mouth. Why not? The truth was, from the minute she'd looked his way on that street in McBride, she'd been smitten. What could he possibly say to her now? Something to establish some distance. Nothing that would hurt her. Something to get him out of there fast. Direct, like, Sorry, I've got to get going.

Like taking her in his arms, kissing her. That's what he did. She was wonderful, she tasted wonderful, which was some kind of miracle after those nachos. A great kisser, better than he'd dreamed she would be, and she'd been fine enough in his dreams. A strong, passionate kisser. Not passionate in a too-knowing way, as though she'd read *Fifty Good Things to Do with Your Tongue*. She just went crazy with her mouth. And then she began climbing him, which got him so aroused he didn't know what to do first—pull off her blue sweater or push her onto the bed. He did both.

In his past, it was only during the most leisurely foreplay that he was able to notice the curve from neck to shoulder, savor the underside of an arm. But this time, wild though they both were, he didn't miss a thing. There wasn't an inch of Lauren Miller that wasn't exquisite. She seemed so perfect for his pleasure it was as if he had submitted specifications: These are the breasts that will get

me most excited; this is the kind of silky skin I must have
for her thighs; these are the sounds I want her to make.
Everything she did to him came as a surprise. Each touch,
each kiss, was exactly what he needed in the particular
instant, her sweet hand caressing his forehead, her belly
against his.

"Lauren." He kept saying it over and over, because he
needed still more of her.

"Charlie."

"Lauren, listen . . ." He was panting so hard it sounded
more like groaning than breathing.

"No, Charlie, wait." She groped around the floor until
she found her jeans. "I hope you don't think I'm a brazen
hussy." She eased a Trojan from the pocket. "I can't imagine what made me buy it." Embarrassed, she could not
meet his glance. "It's not that I was planning—"

He tapped her on the shoulder. "Hey." He fished a Trojan from the back pocket of his jeans and rubbed the foil
of his package against the wrapping of hers. "What
should we do with two of them?"

"Mate them? They could have hundreds of teeny Tro-
jans."

Charlie said, "Let's do it."


He was having a conversation with Lauren, except that he
was under a Ram, putting in a new exhaust. In his head,
Charlie was telling her: All my life I didn't know I was
half of something larger. You're the other half. For the
first time, I feel unbroken. Right . . . The only way he
would ever say something like that was if he wanted to
watch her gag.

But you never know. Here he was, listening to the For-
eigner tape Bill had on and not even minding it, thinking

it was actually kind of romantic. Higher than a kite on zero hours' sleep—and at an age when he would have predicted he was too old to pull an all-nighter. Of course, this wasn't an all-nighter for a chem final or taking care of a sick calf until daybreak. This was reviewing his life. This was falling in love at last, so that his life could mean something.

Like the wrench he dropped, his spirits clunked to the garage floor. He and Lauren might be two halves of some grand design, but he himself was divided in two: Charlie Blair, who belonged with her; Darrell Frederickson, for whom putting in a new exhaust pipe would be the high point of the day. Because when he finished, it would be twelve noon, and he'd drive up to McBride, and Ostergard would be waiting. Shaking in his boots again, terrified of being framed for the Frohman bombing. Or watching out the window for his new blue-eyed boy, Darrell, wanting to see if he'd read *America the Vanquished*. Isn't that some darn book, Darrell?

Driving the slushy, rutted road to McBride, Charlie tried to visualize the guys at that first Wrath meeting. He could picture the two ranch hands, the guy with a greasy face, the skinhead with the lightning bolt tattoo on his scalp, along with his skeleton friend in the leather vest, but the little guy wasn't coming in clearly. Charlie could see the clothes, though, and, yes, the description Lauren got was on the nose. Slacks—like from a suit—spilling over his shoes, the cuffs of a yellow corduroy shirt so long they nearly hid his thumbs. Charlie could see the shoes because the guy had crossed his legs. Ridiculous ankle-high boots made out of some shiny fake stuff stamped to look like alligator or crocodile, shoes that belonged in some other, cheesy part of the country. Real small shoes, he remembered; you could practically have them bronzed and say, Look, Junior's first pair! Why wasn't his face coming in? Maybe because the clothes overwhelmed the man.

What if the little guy was simply a loser with baggy pants who bought five pounds of nails because he was putting up a house for his family? No, because Lauren had found out the clothes were dirty, and Charlie himself thought he remembered a rim of grime on the cuffs—unless his mind was adding a detail. He was always amazed at the nonexistent moles and scars witnesses insisted they'd seen, the thick fringe of gray hair they swore was total baldness. But Charlie did remember the grime. And those shoes had to be hand-me-downs, probably the only men's thrift-shop shoes in his little size. This was not a guy who could afford to build his family a house. In fact, this uncared-for guy probably didn't even have a family. You'd almost think he was a vagrant, but something had kept him from looking like one. What the hell was it?

This time, a single squad car was parked in front of Vern's TV Repair. The same unmarked gray Lumina was across the street. As he drove through town, he noted that someone in Ostergard's shop had strung something up—a sheet, it looked like—so the cops couldn't see in. It didn't matter. He could picture the worktable, the deaf repairman watching TV snow, the white plastic chairs in the middle of the room, Kyle McIntyre's sucky mouth, Ostergard's smiley mouth upturned as he talked so reasonably about the mongrelization of the races. Opening that door was like stepping into hell. And now it was going to be worse. Knowing Lauren was Jewish, how was he going to listen to the shit pouring out of Ostergard's mouth without knocking the fucker's teeth down his throat?

Charlie parked his pickup in the same spot as the day before, a quarter mile away from the shop, and walked down the hill. The whole of downtown McBride was before him. There was Ostergard's shiny truck, around the corner from the shop, which meant Gus Lang was probably there. For some reason, he got a clear image of Lang's face, his nostrils larger than his eyes.

Suddenly, he had it! The face of the little guy: an upturned nose. Not like Gus's snout. A tiny nose. Yes! Charlie recalled thinking that he had the face of one of those boy dolls. For Morning's fifth birthday, he'd taken her doll shopping, and in the two hours it took her to make a selection, he became an expert on doll faces. Boy dolls had shorter hair than girl dolls, less red in the lips and, instead of pink cheeks, a spray of light-brown freckles that wandered up onto the tiny nose. That's why the guy didn't look like a vagrant. He had a baby-doll face.

"You remember what Romans nine, thirteen, quotes God as saying, don't you, Darrell?" Vernon Ostergard chuckled to show that his frantic mood of the day before had vanished, or, with Kyle McIntyre sitting beside him, he was at least back in control. The repairman wasn't there. Neither was Gus Lang.

"Guess it just slipped my mind," Charlie answered, trying to muster equal good nature. He was so tired he didn't know how his neck could possibly be holding up his head. Charlie perched on the edge of the worktable. He wanted to be back in Lauren's bed, sleeping in the spoon position, his arm over her, making sure she couldn't get away, that she'd be beside him when he woke.

"'As it is written, Jacob have I loved, but Esau have I hated.' Now, you may be asking, What does this mean?" Ostergard waited, his eyes on Charlie. The patient teacher, the promising pupil. Today McIntyre wasn't looking at Charlie. He was studying pages in a loose-leaf notebook resting flat on his lap. Studying? Devouring. His head swiveled slowly to the left, then ever so slowly to the right, with every line he read. All Charlie could see was that the pages were handwritten.

"Esau, Jacob," Ostergard prompted. The only thing Charlie could remember about them was that like a bunch of other brothers in the Bible, they didn't get along. His Sunday school memory of Esau was no help: a hairy guy with a giant birthmark on his cheek and a bowl of oatmeal.

"Okay, Vern, I'll bite: What does it mean?"

"It boils down to this." Ostergard adjusted the collar of his green and white shirt as if he were about to be photographed. "Who is the seed of Abraham? The quote Jews unquote?"

"Of course not," Charlie said reflexively.

"Jesus Christ was the seed of Abraham, so in that passage—this is key, Darrell—God is saying He loves the seed of Jacob—Christians—and hates the seed of Esau." All Charlie's energy was focused on looking awake, so he nodded. But the rhythm of bobbing his head up and down was so comforting, like a cradle rocking, that he had to force himself to stop. "So-called Jews are from the house of Esau, the house God Himself hates."

Whatever McIntyre was reading, he was totally wrapped up in it. Page by page, line by line. Charlie tried to fix his eyes on Ostergard, but he stretched out his neck for one fast look at the notebook. Columns. Not numbers. Writing.

What the hell was it? And when would it be a quarter to one, so he could get out of there? How was he going to get through an afternoon of work? Jesus, he had to remember to call Jeanette, tell her he might be able to ID the little guy. If not from mug shots, maybe work with a sketch artist or with one of those computer guys who could call up an infinite number of freckle patterns. Of course, the Wrath little guy could simply be just a pip-squeak racist and have no relation whatsoever to the Plunkett Lumber little guy—although it looked inevitable that whoever the Wrath little guy was, he was going to wind up on TV and in the papers with a nice drawing of his face over "Wanted for Questioning."

Columns of writing. How come McIntyre couldn't even spare him one bone-chilling glance? What the hell was he reading that was so enthralling? Go slow, Charlie counseled himself. Don't jump to any conclusions. An agent with even half a brain had to understand that if he took a huge leap of imagination, he could wind up embracing one theory of a case, fighting for it, staking his career on it, only to discover in the end that it had zip to do with reality.

Ostergard had shut up for a second. Waiting to be appreciated. So Charlie went back to nodding. That didn't seem sufficient, so he asked, "Does the house of Esau have anything to do with the descendants of Cain?" Ostergard was off again.

On the other hand, an agent who was afraid to be a little creative was good for only the most routine assignments, like, Did a man named John Doe work for Goodyear in 1987? You had to be willing to follow a hunch, risk a small leap of faith now and then.

"Did you realize that, Darrell?" Ostergard asked.

"No," Charlie said, automatically. "I honestly didn't."

"Don't feel bad. They don't want you to know."

Columns. At every Wrath meeting, there was a sign-in sheet. Name. Address. Phone. Some men did a John Hancock. Others, from the cautious to the paranoid, pretended they didn't see the paper at all. That's what McIntyre had to be doing—going through months or even years of names, trying to find the one that could be whispered in an anonymous call to the sheriff's office, thereby taking the heat off Vernon Ostergard.

Or was McIntyre, pretending to want to help, searching for a name on a page that he could sneak out of the notebook and crumple up? Would that mean protecting the killer of Eileen Hogan? Yes. Would it mean imperiling Ostergard, leaving Kyle McIntyre free to do with Wrath whatever it was he wanted?

The final dark blue of twilight was deepening to black when Charlie pulled up to Vernon Ostergard's pickup. "Still won't start?" he asked Gus Lang, the very man he wanted to see.

"Deader than a doornail."

Well, that was good, Charlie thought, considering he'd taken a crazy chance when he walked out of Vern's TV Repair after his lunch break: First, check that no one was on the street. Second, say a prayer that no one would turn the corner. Third, pop the hood, pull back the harness wrapping, the sheath that fits over the positive lead going to the distributor; once the lead was exposed, snip it. Fourth, to make sure no one sees your handiwork, slide back the wrapping. One neat trick, courtesy of an

FBI instructor. One lunatic risk. How could he have explained what he was doing if, say, Kyle had chosen that moment for a stroll around the corner? Hey, Kyle, just wanted to check out the Chevy's cylinder arrangement.

"Sorry I had to call you at work, Darrell, but Vern said it would be okay." It sure was. That's why Charlie had done it, to get a few minutes alone with Gus Lang.

"No problem. It was quitting time anyway. Turn the key but don't step on the gas. Let me hear what it sounds like." Gus climbed in and turned the ignition. Excellent. Deader than a doornail. Charlie parked his truck facing Ostergard's Chevy. His vehicle was lower, without a spotlight rack, and did little to illuminate the lifeless engine. He grabbed a flashlight.

"What do you think, Darrell?"

"Let me check it out first, Gus. Come on, get your ass off that cushy seat up there. Give me a hand." The burly man climbed out of the cab. When he walked, his head was thrust way forward. From his posture, it was hard to discern if he was a bully looking for a fight or a big oaf afraid of a whack on the skull.

If Charlie could have copped the loose-leaf notebook, he would have, but he knew Kyle McIntyre would never let it out of his hands, much less his sight. Besides, whatever academic interest a list of names of malcontents might have, it was no good to the bureau unless he could match a single name to the doll face he remembered.

Giving Gus the flashlight to hold, Charlie made a great show of checking every connection under the hood. "Did Vern say when he's having the next public meeting?" he asked.

"Now's not a good time, he says. 'Cause of the bombing."

"No kidding. I would've thought the opposite. Well, just goes to show you why he's Vern and I'm not."

"Well, Kyle's on your side, you know."

"How come?"

"We act pussy now, everyone'll think we're scared, and even the ones who don't think we're scared will think we set the bomb. So what's the point? We came here from Sheridan to make some noise, not to hide." Charlie shifted Gus's arm to move the flashlight's beam. "What's that thing called?" Gus asked.

"Exhaust valve. Know what I was thinking about? What ever happened to those skinhead guys? Remember, the first meeting I went to? They were there. The one with the tattoo on his head and the skinny one."

"Never saw 'em again," Gus said.

"Never came to the Eagle or anything?"

"No."

"Put the light where my finger is pointing, Gus."

"Remember how the skinny guy wore a vest and nothing else?" Lang asked. "How come, do you think?"

"Show how tough he was, maybe. Riding out there half naked on a night that must have been ten below. But ten to one he had a jacket he put on the minute he got to his bike."

"Vern don't like 'em. Skinheads. Says they scare off a better class of joiners."

"What about Kyle?"

"Thinks they scare the shit out of niggers and Jews. They're good, for TV. And some of them don't care about anything. They'll do your dirty work for you."

"Like what?"

"I don't know. Just dirty work that needs doing."

"What do you think, Gus? The skinheads a plus or a minus?"

"You know what they say: 'I don't get paid to think.'"

Charlie laughed. "Me neither. Let's see, who else was there that night? The blond guy and his buddy. The buddy didn't look so white to me. How come you let him in?"

"He *is* white. Says people think he's Mex, and that pisses him off. They've come a few times. Blond guy's Tom and the dark one's Grant."

"Right. I forgot their names."

"Tom's been coming to the Eagle. You ever see him there?"

"I think so. You know, I was pretty sure it would be the spark plugs, but they look okay. Hand me the light, Gus. What do you think about Tom and Grant? I mean, what do they do for a living? They look like cowpokes to me."

"Me too!" Gus agreed happily. "Cowpokes."

"Are they?"

"Beats the hell out of me." With each exchange, Gus Lang sounded less like a killer, more like a kid. Either he was really bent or he was desperate for human contact, Charlie thought, to have hooked up so closely with two men like Ostergard and McIntyre.

"Now, what about that half-pint guy?" Charlie asked.

"You mean Skip or Flip or whatever he calls himself?"

"I think so. The one with the sleeves hanging way down."

"He showed up a couple of times. Haven't seen him for a while. I think it's Skip."

"Point that light over at the distributor."

"Where's that?"

"This thing." Charlie was relieved he wasn't holding the light, because between his excitement and his exhaustion, his hands felt so weak they might tremble, make the beam of light waver. "What does Skip do?"

"I don't know for sure. Vern said he just got out a few months ago."

"Out of jail or the nut box?" Charlie asked.

"Jail."

"No shit. What was he in for?"

"Beats me. You ever in, Darrell?"

"Nothing I want to talk about, Gus."

"Me neither. I was only in juvenile, though."

"You missed the real fun." As Gus laughed, Charlie guided his elbow up a fraction of an inch so the beam illuminated the lead to the distributor. "Skip." Charlie shook his head. "I don't like it when guys have dog names."

"No kidding! Me neither, Darrell."

"It's like calling yourself Fido. What's his real name?"

"I don't know. Did he ever say it?"

"I forget," Charlie said, pulling off his right glove with his teeth. It tasted of motor oil. Using his thumb and index finger, he tested the harness wrapping. "I thought he looked familiar. He a good buddy of Vern's or Kyle's?"

"No. They don't know him. Real quiet guy. Came to two or three meetings. I've watched him listening. Listens real hard. But didn't even stay for coffee except once. Just to hear Vern."

"Don't like the feel of this," Charlie said, tugging at the wrapping.

"What is it?"

"Thing that's supposed to protect the positive leads

that go from here . . ." Gus Lang was definitely more deficient than stupid, Charlie decided. He was no city boy, yet no one seemed to have ever shown him what was what under the hood. "You know what this is, Gus?"

"Battery."

"Right. Now look. The positive lead goes to this thing here. I told you what it was before."

"Distributor."

"Hey, Gus, ever think of auto mechanics?"

"I wouldn't be good at it."

"Sure you would. Good as me, and that's good enough."

"I don't have money for school."

Charlie stripped back the wrapping. "Vern doesn't pay you much?"

"Gives me some spending money." Charlie sensed some emotion behind Gus's disclosure, but whether it was pride or embarrassment or anger, he could not tell. "Room and board. Can't live high on the hog in our line of work. It all goes to the cause."

"Guess so. Here it is, Gus. Look." He pointed to what he had cut earlier. "This isn't worn out or anything. It was cut."

"No shit! I can see it!"

"I can't fix it in this light. Have to come back tomorrow morning before work. Maybe Vern ought to have someone guarding the truck if someone's messing with it."

"It'll be me," Gus said glumly.

"Maybe he'll ask someone else."

"Who? Kyle? Damn it all to hell and gone, it'll be me. I wanted to go into Jackson tonight. Now I'll have to stay with the truck."

"Got a hot date?"

"Not really."

Charlie summoned all the man-to-man camaraderie at his command. "Not really what?" he joshed.

"I'm looking for that Lorn. That reporter. Still going from one place to another to see where she's at."

"What for?" Charlie asked.

"For me, Darrell."

When Charlie couldn't stomach coffee anymore, he switched to Coke to stay awake. By midnight, the police sketch artist who had flown in from Salt Lake had come up with an amazingly good likeness of Skip, from the barbell-shaped pattern of his freckles to the *V*'s of hair that jutted onto his temples. Charlie took a copy to the Sagebrush for Lauren.

"Thank you!" she said, and kissed him. "I'm so glad you're here."

"Did you think I wouldn't show up?"

"Do you mean, did I think somehow they found you out and were torturing you before they killed you? Or that beneath your appearance of virtue is a compulsive womanizer who'd sleep with me and never call again?"

"I don't know what I meant. I'm too tired." He loved it that she took him by the hand and led him to the bed. The spread was still on. On the table, the glowing screen of her laptop computer switched itself off. "Writing your article?"

"Typing the head and 'by Lauren Miller' for three hours." She tugged at his hand until he sat on the edge of the bed. "Take off your boots and get some sleep."

"Gus Lang is looking for you." His eyes stung with fatigue, his head screamed for sleep, but his over-caffeinated heart pounded so hard it forced the rest of his body to stay awake. "It's not a new thing, but he can't seem to forget about you. Someone was supposed to call you to be careful."

"The chief of police did. He didn't tell me who the guy was, though. And insinuated I was in over my head and I belonged in New York. That's when I switched cars and changed motels and started E-mailing my notes to myself in case whoever it was grabbed my computer instead of me. What is Gus interested in? Raping me or buying me dinner?"

"I can't tell. I didn't have time to shower after work. I stink."

"I love the way you smell." She helped him get undressed, opening the buttons he fumbled, taking his clothes and hanging them neatly over the chair he'd sat in the night before. He both wanted her and was profoundly thankful that the kiss she gave him when they were both beneath the blanket was simply tender.

"Maybe you should get out of town," he told her as she turned off the light. The warm curve of her body did not straighten out, but he felt her muscles tense. "We don't have to talk about this now." She said nothing, so he said, "Lauren, I mean get out temporarily. Do you think I want to send you away? But until this thing plays out, I made a commitment to do this job—"

"I understand."

"And after that . . . we'll be together."

"Maybe we should get to know each other for more than twenty-four hours before we sign a lease."

"You know we know enough." Go ahead, he told himself. So he did. "I love you."

"Oh, Charlie."

"Thanks."

"I love you too. You know I do."

He did. "Now look, I'm not saying come to Cheyenne. I admit it's probably not for you. But guess what I was thinking today? Seriously thinking? Leaving the bureau, coming back here. Wouldn't that be—"

"Charlie, my job is in New York. Go to sleep, please. There's no point in talking about this kind of thing now."

"Why not?"

"You're exhausted and you're married."

"Don't you think I know that? I'll deal with it. It's all over but the shouting, and there's not going to be much shouting. Trust me."

"I don't think it's that simple."

"It ain't complex, Lauren. I'll always have a daughter. I just won't be married to her mother anymore." His body's exhaustion was winning the battle against the caffeine. "You can do what you do anywhere." He pointed to the laptop on the table, even though the room was black.

"Sure. *JewNew*'s Jackson Hole correspondent. There's so much Jewish news to write about here, they'll have to change from a weekly to a daily."

"Why are you worried about your paper? You're not happy there."

"But I'm a New Yorker. And a Jew."

"There are Jews here."

"Charlie, I want a real life, I want kids, and I don't want the blood of my blood saying, You know, I think my great-great-something-or-other was a Jew."

"I understand. But why not here? You said you liked it." He didn't want to fight with her. He just wanted her to want what he wanted, so he could sleep.

"I like it, Charlie. It's gorgeous. I'd come back for a vacation." He twirled a strand of her hair around his finger. "Listen, maybe you'd like New York." She said it in her New York way, too breezily, but he could tell she meant it. "Why can't you come to New York, Charlie? The FBI has a big office there. Plenty of business for you."

Maybe he shouldn't have laughed. Him in New York City! But he was too tired not to.

# 17

Charlie held up her deodorant and studied it. "It's for women."

"Do you think it's implanted with slow-release estrogen and over the course of the day your beard will fall out and your testicles will shrivel to the size of Raisinets?"

He spun the roll-on sphere. If he hadn't looked appalled as the Spring Breeze scent wafted up, Lauren would have been disappointed. "Can't do it," he said, and set it on the sink.

What gratified her, sitting on the edge of the bathtub as he got ready for work, was being able to watch undiluted masculinity. Besides being Charlie, he was the all-American naked guy, doing what had to be done—showering, combing—without embellishment. No Euroglop to slick back his hair—had it been long enough to slick back—no pomade or cologne. No citified vanities either, no peering into the mirror to agonize over aging pieces of himself—pouchy eyes, sun-dried skin. Charlie neither added to himself nor divided himself into bits. He was comfortable with his whole, pretty much as it had been handed to him. Oh, she sensed he was sucking in his gut a little, and with his first glance at the mirror, he gave his image the briefest acknowledgment: Howdy, fine-looking dude. No points off for that, she decided, not for a greeting that had lasted but a microsecond. After that, he'd had enough of himself. Now it was time to concentrate on her. He turned to smile, making no attempt to hide how happy he was with her company.

The previous night's exchange that had ended with his guffaw at the notion of New York was clearly forgotten, or at least he'd pushed it out of his mind. Who could blame him? Not her. He had other things to think about. What do you do for a living, Mr. Blair? Nothing much. I fix cars, hang out with psychopaths and risk my life for my country every day. Charlie couldn't see himself in New York, and right now, wherever he was, Lauren had to be—at least to his mind. Well, she thought, from Odysseus to the marshal in *High Noon,* the hero had a good woman waiting. Was that what Charlie's "I love you" had meant to ensure?

"Lauren."

"What? This is not my chronobiological peak, so I hope you're not expecting dazzling repartee."

"I want you to pay attention. I'm not going to ask you to do something. I'm telling you what I want you to do."

"That's the way to treat a woman."

"Okay, this is what I *think* you should do. I don't know if Gus Lang has a big—whatever—crush on you or is stalking you, but he's bad news. I know you're not registered under your name here, but I'm afraid—"

"Afraid of what?"

"I don't know. Afraid he'll come and wave a twenty in front of a chambermaid and describe you. Next thing you know, you walk out your door and you've got an escort." Charlie tried to comb his beard with his fingers but, after a moment, gave up. "I'm giving you two choices, which I know isn't the thing a man is supposed to say to a woman, but this isn't about roles or anything. It's about safety."

"I'm listening."

"You can either stay in my room and do your work—I'll lead you there, check no one's following you, no one's hanging around—or you can go home."

Fair enough. Staying in his room sounded like heaven to her. Going home made some sense too, since *JewNew* was no longer covering her expenses. She was now on her own dime, and she could write the article in the office as easily as she could in the fifty-four-dollar-a-night Wyoming motel room she was paying for. Was there more information to gather on Wrath? There had to be, but Lauren sensed she was coming to the end of her ability to find it. She doubted another day or two would make a difference. On the other hand . . . There was always an other hand for her. Maybe it would matter. And she couldn't bear to leave.

Maybe Lauren Miller was not as sanguine as Charlie Blair that if she left, all they would be doing was hitting the Hold button. What if he had to stay on in Wrath for another six months? Another year? Would he hold her in his heart that long? Would he simply emerge from the Darrell Frederickson life and press Play, so they could start where they'd left off?

After all that time, would he even recall her clearly? Or would she be a barely remembered extramarital interlude, not even qualifying as a full-fledged affair?

"If I stay at your place—" she began.

"It's a real hole, you know."

"I know. You think I've never been in a hole before?"

"It's probably beyond any dump you can imagine, Lauren."

"If I do stay there, wouldn't it get you in trouble with the FBI?"

"If they knew about it? Me, with a reporter covering this case? What do you think? Of course, is the answer. But they're not going to know. All the agents they've got here are looking for the guy who set that bomb, not checking to see who's been sleeping in my bed."

While Charlie dressed, she made coffee in the pot in the room, yearning for Starbucks, or even an all-night diner. It smells a little like coffee, they both conceded. Both of them used the powdered coffee lightener, both made faces at the white coating it left on the plastic stirrer. "What do you think the main thrust of your article is going to be?" he asked.

"I liked what you said about Ostergard's poison being the price we pay for free speech." Charlie lifted his cup in acknowledgment. "I guess that's the official FBI response to every sniveling liberal."

"It sure is, but that doesn't have to be in your article."

"I'll probably lead off with a couple of quotes from Ostergard. What I want to get across is his belief that there's an all-powerful enemy manipulating everything in the world. ZOG. ZOG controls what we see on TV and in the movies. It controls what we read in the papers. It controls international finance. The government. The United Nations. The educational system. Now, if there were just one Ostergard, you'd say: God, is he paranoid! Put him in the funny farm, next to the guy who thinks he's Napoleon. Right?"

"Right."

"But somehow, ten, twenty, thirty people get convinced by this man that this vast conspiracy actually exists. And for every two-bit demagogue like Vernon Ostergard, there are a couple of hundred speaking the same party line to *their* followers. So what is mental illness in one guy becomes a political movement. Okay, good old Vern concentrates more on anti-Semitism. Some dipshit in camouflage, in Michigan or Arizona, leans more toward the federal government as the Great Satan."

Charlie traced the rim of the paper cup with his finger. "Remember about ten years ago, when Japan was at the height of its power? Same thing—talk about how Asians were going to run the world."

"I remember. Always couched in economic terms, but it really came down to the Yellow Peril."

"But the numbers you're talking about aren't dangerous. I mean, if between ten and forty thousand people are doing Heil Hitler salutes or running around in militia uniforms, looking for UN troops, that's not a big percentage of the people of this country."

"Numerically, I guess you're right," Lauren said. "Numerically, how many National Socialists were there when Hitler came to power? For Jews, that's always the point of reference."

"I guess it has to be." He took a sip of coffee and made the same face she was sure she was making. "How dangerous are you going to say Ostergard is? Because he can set guys like this off?" Charlie reached over to the nightstand and picked up the copy of the drawing of Skip he'd brought.

Lauren's eyes followed his hand to the nightstand but continued to the bed. She felt a flush of pleasure heating her again at the sight of their occupancy: pillows touching, sheets rumpled, blanket no longer tucked in. Then she turned to the sketch. Alfred E. Neuman minus the smile.

"Listen," she said, "if you or I were inclined Ostergard's way politically—to be anti-Semites or racists—listening to him wouldn't make us set a bomb. We'd be relatively stable anti-Semites or racists. We'd go to meetings, maybe donate a few bucks, maybe get angrier than we were. But if someone is on the brink, Ostergard's message can send him over. *Did* send him over. Eileen Hogan died an unspeakable death and some guy's dream house was blown to smithereens because a person who's either very sick or very wicked thought a Lutheran was a Jew. What's so bad about Ostergard's message is, he pushes the idea that danger is imminent. Watch out! It's coming! Oh God, it's here!"

"I know. The Skips listen." He shook his head. "The McVeighs. The Rudolphs. And when the Ruby Ridge stuff happened, I remember thinking it was their feeling about there being an immediate threat that made them hole up like that."

"I agree," Lauren said.

Charlie set down his cup, using the Wanted circular as a coaster. "But now I'm also thinking how that imminent danger stuff makes the Skips, the McVeighs, the Rudolphs, the Randy Weavers feel incredibly important. They're saying, Hey, if I can strike a blow against the all-powerful whatever, then there's hope for the white race. One small step for mankind."

Lauren nodded, then shook her head. "I don't think it's that altruistic. They're really saying, If I strike that blow, I'll be the hero. Ostergard will love me, look up to me, even. The whole white world will be at my feet."

"Ostergard's not the worst of them. Sure, he's bigoted, but he's boring. The danger comes from other Verns in other Wraths, who might know when to shut up. They'd have a broader appeal. But in Wrath itself, the real danger is probably Kyle McIntyre. He's effective, ruthless. Whatever their bond, he's using Ostergard to get what he wants."

"Which is what?"

"I don't know. Chaos? Death? Power for the sake of power? I have no idea."

"Tell me how this sounds to you. I'm going to say that the problem with these groups is that they can't bear having rationality interfere with their paranoia. It's not so much that their members tune in to one or two Oster-gards, or read some porno-militia trash describing the Final Battle—with disembowelings and other graphic disgustingness. It's that they're living isolated lives, up in the mountains or in jail like Skip. Even in cities, they isolate themselves. All they hear—all they allow themselves to hear—is conspiracy. Everything else gets cut off, shut out. The experience, the hate, becomes intensified. That's all there is for them, hate. There's nothing to counter it. There's no 'Have a nice day.'" Lauren studied Charlie for a moment. "Look at you."

"Look at me." He smiled.

"Devilishly handsome. But let me interview you now. What is your life like, Darrell?"

"Darrell's life?" Charlie's smile faded. "Work. Wrath."

"But you're not Darrell Frederickson, are you? You have another life."

"I have you now."

"You have a family who loves you—"

"Except for my wife and father," he interjected, a little too coolly.

"Deep roots in this part of the country. A religious background that's taught you to love your neighbor."

"How do you like the way I do it?"

"You certainly know how to make your neighbor love you back. Wait, don't let me lose my train of thought. What else do you have?"

"A college education."

"Right. A real job that pays you decently—"

"Semidecently."

"—and gives you a certain status in the community, although God knows not in Ostergard's community. You also have cultural ties. I'm not talking about the ballet, so don't feel threatened."

"Stop. I'm not a macho moron. When this is over, I want you to take me to a ballet. Deal?"

"Deal. Now let's not stop. You watch the news, don't you?" He nodded. "You watch sports. What else?"

"The History Channel. And? You want more? Okay, all those *This Old House* shows. *Seinfeld* reruns, so I know everything there is to know about New York. Some nights I just listen to music, mostly country. Would you give it a shot?" He stood to pour another cup of coffee.

"How do you know I don't listen to Merle Haggard every night?" Lauren demanded.

Charlie beamed. "You brought Merle Haggard up, so listen. There was a guy who was a huge influence on Haggard. The greatest honky-tonker who ever lived. Lefty Frizzell. That's my artistic equivalent of the ballet. Deal?"

"Deal."

Instead of beaming some more, or looking pleased at their bargain, Charlie got a faraway look. He was staring out the window, except the curtains were drawn. Either he was hearing honky-tonk or he was thinking about what he was going back to. "Sorry," he said after a moment. "Where were we? Oh, all the different influences on me. I guess that's what you're getting at."

"Right. Charlie Blair goes to movies?"

"Yes. Is this an interview to test if I have enough culture for you? Because you know I'll tell you whatever it takes: I listen to Bach five nights a week. I can't read enough Yeats."

"My point is, you have a million influences on you from all directions. You've probably even heard some Bach and read a line or two of Yeats." He did not deny it. "You read the newspaper, magazines, books."

"Right."

"So imagine yourself in a world without all this richness. Without a job or with a crummy job."

"Lauren, don't you of all people make excuses for them."

"Forget excuses. Explanations. Let's get back to that isolation business. If you're a loser who is overwhelmed by the world, what do you do? Face the world? No, you cut that world off as best you can. And while you're at it, you cut off any old friends and family who tell you maybe it's not as bad as you think or, worse, maybe your problems are your fault. You stop reading the papers, stop listening to the news. Or you read or listen only to get fuel for your fire, like the Clinton conspiracy nuts. Or you only read papers that tell you, Yeah, pal, you *are* being fucked up the ass—and guess who's responsible? You watch cable and listen to talk-radio guys who say the same thing. And who do you fall in love with? Do you know they have Internet matchmakers for Jew-haters and racists?"

Charlie shook his head sadly. "I got stuck with you, when I could have had an anti-Semite?" Lauren leaned over to kiss him and splashed coffee on her nightshirt. "But listen," Charlie said, "don't most of us do that? Live where we're comfortable, read what echoes our beliefs? Do you read . . . what's the name of that conservative thing? The *National Review*? No. Do I read the *ACLU Daily Hysteric*? No."

"My parents happen to belong to the ACLU."

"Why doesn't that surprise me? And as for you, you're not with the *Daily News*. You're with the *Jewish News*. Your readership isn't a cross-section of America."

"No, but I read the *Daily News*. I read five newspapers a day. Ask yourself this, Charlie. What is there beyond all our special interests? What do you and I have in common? No smart-ass answers. What do you and I have in common with, say, a bus driver in Iowa and a coal miner in Pennsylvania and a computer programmer in California? A common citizenship, right?"

"That's right. And is that what you're going to write? That we have a common culture? Watching the white-Bronco chase. Seeing *Titanic*."

"And watching the Oscars and the Super Bowl and talking about it the next day at work. Hearing the same news, worrying about global warming or the President's sex life or the designated hitter rule. Okay, I might go to a Seder, you might have Easter dinner, but we share most of the same holidays. Your ancestors and my ancestors came from different places, but we share a history that transcends their origins. We don't just share. We celebrate. Thanksgiving and the Fourth of July are celebrations. Memorial Day is a commemoration. My grandfather was killed in the Battle of the Bulge. Every year, we go and put a flag and flowers on his grave. But whether or not someone died in battle in your family, Memorial Day is your holiday too."

"But Ostergard and those guys have that."

"No. They reject most of our culture. Some of those groups appear to practically worship the Bill of Rights, but they hate America as it is. The America they claim to love never existed. They can't celebrate anything American because America is run by ZOG. They want to overthrow the government. The FBI is a Zionist tool. The army is run by blacks. They don't like the Oscars because Hollywood is run by Jews. They don't go in for sports because guess who's whipping the white boys' asses? They don't trust the schools because the schools are teaching ZOG propaganda—tolerance for homosexuality and interracial relationships. So they home-school their kids, which, depending which side you're on, protects or isolates the next generation."

Charlie leaned forward. "Some of them teach—like in those communities in Montana and Idaho. They teach their kids to shoot to kill. I'm not talking about father-son stuff. Hunting. I'm talking about kids who are brought up with a siege mentality, taught to fight. You know, in the bureau, when new agents learn to shoot, it's at shapes." His hands outlined a bottle. "The shape represents the kill zone, the center mass of the body. These kids don't learn to shoot at abstract shapes. Their targets are blown-up photographs of actual people. They can handle an assault rifle by the time they're ten years old. The little tykes are shooting at heads and hearts."

"Scary."

"Did you ever see the mess an assault rifle can make?" She watched him decide this was one memory he would not share with her. "And if you want more good news, they're sending their kids into the armed forces, to learn advanced kill techniques—and to operate the heavy weaponry they've stockpiled."

"Well, this certainly is a happy beginning to my day," Lauren said.

"Glad to oblige. Okay, we agree they're isolated, their families are isolated. Then what?"

"Some of them just hang out, waiting for the end of the world, for the big race war—ZOG having blacks and Asians do their dirty work. I guess the Israeli Army will get a three-day pass. The others want to tear down the government, tear down our institutions, destroy our arts, our educational systems. What they want is a regime where guys like Gus Lang are the elite. And you know what helps them? The new technologies. They can spread their views on a global scale, network like crazy. Their conspiracy theories become so prevalent, so familiar—just because they're out there on the Web, in print, on the airwaves—that so-called legitimate politicians pick them up. They start talking about government as if it's the work of Satan, evil, not just a clunky institution that may need reform."

"Sounds like my old man. The Honorable Chuck, my sister and I call him."

"Well, the honor skipped a generation. Your father may buy into this—"

"Or be bought."

"—but most of us, you and I and the Iowa bus driver, laugh at their belief that the federal government is evil. This kind of thinking keeps spreading, though. It makes people give up on Washington. It keeps the finest and the brightest out of public service. And in each community where that ZOG crap reaches a critical mass, the Skips and McVeighs start exploding more often." Charlie shook his head. "We're not dealing with loners with a rifle and a handful of bullets, like Lee Harvey Oswald. Not even with five pounds of nails and forty sticks of dynamite. We can really never protect ourselves against that kind of attack by one crazy person unless we're willing to go through a metal detector and have our purses searched every time we buy panty hose at Macy's."

"And then there are the Ostergards. Where do they fit in? They don't buy five pounds of nails or a load of fertilizer."

"The Ostergards are scary too," Lauren said. "They're high-tech. Armed and well financed. Do you think they're just passing around the hat at meetings? No, they commit crimes to bankroll their armaments. They get money from rich nuts, or under the table from so-called legitimate groups who want to use them."

"Or who get used by them," Charlie interjected. "You should write this, or at least hint at it: Ostergard has probably conned two or three ultra-right foundations or groups into thinking Wrath has one thousand, ten thousand members. The foundations can hand over some serious money. That's probably where Ostergard's thirty-thousand-buck Chevy comes from. That's who pays for his damn arsenal we still can't find."

"But the Frohman bombing, Oklahoma City—it's not just stockpiles of bazookas or whatever you call those guns. Do you think Waco and Ruby Ridge were the end of it? Even if the government wimps out and stops confronting these people, won't take their weapons away, won't even enforce the ban on assault weapons, how many years do you think it's going to be until these people confront the government anyway? Those arsenals are a war waiting to happen. Time after time, History Boy, the leaders who believe in Doomsday have a literal Doomsday mentality. They wind up leading their people to some form of suicide. With some of those cults like Jonestown and those weird comet guys in California, they turn their aggression on themselves. They take drugs and just die. With guns or bombs on the brain, they're going to take others with them. When they start coming out of their strongholds and attacking, are the Jews or blacks or gays or whoever's in their line of fire going to get their own arsenals so they can kill themselves a hundred or a thousand white guys? And who's going to stop it?"

After he'd gone, Lauren showered, pleased the soap was still wet from Charlie. Dressed, she was restless: the motel room was too small to do much wandering about in, but she wandered as best she could, from bed to table to bathroom to closet. Glancing into the palm of her hand, she found herself hefting her car keys. As if she, like Charlie, had someplace important to go. Well, hadn't she? A couple of days left, then back to New York. Still time to pick up a stray fact or two in Jackson Hole. At least time enough for more local color.

Breakfast at a truck stop. When she asked for unbuttered whole wheat toast, just jam, the waitress looked at her with pity rather than contempt. She drank more coffee, holding the mug with both hands, relishing its warmth, and thought about Charlie. He had to be at work at six-thirty. But he'd told her he was going to stop back at McBride first, just for a few minutes. Need-to-know-basis language, not saying why he had to go back, not mentioning whom he was seeing. All Lauren had to go on was his "few minutes." Still, she figured that meant he'd be safely at work by seven. Then she could find her local color.

Her watch said six twenty-five. Another half cup of coffee to assure heartburn. Get the check, pay. Six-thirty. Too early yet. There was one road to McBride, and the last

thing she wanted was to pass Charlie on his way to the
garage. She bought *USA Today* and read about how much
the members of the cast of *Buffy the Vampire Slayer* adored
each other. Finally, it was time.

Local color, that's what she was after. In this case, the
local color was metallic blue. From the base of the mountain where she had parked, at the end of a dirt road, she
could look down on most of McBride and see Vernon
Ostergard's big blue pickup truck. All she had to do was
wait for it to roll, so she could roll along with it. Okay, a
risk. But if it didn't head toward the main road, if it went
on some off-road, four-wheel-drive expedition, she
wouldn't be crazy enough to follow it, even assuming the
Geo could comfortably navigate any terrain rougher than
a pebble.

God, were stakeouts boring. She sat with her braid
tucked into her pullover, the damn baseball cap on her
head so no one would spot the red hair. She didn't want to
play the radio for fear of killing the car's battery, and she'd
already sung the entire score of her fifth-grade production, *Oklahoma*. She had wanted to play Ado Annie but
lost out to Cathie Morvillo. Adam's class had done *Fiddler
on the Roof*; her brother got to play Tevye. The lead. He
never let her forget it. She supposed she'd have to sing
that next, then *Grease*.

If the pickup headed for the main drag and she tailed
it but it turned off at one of those mountain roads with a
lot of corroded mailboxes, she wasn't going to follow it.
The only risk was that he'd spot her in his rearview mirror and pull some western dangerous driving maneuver
that would end up with her car in the ditch and her ass in
a sling. Assuming the "he" in question was Gus Lang, the
person she'd seen driving the truck that first day in

McBride. Because if he was looking for her, why not l[...] him find her—as long as they were in some public spot? Could he still take out a gun and threaten her unless she got into his pickup? Yes. But she knew that people who got into the vehicles of knife- and gun-wielders were more often than not found dead, so she would not go.

Oh my God! Was that him? Too far away to tell, but someone was getting into the truck. Someone was pulling out.

Five after eleven. Great, the truck was getting onto the main road toward Jackson. Lauren stayed behind it. Considerably behind. She wanted to be far enough away to be a speck in his mirror. For a westerner, he was a lousy driver. Not just hogging the center of what admittedly was a deserted road but weaving back and forth in snakelike fashion. Every once in a while he'd speed up, doing eighty, and she'd lose him, but then, over the next rise, there he'd be, tooling along at sixty.

Here he was, coming up to Bill's Auto. Was he going to stop? Because there was no way *she* would. Each time she thought about what Charlie's reaction to this . . . the word "escapade" kept coming to mind . . . she wanted to quit. Are you crazy, Lauren? would be just the beginning. But on her way up to McBride, when she kept thinking about Charlie, wanting to make a U-turn and floor it back to her computer, she devised a test for herself: If Charlie Blair were just another FBI agent, with the personality of a lox and the looks of J. Edgar Hoover, would she go back? And if she weren't in love with him, would she turn around? Her answer to both questions was no. She was a reporter on a story, and she had to keep going.

Fabulous, fabulous! The pickup was driving past Bill's without even a honk of greeting.

On and on, another ten miles toward Jackson. His brake lights were coming on. He was heading into a Texaco station. All right! She slowed down to ten miles an hour so she wouldn't be pulling in right behind him, so it wouldn't look as if she'd been tailing him.

Good. He was getting out of the pickup, going into the office. Gus Lang! Lauren pulled over to a different service island, and as he came strolling out of the office, she emerged from her car, walked toward him and did what she hoped was a subtle double take. "Oh, hi," she said. Lang blinked a few times. He looked more frightened than surprised. "I'm that reporter that interviewed Mr. Ostergard. Didn't we meet?" He nodded. "I'm Lauren Miller." He wasn't tall, but he was incredibly muscular and massive. Standing before her, he reminded her of a photograph she'd seen in a book about the D-day invasion: the concrete fortifications the Germans built along the Normandy beaches. Low, hulking structures with thirteen-foot-thick walls. "I'm sorry, but I can't remember your name."

"Gus."

"Right. And your last name?"

"Lang. What are you doing here?"

"Getting gas," she said. "Then going into Jackson. What about you?"

"Gas too."

"Well, nice seeing you." Lauren went into the office and handed over ten dollars. When she came out, he was still in the same spot. She gave a small wave and headed toward the pump, but he stepped into her path.

"Want to go for a ride in my truck?" It was the least tempting invitation she had ever received. Not because of the intimidating effect of his size, or even his low-browed, beady-eyed *Of Mice and Men* appearance, but because of the way he spoke, thick—as though his tongue was too big for his mouth—and mechanically, without any inflection.

"No, thanks," she said. "I have my own car." Before he could come up with a response, Lauren said, "I'm going to stop for a cup of coffee before I go to my next interview. Want to join me? There's a truck stop on the left just before you hit town. I think it's called the Frying Pan."

When Gus Lang walked into the Frying Pan, the waitress who had served Lauren breakfast earlier did the small, nervous shuffle of a woman who has seen trouble walk in many times. When he headed toward Lauren's table, the waitress went behind the counter and stood beside the door to the kitchen.

Lang turned the chair around, so its back was against the table, and straddled it. It was an action out of so many old westerns that Lauren couldn't tell if he was aping them to look as butch as old-time bad guys at a poker game or if this was the way he always sat. "What do you want?" he asked.

She knew he didn't mean coffee or tea. "Nothing much. Thought we could talk a little."

"Want to go out?"

"Out where?"

"Out with me." Just as his speech had no inflection, his expression did not alter. She could not read him at all.

"I'm sorry; I can't. Journalists have to keep a distance from people they may be writing about . . . or people who work with people they may be writing about."

"What if you wasn't?"

"I don't know." Since she couldn't read him, she decided that to risk condescension was foolish. He might be physically slow and have a one hundred eighty IQ. Okay, dubious. But even if he was a little slow, he would have to have learned that most women reacted to him the way the waitress had, with trepidation rather than desire. "Can I call you Gus?" He nodded. "Okay. Gus, I think you may be operating under some false assumptions about New York women. That we're fast, easy, loose, whatever word you want to use. I'm not like that. I don't go for rides in trucks with men I don't know. I don't go out with men I don't know, even if they weren't part of a story I'm covering."

"I didn't . . ." he said. It seemed to be an apology.

"Well, then, I'm sorry for misjudging you. What brings you into Jackson?"

"Time. I had some time."

"Well, it's nice to get out and about. How are things up in McBride?"

"Okay."

"Okay?" She smiled. "I hear they're talking about Mr. Ostergard in connection with the Hogan murder."

"What murder?" He looked puzzled.

"With the bombing at the Frohman ranch."

"Oh, the bombing."

"Frohman's housekeeper died in the blast. That makes it murder. Her name was Eileen Hogan."

"So did his dogs," Lang said.

"I heard. So Mr. Ostergard must be pretty upset, people thinking he did a thing like that." Lang was looking around as if he were a lighting fixture inspector. Lauren called over the waitress, and since he could not or did not want to say what he wanted, Lauren ordered two coffees. "Pretty upset," Lauren repeated.

"He didn't do it."

"Well, everybody said he did the first one, in the video store, so it's natural to assume he did the second."

"He didn't do the first one either."

"Okay, he had someone else do it." She raised her eyebrows, a little flirtatiously. "You, Gus? Off the record. I swear I won't print it."

"Not me." She thought she saw a tentative smile, but it disappeared so quickly she could not be sure.

"Want to tell me who?"

He shook his head slowly. "Whoever. They wouldn't still be around, would they?"

"I guess not," she replied. "Tell me, where does Kyle McIntyre fit into all this?"

"What do you mean?"

"He looks like a very smart guy."

"Kyle is very smart."

"So who's running the show? Ostergard or McIntyre? Who's the boss? Ostergard's out front, but who runs things behind the scenes?"

He stuck his finger into the coffee, then picked up the cup and drank. "Maybe you're too smart for your own good."

"Is that the way you talk to a woman you want to go out with? Threatening her?"

"I wasn't threatening you." He set down the cup. "I meant you're smart, that's all. Vern was the whole show up in Sheridan. That's where we're from."

"When did Kyle come in?"

"I don't know. I'm not good on years. He just started doing things for Vern. Like I do. Drive. Pick things up. Drop things off. But after a while, they got real close. Like brothers or something. Kyle was making suggestions. Why don't you try this, Vern? Not, like, about the meetings, because Vern knows what he wants to say and nobody can stop him."

"I know. I heard him." She smiled. This time, Lang smiled in return, but he kept his lips together. She was sure he was ashamed of his teeth. "What sort of suggestions?"

"About stuff we needed to buy."

"Weapons?"

Another close-lipped smile. "Mailing lists. He wanted to buy somebody's mailing lists. I didn't listen that close."

"Kyle seems to have wanted to take Wrath to a new level."

"He wanted to get bigger. To get more influence. But we couldn't do it in Sheridan, because Vern had been doing it there for eight years and nothing new was going to happen. That's what Kyle said."

"So Kyle was the one behind the move down here."

"To get more members. To get some publicity. The more you get, the more people come. The more people and stuff, the more money comes in. That's what he says."

"And with money you can . . . what? Buy a beautiful truck like the one you have?"

"Right."

"Buy surface-to-air missiles?"

He smiled and shook his head. "We don't have those!"

"Okay. Well, now you've made the move from Sheridan, you're here, and the upshot is Ostergard is being talked about in a murder case. Does he blame Kyle McIntyre for that? I mean, it would only be human."

"I guess."

"Does he want to get rid of him? Can he get rid of him? Or is McIntyre the one who's running Wrath now?"

"Kyle can't talk."

"You mean, he can't be a public figure the way Vernon Ostergard can."

"Right."

"But he can do everything else, can't he?" Lang said nothing. He seemed mesmerized as Lauren took her braid and refastened the elastic around the bottom, then flipped it back behind her. "He can buy whatever guns he wants. He can deal with people who want to make donations. Not five-dollar donations. Bigger stuff."

"How do you know that?"

"I'm a reporter. It's my job to know. And he can tell Ostergard, 'We're not leaving Jackson Hole,' even though Ostergard wants out."

"Vern says nothing's gone right here."

"He's gotten publicity. He's gotten new members."

"That's true."

"That guy who walked in when I was there, the mechanic. Darrell. He looked as if he's enthusiastic about Wrath."

"Kyle says he's no good."

"Kyle doesn't like him?"

"Hates him."

"Why?"

"Thinks he's a tool."

"What do you mean, a tool? Like a jerk?"

"No. A tool of the Zionists."

"Darrell?" Her every sense was on alert. She heard Gus Lang's mucusy breathing, smelled fresh coffee being brewed. "What does Ostergard think?"

"Oh, he likes Darrell. Says he's got a future."

"I guess they must disagree. Fight over Darrell." Lang shrugged. "Who do you think is going to win?"

"Maybe Kyle."

"How come?" He shrugged again. "I promise you, Gus, I won't print one word of this."

"I like Darrell. He's a good guy."

"But Kyle doesn't. So how is he going to win?"

"Kyle? Take him out."

"'Take him out'?" Lauren asked. She couldn't afford to show fear, but she did show surprise. "No kidding! You think he's really got the guts to do something like that?"

"Won't be the first time." Lauren leaned in toward him. "You know," Gus confided, leaning forward so his neck and head came past the back of the chair, nearly halfway across the table, "Kyle's okay. Most of the time. But sometimes . . . It's not that he has a temper. He doesn't. Never. Vern has a temper. Kyle just decides something has to get done. And he gets it done. Or has it got done. Know what I mean? Off the record, Lorn?"

"Off the record."

"The guy who made the first bomb. The one that didn't go off. That was Russ. It wasn't supposed to go off. Vern didn't want it to."

"Did Kyle?"

"I don't know."

"Do you think Kyle gave Russ different instructions?"

"I don't know."

"What happened to Russ?"

"He went out to get burgers with Kyle the next night."

"And?"

"Kyle came back with the burgers."

"Did anyone ask 'Where's Russ?'"

Gus Lang laughed, and this time his teeth showed. "We didn't have to ask."

"You knew."

"We knew."

# 18

Charlie was in his truck, regretting he didn't have a Lefty Frizzell tape. He tried to take a bite out of a roast something sandwich—the woman in the store had claimed beef—but it did not want to get bitten. Lauren. He loved her girl stuff in those little zipper cases. One for makeup and two miniature jars of some slimy stuff, another for shampoo and hair stuff, and one chock-full of everything else, like deodorant and tweezers and toothpaste and Advil. No other drugs, prescribed or recreational. No plastic case with a month's worth of the Pill.

Okay, he shouldn't have gone through her things, but when he'd closed the bathroom door to take a leak, they'd been lined up on the sink as if waiting for inspection. He gave them a quick, neat going-over. He wanted to know her better, although what he found added nothing to what he already knew: Lauren took care of herself but wasn't vain. Lauren was organized but a little messy. Lauren didn't spend the national debt on cosmetics, the way Stacey did, with her twenty different lipsticks, all brown. Lauren was healthy. Lauren was the woman he had been waiting for all his life; he'd felt it when he first saw her, he'd known it when he spoke to her. He was going to get a divorce and marry Lauren Miller.

He hoped Morning would get to like her. And he hoped Lauren's ACLU parents would like him and not throw a fit about her marrying an FBI agent. Her Jewish parents. That was another thing he'd have to deal with, reassure them about whatever they needed reassuring about. What? He had no idea. That he wouldn't hang pictures of Jesus all over the house? The whole marriage subject was not something he was going to bring up with Lauren now, because she would give him an argument about—

Was that his cell phone? Smiling, thinking how he wanted to answer with I love you but how, because it could be official business, he'd just say hello, Charlie reached under his seat, then realized he hadn't given the number to Lauren.

"Johnny, hi, it's Christie." Jeanette Wagner.

"This isn't Johnny, honey pie." The bureau's codes were so pathetic. He imagined an endless list of them, compiled by some doddering, degenerate Hoover crony in 1951.

"We want you to come home," she told him. "Now."

"*What?*"

"Turn around and come home."


"Did you have any sense at all that Kyle McIntyre thought you weren't what you said you were?" Jeanette Wagner asked.

Immediately after her conversation with Gus, Lauren had made three calls: to the sheriff, to the chief of police and, just to be sure the right person got word, to the FBI office in Cheyenne. Her message: Kyle McIntyre may be looking to kill an FBI agent named Charlie Blair.

Now it was the third hour of Charlie's debriefing, and Jeanette Wagner still hadn't sat down. She stood a head taller than the other agent, an older guy out of the Denver office, Nick Garcia, who was lounging against the door. Charlie, at a paper-strewn table, talking into a pea-sized microphone, watching a tiny tape slowly revolve, felt like a suspect being interrogated by a good cop/bad cop team. The question was, who was who? When he walked through the door of a half-deserted Park Service building the FBI was using, Jeanette had made a beeline toward him, grasped his arms and said, I'm so glad to see you, Charlie. Actually called him by name, which might have been gratifying, except now he was wondering if it was a signal that they weren't going to let him go back. Now, though, she was the bad cop, asking the same question in its one hundredth variation, her voice raw despite the cherry throat lozenges she kept popping.

"I told you, I got no sense he knew anything specific. I got every sense that he didn't like me, that he resented Ostergard's interest in me and that he wanted me out of there."

Direct. Low key. But inside, he still had the shakes, although it wasn't because Kyle McIntyre might be planning to take him out. That wasn't news. Taking out was what psychopaths did for pleasure. It was disturbing. All right, scary. But what was really spooking Charlie had nothing to do with McIntyre.

Lauren. When she called the Cheyenne office, they'd patched her right through to Jeanette. Lauren told her everything: that she had actually gone after Gus, tailed him, invited him out for coffee, for Christ's sake. Every time Charlie thought of her with Gus, of what Gus could have done to her, his hands got clammy. He recalled the light in Gus's small animal eyes when he talked about Lorn. He had to steel himself to keep from shuddering.

"*Why* doesn't McIntyre like you?" Garcia was demanding. He was a round-faced man with flat, unremarkable features. His eyes were some vague shade between hazel and gray. But his long dark hair had turned a lustrous, dramatic silver at the temples, as if the bland-looking agent had confiscated a matinee idol's hair.

"He didn't tell me."

"Charlie," Garcia said, smiling to show that now Jeanette was the bad cop, and he was switching over, becoming good, "we haven't been there. You have. We need some sense of the immediacy of the threat before we can think of letting you back. Hey, do you want another Dr. Pepper? I'll have someone run out for it. We should've bought a six-pack."

"Where's Lauren Miller?" Charlie asked.

"Where she was an hour—" Jeanette snapped, then looked at her watch. "Two hours ago. She said she'll wait for you. I don't like this whole business."

He'd bet anything Lauren had not mentioned their relationship to Jeanette. His guess was that Jeanette was just this side of steaming over Lauren because Jeanette, besides being smart, had terrific woman's intuition. She'd put one and one together: Lauren plus Charlie, add a room in the Sagebrush Motel and come up with a ten-hour gap between the time of their scheduled meeting and Charlie's reporting on it. Or maybe Jeanette was simply not liking the whole Lauren business because the information on Kyle's possible plans for taking out Darrell had come not through some reliable law enforcement source but through a journalist, a source Jeanette and the bureau could not control, the very enterprising journalist who had broken Charlie's cover.

"Don't act like it's a bolt out of the blue, Jeanette,"

Charlie said. "You knew all about the reporter. I told you Gus Lang was talking about going around to motels looking for her. You told me you passed that on to her."

"I did," she replied somewhat huffily. "Through Vultaggio. The chief of police in Jackson."

"You gave me permission to talk to her, to go to her motel, so I don't get why you're coming back to me saying—"

"I know, I know. I only said I don't like it, for Pete's sake. It's not your fault. It's not even her fault. Personally, I admire her guts, although I think she's a little too Brenda Starr, Girl Reporter. To have gone looking for Gus Lang, who was looking for her! It shows questionable judgment. She'd been warned someone from Wrath was stalking her. She knew for herself what these people are."

"But aren't we glad she did," Garcia, the peacemaker, cut in. "Now, Charlie, I asked you two questions."

"I wouldn't mind another Dr. Pepper."

"Good." Garcia opened the door and hollered for Dr. Pepper. "How would you weigh the McIntyre threat that he might take you out?" he asked.

"I don't know. I'm sitting here over two hours, and you still haven't given me the context."

Jeanette and Garcia glanced at each other and nodded simultaneously, giving each other permission to disclose more intelligence, offering Charlie a glimpse of yet another Denver-Washington power squabble Washington would inevitably win. "Gus told the reporter a man named Russ was responsible for the first bomb," Jeanette said.

"No kidding! What about the second?"

"Nothing about that," Garcia said. "Denied any connection. But when the reporter pressed Gus a little on why he thought Kyle would be willing to"——he looked at Charlie apologetically——"take you out, he told her that one night Kyle and Russ had gone out for hamburgers, and only Kyle and the burgers came back."

Jeanette exhaled slowly, showing how patient she was being. "How would you weigh McIntyre's threat now?"

"I'd say pretty threatening."

"I'd say so too," Garcia agreed.

"I'm glad to hear you agreeing with us," Jeanette said to Charlie. "I was concerned you might be taking the danger too lightly."

"No. I've considered Kyle McIntyre a danger from day one. Maybe day two. But there's long-term and short-term danger. I don't think we have to say, Uh-oh, this is it—call the operation off. Maybe he's one of those slow-burn guys and I have another four or five months before his fuse runs out. I don't know."

What Charlie did know was that he wanted to see Lauren. He knew she was no fragile flower, but after Jeanette debriefed Lauren, she'd handed her over to a couple of other agents for further questioning. He didn't know how aggressive they'd been with her. Their natural assumption would be that a reporter was holding something back, and they could be pretty rough. That's how he would be. The minute he saw her, he'd be able to tell how it went. What he also knew was that just having asked about her two minutes earlier, he could not now demand to see her. Instead, he imagined her in his arms, her head resting on his chest. He would slip his hand under her hair and massage the back of her neck. It would be so warm.

"What I'd like to do is give Ostergard a call," Charlie

finally said. "I've been up there for my lunch hour almost every day. I don't want him to think I'm losing interest. He's a guy who needs an audience. If it's not me, he may have to fall back on Kyle. Once that happens, I won't be able to get in again." Another simultaneous glance and nod, although if he'd had to bet on it, he'd have said Garcia nodded first. "By the way," Charlie added, "did anyone do anything about Lauren Miller not using the car Gus saw her driving? Even if she's only going to be around another day or two, we can't have her in something Gus can ID." Glance, mutual shrug, mutual nod. Garcia slipped out the door. "Any news on the Skip front?" Charlie asked.

Both of Jeanette's thumbs went up. Her face brightened. She seemed to forget she was the bad cop. "Philip Edgar Platt, aka Petey, aka Flip. Released from the Wyoming State Pen on December nineteen. Served five years for aggravated burglary."

"Excellent."

"Five feet five inches. I forget how many pounds. Less than I weigh."

"How much is that, Jeanette?"

"None of your business. Yikes! What's the matter with me? I forgot to show you. . . ." She searched through the papers and files covering the table. "We found those two men, Blondie and Brownie, the ranch hands, who were at that first meeting you went to."

"Tom and Grant?"

"Right. Sheriff knew who they were right off the bat. Small-time pains in the neck, long history of drunk-and-disorderlies. Their MO is they go to a bar, egg some guy on until he finally says okay, I guess Brownie's not a white man. Then they get mad as hell at the guy and beat the living daylights out of him. Anyway, they both identified Flip as having been at a couple of Wrath meetings." She retrieved a prison mug shot. *"Voilà!"*

Yes! But was this really the bomber? The murderer of Eileen Hogan? Philip Edgar Platt, aka Petey, aka Flip, lacked the familiar feral look of the deadly loser, part man, part rodent, like Oswald or McVeigh or James Earl Ray. All Charlie could see in the photograph was the third-rate cuteness he recalled from the Wrath meeting. The full face and profile in the mug shots were those of a boy doll some child might have dressed up in a little prison outfit. "That's the guy."

"Known to have been on the fringes of a white supremacist group in prison. No known close associations while in. No known family. No record of any visitors during the entire length of his sentence. Attended one AA meeting at the beginning of his time but never went back. Worked out on the weight machines, in very good shape, so in spite of his size he wasn't picked on."

Charlie smiled. " 'Picked on.' I like that. Any trace of him in Jackson Hole?"

"Good news or bad?"

"Get the bad over with."

"We can't find him."

"The good?"

"He was here, working as a janitor in a small medical building. Erratic work habits, not quite enough to get him fired. He was living right across the border, in Idaho. Renting a room. He's gone from there too."

"How long?"

"He hasn't been seen since the day before the bombing."

\*      \*      \*

He'd had such fantasies of having Lauren in his room. In the single bed, first with him on top, then her. Maybe on the chair, definitely in the shower, even though he had a feeling that whatever fungal growth was furring up all the grouting would put her sex drive into negative numbers. He'd imagined talking too, talking through the night as they lay beside each other in the dark, holding hands.

But the FBI put a stop to that. He'd placed his call to Ostergard: Sorry I couldn't drop by during my lunch hour, Vern, but I had one heck of a toothache. Had to go into town, get it fixed. When Ostergard said, Well, Darrell, hope I'll see you tonight at the Eagle, both Jeanette and Garcia, hunched over, earphoned to listen in, nodded simultaneous emphatic yeses. Go. Not for Ostergard, they explained after he hung up. To see Gus. To get Gus. Gus was clearly the weak link. Vernon Ostergard was the leader, the paranoid schizophrenic, and Kyle McIntyre the general, the psychopath. Not the likeliest or the best government witnesses. But Gus might be convinced to testify if he could be persuaded that his loyalty to Wrath would buy him nothing but consecutive prison sentences on state charges of being an accessory to the murder of Russell Dillard and on federal charges of conspiring to violate Mike Pearlstein's civil rights. But before the FBI could go to work on Gus, they wanted to unsettle him. Charlie was to go to the Eagle and manage to let Gus know that Kyle McIntyre was becoming a real concern. Not the fact that Kyle had it in for him, Darrell. No. That he knew about, that he could deal with. What was bothering Darrell was this deep-down bad feeling that Kyle was harboring some grudge against Gus Lang. Just watch yourself, Gus.

At first Lauren was acting as if she was taking his going off in stride. She told Charlie the agents who had questioned her were pussycats—okay, they had abided by the rules of the Geneva convention. She appeared enchanted with the Jeep she'd gotten in exchange for the Geo that Gus could ID—a double upgrade, she informed him three times. "It drives so quietly you can actually hear the radio." After she'd followed his truck from Jackson to where he was living, she was still bubbling as she got out of the vehicle. "I'm ready for an off-road experience!"

"You could have had one with Gus Lang."

"I think he was too shy."

Charlie led her up the stairs to his room. "I'm talking about an off-road experience that would have ended with me identifying your body."

"I know. You would have told the medical examiner, 'I know this body! It's terrific.'"

"I would have."

She peered around the hundred square feet of squalor he was renting, put on what she was convinced was a western accent: "Right purty place you got here, Slim." He laughed as he started kissing her. Everything was fine until his cell phone rang. Jeanette, telling him everything at the Eagle was set. Give them an hour, then get going. When he hung up, he knew his instincts were right: Lauren's high spirits were being forced.

"I wish you didn't have to go," she told him, but calmly. She seemed to be half hoping he was going to say "I won't go if you don't want me to." Her eyes were bright in anticipation, although in truth they were pretty much always bright. Did she think he was going to say "Okay, I'll stay," so they could go ahead and spend the night doing it two ways on the bed, one on the chair? Not in the shower.

"You know I have to go," he replied. Not argumentatively. As calm as Lauren was.

Looking at his room through her eyes, he saw it was even uglier than through his—cramped, uncomfortably narrow, like an old railroad car, ominously low-ceilinged. Each day, more yellow paint from the cracked and dried window frame flaked onto his pillow, so that someone coming into his room might think he had a disgusting scalp condition. Naturally, he made a big deal of pointing out the peeling paint above the pillow, only to find he didn't have her attention; she was staring at the mouse hole he'd plugged up with steel wool. It didn't help that his landlady was cooking something for dinner that smelled like carrion and onions. And Lauren hadn't even seen the bathroom yet.

"Why are they letting you go to that bar when they know Kyle McIntyre wants you dead?" To her credit, she was pretty relaxed. She sat on the bed Indian style, which seemed to be how she was most comfortable. He stretched out along the length of the bed, and she looked down on him, tracing his mustache with her finger. "Don't you think they're being a little blithe about your safety?" She posed the question matter-of-factly, as if genuinely curious to learn the answer. True, he could hear some strain in her voice, but nothing that would qualify as even pre-hysterics.

"This is their thinking," he started to explain. "No matter how much Gus may admire Kyle's viciousness, he's got to be uneasy about him. It wouldn't be human not to be. There's something wrong about Kyle. They need me to go in there and ratchet Gus's unease up to nervous—or even frightened." He snaked his hand under her jeans, up her leg. She didn't push his hand out, but caressing her calf wasn't distracting her the way he'd hoped. "Also, they're counting on it being a normal night at the Eagle: Ostergard and McIntyre sitting at a table, and the rest of us hanging out around the bar until we're summoned—or until Ostergard starts holding forth. Hopefully, my saying something to Gus at the bar will give him the opening to say something to me about McIntyre wanting to take out Darrell."

"If Kyle does take out Darrell, might I remind you that Charlie Blair would go out with him."

"Thank you."

"In case you forgot."

"What my handlers are hoping for is this: I'll be able to come up with a better assessment of how serious the McIntyre threat is, so they'll know whether or not to pull me out. And while I'm at it, get to be better buddies with Gus. That way, if he feels easy with me, it could be used during the process of turning him."

"What if it's tonight?" Lauren asked.

"McIntyre going after me?" She nodded. He liked her hair back in the braid during the day, but now that it was dark, he wished he could reach up and around, take off the elastic thing, take out the braiding.

"Yes, McIntyre going after you." Okay, she didn't seem as if she wanted her hair loosened.

"I'm going to be in a bar. There'll be ten, fifteen guys. He's not going to shoot me in front of them. He's a psychopath, not an idiot."

"Are you going to have a gun?"

"Lauren, do you think this is *Shootout at the O.K. Corral*?"

"I just asked you a question."

"Yes is the answer. Now listen. The FBI is not a wild and crazy bunch of risk takers. They don't want me to die. They're going to be sending a couple of sharpshooters into the Eagle early, about seven. They'll pose as hunters. Not that they'll even have to shoot. Just the fact that they're strangers will be a deterrent. The upshot of it is, by the time Ostergard and McIntyre come in, the bartender and the other guys will have time to talk with the sharpshooters a little, they'll all have a couple of beers—"

"So your sharpshooters will have point-oh-eight blood-alcohol levels and won't be able to shoot straight."

"—and we'll have a few people who'll move into the parking area just as soon as McIntyre and Ostergard go inside. Just in case Kyle decides to follow me out of the bar at the end of the evening. I'm covered, Lauren."

Charlie extracted his hand from under her jeans and drew her down so she was lying beside him. He took her heart-shaped face in his hands.

"Did they order you to do this?" She was questioning him as though they were sitting on opposite sides of the room. He sensed that at this rate, he was not going to get a quick one in before he had to leave for the Eagle. At this rate, not even a quick kiss. "Or did you volunteer?"

"It was their idea."

"Was it an order? Did you feel pressured? Could you have said 'No, I think Kyle McIntyre is too volatile'?"

"They wouldn't order me to do something like that. They can't read this thing. They have to rely on my judgment. Basically, they made a suggestion and wanted to know what I thought of it. I thought it was a good idea." If he kissed her now, she would think he was kissing her to divert her, to avoid answering her questions because he was afraid she'd perceive how chancy a situation it really was, not because he thought she had really beautiful lips. "It *is* a good idea," he continued, talking to her lips. "If we can turn Gus, have him give information and agree to testify against Ostergard in the Pearlstein matter and against McIntyre in the murder, then I'm out of there. Free." He waited for her eyes to widen with delight at the prospect. Maybe she didn't get what he was saying. "Then we can be together."

"Can you wear a bulletproof vest?"

He let go of her face. "No."

"Why not?"

"Because someone might pat me on the back and feel it. Because if for any reason Kyle is really convinced I'm a ZOG tool, he might decide tonight's the night to check if I'm wired."

"I guess we do have to give him credit for being intuitive. He asked me if I was a Jew. He thinks you're an undercover something-or-other."

"I'll be fine."

Lauren took his hands in hers. "Charlie, I'm so scared." Fear stretched out her voice so it was higher, almost unrecognizable.

He sat up and moved to the edge of the bed so his back was toward her. He didn't know what to say. He felt her moving over. She leaned against his back and put her arms around him. Her head rested on his shoulder. "I have to go," he said. "It's my job." He took her right hand, brought it to his mouth, kissed it, then lifted himself up and out of her embrace. "I think I'll change my shirt."

She was holding back. He could feel it. "Charlie," she said at last.

He pulled aside the curtain that hid the shelves his clothes were on and stared at his shirts. He just stood there, unable to make a decision. Three shirts, and he was stymied. Turning, he saw that she was standing beside the bed now, rubbing her upper arms as if she were freezing, when the room, for once, was merely cold. "What?"

"I wish . . . you know what I wish, Charlie."

"Don't you think I wish that too?" He looked back at the shelves, grabbed the blue shirt and began to change. "I'm not planning on dying tonight. I'm going into a situation that's pretty much under control. But okay, I have to assume something might go wrong. What would you do in my place?"

"I don't know if I could be doing what you're doing."

"You told me your grandfather was killed in the Battle of the Bulge. Can you see yourself—under any circumstances—willing to risk your life for your country the way he was? Give your life, if it came to that? Or would you only be willing to get wounded for your country? Can you say it? 'I, Lauren Miller, whose ancestors came here looking for freedom, would be willing to sustain light injuries for my country. But not risk my life. No, a person has only one life, and these aren't like the days when people were naive and threw everything away for a cause. Nothing's worth dying for.'"

"That's not fair."

"It's not?"

"I would die for my country. If there were a war—"

"I'm not even going to say to you 'This is a war.' You know more than anyone else what I'm up against. Tell me what you want done about it, then. Do you want the FBI, the cops, to back off, let Ostergard get away with that little flash that didn't blow up? Go ahead, Vern. It was only a little intimidation, a little civil rights violation. Boys will be boys. Do you want to give Kyle McIntyre free rein to take out whoever pisses him off?"

"I want . . ." She turned to look at the window, but it was dark and, anyway, he knew she was looking away to try and keep from crying. "I want not to lose you."

"If I backed out now, would you still want me?"

# 19

"Remember what Newton said?" Charlie asked. "For every action, there is an equal and opposite reaction. You have to get a good enough grip on the gun to absorb the recoil."

"I don't want to touch it."

"Listen to me, Lauren."

"Not on this!" She didn't want a fight, not now. "You have to leave, and I don't want a crash course in shooting a weapon I don't believe in—"

"It's not like leprechauns!" he yelled. His sound was too big for his small room. Lauren imagined his landlady on the floor below, looking up at the ceiling. "It's not a question of believing. Look at it!" He modulated his voice so it boomed less. "It's just a gun!" His forehead and his ears were bright red. "What would happen if Kyle McIntyre figured out where I lived and came and found you? If you heard someone coming up the stairs—"

"Probably your landlady, and I'd blow her straight to hell!"

He had pulled back the thin mattress, and there it was, stuck in one of the springs, his second gun, big, ugly, the menacing gray of a storm cloud. Charlie lifted it out. Lauren backed away from it. "You'll keep the door locked," he told her. Recognizing that his methods were not working, he chewed his lip for a thoughtful second, then became temperate. "If somebody won't identify himself or tries to break in, wouldn't you feel better if you were armed?"

"Obviously not."

Moderation gave way to charm. He offered her his lop-sided smile. "I know I'm being overly cautious. I don't want to scare you."

"Then put down the mattress."

"I just want you to hold it for a minute."

"Yeah, yeah. That's what all the boys say. Well, I'm not going to."

Charlie looked from her to his watch and back again. "Will you please listen to me?" he asked.

Her heart was hammering. Gun lesson or no gun lesson, Charlie would be going soon. Very likely he was right. There was next to nothing to worry about. Her fear was simply a delayed reaction to the past few months, from all she had done to prepare to write her article. Surfing the Net, spending the fall and winter reading ferocious anti-Semitic tracts, revolting hate jokes printed over a picture of the red, white and blue. Interviewing Ostergard, listening to him spew. Having to steal away from the Buckin' Bronc because someone was looking for her. Chasing after Gus Lang.

Okay, she'd been scared, sometimes out of her wits. But not immobilized the way she felt now, a slab of stone with a pounding heart. Maybe she was simply on overload. Another few hours of self-inflicted torment, and Charlie would be back with her. He'd climb up the stairs and call out, with pretend panic—she could even hear the laugh in his voice—Don't shoot! It's me.

"I'm listening," she said.

"I'm going to leave it on this shelf here." He yanked his shirts off the shelf and dropped them onto the floor.

"I'm turning off the safety mechanisms on the gun. That means— Damn it, Lauren, you said you'd listen." She nodded once, both as an apology and as a sign she was paying attention. "Do you see this thing? What is it?"

"The trigger."

He lifted the gun. "See where I'm putting my finger? Where is that?"

"Not on the trigger."

"Right. That's where you keep your finger when you pick up the weapon. Want to get the heft of it? It will probably feel heavy to you."

"I told you, no." His beard didn't hide how his lips compressed in anger. "There's no point in me touching it."

"Keep your finger off the trigger until you're ready to fire," he explained coldly. "Rest it where my finger is. Assume that anytime your finger is on it, the trigger can go off, so even if you have it pointing down—not at your foot—you could accidentally get off a couple of bullets, hit someone on the floor below. All right, you're holding it tight so you can take the recoil, but not in a death grip. You hear someone coming up the stairs. What do you do?" She didn't answer. "You goddamn ask who it is, Lauren. Anybody but me, tell them to go away, I'm not here. If Kyle comes through the door? Aim the gun. If he's armed—"

"I'll tell him I believe in gun control."

"Stop it!"

"Stop shouting at me!"

"If he's armed," Charlie boomed, "you shoot, because he's damn well going to shoot you. If you see he's not armed, tell him to halt. If he doesn't, then you shoot. Aim for his chest or a little lower, right here, a big area. Don't try for his arm or his leg. Give the trigger a good pull. It takes about five pounds of pressure. Is there anything you don't understand?"

"One thing."

"Go ahead," Charlie told her.

"If you're so sure there's nothing to worry about, why are you so frightened?"

He checked that the safety mechanisms were off, placed the gun on the shelf and, without another word, walked out on her.

The bang of the door he slammed made her heart pound even harder, so it was a moment before Lauren thought to go to the window. Wave to him. Good luck, Charlie! I'm sorry! I'll be here, waiting! Don't worry, you'll be fine! So will I! A wide, generous wave. But by the time she knelt on his pillow and looked outside, his truck was pulling off. She slumped and rested her arms on the sill, barely noting the chips of paint scraping them.

The street below was a profound black, as dark as the terrible shadows that fall over the doomed in horror movies. Not a streetlamp, of course. No lights from the other houses, because there were no other houses. Just this one house in the middle of nowhere, a place that looked as if it had been made from Lincoln Logs.

What was that down there? A light? Not bright, not a headlight. The red of a reflector moving by. Another truck coming around the corner, except the jerk didn't have his lights on. Going in the same direction as—

A big Chevy truck. Too dark to see the color, but she bet it was blue. Just like Ostergard's. No, not just like: Ostergard's truck, and it was following Charlie's. Not crazily, like a car chase. Slyly, keeping its lights off so nothing would show in a rearview mirror. Who was driving the Chevy? Too dark. No time. She grabbed her coat and her car keys, raced down the stairs and into the Jeep. She pulled away from the curb. As she backed up to straighten out after making a U-turn, the rear of the car felt as though it was sinking into something. Air? Snow? She shoved the Jeep into gear and drove.

Lauren's hand kept inching forward, then jerking back as it fought its natural inclination to turn on the Jeep's headlights. No, they would alert the Chevy's driver. Except he had Charlie's taillights to follow, and she had only darkness. Now all three of them were on the road. Gravel crunched beneath her tires, pinged against the metal of the Jeep. The road began rising so fast that the vapor from the Chevy's exhaust seemed to be blowing straight at her window. All she could do to keep herself on the road was to follow it.

So dark. The shadow of death. "The Lord is my shepherd—" No, not that one. Comforting, maybe, but it was also the one they said at funerals. The opening words of another prayer sprang into her head, something she had heard covering what? A colloquium on the Palestinian Talmud at the Jewish Theological Seminary? The opening of Kosher Kookies in Forest Hills? "'O God and God of our fathers . . .'" Lauren spoke aloud into the dark. "And our mothers." Then she realized: She had left the gun in Charlie's room. "O God, please help us."

Don't think about the gun, she instructed herself. It's gone. Should she start leaning on her horn? What would Charlie do when he heard it? Think someone was in trouble, signaling for help? Maybe stop, get out of his truck to look. Get run down by the lightless Chevy. She couldn't risk it.

How fast was Charlie going? Was he nuts? These

weren't smooth tourist roads out here. Rutted from winter's wear, crumbling from neglect, winding uphill. Whoops! Snaking downhill. Who the hell would drive fifty miles an hour on them in a crummy old Ford pickup? Someone who had grown up driving such roads. Charlie Blair. And who else? Who was driving that Chevy? If it was Gus . . .

She had tailed Gus once. A lousy driver, weaving back and forth. But the big pickup seemed to be cruising straight after its target. What was this? The road was winding and winding around some mountain or giant hill or something. The driver ahead of her was moving with the confidence of someone on a six-lane interstate in broad daylight. Not like Gus, speeding up, slowing down, braking suddenly. Or was this a different Gus, Gus on a mission, Gus chauffeuring Ostergard and maybe Kyle? This was no hill. The road kept corkscrewing up and up, with no end. So narrow. How could a car coming the other way possibly pass?

Don't look off to the side, Lauren warned herself. Because next thing you know, the Chevy will round some corner, and if you lose sight of its smoky trail, you'll— Don't think about it. It's not like you have a choice. What could you do? Shift into reverse and back down the hill? Forget about Charlie Blair? So just keep going and don't look off to the right, because you'll see there's nothing there except two thousand feet of air. Oh God, what if it is Gus and he makes some stupid driving mistake and goes off the mountain and I'm following his vapor? Four-wheel drive and an air bag won't mean squat if I'm driving on oxygen. "I'm so scared!" she announced to the night.

Stop it. Sooner or later the road will flatten out. Sure,

when it gets to fucking Kansas. Relax. Take a deep cleansing breath through your nose, exhale slowly through your mouth. The minute it gets flat, you'll pass the Chevy and warn Charlie. Even if Chevy guy sees you, he'll think—maybe he'll think—you're just another driver passing two pickup trucks. How can you let Charlie know what's happening? With your thumb, like a hitchhiker, gesturing behind you: Look! Back there! Open the window and scream "Danger! Behind you!" Blow your horn like crazy. Relax. If he sees you, he'll know you're not following him to blow kisses.

How could she still not have gotten his cell phone number? What the hell was wrong with her? She could have called him in his truck from his room. No phone there. Okay, pounded on the landlady's door. Charlie, Ostergard's blue pickup truck is right behind you! Oh, Lauren, thanks for telling me! At the very least she should have called the sheriff. Why hadn't she thought to call the sheriff? Ten squad cars, sirens screeching, lights flashing. Oh God. So hard to see. Where was the moon?

Going down now. Scarier than going up, easier to lose control. If they ever got out of this, she'd give him such hell for racing down a mountain. What kind of a maniac—

Ice. A patch of ice, and the Jeep's skidding. Horrible, sliding first one way, then another. Wheel steady. No, don't brake! The ice can't go on forever. I have no control, I'm out of control on a mountain road— All right. Thank God. But why is the road winding down longer than it went up? Around and around, like one of those nightmare municipal garages that spiral forever.

Is that the vapor trail? Or fog? We're getting lower, and it looks thick. Am I following the truck or fog? The

Chevy! Too close. Stop. Don't brake. Shift to D3, what I should have done a hundred or a thousand feet before. Shift slowly. Follow. Okay, getting flatter. Straighter. Yes, when she steered closer to the edge of the road, she could see Charlie's taillights!

Pass the truck, that's all she had to do. And fast, because in the broad beam of the headlights, Lauren saw the flat stretch of road veering slightly to the left, then narrowing and, once again, rising. She shifted back into Drive. Turning the wheel slightly to the left, she started to press the gas pedal to the floor. Suddenly, the Chevy shot out from behind Charlie's Ford, passed it and, squealing to a stop, cut it off, at right angles to Charlie's truck. The Chevy blocked the entire road. Its lights flashed on. It was like a giant sleeping animal awakening. Gleaming blue, the idling engine growling its eagerness for the hunt.

The Chevy's headlights illuminated a grassland to the right; its giant searchlights shone down onto Charlie's smaller truck. Lauren pulled the Jeep off the road, to the left, into the darkness, onto the flat, dry grass. She dropped to the ground and crept on her stomach, the way they do in war movies. She got nowhere fast, so she got up into a crouch and started heading toward the trucks.

Charlie's pickup was all lit up, every scratch, every dent visible. But where was he? Had he dropped onto the floor? Then, in that terrible light, Kyle McIntyre, in a camouflage uniform with black boots, appeared. A big rifle rested on his shoulder. He began to run with the rifle toward Charlie's truck, a soldier about to shoot. She couldn't scream. She didn't have to. Charlie would understand what was happening. He has a gun, she told herself. He must be a good shot. He's from Wyoming. He's in the

FBI. He's probably aiming at McIntyre right now and—

The terrible sound! Not a zing of a bullet. A crashing *rat-tat-tat-tat*, like a machine gun. McIntyre was running toward the driver's door, shooting at it. Oh dear God, the horrifying noise as one bullet after another tore into the metal and glass. Then nothing. No sound. No movement. Lauren waited for the explosion of a bullet out of Charlie's gun. There was none. Closer, she moved in closer.

The rifle still on McIntyre's shoulder, but lowered now. His mouth wide open, as if he were screaming an O! of jubilation, McIntyre strode over to the driver door and jerked it open. Was Charlie in there? Maybe he'd jumped out the passenger door and was circling around. He'd fire one shot, and everything would be okay.

McIntyre's left arm reached in toward the driver's seat. Then he propped his rifle against the truck and, with both hands, dragged out Charlie Blair. Oh God, Charlie wasn't moving. Didn't flinch, didn't wince, when McIntyre let him drop onto the road. Lying there. She could see a dark stain on the shoulder and chest of his khaki jacket. Left side. Lying there, like he was dead. And McIntyre stood, feet apart, fists on his hips, like a conquering hero. What was he going to do? Lauren knew. Savor the moment. Then he was going to take the rifle and shoot Charlie more, fill his body with bullets, watch it twitch.

Over my dead body, Lauren told herself. As McIntyre's right hand reached out for the rifle, she began moving toward him, as fast, as silently, as she could, although not fast enough. He was lifting the rifle to his shoulder—

And she was behind him and her arm reached around and her hand was in front of his face and she shut her eyes tight and shot the pepper spray. McIntyre screamed, a shrill, unearthly wail, dropped his rifle and clapped his hands over his eyes. Lauren grabbed the rifle as he staggered around the road. Was the safety off? On? He wouldn't stop screaming. Do these things have safeties? "Shut up!" she yelled. She raised the rifle, took aim and a single shot rang out. McIntyre dropped onto the road.

Except she hadn't touched the trigger.

"Lauren." Charlie was up on one elbow, his left, the side that was all bloody. His eyes closed tight for a moment, as if the pain was unbearable. She was beside him, touching his face, taking off her coat to put around him. "He ought to be dead," Charlie could only whisper. "Anyone else in the truck?"

"I didn't see anyone."

"I'll keep him covered. I want . . ." He took a deep, gasping breath. "I'm okay. A couple of bullets, I think. Shoulder and armpit. Maybe chest. Hurts like hell. Go over there, feel for a pulse. Under his ear. Do you know where?"

Slowly, she walked over to McIntyre, hunched down and pressed the pulse point behind his ear. Still warm, but she felt nothing there. And nothing in herself. No revulsion, no fear. Certainly no elation. "Nothing," she called. She put her fingers under his nose and waited. "Nothing." She looked down the length of the dead body of Kyle McIntyre. No blood at all on his camouflage fatigues. Just a single black hole right in the middle of his forehead. Then she went back to Charlie. He waved her away.

"Get me his rifle. In case anyone else . . ." She picked it up and handed it to him, touching nothing near the trigger. "Under the driver's seat," he said. "Phone." She moved to the truck. Blood all over. The phone was in a small compartment almost flush with the bottom of the seat. "Dial Recall seven-seven."

A man answered, and Lauren, without hesitation, was able to tell him that an FBI agent, Charles Blair, had been wounded, probably by a couple of bullets and was bleeding. He'd been shot by Kyle McIntyre, who was dead. They were all on a flat stretch of road between Agent Blair's room and the Eagle bar. When asked, she said her name was Lauren Miller. A reporter.

"They'll be here in a few minutes," Lauren told Charlie. "The man who answered was Nick Garcia. He said you know him. They were waiting for you outside the bar." She sat slightly behind him so he could lie back against her.

"Thank you," he whispered.

"Anytime."

"I got blinded by his lights and the next thing I know I was shot. I must have passed out. When I came to, on the ground, I couldn't get to my weapon fast enough. If you hadn't—"

"Take it easy."

"You're the one in shock, Lauren. You'll fall apart later. Did I say thank you?"

"Don't talk, Charlie."

"I love you."

"I love you too. Now be quiet."

"Pepper spray?"

"Yes, pepper spray. Shush."

"Talk to me."

So she told him what had happened, and even for a time when he slipped into a state between sleep and unconsciousness, she talked. About being so sorry about their fight, although she still believed in gun control and always would, and about following the vapor trail and skidding on the ice going downhill and seeing McIntyre with his automatic rifle raised, running and shooting, and how she knew Charlie was a great shot, how she knew he could have just wounded McIntyre and stopped him cold. Was the FBI rule Shoot to wound or Shoot to kill? She didn't know, but she guessed he aimed right for his head because Kyle McIntyre might have been wearing a bullet-proof vest and Charlie Blair wanted him dead. "Frontier justice," Lauren was saying when the feds came over the hill. "Or maybe you did it for me."

Charlie felt a cool, soothing hand on his cheek, and when he opened his eyes, he saw it belonged to his mother. "Don't cry," he told her.

"She already is," his sister said.

"I'm all right," he said. "I was just sleeping." The hospital room felt like a bed in a deluxe hotel. Incredibly luxurious. Clean sheets, no yellow paint flaking onto his pillow; nurses coming in every five minutes to take his pulse or give him pain pills that made him lose all sense of time, smiling at him when they came to change the antibiotic bag. "I didn't lose that much blood."

"The doctor told us"—Judy Blair wiped her tears with her index fingers—"five bullets."

"They got them all out, Mom." He guessed it must be about noon, but when he looked outside, it was twilight. With his right arm, he reached over to the nightstand and got her a tissue.

"I'm sorry to carry on like this," Judy Blair said. "I was at the bank, in a meeting, and Stacey called and said you'd been shot. Not 'Charlie's okay but he's been shot.' Just

'He's been shot and he's in Saint John's Hospital.' And I started crying and yelling, 'What? What? He's here? Shot?' in front of five people in the conference room. Finally, I was able to ask, 'How is he?' Then she said, 'Oh, he's okay.'"

"I am okay. I'm getting out tomorrow. They just wanted to give me the intravenous stuff for a day."

"You've been here in Jackson Hole all this time. I can't believe it."

"I know, but one of the conditions of my being here was my not contacting you. I had to live like the guy I was. No family ties. If someone was tailing me, I couldn't risk exposing you."

She touched his cheek again. "You didn't call."

"I did call."

"But I thought you were calling from Cheyenne." Kaylea rolled her eyes to say, Mom being Mom. "I can't get over you in a beard." Judy patted it once, as if it were some new pet he'd brought home that she wasn't quite sure of.

"I've got to keep it for a while, or grow it back before I testify at any trials."

"Why?" Kaylea asked.

"Because there's no point in any of the Wrath guys seeing me as I normally am. They should only remember me one way."

"Looking like Paul Bunyan," she said. "All you need is a blue ox."

"Babe," he remembered. "You wanted to be Babe one year for Halloween. You were always nuts, Kaylea." His sister looked good, her skin almost walnut from a lifetime of skiing and hiking, her eyes a startling blue against the dark skin.

"Here, Charlie." His mother held a cup of water and eased a straw into his mouth. She was still pretty, he thought, like the head cheerleader for some winning middle-aged team. No, not pretty. Cute. Small and smiley.

"It's okay, Mom. I can hold things."

"The nurse said you need fluids." He let her hold the cup while he drank. "Is Stacey coming up?" she asked.

"No. Morning has a competition in Anaheim this weekend."

"What does that have to do with Stacey being here now?" There was a sharpness to his mother's voice, the same edge as when she spoke of his father. He and his sister exchanged another Mom-being-Mom look. "She's your wife."

"Not for much longer."

Kaylea's eyebrows rose about a foot. His mother's eyes narrowed slightly, which only intensified the I-knew-it light that shone in them. "Someone else, Charlie?"

He knew he should present the news soberly, but he found himself grinning like a fool. "Someone for me."

"Fuck you, Darrell," Gus Lang said for at least the tenth time.

"I'm a piece of cake," Charlie told him from across the table in the interrogation room at the sheriff's office, where Lang was being held.

"You're a piece of shit."

"I want to help you out of this mess, Gus." His chest and shoulder hurt, more than an ache, less than agony. Some nerves must have gotten demolished, he thought. The pain kept zinging him in different areas; now it was traveling up his neck, right into his ear. What he wouldn't give for an ice pack! He was dying to pop another one of the pills they'd given him in the hospital, but he needed a clear head for the interrogation. "Wait till you start talking to the state guys about the Russell Dillard homicide. We only want you for a civil rights violation and accessory in the attempted murder of a federal officer."

"Fuck you."

"Gus, I know you're upset." Jeanette's voice was so tender, so caring, like every sitcom mom on Nick at Nite. "This must be rough on you." With that confectionary voice, it sounded as though she were being operated by a ventriloquist.

"Fuck you too."

"I know Vernon Ostergard was like a father to you," she told him.

Gus Lang smirked. "I know what you're trying to do."

Jeanette put her hands together as if in prayer and rested her chin on them. Thoughtful. Maternal. Well, they'd agreed they wouldn't win Gus over by intimidation, so they decided to play good cop/good cop for a while. "After you got out of juvenile, your own family wouldn't take you in. Vernon Ostergard did. That's to his credit, Gus." Of course, if the sweetie-pie approach didn't work, she'd be roaring, Don't you give me that crap, you no-good murdering piece of shit! "And it's to your credit you're so loyal to him."

"Then don't expect me to talk," Gus snapped. He folded his hugely muscled arms over his barrel of a chest. "Where's Vern?"

"Under arrest."

"Here?"

"For the time being."

"Can I talk to him?"

"No," she said sweetly.

Gus glanced over at Charlie. "I'm especially not talking to you, you fucking phony."

"You know, Gus," Charlie said, "I have the advantage of knowing you. I like you. You're a good guy."

"You can't jerk me off, fuckface."

"The times we talked, you know what struck me?" Gus started humming a tuneless song and looked up at the ceiling. "You were a good guy who was being underused. Let me tell you what I mean." Gus hummed louder. "Sure, Vernon Ostergard and his wife, his ex, gave you a place to stay, but you worked like a dog for them. Worked in his shop, helped with all the chores, did everything he asked you to do for Wrath. You didn't get a free ride." The humming faded, although Gus's head remained tilted back. His neck was huge. The muscles in it bulged with such clear definition they resembled an anatomy drawing. "You busted your hump for Vernon Ostergard." Charlie leaned forward. The pain was getting worse, moving toward his back now, a hot knife stabbing into his shoulder blade. "But what pissed me off was how he paid you back. You were his number-one man. Then Kyle McIntyre comes along, and what happens? You get pushed into the background." Gus's small eyes fixed on Charlie. "You get to be Vern's chauffeur, and crazy Kyle gets to sit at his right hand. Gets to take part in the decisions. Gets to run Wrath. And what do you get? A little pocket money. A grown man, a hard worker like you. You'd be making good money in a regular job. Have a nice car, a girlfriend. But no, you're working your ass off."

"Shut up."

"Once Kyle came into the picture, nothing you did was right. I heard Vern, getting after you about your driving. What the hell was he talking about? You're a good driver. I told you: With your brains, you could be a class-A mechanic."

There was a knock on the door, and one of the deputies came in with the coffee and doughnuts Jeanette had ordered. If Gus didn't start talking in a minute, she'd probably shove one down his throat. "Yours is regular, right, Gus?" she asked, passing him the cup, giving him first choice from the bag of doughnuts. He glommed two.

"Let's talk about that bomb in Big Elk Video."

"The girl said something about it, didn't she?" Gus demanded. His lips and nose were coated with powdered sugar. His mouth was full. "The reporter. She lied. She told me it was off the record."

"Off the record means it won't be printed," Jeanette explained. "I've spoken with the reporter, and she says she absolutely will do as she promised, not write a word about her conversation with you."

"Not *a* word and not a lot of words," Gus said. "Both." Jeanette nodded.

"We need you, Gus," Charlie said. "No two ways about it. We're federal, so we're not dealing with murder. That's Wyoming. But because of the terrorism angle, we're involved with the Frohman bombing and Eileen Hogan's murder."

"That's Skip!" Gus wiped his lips with the back of his hand. "I don't know shit about that!"

"Flip. But he was a member of Wrath. We want to know more about his connections. We want to know about a lot of things. We're interested in any weapons violations, where Ostergard was getting his hardware from. And like I said, the video store bomb. And where Vern was getting his money, where he was spending it—

to see if there were any income tax violations. We need to know the identities of any other members of Wrath involved with these crimes."

"We want to know where the weapons are being kept, Gus," Jeanette said. He shrugged. She offered him another doughnut, the custard one Charlie had his eye on. Gus grabbed it.

"We'd like to work something out with you, Gus," Charlie told him.

"I bet you would."

"We can try to see you're not prosecuted at all on any state charges. We can ask the U.S. attorney to work on folding the state charges into the federal. But you would have to testify against Vernon Ostergard."

For a long moment, the only sounds were Gus's chewing and the flush of a distant toilet. At last he asked, "Would I do time?"

"You might have to go away for some time on the civil rights violations," Jeanette said, managing to sound sad.

"What civil rights?"

"The owner of Big Elk Video."

"That's civil rights?"

"Yes. But I promise you, Gus," Jeanette said, "we'll do the best we can for you on that." Gus leaned his elbow on the table and leaned his chin on the fist that was holding half the doughnut.

"With Kyle dead," Charlie said softly, "once Vern goes away, I don't know what kind of threat there would be from Wrath. We have to talk more in order to figure out if there's any danger. But we can put you into the Witness Protection Program."

"Florida?"

"Florida? Could be." Jeanette smiled, as if she could

picture Gus under a palm tree, sipping a rum and Coke. "We have to look into that. We definitely can get you into a trade school. Any kind of a school you want, anything you want to learn."

"We'll go to bat for you, Gus," Charlie promised. "You work with us, we'll make it happen."

"You read him his rights?" Lauren asked.

"No. I beat him with a rubber hose. Why are you so worried about Gus? Do you secretly have the hots for him?"

"Yes. I only took up with you to make him jealous." She was finishing her article, typing over words on her computer, making elaborate notes to herself on a pad with a pen she kept sticking back in her hair, right above the elastic band of her ponytail. "There's one thing I don't understand, Charlie. He's a criminal, right? I mean, he consorts with known criminals. He spent years in kiddie jail."

"Right."

"So how come he's willing to talk? He's been in the criminal justice system since he's been fourteen years old. He must have heard all the jailhouse wisdom. Then you come along and tell him, You have a right to counsel, and if you can't get your own lawyer we'll get one for you. And *still* he blabs. Explain that to me."

When, after that first night they were together, he told her he loved her, he'd meant it, but he had no idea then just how much he loved her. Lauren wasn't just good; she was excellent. What he'd thought was gutsiness turned out to be physical courage. No, more than that. Fierceness. She'd believed he was dead, yet she'd gone after McIntyre with the pepper spray because she thought he was about to desecrate Charlie's body. What he'd regarded as her New York charm turned out to be a genuine warmth and openness to people. And what he'd believed was a reporter's curiosity was really a passion to understand how the world worked.

"You mean, why didn't Gus say, Get me a lawyer, and then keep his mouth shut? Because when you're with other people, talking is natural. Not responding isn't. Look, if a kid gets caught with his hand in the cookie jar, what does he do? Usually, he says, I did it and I'm sorry, or else he lies. He doesn't tell his mother, I'm not going to answer your questions, and I'm going to sit in the kitchen with you in total silence until my lawyer comes."

"I like that analogy," she said.

"Thanks."

"So go rest on your laurels. Come on, you got out of the hospital this morning, you're with Gus Lang all day and your whole upper-left quadrant looks like it hurts like hell."

"I took a pill when I came in."

"You sleep. I'll finish my article." She found a blanket on a shelf in the closet and covered him. The room was dark except for a small lamp and the light of her computer screen. The only sound was the soft click of the keys as she typed.

His mother, although slightly miffed he didn't want to stay at her house, had found them a room in a bed-and-breakfast. A girlie, non-western kind of room, with pink and purple roses all over the wallpaper and the chairs. But it was as clean as the hospital and had a king-size bed. As he fell asleep, he thought that he wanted to stay there with Lauren forever.

When he awakened, two hours later, she was beside

him, fully dressed, sound asleep herself, her hands under her face forming a pillow for her cheek. For the first time since he'd known her, the lid of her laptop computer was closed. She had finished her article.

He debated between a two- or three-week vacation with her—did she ski? did she like to hike?—starting the next morning; or first going down to Colorado Springs to see Morning and speak to Stacey. He was leaning toward getting it over with, which would mean Lauren could either hang around for a couple of days or go home to get her life in order before coming back—

The phone rang. Almost midnight. He knew what it was. "Charlie," Jeanette said, "Gus wants to talk."

# 20

Gus had spiffed up for the questioning. Not only had he shaved, he had also combed his hair straight back, plastering it down with water. At first Charlie thought it was because he knew the session would be videotaped. It was not for the camera, though. Each time Charlie asked him anything, Gus would glance his way for only an instant, then shyly offer the answer to Jeanette, as if it were a bouquet. "When was it decided to put a bomb in Big Elk Video?" Charlie was inquiring.

"There was something in the paper about how it was going to open Thursday. The store."

"I see," Jeanette said. "Was there any kind of discussion about it?"

Gus's response was a grunt, although Charlie assumed it was a chuckle. "Discussion, yeah. Like Kyle said, 'Look. A Pearlstein. They're coming in, taking over. That's how come we had to move our base of operations to Jackson Hole. Wherever they go, their media goes too.'"

"Who did he say this to?" Charlie asked.

"To Vern. Vern said to use their media against them before Kyle did. Not that he really wanted to come down from Sheridan, but Kyle made things sound so good that Vern just picked up and left."

"You were in the room when they had this conversation?"

"Sure."

"Was anyone else there?"

"I don't know. Maybe Mickey. Mickey Hartman, the guy who does the work. TV work. We call him Mickey Mouse."

"Isn't he deaf? I got that impression."

"If you yell, he can hear you."

"Do you think he heard them talking?"

Gus shrugged. "Ask him," he told Charlie, and turned back to Jeanette.

"Is this Mickey a member of Wrath?" she asked.

"No. He just works." Gus was clearly not a man used to talking. His speech sounded as though it were being generated by a primitive computer. "Worked for Vern up in Sheridan and came down here. Gets good wages."

Jeanette smiled. Gus's lips shifted slightly in response. "How did Ostergard respond to Kyle McIntyre's talk about Jews in Jackson Hole?"

"Like, 'Yeah, well, there's money to be made here, what do you expect?'"

"And then? How did the bomb come up?"

"Kyle said something about he'd like to blow the store off the face of the earth. Not just because it was here. To show they just couldn't come in where they're not wanted. They got to learn to stay where they belong. He said a firebomb would be good. A good way to let people know we're here. Wouldn't have to kill the guy if Vern didn't want it, but Vern told him no way."

"Why didn't Vern want to do it?" Jeanette asked. She was looking at Gus as if enthralled by his story, her eyes urging him, Please go on, I can't wait to hear more. This was no eyelash batting. Even though Charlie knew she was doing her job, her interest in—no, her devotion to—Gus felt absolutely real. Charlie himself believed it.

"It's like this. Vern said, like, right now we're the only group in town like us."

"Like what?"

"You know. Who understands about ZOG."

"The only organized anti-Semitic group in the area."

"Right, except they're not Semites. Vern says the white race comes from Noah's son—his name was Shem. I guess they called him Sem. Whites are the real Semites, so how can we be anti-Semitic? Then we'd be against ourselves."

"Well," Jeanette said sweetly, "we'll call Wrath anti-Semitic just for simplicity's sake. Ostergard said you were the only game in town. Then what?"

"If there was a firebomb, there'd be, like, the biggest investigation. We'd be the main suspects. We'd get arrested. So he said it wasn't going to happen. Except Kyle must have talked to him when I wasn't there, because a day or two after, Vern said, Okay, we'll put a bomb in there to scare them, but it won't go off. We'll make sure it won't go off."

"How could he be sure?" Jeanette wondered.

"Because Russ—Russ Dillard—he was in the Gulf War. He was a demolitions man there, so he could do that. Easy for him. And then Vern said he'll make up a name for a make-believe group, an anti-Semite group, and he'll call in to some radio guy and say, Hey, *we* did it. So's they won't connect it to Wrath."

Jeanette rested her chin on her hand and gazed at Gus with something between joy and pride: You're mine, the look seemed to say, and you're doing so well. She was terrific, Charlie decided, the best he'd ever seen. Taken with Gus, charmed by Gus, loyal to Gus, but without being falsely flirtatious, without offering a friendship that was impossible and ridiculous. Charlie hated to interrupt the relationship, but he asked, "What did Kyle think about Vern's plan?"

"He thought it sucked. They had a fight. Kyle never yells or nothing, but Vern does, but they were both fighting mad. Kyle said it was stupid to make up a group, because Wrath wouldn't get credit, and then Vern told Kyle he was stupid, that if we got suspected, it would scare away big contributors. But Kyle said . . ." Gus scratched his head, then quickly smoothed back his still-damp hair. "I think he was saying something like, a firebomb was what the big contributors *wanted* from us, because they couldn't do it themselves, but they was scared to come out and say so."

"And what did Ostergard say to this?" Jeanette asked.

"That even if a bomb didn't go off, everybody still would be talking about it, and how it would create an atmosphere that was right for us because we were the only ones standing up and telling the truth about ZOG."

Gus wouldn't be a half-bad witness, Charlie decided. He was not as stupid as he looked, not with his memory for conversations, his comprehension of what had been discussed. Still, he was not smart enough to appear slippery—a leader masquerading as a follower to avoid a long prison sentence. And clearly he wasn't smart enough to think of questioning Ostergard's teachings. Actually, now that the Bible story was starting to come back to Charlie, Gus reminded him of Esau, the dim, hairy brother even a mother couldn't love.

"Were you around when Vern and Kyle or Vern alone discussed planting the bomb with Russell Dillard?" Charlie inquired.

"No." Gus turned to Jeanette to answer. "But I drove him."

"Drove Ostergard?" she asked.

"No. I drove Russ to the video store. But not in the truck, because Vern said not to because someone could get the license, even though it was two-thirty in the morning and nobody would be up."

"What did you drive him in?" she asked.

"I borrowed a car."

"Whose?"

"I don't know. Not in McBride. Vern said don't take anybody's car in McBride, so about eleven that night, I came into Jackson and looked around till I found a car with the keys behind the sun thing. Then I had to drive it back and hang out till Russ was ready and then drive him back to Jackson."

"So you drove him to Big Elk Video?" Gus nodded. "Did you go in with him?"

"Vern said I was supposed to stand with him outside while he did something that would make the burglar alarm not go off. But Kyle was there when we drove up. He told me to drive around for a half hour. I came back and Kyle was gone. Russ was waiting for me."

"What time was this?" she asked.

"A little before three."

"And what did Dillard say?"

"He was all shook up. Said Kyle told him to make it blow big. Ordered him. Russ told Kyle he only had a little stuff. Couldn't make a big blast even if he wanted to. He said Kyle grabbed him and started shaking him so hard his head was going goink! goink! goink! He said Kyle said, 'I told you it had to blow big.' Russ told him he couldn't do that without Vern's orders, and Vern didn't want it. Kyle took off. Russ said his hands was shaking so bad he could hardly set the thing that made the bomb go off."

"What happened to the car you took?"

"I had to drive back to McBride, so Russ could report on the operation to Vern. Then I had to take the car back to Jackson, where it came from, before the people woke up. Vern had to wake up Mickey to follow me down there and drive me back, because they didn't want me hitching a ride out of Jackson the morning of the bomb."

They paused for coffee. Jeanette apologized that there were no doughnuts; it was late, and the ones in the little store that stayed open till eleven looked stale. But she'd bought a box of cupcakes. She hoped Gus liked cupcakes. Charlie had to leave the room so he could laugh. When he returned, he grabbed a chocolate cupcake from the box, because he saw Gus had one in his mouth and another ready to go. Jeanette was asking, "Where do you keep your weapons?"

"In a holster," Gus answered. If he hadn't been sitting, he would have swaggered. When he saw Jeanette shake her head sadly, disappointed by his showing off, he blustered, "It's legal to have guns. It's legal to have all the hunting rifles you want. You could have a million, a billion."

"But it's not legal to be buying semiautomatic assault weapons like the one Kyle McIntyre used on our friend here." She looked over to Charlie. "You know what he shot you with?" Charlie shook his head. "A Galil. Comes standard with a fifty-round magazine. It can take a grenade-launching attachment. Made in Israel."

"You're kidding."

She raised her right hand—I swear—then turned back

to Gus. "We're interested in Galils, AK-47s, whatever you've got that can spray bullets at close range."

"Is this extra? Besides civil rights?"

"Another charge? I think it could be," she said. "But we're working with you, Gus, not against you. Did you do the buying? Or did you just drive the truck?"

"I drove."

"Who did the buying?"

"Kyle. He knew more about it than Vern. Vern didn't even like to hunt. Hardly ever took target practice."

"Did Ostergard ever go with Kyle McIntyre to buy these kinds of weapons?" she asked.

"Sometimes. Vern had to watch the money. He said Kyle was too free with a dollar."

"Do you know what weapons they bought?"

"What you said. And Stairoggs."

"Steyr Augs, right?"

"They're real good to shoot from cars. I forget the rest. Kyle liked the Gals, and I liked the AR-70s. We have some of those too."

"Vern and Kyle picked up some weapons a couple of weeks ago," Charlie said. "Remember, Gus? The day we were going around putting all those circulars for a meeting on cars."

"I remember. It was snowing."

"Right. Did you ever get to see those weapons?"

"Sure."

"When?"

"The next day. Kyle and Vern went to pick them up from the guy who was selling them. Nervous guy, so just they went. But the next morning, we brought them to what Vern calls the armory."

"Where is the armory?" Jeanette asked.

"We used to keep them in a barn in Sheridan. I mean, it looked like a barn, but it wasn't."

"But they're not in Sheridan anymore," she observed. "So where are they?"

"Then we had them in the shop. Kyle wanted them where we could get our hands on them fast. But Vern said to move them."

"Where is the armory?" she asked patiently.

Gus Lang hesitated. "In Jackson," he finally muttered. Jeanette waited. "That mini place." He hung his head, embarrassed.

"A ministorage place? What's it called?"

"Timber Storage. It's a pain in the neck. How can you have an armory there? It's like a place where people keep sofas. We're looking for something closer to home, but not home, because, you know."

"And what name is the storage under?"

"V. Towers." He leaned forward toward Jeanette. "You know, I know a lot."

"I can see that, Gus. I'm impressed with your memory."

"Vern and Kyle talked a lot in front of me. Sometimes they told Mickey, who can't even hear, to get out, but they never told me."

"I guess Ostergard felt he knew you a long time," Jeanette said encouragingly.

"I guess different." Gus chewed on a wooden coffee stirrer. "I guess they thought I was so stupid it didn't matter. Like you talk in front of a dog."

"I don't like to hear you say that, Gus," Jeanette told him.

"That's how it was. Vern never tried to teach me stuff, like he did with everybody else. He didn't tell me stuff and give me stuff to read, like, with . . ." He pointed to Charlie. "I heard it when he talked. That's how I learned it."

"What else did you learn?" she asked.

"I didn't learn about any money, if that's what you mean. I don't know about income taxes. I was there when they talked about money, but I didn't listen to that part. It was too boring."

"Do you have any idea where Ostergard keeps his business records?" Charlie asked.

"No. I don't know if he got records."

"What about cash? Does he have a safe?"

"No."

"No hiding place?"

"No."

What were their lives? Charlie mused. The shop and a place to sleep. And the nightly trek to the Eagle. "What about at the Eagle?" he asked. "Is there a safe there?"

"In the Eagle? In the back, in a little room."

"Did Vern or Kyle ever use it?"

"Vern, not Kyle. Sometimes he gave me envelopes to drive over there and give to Timmy. The owner. He's the bartender too." Gus yawned. "That's all I know. Can I go to sleep now?"

"I'm so sorry we kept you up so long." Jeanette reached over and touched his shoulder, a sweet apology. "We'll talk more tomorrow." Gus nodded, looking pleased. "One more thing before you go. This Flip. Philip Edgar Platt. We could really use your help. Do you know anything more about him? Anything at all, even if it seems silly."

"He only stayed for coffee one time."

"Okay," she said. "Thank you."

"He didn't talk much. One time, though, I guess the time he stayed for coffee, somebody was talking to Vern about how he heard there were folks who spent the winter in tents, even when it got to thirty below. Like, you know, survivalists. A lot of them in Idaho, for some reason. Cold there too. Vern said, 'When it's time to fight, if we got to stay in tents, we'll do it. We'll do whatever it takes.' And then little Flip piped up and said, 'I do it some nights, in a lean-to. If your tent's wove tight, and you got a stove, it's not so bad. It's just if the stove goes out, it gets cold fast.'"

"Did he happen to say where he put up the lean-to?" Jeanette asked.

"Nobody asked," Gus told her. "Nobody believed him."

"People here eat dinner at five-thirty?" Lauren asked. She hung her coat in the closet lined with the same flowery paper as the bed-and-breakfast's walls. Their room made her long for home. The rose-covered chintz chair reminded her how, at the end of every winter, right around this time, her mother would sit at the kitchen table overlooking the bleak, brown backyard and pore over nursery catalogs, oohing at blooms of pink and red and yellow and apricot-edge white, looking for that year's new rosebush.

"What's wrong with five-thirty?" Charlie asked.

"In New York, that's late lunch." They'd had their first restaurant dinner together, at Sal & Hal's, and had been treated to a drink and à la mode on their apple pie.

"Wasn't it funny how Sal kept finding excuses to come over to our table? 'That salt shaker pouring okay?' And how Hal came out of the kitchen three times to stare at us. Like, *Lauren with Charlie Blair?*"

Now that Ostergard was in jail and Gus Lang was

cooperating, now that her article had been E-mailed to Eli at *JewNew,* Lauren sensed that instead of their coming together, some force was pulling them apart. Maybe it was that after the adventure, they couldn't abide the ordinary. They had had no time together when they were not swimming in a sea of their own adrenaline. Tranquility and loving Charlie Blair seemed antithetical. Throughout dinner, she kept looking across the table at a handsome man, a beautiful, beguiling man, who was telling her of his marriage plans with the woman he loved: I doubt if the divorce will take that long, because we've been separated for three years. That's up to the lawyers. Meanwhile you and I can be together. That's the important thing. And we have to talk. It's important that we talk. I don't know, maybe you'll like it in Cheyenne. There's a Jewish temple you could go to. But with this case, I can be out of there. I'm pretty close to golden now. I can write my own ticket. The question is, do I want a ticket for Denver or Salt Lake or someplace? Or do I just say goodbye, thanks for the memories, thanks for the pension, and settle down here? You know that's what I really want to do, Lauren, be here. But it's not my decision. It's our decision.

When she asked what about New York, or Washington? Charlie's usual irresistible smile became even more dazzling. Can you see me in New York—I mean, apart from going to the Statue of Liberty? Then the smile faded. He reached across the table for her hand. I love you. If that's what it takes . . . She could see him, exhausted from the long interrogation, still hurting from his wound, trying to force himself to finish the sentence. He could not. Lauren, I don't know.

And the truth was, yes, she could see him going to the theater, to a Mets game, but she could no more imagine

Charlie going through a subway turnstile twice a day or standing on a Long Island Rail Road platform, holding an attaché case, than she could picture him dancing the tango with a rose between his teeth.

The phone rang, and he sauntered over to pick it up. His saunter was perfect. Whatever Charlie did was perfect to her, from his walk to his physical and moral courage. His perfection was not a love-blind chimera but a true seeing of what was there. She knew there was no other man on earth she could ever love like this.

He covered the phone with his hand. He was smiling and shaking his head. "Your editor. He asked me, 'Who the hell are you?'"

"Feh!" Eli said when she got on the phone. "You had to sit there and listen to that Nazi say those disgusting things, enough to make you *brech*. So okay, Lauren, you'll come back and then we'll talk."

"What did you think of the piece, Eli?"

"What did I think? I said we'll talk. That means it's a good piece and maybe you should get a raise."

"That means when you finished it you got a vision of my walking down Forty-third Street and knocking on the *Times*'s door and them opening it up and saying 'Welcome!'"

"Lauren, come home with an open mind, and soon. We'll talk."

The first time they made love that night, Charlie tried to bewitch her and did, using every trick in his very long book. Oh, he was so masterful, so knowledgeable as to where every button on a woman was located and precisely the amount of pressure with which to push it. He was demonstrating with his kisses and caresses, proving with his thrusts, that she would never find what he had in New York. But afterward, he knew without her saying a word that while slick tricks of the tongue could make her weep with pleasure, they were not what she had to have from him. In the middle of the night, they wrapped their arms and legs around each other and, just before dawn, they became again the one they were meant to be.

At sunrise, the telephone rang again. A search and rescue team had found Philip Edgar Platt, aka Petey, aka Flip, in a lean-to north of Shadow Mountain. He was at least four days dead. Frozen solid.

When the sun was up, Lauren packed her duffel bag. Charlie stood by the window and looked out at the mountains. When he heard the sound of the zipper, he turned and said, "Can't you even give it a try?"

"I could ask you the same thing. And then what, Charlie? What if we gave it a try? You'd find fifty different places to fish in New York? I'd find ten liberals and five journalists in Jackson Hole, and we'd form a book club?"

"We belong together."

"I know we do, but we'd have to be in a place that hasn't been invented yet."

"We can invent it."

"How? I look at this wallpaper, and all I can think of is home. My mother's rosebushes, the cushions on our porch glider. Everyone here is so hearty and straightforward and clean. 'Howdy! Good merning, and how are you today? Goin' fly-fishing in backcountry or ya thinkin' 'bout huntin' buckwheat?' I admire it, but I could never be it."

"No one's asking you to be it. I didn't fall in love to find a fishing buddy."

"No matter where I've ever been, I'm always pulled east."

"You've never been with me."

"But I don't belong here any more than you belong in New York. The first snow of the season? You wouldn't think it was beautiful and peaceful, the way I do. You'd be longing to go west, up to your mountains. You need grandeur. When the buds started popping on the oaks and maples, you'd only want to be here, where you belong, watching the aspens get green."

"Can't you just try, Lauren?"

"Can you, Charlie?"

# 21

She won't let him go to the airport with her. No *Casablanca* scenes, she tells him. He carries her duffel bag and laptop to the Jeep. They do not kiss goodbye. They are crying. Their faces are soaked, and their noses are running. They hug. He says, "I'll love you for the rest of my life." She says, "I'll love you too, the same way."

She looks straight ahead as she drives to the airport. She cannot bear to look left, at the mountains. She returns the Jeep, buys three newspapers and boards the plane. She is in control. In Denver, she stops at the Departures board to look for the gate for her flight to LaGuardia. She begins to sob. Four people hurry over to see if she needs help. This is not, after all, New York.

He spends the morning with Jeanette and an assistant U.S. attorney. During a break, Jeanette asks, "How's your reporter friend doing?" He says, "She went back to New York." He feels like a dead man. He tries to think of good things: his daughter coming to Jackson Hole for a visit, a really tough hike with his sister, being with his mother and her family again for Thanksgiving. None of it can restore his life. He tells himself this is natural. If he didn't feel as if his soul had flown out of him, he'd be an insensitive jerk. It takes time to heal.

Jeanette says, I'll buy you lunch. He says he's not hungry, that maybe he needs a couple of days to get back to himself. He gets in the Chevy Blazer they gave him after his truck got shot up and finds himself on Highway 191, on the way to Cheyenne. He gets home at eight thirty at night, shaves off his beard and drinks three beers on an empty stomach. He can't believe he'll never touch her again.

He gets up at five the next morning and still feels dead. He looks over his CDs, but there is no music he wants to hear. He sits on the edge of the couch for five hours. Then he gets up and puts on his best suit, goes to the airport and buys a ticket to New York. After he changes planes in Denver, the flight attendant serves him breakfast. She asks him if he's going to New York on business, and he says no, I'm going to see my . . . He gets so choked up he can't speak anymore, and the tears come into his eyes, and she smiles at him as though this is something that happens on every flight.

He lands in New York and finds a suburban taxi that takes him to Long Island. He knocks on the door of a white-shingled house. A dog begins to bark. A man with white hair that once might have been dark-red hair answers it. The beagle beside him wags his tail. Sorry to bother you, Charlie begins. I'm a friend of Lauren's. From Wyoming. A woman with Lauren's eyes comes up behind the man and says hi. The man says, He's a friend of Lauren's from Wyoming. The woman asks, Would you like to join us for dinner? Turkey burgers, which I know may not sound tempting, but with enough tomato and onions . . . She talks so much and sounds so much like Lauren that he chokes up again. Come in, the man urges. They do not yet know his name. He asks, Is Lauren around? and they tell him, Oh no, she's still in Jackson Hole. He's frightened. He can't imagine what could have happened. He put her in her car to the airport. But he doesn't want to frighten her parents, so he smiles and says, I'm Charlie Blair.

Then—thank you, Lord—she phones in the middle of the turkey burgers and says she could not imagine a life without him, so she took the next plane back to Jackson Hole. She's been so frightened. No one knew where he was, or maybe the FBI just doesn't talk. Oh, Charlie!

You went back to Jackson Hole? he asks.

She says she is willing to give it a try, because she understands how much this one particular place on earth means to him. She loves New York, but her passion is not so geographic. She realizes that if everyone she loved there picked up and moved to Circleville, Ohio, so would she. I'll give Jackson Hole time, she says, I promise you, Charlie. But if I can't put down roots—

New York, he tells her. No arguments, no recriminations. You have my word.

He watches a Knicks game with Jed Miller and Lucy the beagle, and they talk sports. He spends the night in their house, in Lauren's brother's room, beneath an R.E.M. poster. He is no longer a dead man.

Her flight comes in the next afternoon. At the gate, he flashes his credentials and walks out onto the plane. Before she knows what's happening, a tall, clean-shaven man in a dark-gray suit is taking down her duffel bag from the overhead compartment. She recognizes him now. Grabbing her hand, he walks off the plane with her.

When they get into the terminal, he says "Lauren." She says "Charlie." The great-great-grandchildren of Dora Schottland kiss and go off together for the rest of their lives.

# Afterwords

The final paragraphs of an article in the *Los Angeles Times Magazine* written by Lauren Miller, after the sentencing of Vernon Ostergard on counts of federal income tax evasion, violations of the Violent Crime Control and Law Enforcement Act's ban on the transfer and possession of assault weapons and the civil rights violations of the United States Code:

. . . When I first came to Wyoming to try and see what groups like Wrath were all about, I asked myself, Who are these people who claim to own America? But since the arrest of Vernon Ostergard and Gus Lang a year and a half ago, I began thinking not so much about them but about us. Americans. What holds us together? What do all of us have in common?

Love of freedom? Of course. But even deeper than that, the one quality we share is optimism. Think about it. Haven't we always been able to imagine something better—freedom of religion, streets paved with gold? Land of our own for a split-level, a farm or a ranch? We not only imagined it, we had the guts to go for it. Admittedly, the people who came here were often leaving appalling conditions behind. But not everyone did leave. Did all Germany and Ireland empty out during the potato famine? Were the shtetls in Russia deserted after the Kishinev pogroms? No. Most stayed.

So think what optimism it took for the people who did make the journey to uproot themselves, to start a new life here. And for so many of those who did not come freely: Look how they not only survived but prevailed. Whether it's nature or nurture that breeds this spirit, we Americans are the children of these tough critters. We have their genes and that quality of theirs that is either confidence or naïveté. But we believe in happy endings. We root for the underdog, and if the underdog loses we say, Wait till next year. We truly believe we can discover a Northwest Passage, get to the moon, cure a disease, find true love. And when times are hard and we realize we ourselves will not reach our goal, we have an abiding belief that our children will.

Vernon Ostergard and his ilk lack that American gift for dreaming. They can only cling to recycled nightmares of destruction and vengeance. They have abandoned all hope for themselves and their children, except the hope to get rid of Jews and African-Americans and Asians and Indians. Not only do they hate their neighbors, they despise their own democratically elected government.

Vernon Ostergard and his ilk are certainly citizens of the United States. But really, they are not Americans.

—*Lauren Miller is a freelance writer. She lives in Jackson Hole, Wyoming, with her husband, Charles Blair, who was recently elected sheriff of Teton County.*

# Acknowledgments

On occasion, a novelist may feel like a minor god fashioning her own universe: This is *my* Wyoming, *my* Lower East Side, *my* heroes, *my* monsters. But she soon recognizes her limitations. She needs facts to make the worlds she is creating feel authentic. And she needs support in those times when her invention fails her.

I sought information and aid from the people listed below. Being a novelist and not, like Lauren, a reporter, I now and then twisted or even ignored their facts to serve my fiction. I appreciate their kindnesses and apologize for my inaccuracies.

Thank you to the men and women of the Federal Bureau of Investigation who were so articulate and so generous with their time: Robert B. Bucknam, John M. Cosenza, Dean Fletcher, Bradley J. Garrett, William Hagmaier, Charles E. Hoyt, Susan E. Lloyd, Xanthie C. Mangum. Also, thanks to two former agents, Michael J. Slattery, Jr., and Arthur Viviani. And while I'm on the subject of the good guys in the white hats, I'd like to express my indebtedness to Dean Parks, Sandra C. Mays and their colleagues at the State of Wyoming Division of Criminal Intelligence and to Sheriff Roger Millward and Deputy Sheriff Lloyd Funk of Teton County, Wyoming.

I am grateful to the journalists I spoke with: David Bernknopf and Carol Buckland of CNN; Robin Cembalest, formerly with the *Forward*, now with *ARTnews*;

Roger Hayden of the *Jackson Hole Guide*; Mark Huffman of the *Jackson Hole News*; Stewart Kampel of the *New York Times*. My novelist pal Sparkle Hayter, a former reporter, was also a great help.

I spent a fair amount of time in Wyoming. Still, to me it was not, like Brooklyn, *terra cognita*. These people gave me a deeper understanding of the West: John Cooney, Dorothy Feldman, Wes Harris, Bill Heninger, Doug Hixson, Roslyne Kaufman, Bill Rawlings, Larry Rieser, Connie Roosevelt, Theodore Roosevelt IV, John Shannon, Frank Wohl, Lisa Wohl and Judy Woodie. Joe Infanger and his family were both helpful and hospitable. And a special thank-you to my dear friends Herschel Saperstein and Saundra Saperstein, born and raised in Ogden, Utah, whose stories of their forebears sparked my imagination.

My buddy Charles Stillman was kind enough (as he usually is) to introduce me to Abraham Foxman of the Anti-Defamation League. Mr. Foxman offered me invaluable insight into the mentality and workings of hate groups and also helped in steering me to his able colleague Gail Gans. Thanks as well to Kenneth S. Stern of the American Jewish Committee for sharing his knowledge.

More thank-yous to Woody Allen, George Asher, Neil M. Barofsky, Paul Blackman, Marshall Brickman, Shirley Strum Kenny, Deborah LaMorte, Lenny Maestranzi, Elaine Pesky, John Royster, Warren Rubin, Bill Scaglione, Rabbi Toni Shy, Robert Stoll, Beryl Stoller, Maria Terrone, Edith Tolins, Janis Traven, Julie Walsh, Bill Walsh, Matthew Weinberg, Alan Willinger, Bernice Wollman, Walter Zellman, Susan Zises and the folks at the Port Washington (New York) Animal Hospital.

Emily Rose is a librarian who can find anything. I

thank her as well as the staffs of the Port Washington (New York) Public Library, the Navy Office of Information (especially Commander Tim O'Leary), the Naval Historical Center and the Teton County (Wyoming) Library.

This is a work of fiction, so I will offer no bibliography. However, I would like to acknowledge some books I found particularly helpful. For information on hate groups, I recommend *A Force Upon the Plain: The American Militia Movement and the Politics of Hate,* by Kenneth S. Stern; *Gathering Storm: America's Militia Threat,* by Morris Dees and James Corcoran; and the title work in *The Paranoid Style in American Politics and Other Essays,* by Richard Hofstadter. For those who are interested in history, T. A. Larson's *History of Wyoming* is a good place to start, as is Irving Howe's classic on the emigration of Eastern European Jews to the United States, *World of Our Fathers.* Kenneth Libo and Irving Howe's *We Lived There Too: In Their Own Words and Pictures—Pioneer Jews and the Westward Movement of America, 1630–1930,* is another good resource.

The following people made generous contributions to Long Island charities. Their prize (I hope they'll find it so) was to be characters in this novel. Note that all four are terrific and their namesakes in *Red, White and Blue* are purely my inventions: Jane Shalam, Denise Silverstein, Don Vultaggio and Jeanette S. Wagner.

This is my seventh novel with Larry Ashmead. He is a publishing legend for a reason: he is a splendid editor, a delight to be with and a true friend. I am also indebted to his colleagues Bronson Elliott, Jason Kaufman and Allison McCabe, as well as the rest of the resourceful, good-hearted people at HarperCollins.

There are a fair number of clever literary agents. Owen Laster, who represents me, is not merely smart. He is wise and kind.

I cannot list what my assistant AnneMarie Palmer does, because she does everything. My life as a writer is possible because of her hard work, equanimity, diplomacy and benevolence.

I am blessed with extraordinary children. I thank Andrew and Elizabeth Abramowitz and my daughter-in-law, Leslie Stern, for their love, hilarity, humanity and perspicacious editorial comments.

Lastly, my love and gratitude to my favorite cowboy, Elkan Abramowitz. He is the best person in the world.